Also by Jude Deveraux

Jude Deveraux

The Awakening

POCKET BOOKS
New York   London   Toronto   Sydney

This book is a work of historical fiction. Names, characters, places and incidents relating to nonhistorical figures are either the product of the author's imagination or are used fictitiously. Any resemblance of such nonhistorical incidents, places or figures to actual events or locales or persons, living or dead, is entirely coincidental.

An *Original* Publication of POCKET BOOKS

POCKET BOOKS, a division of Simon & Schuster, Inc.
1230 Avenue of the Americas, New York, NY 10020

ISBN: 13: 978-0-671-70679-1

First Pocket Books printing June 1988

18 17 16 15 14 13 12 11 10

POCKET and colophon are registered trademarks of
Simon & Schuster, Inc.

For information regarding special discounts for bulk purchases,
please contact Simon & Schuster Special Sales at 1-800-456-6798
or business@simonandschuster.com

Front cover illustration by Shasti O'Leary Soudant

Printed in the U.S.A.

Chapter One

∞

Kingman, California
July, 1913

$\mathbf{A}$ gentle breeze stirred the grasses on the flat, rich farmland of the fifteen hundred acres of the Caulden Ranch. The leaves on the fruit and nut trees moved; there were peaches, figs, walnuts and almonds. Cornstalks dried in the scorching heat. As usual, it hadn't rained a drop in two months now and everyone in the Kingman area was hoping the rains would hold off another few weeks until the hops were in.

The hops, the major crop of the Caulden Ranch, were close to peak ripeness, hanging off fifteen-foot-tall poles, beginning to turn yellow and bursting with their wet succulence. In another few weeks the pickers would arrive and the hop vines would be torn from their strings and taken to the kilns to dry.

It was very early morning, with the many permanent farm workers just beginning to rise and start about their chores. Already, the day was hot and most of the workers would be in the fields, long flat acres with no relief from the sun. Some luckier workers would be spending the day in the shaded hop fields, the vines overhead forming a canopy of shelter from the blazing sun.

Through the middle of the ranch ran a well-used dirt road with other roads branching off it, all roads leading past enormous barns, barracks for the workers and the huge, chimneyed hop kilns.

In the middle of the ranch, facing north, stood the big Caulden house, constructed of local red brick, with a painted white verandah around two sides, balconies protruding from the second story. Tall palm trees and an old magnolia sheltered the house from the sun and kept the darkened interior cool.

Inside, in the west bedroom on the second floor, Amanda Caulden was still sleeping, her thick chestnut hair pulled back into a respectable braid. Her sedate, characterless nightgown was buttoned to her chin, the cuffs carefully covering her wrists. She lay on her back, the sheet folded perfectly across her breasts, her hands clasped across her rib cage. The bedclothes were only barely disturbed, the bed looked as if it had just been turned down—yet a twenty-two-year-old woman had spent the night here.

The room was as tidy as the bed. Apart from the young woman lying so utterly still, there were very few signs of life. There was the bed, expensive and of good quality—as was the woman—and two chairs, a table here and there, a closet door, curtains on the three windows. There were no lace doilies on the tables, no prizes won by a male admirer at a fair, no satin dancing slipper hastily kicked under the bed. There was no powder on the dresser, no hairpins left out. Inside the drawers and the closet, everything was perfectly neat. There were no dresses shoved to the back that had been bought on the spur of the moment then never worn. There were eighteen books in a case under one window, all leather bound, all of great intellectual importance. There were no novels about some pretty young thing's seduction by some handsome young thing.

Up the back stairs, bustling, straightening her impeccably neat blue dress, came Mrs. Gunston. She straightened her spine and calmed herself outside Amanda's door before giving one quick, sharp knock then opening the door.

"Good morning," she said in a loud, commanding tone that actually meant, Get out of that bed immediately, I don't have time to waste pampering you. She rushed across the room to thrust aside the curtains as if they were her enemy. She was a big woman: big-boned, big-faced, big-footed, hands like gardening plows.

Amanda woke as neatly as she slept. One second she was asleep, the next she was awake, the next she was standing quietly by the bed looking at Mrs. Gunston.

Mrs. Gunston frowned, as she always did, at the slender delicacy of Amanda. It was amazing to think that these two people were of the same species, for, just as Mrs. Gunston was heavy and thick, Amanda was tall, slim and fragile-looking. But Mrs. Gunston only felt a kind of exasperation in Amanda's femininity because she equated her delicacy with weakness.

"Here's your schedule," Mrs. Gunston said, slapping a piece of paper on the table under the west window, "and you are to wear the"—she checked another piece of paper she'd taken from one of her numerous pockets—"the *vieux rose* dress with the lace yoke. Do you know which one it is?"

"Yes," Amanda answered softly. "I know."

"Good," Mrs. Gunston said curtly, as if this were a big accomplishment for Amanda. "Breakfast is promptly at eight and Mr. Driscoll will be waiting for you." With that, she left the room.

As soon as the door closed, Amanda yawned and stretched—then cut off both halfway and looked about guiltily as if expecting someone to have seen her. Neither her father nor her fiancé, Taylor Driscoll, approved of yawns.

But Amanda didn't have much time to contemplate whether or not a yawn and stretch would merit disapproval, for she had no time to waste.

With unconsciously graceful movements, she hurried across the room to look at her schedule. Every night Taylor made out a new schedule of courses for her, for Taylor was not only to be her husband, he was also her teacher. Her father had hired him years ago when Amanda was only fourteen, saying that Taylor's instructions were to make Amanda into a lady. At twenty, when Taylor deemed her educated enough to be called a "gentlewoman," he asked her father for permission to marry her as soon as he had further educated her enough to be his wife.

Amanda's father, J. Harker Caulden, had been delighted and had accepted promptly for his daughter. No one had found it necessary to ask Amanda so important a question. One evening at dinner Taylor had interrupted a stimulating conversation on the influence of baroque art on the world today to tell her they were to be married. At first she had not known what to say. J. Harker had said, with a touch of disgust, that she was now engaged to Taylor. Taylor had smiled and said, "If you agree to the marriage, that is."

J. Harker had been horrified at the idea of giving a woman a choice. "Of course she wants to!" he'd bellowed.

Amanda, her cheeks pink, had held her hands tightly together and looked at her lap. "Yes," she'd managed to whisper.

To *marry* Taylor! she'd thought all through the rest of dinner. To *marry* this tall, handsome man who knew everything, who had been her teacher and her guide since she was an adolescent! It was a dream she'd never allowed to cross her mind. After dinner she'd pleaded a headache and gone to her room. She had not heard her father's angry mutterings of, "Just like her mother," for Grace Caulden spent most of her life reclining alone in her little sitting room at the back of the top floor.

Amanda had not been able to sleep that night and so had done poorly on a test on the French policies of Charles I that Taylor had given her the next day. Justifiably so, he had berated her rather fiercely and Amanda had vowed to make herself worthy of the great honor of being his wife. She would work and study and learn all that she could and someday she might be worthy of him. Of course, she'd never know half as much about life and the world as he did, but then a woman didn't need to know as much as a man. All she wanted to do was please Taylor and be the best wife she could be.

She picked up her schedule. Once again, a little shiver of gratitude went through her as she saw the list written in Taylor's own neat, even, small handwriting.

Every evening he took time out from his busy schedule of learning how to run the ranch that would
someday be his to write out her curriculum. She began
to memorize today's schedule.

7:15 A.M.	Rise and dress
8:00 A.M.	Breakfast: one three-minute egg, one piece of toast, coffee with half milk. We will discuss President Wilson's tariff revisions.
8:42 A.M.	Study for examination on French irregular verbs. Complete essay on Puritan ethics.
11:06 A.M.	Gymnastic exercises with Mrs. Gunston
11:32 A.M.	Bathe
12:04 A.M.	Review for examination on identification of birds of the finch family
1:00 P.M.	Luncheon: steamed chicken, fresh fruit, lemonade. We will discuss the symbolism in Gray's "Elegy in a Country Churchyard."
2:12 P.M.	Examination on French irregular verbs
2:34 P.M.	Watercolors if examination score is 96 or better. If not—study!
3:11 P.M.	Rest
4:37 P.M.	Sewing with Mrs. Gunston. Practice in cut work.
5:39 P.M.	Dress for dinner. Wear the pink Jeanne Hallet dress—do not forget the rose belt.

6:30 P.M. Dinner: two steamed vegetables,
broiled fish, skimmed milk.
Discussions will include
late-nineteenth-century literary
masterpieces.

7:38 P.M. Reading aloud in the parlor; tonight's
passage is from Thoreau's *Walden*.
(Be prepared to discuss that region's
flora and fauna.)

9:10 P.M. Prepare for bed (including breathing
exercises)

10:00 P.M. Bed

At last, dressed in the elegant dress Taylor had
chosen for her, both chosen from her closet and
chosen from her dressmaker, Amanda left her room to
go to the bathroom at the end of the hall. She glanced
quickly at one of the clocks Taylor had insisted upon
being distributed throughout the house and saw that
she was exactly on schedule. The morning time in the
bathroom was four minutes—Taylor had timed her,
then subtracted a minute for efficiency's sake. She
checked her hair in the mirror to make sure there were
no stray strands escaping. Taylor believed that un-
kempt hair was the sign of a wanton woman.

She left the bathroom, saw she was a full forty-five
seconds overtime and began to hurry down the stairs.

"Amanda!"

It was Taylor's voice, low, deep, and full of disapproval. He was standing in a shadow at the foot of the
stairs, his pocket watch in his hand, a scowl bringing
his dark brows together. Immediately, Amanda
slowed her pace, hoping her wildly beating heart
couldn't be heard.

7

"Were you running, Amanda?" he inquired in the same tone one would ask, Were you trying to cut off the cat's tail? It was a mixture of horror and disbelief.

Amanda had never thought of lying to Taylor. "I was hurrying, yes," she said softly. "I apologize."

"Good." He put his watch back in the vest pocket of the dark suit he wore. Taylor was always immaculate, with never a wrinkle or dust spot to be seen on his person. He could ride in the back of an open auto along dusty roads and come out as clean as when he stepped into the car. No matter how hot it grew, Taylor never perspired. He also never bent. His back was straight and rigid, his shoulders back as far as any soldier's. He was tall, very thin (which he said showed that he had control over one of the primitive aspects of man—hunger) and handsome in a dark, almost forbidding way. Sometimes Amanda thought Taylor looked a bit like a photograph of a handsome man that had come to life.

Taylor turned to Amanda and inspected her. He made sure every hair was pulled back, that her dress was perfectly ironed, that her stocking seams were straight, her shoes polished. He saw that she stood up very straight—no slumping in the woman he was to marry—and frowned briefly at her breasts. When she stood with her shoulders back like that she looked too . . . too feminine.

He turned on his heel and went toward the dining room, and Amanda breathed an inaudible sigh of relief. She had passed inspection and, what is more, he had not been angry with her for rushing down the stairs in her hoyden manner that he hated so much.

Courteously, Taylor held her chair out for her in the dining room, then took the place at the head of the table. As always, her mother took breakfast in her sitting room while her father ate earlier. Sometimes Amanda thought her father didn't *want* to eat with her and Taylor, that perhaps their enlightened discussions bothered him. After all, J. Harker had quit school in the eighth grade to support his family and that was why he was so insistent that his daughter be educated and that she marry an educated man.

The maid placed Amanda's egg before her, her single piece of dry toast to one side, and Amanda knew she was to start the conversation. Taylor liked to know that she had memorized the schedule he had so laboriously prepared.

"I believe free wool was one of the major issues of President Wilson's tariff reform, that is, the removal of a duty on imported raw wool."

Taylor didn't speak but he nodded, so she knew she was right. It was so difficult remembering all the topics of current events.

"And the duty on manufactured woolen goods has been reduced to thirty-five percent. This, of course, puts a burden on American farmers who sell wool, but on the other hand American manufacturers can buy wool from anywhere in the world."

Taylor nodded. "And the sugar?"

"The tax on imported sugar protects the Louisiana cane growers and the Western beet farmers."

He raised an eyebrow at her. "You know nothing else about the sugar tariff?"

Frantically, she searched her memory. "Oh yes, the sugar tariff will be lifted in three years. The Western beet farmers say—"

They both looked up as J. Harker burst into the room. He was a short, squat, angry-looking man, a man who, a long time ago, had found out that the only way to get anything was to take it. He had brought himself up from nothing to owning the largest hop ranch in the world. He had fought every step of the way—even when there was no need for fighting, he had fought—and every punch he had taken had made him angrier.

"Look at this," Harker said, holding out a letter toward Taylor. There were no preliminary courtesies of, good morning, nor even any acknowledgment of his daughter, merely the handing of the letter to Taylor, whom he, quite simply, thought was the smartest man on earth. Taylor's illustrious family— albeit a penniless one—his education, his manners, his ease in society, were things that awed J. Harker.

Carefully blotting the corners of his lips, Taylor took the letter and read it.

"Well?" J. Harker demanded in his blunt way.

Taylor carefully folded the letter and took his time answering. The letter was from the governor of California, stating that he was afraid there might be labor trouble this year with the migrant workers who came to pick the hops. The ULW, the United Laborers of the World, were talking of coming to Kingman and seeing if they could get the laborers to strike against the hop growers and, since the Caulden ranch would be the first to be picked, the governor suspected the trouble would start there.

Taylor ignored J. Harker's glaring and continued to give the matter some thought. This year hop prices were at rock bottom and the Caulden ranch was going to have to cut corners to make ends meet, and these cut corners would, no doubt, cause problems with those crazy labor leaders. But those men could be handled. Didn't J. Harker contribute enough to the various causes in Kingman to be able to ask for a little protection from the sheriff and his deputies? Yes, the labor leaders could be dealt with.

It was the second part of the governor's letter that bothered Taylor—and what was no doubt enraging J. Harker. The governor wanted to send some college professor, some man he'd just appointed Executive Secretary of Immigration and Migrant Labor, to Kingman to see if the professor could prevent any trouble. It would be all right, Taylor thought, if this man were stupid, but, somehow, Taylor doubted that he was. A Ph.D. in economics from Heidelberg University in Germany. No doubt this man had spent the last forty years of his life studying labor problems and had never been two miles off a college campus. No doubt he was all for the laborer and had never given a thought to the problems of the ranch owner, never considered the amount of money it cost to grow hops, just expected the "rich" owner to pay exorbitant wages to the "starving" pickers.

Taylor looked up at J. Harker. "Invite the man to come here," he said.

"Here? To Kingman?" J. Harker's face was getting red. He hated the concept of the government telling him how to run *his* ranch. It was his land, wasn't it? And the pickers were free people, weren't they? If they didn't like what was going on, they could leave, yet the governor seemed to believe he had a right to tell J. Harker how to run his own ranch.

"No," Taylor said, "I mean, invite him here to this house." Before Harker could protest, Taylor continued. "Think about it. He's a poor college professor, makes perhaps twenty-five hundred, three thousand a year. I wonder if he's ever seen a ranch like this or visited a house like this. Bring him here now, weeks before the pickers arrive, and let him see that we aren't monsters, let him see—" He broke off to turn his gaze on Amanda, who had put her hand out for the jam jar. "No," he said simply, and Amanda withdrew her hand guiltily.

"A college professor?" J. Harker said. "Who'll take care of the old guy? With the hops about ripe, I can't spare a minute and I need you to—"

"Amanda," Taylor said, making Amanda start.

She'd been only halfheartedly listening to the conversation since it didn't pertain to her and now Taylor had caught her daydreaming.

"Amanda will entertain him," Taylor said. "She can discuss several different aspects of economics with him and, if she doesn't know enough, he can teach her. She can also show him Kingman. You can do that, can't you, Amanda?"

Both Taylor and her father were staring at her with the intensity of hungry hawks watching a rabbit running across an open field. These were the two people she most wanted to please, but she knew she wasn't very good with strangers. She didn't meet too many people—rarely was meeting someone put on her schedule—and when she did, she didn't have much to say to them. People didn't seem to want to discuss what had made the Nile flood. They liked to talk of dances (something she'd never attended) and clothes (Taylor chose her clothes) and moving pictures (she'd never seen one) and baseball (never seen a game but she knew all the rules; she'd made 98 on that exam) and cars (she rarely went anywhere and then only with Taylor and a chauffeur, so she knew little about automobiles). No, she wasn't good with strangers.

"Amanda?" Taylor said louder.

"Yes, I will try," she said sincerely. Perhaps a college professor would be easier to talk to than other people.

"Good," Taylor said and seemed disappointed in her hesitancy. He glanced at the tall clock at the end of the dining room. "You are three minutes off schedule. Now go and study."

She rose immediately. "Yes, Taylor." She glanced at her father. "Good morning," she murmured before leaving the room.

Alone in her room, she sat down at her little desk, opened a drawer and took out her notes on French irregular verbs. At ten A.M. she worked on her essay on Puritan ethics. Twice she miswrote a word and had to start over again. Taylor insisted that each of her papers be in perfect form, with no errors.

At eleven A.M. Mrs. Gunston was waiting for her in a basement room. Amanda wore a blue serge gymnastic dress that reached only to mid-calf. Taylor had said this dress was necessary but he had designed a modest, long dress to be worn over it while Amanda walked down the back stairs—*not* the front stairs where she might be seen—to the basement.

For thirty minutes, Mrs. Gunston put Amanda through a rigorous program using heavy Indian clubs and weighted pulleys attached to the wall.

At 11:30, faint with hunger and fatigue, Amanda was allowed seventeen minutes in a tub full of cool water (Taylor said hot water aged a person's skin).

According to her usual schedules, then she had to dress, study for tomorrow's exam and be at luncheon at one sharp.

But today was different.

When Mrs. Gunston appeared in Amanda's room at 12:45 with a tray of food, Amanda was immediately concerned.

"What has happened to Mr. Driscoll?" she asked, fearing that only death could make Taylor upset the schedule.

"He is with your father," Mrs. Gunston said, "and he has given you a new schedule."

With her eyes wide in wonder, Amanda took the new schedule.

From 1:17 to 6:12 read the following:
   Veblen's *Instinct of Workmanship*
   Hoxie's *Scientific Management*
   Royce's *Philosophy of Loyalty*
   Montgomery's *Labor and Social Problems*
6:00 P.M. Dress for dinner. Wear the blue chiffon with the pearls.
6:30 P.M. Dinner: two steamed vegetables, broiled fish, skimmed milk, a one-inch piece of chocolate cake.
7:30 P.M. Discuss what you have read
9:30 P.M. Prepare for bed
10:00 P.M. Bed

Amanda looked up at Mrs. Gunston. "Chocolate cake?" she whispered.

A maid walked in, set the four books on a table and left the room. Mrs. Gunston picked up one of them.

"This man, this Dr. Montgomery, he wrote this one and he's coming here. You're to know something to talk to him about, so you better stop dreaming of cake and get to work." She turned away with an officious bustle and left the room.

Amanda sat absolutely rigid on a hard little chair and began to read the book by Dr. Henry Raine Montgomery first. At first it seemed such an odd book that she didn't understand it. It was all about how the strikes of laborers were actually caused by the owners of the mines and factories and ranches.

Amanda hadn't thought much about the men who worked in the fields. Sometimes she'd look up from her book and see them, far away, looking like toys, moving about under the blistering sun, but she'd always looked down at her book again and never given them another thought.

She read all afternoon, making her way through two of the books on the list, and by dinner time she felt confident she could discuss labor management with Taylor.

She was unprepared for his anger. It seemed she'd read the books incorrectly. She was to read the books from the *management's* point of view.

"Have I taught you nothing?" Taylor had said to her in a cold voice.

She was sent to her room without the chocolate cake and she was to write a long essay on why the books of Montgomery and the others were wrong.

At midnight Amanda was still writing and she was coming to greatly dislike the name of Dr. Montgomery. He had turned her calm household upside down, made Taylor angry at her, cost her many hours extra work, and worst of all, cost her a slice of chocolate cake. If this was what his *book* did, what in the world was the *man* going to do?

She smiled in weariness and told herself she was too fanciful. Dr. Montgomery was merely a poor, old college professor who knew nothing about the economics of the real world, only the economics of a paper world. She imagined a gray-haired man bent over a desk, a dusty pile of books around him, and she wondered if he'd ever seen a moving-picture show. Perhaps the two of them could go into Kingman and . . . She stopped that thought. Taylor said moving pictures were mind-deadening and people who went to them were lower-class buffoons, so of course this college professor wouldn't want to do something so unworthwhile.

She turned back to her essay and continued to write about how wrong Dr. Montgomery's book was.

Chapter Two

It was the sixth day of the Los Angeles to Phoenix Harriman Derby and the two men in the Stutz were growing weary. What time there was for rest had been used for repairing the stripped-down racer. This morning they had hit mud, and the red racer—and the men—were now covered in dried, caked earth, only their lips clean, licked clean, and their eyes under their goggles not covered.

It had been a grueling race, with the path of the race unmarked and the citizens of the towns on the course not warned of the approaching speeding cars. The towns that were forewarned were worse, because the people stood in the middle of the road awaiting the approach of the cars. They had never seen autos that could do sixty miles an hour and had no understanding of how fast that was. Many drivers had been given the choice of hitting a tree and dying, or hitting the spectators and taking them along. Most chose the tree.

Sometimes spectators were angry at the drivers or at autos in general and threw rocks at the drivers. Sometimes they tried to slap the driver on the back in congratulations. However they did it, spectators caused drivers to lose their lives.

Hank Montgomery, the driver of the Stutz, was cautious as he slowed down to forty to enter the little cowtown on the Arizona border. Next to him, his mechanic, Joe Fisher, leaned forward and strained to see what was ahead. Nothing seemed to be moving, and then, just as they passed the first building on the edge of town, they saw the reason for the empty street. To their left, slammed into a building, was Barney Parker's Metz. The dust hadn't settled from the wreck, and Barney lolled against the seat looking more dead than alive.

Hank downshifted and started to slow the Stutz when Joe yelled and pointed. An angry-looking group of citizens, clubs, sticks and rocks in hand, not to mention a few rifles and shotguns, were approaching Barney's car, but when they heard Hank's motor, they began to turn toward Hank's Stutz.

"Get out of here!" Joe shouted.

There were angry, armed people in front and in back of Hank and buildings on both sides. He could slam the car into gear, floor the accelerator and plow into the people, or he could—

Hank did some of the fastest thinking he'd ever done, and some amazingly quick turning of the heavy steering wheel. He turned down an alley even as Joe yelled at him not to. If the alley was a dead end, they were done for. This was obviously one of those sleepy towns that wanted to stay that way and they resented autos tearing through their streets at all hours, scaring horses and making even the sidewalks unsafe. If they ever caught up with this race driver, Hank might not live to tell about it.

There was a light at the end of the alley. It opened into a fenced yard where a woman stood feeding her chickens—or had been feeding them, because now she was paralyzed at the sight of a filthy auto traveling at a breathtaking speed coming through her fence.

Both Hank and Joe ducked in unison from long practice as the fence hit the front of the car. When the men came up, they were attacked by squawking, flying chickens. Hank knocked one chicken off his lap then leaned out to brush two off the hood. Joe lifted a chicken from the floorboard and tossed it out.

After they got through the other side of the fence, Hank slowed down and turned to look back. The farm lady was shaking her fist at them as her chickens flew everywhere and behind her came running a group of outraged citizens.

"Are you crazy?" Joe yelled over the roar of the motor as Hank turned the car back toward the town. "Let's get out of here."

"I'm going to see if I can get Barney," Hank yelled back.

"No, you—" Joe yelled, then slammed back against the seat as Hank took off. Who was he to argue? He was only the mechanic while Hank was the owner and driver. What did it matter that it was his neck too? Hank did what he wanted.

Joe held on to the side of the car as Hank revved up the car to forty, fifty, sixty. Joe saw the turn that led back toward the road where Barney's car was wrecked and he prayed Hank wouldn't try to take the corner at—

Joe knew he aged twenty years on that turn as Hank took it at seventy miles an hour, barely missing the boardwalk on the far side. Joe smelled rubber and cursed as Hank pulled on the brake as he approached Barney's Metz.

"Get the gun!" Hank yelled.

Joe obeyed as he reached for the pistol that Hank kept lashed to the floorboard but he knew that his hands were shaking too hard to use the thing.

There were only three citizens standing near Barney, who was now limping out of his car. His mechanic had quit on him two days before. Barney was dazed, but as he saw Hank and Joe, then saw a furious mob turning the corner behind them, he knew what was going on. Without a backward glance to his destroyed car, he jumped into Joe's lap as Hank sped ahead.

It was difficult trying to get around the little town, driving over prairie-dog holes, dodging cactus, stopping to open and close gates. Joe complained about Barney's weight while Barney bragged about how he would have beaten them except that he swerved to miss a dog and rammed into the side of the building.

Joe was thinking Barney wasn't so bad after all.

"Damned animal bones are hell on tires," Barney said.

Joe and Hank exchanged looks, and an hour later, about six miles outside another little town, Hank stopped the car and told Barney to get out.

"You can't leave me here!" Barney said. "I'll die of thirst."

"Only if you've forgotten how to walk," Hank said as he put the car in gear and started moving.

Joe leaned back and sighed. "Never felt so light in my life. Where to now, boss?"

"To the finish line!"

Hank Montgomery won the Harriman Derby and flicked mud off of himself as he walked to the platform and accepted the three-foot-tall silver trophy from the mayor of Phoenix.

Joe stood at the bottom of the stairs waiting for him. They had been racing for eight days, with no sleep to speak of, and all Joe wanted was a bath and a bed. "You did get us rooms here, didn't you?" he asked wearily between people congratulating them.

"I got you a suite and me the top floor of the Brown," Hank said, grinning.

"Top—?" Joe began, then stopped. Sometimes he forgot that Hank was loaded, but then he guessed that was a pretty good compliment to pay to someone. Hank didn't act like a rich guy—nor did he act like a college teacher.

"Well, I'm going to bed. You comin'?"

"In a while," Hank said, removing his leather cap and doing his best to neaten hair that was dark blond when it didn't have five or so pounds of mud in it.

Joe followed Hank's eyes to a very pretty young woman standing by the edge of the crowd. "You're going to get into trouble," Joe warned, then shrugged. What Hank Montgomery did was his own business. He paid Joe well and he shared the winner's purse with him, and that's all Joe wanted. He turned and made his way through the crowd.

Dr. Henry Montgomery gathered his papers and books, slipped them into the heavy leather satchel and left the classroom. He was a tall, broad-shouldered man and his dark brown suit fit him perfectly, showing off the muscular body he had developed through years of exercise. Very few of his colleagues and, he hoped, none of his students, knew his background. To them he was an economics professor with excellent credentials who gave difficult tests and expected a great deal from his students. Some of the other teachers didn't like his ideas on labor and worried that he might anger some of the richer alumni, but since Dr. Montgomery remained quiet and wasn't involved in any scandals, they accepted him. They did not know of the wealth in his family or that during his holidays he raced automobiles, nor did they guess there was another side to Dr. Montgomery.

Hank walked the mile and a half to his house, a pretty little brick building set at the end of a quiet dirt lane, heavy shade trees towering over it and everywhere lush greenery growing beautifully in the California sun. Hank smiled as he saw the house, as he was looking forward to its tranquillity and the hovering, maternal care of his housekeeper, Mrs. Soames. He had student essays to read and grade and he was working on his second book about labor and management.

As soon as he opened the door, Mrs. Soames came rushing into the room, a heavy cloud of powdered scent hovering about her, her face bursting with smiles—as was the rest of her bursting. Mrs. Soames was an excellent cook but she "tasted" the dishes a little too often.

"You're home," she said happily, then held out a letter to him. "It's from those people up north, the ones the governor wants you to take care of."

"That's not what he said," Hank began. "He—" Hank stopped because it was no use explaining again to her what his job was to be. He opened the letter while Mrs. Soames stood there and watched, knowing it was no use asking her to leave.

He frowned when he finished reading. "It seems the Cauldens want me to come and stay with them. They want me to be their guest until after the hops are in."

"They're up to something," Mrs. Soames said suspiciously.

Hank rubbed the back of his neck. "Probably just want me to get to know them and like them. I'm not likely to take the laborers' side if I'm staying in the luxurious quarters of the management."

"So, are you planning to stay with them?"

He put the letter down on a table. "I think I'll decline their gracious offer. I need to do some extra work with a few students anyway, so I'll stay here until just a few days before the workers are due to arrive to pick the hops."

"Good!" Mrs. Soames said firmly. "Now you sit there and rest. I've fixed you a nice dinner."

He watched her hurry out, then poured himself a large whiskey, removed his jacket and sat down to read the evening newspaper.

Mrs. Soames, in the kitchen, wasn't nearly as calm as Hank was. She slammed pie dough down on the table and attacked it with a rolling pin. Too many people took advantage of her Dr. Hank. They seemed to think he could do everything at once. They thought he could teach those ungrateful students of his, be the Executive Secretary of whatever-his-title-was, race his cars—the only fun he had—and, in his spare time, prevent labor strikes. It was more than one man should be asked to do.

But Dr. Hank believed in helping people less fortunate than himself and he would risk his life to help them. And didn't she know that to be true! Six years ago she was married and living in Maine with the odious man who had been her husband for nearly twenty years. He drank; he beat her. She bore scars from his abuse but no one would help her get away from him. Her family said she was his wife for better or worse and she just happened to get only the worse. They were sorry to see her wounds but there was nothing they could do to help her. The police wouldn't help; the hospital where she spent a week once when he'd nearly killed her gave her back to him. She ran away from him three times, even managed to get two hundred miles away once, but he always found her again. She had almost given up hope until Dr. Montgomery, driving by in one of his motorcars, happened to see the old man strike Mrs. Soames.

Dr. Montgomery stopped his car, jumped out, hit her husband in the face and escorted Mrs. Soames to his car. Mrs. Soames was suspicious of the handsome young man at first, but then she asked herself, What could he possibly want from her?

He drove her home to his family, who lived in a long, sprawling house that his family had owned since before the American Revolution. Dr. Montgomery's mother, a breathtakingly beautiful woman, had swept down the stairs and looked Mrs. Soames up and down. "Another stray, Hank?" she'd said, then gone on her way.

Mrs. Soames stayed with the lovely family for three months, making herself as useful as possible until Mrs. Montgomery began to say she couldn't run the house without Mrs. Soames.

Dr. Hank obtained a divorce for Mrs. Soames and then, to make sure she wasn't bothered again, he asked her to go with him when he went all the way across the country to California to accept a post as an economics professor. Mrs. Soames had readily accepted and these last five years had been the happiest of her life.

But the very trait in him that had made him save her was what also worried her. He cared about people less fortunate than he was. He cared about the man who delivered the coal and always had Mrs. Soames save a piece of pie for him. Yet there were several men Dr. Hank worked with, illustrious men, educated men, who he wasn't particularly polite to.

Last year that book of his that had caused such a stir had been published. All she knew was that it was something about being on the side of the maids and delivery men of the world. Mrs. Soames was sure it was a good book but it certainly had caused trouble.

Union organizers, men who all seemed to be nervous, their eyes jumping around, came to see him. Mrs. Soames counted the silver when they left.

She put the pie in the oven then grabbed the potatoes to mash. And now these rich farmers wanted her Dr. Hank to come and stay with them. Corrupt him, that's what they wanted to do. Give him wine with his every meal, feed him French sauces and give him indigestion.

And worst of all, she thought, as she slammed the masher against the innocent potatoes, they wanted to endanger her dear Dr. Hank's life with that union riffraff. Her dear, saintly Dr. Hank needn't risk his life for a bunch of people he didn't know. He had enough to do at his college.

She put the massacred potatoes aside and went into the parlor. He was sitting quietly on the sofa, reading his paper and sipping his whiskey. The setting sun came in through the west window and made his hair glow like an angel's. Like the angel he was, she thought, looking at his profile. Such a handsome man, she thought. Such a good, kind, lovely man.

She walked across the room to pull the curtains closed so the sun wouldn't shine in his eyes and she saw a long white open-topped limousine pull up outside. A chauffeur in a spotless white uniform and cap sat in front and in back was a beautiful young woman wearing a white silk dress, an enormous-brimmed white hat with white ostrich plumes curling around it and softly framing the woman's face. Her hair was a deep shade of red, the only color on her, the car or the chauffeur.

Mrs. Soames jerked the curtains shut and gave a glare at the back of Hank's head. There was one area where her Dr. Hank wasn't so innocent and that was when it came to women. She never asked, of course, exactly what he did on those automobile races of his, but twice he had returned with articles of ladies' undergarments in his luggage. Once there had been a black silk stocking inside his trouser leg.

She turned to peep back out the curtain and saw the chauffeur helping the young woman out of the car. And in the woman's hand was—oh no!—it looked to be a book of wallpaper samples.

Mrs. Soames closed the curtain and rolled her eyes skyward. He had done it again. She had tried to explain that it was all right to save fat old women like herself from unpleasant situations, but when he started saving young women they expected something from him—like marriage and a family, for instance.

She gave the back of his head a look of disgust. He was much too old to be getting himself into these predicaments.

She walked to the front of him and took the newspaper out of his hands and began folding it. "You have a guest coming," she said sternly. "Tall, red hair, henna I would say, very pretty."

Hank finished his whiskey and looked puzzled. "I don't seem to remember . . ."

When men had flaws they had *flaws*. Were there so many women in his life that he didn't remember this stunning woman? She narrowed her eyes at him and slipped his empty glass into her apron pocket. "She has a bosom like the prow of a ship."

Hank grinned in memory. "Blythe Woodley."

Mrs. Soames's mouth made a disapproving little line. "She has a wallpaper sample book."

Hank's face lost its color. "She's in front? I think I'll go out the back. Tell her—"

"I will *not!*" Mrs. Soames said indignantly. "You have made that poor woman believe something that isn't true and now you must face her like a man and not take the cowardly way out." She started to say more but she didn't as she turned on her heel and left him alone in the room.

Hank slowly slipped on his jacket and prepared to face what he knew was coming. Three years ago Blythe had been a student of his and he'd been impressed with her intelligence, her curiosity, the thought she put into her essays, her questions asked in class, and, not least of all, her magnificent bosom. Not that he ever was forward with her in the least. Even when she stayed after class and asked him questions and gave him every opportunity to make their relationship a more personal one, he had remained aloof from her. He didn't touch his students.

At the start of the next school year, he had expected to see her again but he hadn't seen her on campus. Then one day he saw her walking across campus wearing some frothy sort of dress more suited for a dance than for study. He'd stopped her and asked her how she was. He didn't like what she told him. Her family, which had a little money—nothing like Hank's, though—had introduced her to the son of an old friend of her father's. They'd spent all summer together and one thing led to another and at the end of the summer they'd become engaged. It was only after the engagement that Blythe found out that her fiancé didn't want her to go to college. Under pressure from him, her family and his family, she'd left college and entered a cookery school.

Hank hadn't liked this idea; he hated the idea of someone else controlling another person's life, but if it made Blythe happy, it wasn't any of his concern.

She said she was on her way to luncheon with her fiancé and, on impulse, she asked him to go with her.

Also on impulse, Hank accepted her invitation. Maybe it was impulse but it might have been a tone in Blythe's voice, a kind of urgency and pleading, or maybe it was the touch of sadness in her eyes.

He went to lunch with them and it was worse than he feared. Blythe's fiancé was obviously scared to death of a woman who might be as smart—or smarter —than he was. He condescendingly explained the items on the French menu to Blythe, yet Hank knew Blythe spoke and wrote French fluently. He asked Hank about his book, then, before Hank could answer, he patted Blythe's hand and said they'd better not bore her with an intellectual conversation. And Blythe was the woman who'd last year missed only one question on the toughest final exam he'd ever given!

He didn't like what he saw but he wasn't going to interfere. He'd already learned that when you stepped between a pretty woman and her fiancé or husband or father, pretty women expected you to marry them. Ugly women thanked you ever so much for freeing them and went on their way, but pretty women expected you to spend the rest of your life with them.

So he'd walked away from that luncheon and done nothing, not so much as said one word to Blythe about how she was throwing her life away for this pompous young man.

But then, the best-laid plans . . .

He'd come in the winner of the Harriman Derby and he was exhilarated with winning and he didn't remotely feel like a professor of economics. He was just a happy, healthy, energetic young man with a silver trophy in his arms and people cheering him, and there, on the sidelines, had stood Blythe Woodley wearing a white dress and all that red hair of hers hanging down her back with this cocky green feather curving around her head. He didn't think. He just put his free arm out and she came to him, curving her body to his so well that she was like a second trophy he'd won.

At the hotel, after the door was closed, for just a second he'd had a return to sanity and told her she'd better leave. But then she'd slowly raised her skirt above her knee and revealed a black silk stocking. He could resist most anything, but black silk stockings on long, slender legs was not one of them. He thought he might betray his country if a woman asked questions of him while revealing a pretty leg.

They had spent the weekend together—a wonderful, exciting two days of champagne baths and, one morning, a wild ride across the Arizona desert in his newly cleaned racer, then a picnic and lovemaking beneath a saguaro cactus. On Monday he'd kissed her goodbye and had returned home and she, he assumed, had gone back to her fiancé.

But now, a month later, she was at his doorstep bearing a wallpaper sample book, and he knew that wallpaper samples or fabric samples meant marriage.

He glanced longingly at the whiskey decanter but a knock sounded at the door and there was no more time.

Mrs. Soames found him later, sitting in the darkness, sipping more whiskey and, to her dismay, the decanter was half empty. She turned on a table lamp and, except for blinking his eyes, he didn't move. Scattered about the room were torn pieces of wallpaper as if someone, in fury, had torn sheets and thrown them—which is probably just what happened, she thought with a grimace.

She was not going to let him sit there and feel sorry for himself. "You deserved it, you know," she said angrily. "You lead these young women on. You make them love you, then you refuse to marry them. And while we're on that, why *don't* you marry one of them? That young lady, Miss Woodley, looked perfectly respectable to me. You're twenty-eight years old and it's high time you thought about settling down and raising a family. Maybe then you'd stop this foolish racing of cars and stealing women away from other men."

She stopped her tirade when she saw how sad he looked. She sat down beside him and patted his hand. "There, dearie, you meant well."

"The funny thing is," he said softly, "I would rather like to get married. It's just that I haven't found her yet. I can't think of a thing wrong with Blythe. She's really quite perfect. She's smart and interesting, dazzling to look at, great in—well, good company, and she's from a family good enough to please my grandmother."

"So marry her," Mrs. Soames said. "Or at least court her. I don't think it will take much to fall in love with her."

He sipped more whiskey. "I could never love her. I don't know why, but I know she isn't the one. I have this feeling that someday I'll see her and I'll know her." He turned to grin at Mrs. Soames. "That sounds somewhat metaphysical, doesn't it?"

"It sounds to me like a man who's had too much whiskey on an empty stomach." She heaved herself up. "You come in and eat now."

Hank didn't move but just stared blankly ahead. "I'm going to go to Caulden's ranch," he said. "I think I'd like a little vacation from this place."

Mrs. Soames sniffed. "You want to put some distance between you and that poor Miss Woodley is what you want."

Hank began to look sad again. "I never meant to insinuate marriage. She just—"

"Come on and eat," Mrs. Soames said, exasperated.

"I just pray this Mr. Caulden doesn't have a daughter who is oppressed or repressed or anything else, so that you feel like saving her."

Hank smiled crookedly and got off the couch. "If he does have a daughter, I'll stay away from her, I swear. I don't care if she wears nothing but black silk stockings and walks into my room in the middle of the night, I'll still stay away from her."

Mrs. Soames chose to ignore that remark.

Chapter Three

Amanda suppressed another yawn and tried not to look with dismay at the tall stack of books on her desk. For days she had done nothing but read books on economics in preparation for the professor's visit. Both her father and Taylor had drilled her about the importance of this man's visit and how Amanda was to be a gracious hostess. "And keep him away from here," J. Harker had said. "I don't want him snooping around my land."

Taylor had given her a list of museums and places of interest to visit. Perhaps she might go with him to Terrill City to visit the library there. He wanted Amanda to brush up on her local history so she could act as a knowledgeable tour guide.

Amanda so wanted to please the two men in her life but it seemed to be almost impossible with this Dr. Montgomery coming. The fear that her father and Taylor shared—that Amanda might act like her mother—was beginning to worry Amanda too. She must not, under any circumstances, forget herself. She must make her father and Taylor proud of her. This professor was a man of great learning and she must not disgrace herself with him. Taylor said Amanda had a frivolous streak in her—no doubt inherited from her mother—that must be suppressed. And he said that the outcome of what happened with the union leaders depended on Amanda's favorably impressing Dr. Montgomery. A great deal depended on the high caliber of Amanda's intellectual stimulation of Dr. Montgomery.

She returned to the books.

Hank drove through the beautiful California countryside south of Sacramento, the little Mercer open all around and allowing him to smell the flowers and enjoy the fragrant breezes. It was a beautiful little summer car, no top, no doors, just a bright yellow body, yellow wheels, and black leather seats. It was a man's car, low to the ground, very fast when pushed, the heavy steering improving the faster it went. The car did have a flaw in the fact that the brakes were next to useless, but its speed and torque (it could climb very steep hills in fourth gear) made up for the bad brakes.

Hank was looking forward to a few weeks of rest on a hop farm. He imagined Caulden's plump wife serving hot biscuits and gravy in the mornings. He imagined lying in a hammock and dozing in the sultry heat. It would be nice to get away for a while from books and students and papers to grade.

North of Sacramento was Kingman, and he slowed down to look. It was a medium-sized town built around five railroad tracks, and from the hustle and bustle of the people, the place looked to be thriving. There was the Opera House that played motion pictures every Friday and Saturday night and matinees during the week. He passed a rich-looking residential area with big, well-kept houses.

At a filling station on the west side of town, he asked where the Caulden ranch was. The attendant turned and pointed toward the horizon. All Hank saw across the flat land was another town in the distance.

"It's near that town?" Hank asked.

"That 'town' *is* the ranch," the attendant replied.

Hank stood and stared at it for a while, looking at building after building spread along the horizon, and he began to understand why the ULW wanted to start at this place. Make a ruckus here and the world would hear the noise.

He got back into the Mercer and started driving toward the Caulden Ranch. He passed several side roads that no doubt led into the ranch but turned when he came to a wide road bordered by palm trees and flowering shrubs. The road led half a mile to a two-story brick house with a wide, deep verandah around most of it.

No one came out at the sound of his car and so he went to the door and knocked. A maid answered, an unsmiling, lusterless-looking little woman who politely took his straw hat, led him out of the dark panelled vestibule and into the big hall. To the left was a pair of french doors, and the maid politely knocked, then slid one door open.

"They are waiting for you," the maid murmured and Hank moved past her.

In the library, directly before him was a fireplace flanked by two floor-to-ceiling windows that looked into the green lushness of a conservatory. He smiled slightly at the sight and thought he'd like to explore the place. To his right were two more doors, both shut.

To his left, he could feel the eyes of people, so he turned slowly and saw two men. The older one had the belligerent look of a mean little kid who was being made to do something he didn't want to do, while the other one looked as perfect as a store mannequin. He's a cold fish, Hank thought, and immediately liked the older man better.

"I'm J. Harker Caulden," the older man said, as if daring Hank to challenge him. "And this is my son-in-law, Taylor Driscoll."

Hank held out his hand to shake, but Caulden ignored him, so he turned to Driscoll. Driscoll's hand was as cool as his looks and his hand felt fragile in Hank's.

"You don't look like a college teacher," J. Harker said daringly.

Before Hank could speak, Taylor stepped forward. "What Mr. Caulden means, Dr. Montgomery, is that we assumed you'd be older, a bit more mature."

Hank grinned. "I hope I'm not a disappointment."

"No, of course not," Taylor said. "You are welcome. I imagine you'll want to get settled before luncheon. Martha will show you to your room."

Hank knew he'd been dismissed. He nodded and left the room. You aren't any more disappointed than I am, Mr. Iceberg, he thought, I was hoping for a pretty little farmhouse. Oh well, he could always leave in a day or two. He followed Martha up the stairs.

J. Harker was chewing on an unlit cigar and pacing the library. "I don't like it one little bit," he said. "He doesn't look like a college professor should. He looks too young, too healthy. He looks like he might go out in the fields and lead a strike himself."

"All the more reason to keep him where we can watch him. I admit his age and looks threw me for a moment, but I will try to make up for the rudeness of both of us. He *must* be kept away from the fields. We have to save every penny we can this year or we'll lose everything."

"You don't have to remind me," J. Harker said bitterly. "It's just that he don't—"

"Doesn't," Taylor corrected him automatically. "Doesn't look as a professor should. Amanda will—"

"Amanda! Surely you don't think I'll let her go out alone with *him.*"

Taylor's face showed little emotion. "I have taught her well and she is obedient. She will help us now that we need her."

J. Harker looked hard at the man who was to be his son-in-law. Taylor seemed to have supreme confidence that he was going to get everything he wanted out of his life. Years ago Harker had tried to get him to marry Amanda, but Taylor wanted to wait until she was "trained properly." Harker hadn't protested, but now he thought Taylor was making a mistake if he let Amanda go out alone with this good-looking young buck. "I think you'll be sorry for this," Harker said. "She has the blood of her mother in her."

"I know Amanda," Taylor said. "There's something . . . insolent about that man that Amanda will greatly dislike. Trust me. She will help us."

"You have more faith in women than I do," Harker said, clamping down on his cigar.

The bedroom the maid led Hank to was quite nice. It was at the front of the second floor, looking north with east and west windows. There was a pretty little private balcony with two wrought-iron chairs and a tiny table. While standing on the balcony, to his left was the roof of the first-story verandah wrapping around the windows of what he assumed was another bedroom.

His room was dark and clean and the furniture of good quality, but it had none of the homey touches that Hank had grown used to with Mrs. Soames. He looked at the books in the bookcase and found nothing of interest and so began to hang up his clothes. He had refused Martha's offer of help.

He removed his dusty traveling jacket, rolled up his shirt sleeves and headed for the bathroom Martha had pointed out to him. The door was closed, so he knocked.

"Yes?" came a woman's voice.

"I'm sorry," Hank said, "I'll come back."

"I will be out in three and a half minutes," said the woman.

Hank was already on his way back to his room when he heard this. A *woman* who knew *exactly* how long she was going to be in the bathroom? Hank stopped where he was and lounged against a wall where he could see the tall clock and the bathroom door.

As the hands neared three minutes, he reached into his pocket for a coin to flip to lay odds with himself whether or not she'd be punctual.

At exactly three and a half minutes the bathroom door opened and out stepped what Hank thought was surely the most beautiful woman he'd ever seen. Tall, thin—too thin—big brown eyes that looked wary, sad, frightened and curious all at once. Deep, dark chestnut hair. He didn't see what she was wearing, for he seemed to see her in several gowns: medieval velvet, Napoleonic muslin, Victorian taffeta, Edwardian linen.

The coins in his hand fell to the floor.

"May I help you?" the woman-vision asked.

"I . . . ah, I . . ." Hank stuttered stupidly.

The next second the vision was gone and he was able to see again. No, she wasn't the most beautiful woman in the world. She was very pretty, true, but, technically, she wasn't as beautiful as Blythe Woodley. But he couldn't stop staring at her.

"Are you Dr. Montgomery?" she asked.

He began to recover. "Yes, I am, and you are?"

"Amanda Caulden. Welcome to my home."

She held out her hand to him and he almost didn't take it. What in the world was wrong with him? "Thank you very much. I met your father and his son-in-law. You must have a married sister." He was doing his best to make conversation but he was getting lost in her eyes. Not again, Montgomery, he commanded, thinking of what had happened with Blythe Woodley. Don't even consider it.

"Taylor is my fiancé. Now, Dr. Montgomery, if you'll excuse me, I'm late."

"You're leaving?" he said, then cursed to himself because he sounded like a little boy whose mother was leaving.

"No, I shall join you at luncheon. Shall I help you pick up your coins?"

"No, I can," he said quickly, and immediately went to all fours and reached under a table for a coin, then turned to look up at Amanda and bumped his head. She took a step forward and saved a vase of flowers from falling to the floor.

"Perhaps I should call a maid," she suggested.

"No, I'll be fine," he said, then bumped his head again.

Amanda just looked at him, expressionless, then opened the door to the room next to his and went inside, closing herself from his view.

Hank sat on the floor and cursed for a full five minutes, but he couldn't get the image of her from his mind. He saw her as something from a painting from Fragonard: on a swing, laughing, satin skirts blowing, exposing lacy petticoats and tiny shoes with jeweled buckles. He saw her running through fields of golden wheat, long hair streaming out behind her. He saw her dancing a tango, wearing a slinky dress.

He saw her in his arms.

He stood, his eyes on the door to Amanda's room, and, without conscious thought, he walked softly to her door and put his hand against it.

It was at that moment that Amanda opened the door to her room—and almost got Hank's hand in her face.

She was too startled to do anything but stare at him, her eyes wide.

"I . . . ah, the coins. I, ah . . ." Hank stammered, then gave her a weak smile.

"It is time for luncheon," she said firmly and turned sideways to get past him. She halted on the stairs and put her hand to her breast and willed her heart to stop pounding. Was this man insane or just very eccentric? He didn't look like a college professor. In fact, he didn't act as if he had a brain in his head. She had left the bathroom and there he had stood, staring at her as if he'd never seen a woman before. Amanda had looked down to see if perhaps she had forgotten some important article of clothing. Then he'd thrown coins on the floor and floundered about, nearly knocking over furniture as he tried to retrieve them.

What he had been doing when she opened her door and nearly walked into his hand, she didn't like to think about. She continued down the stairs.

"Amanda, you are late," Taylor said sternly.

"I . . . I met Dr. Montgomery."

Taylor was watching her. "He is younger than we anticipated and therefore more dangerous. He must be kept occupied. Have you studied the topics for today's discussion?"

"Yes," she said in a faraway voice. She couldn't possibly voice her complaints to Taylor. She couldn't say that she didn't *like* Dr. Montgomery, or that she was even a little afraid of him. Taylor wanted her to spend time with him and she had to do it—for Taylor.

Dr. Montgomery sauntered down to the dining room at five minutes after one. At least this time he was fully dressed. Even though Taylor had lived in the same house with Amanda for eight years, had shared the same bathroom, she had never seen him in his shirt sleeves as Dr. Montgomery had first appeared to her.

Now he wore a simple, rather too casual tan suit and he had a way of sitting in his chair that was not quite proper.

"Was I late?" he asked. "Sorry. It took me a while to find all the coins. I can't afford to lose anything, not on my salary," he said, smiling at Amanda as if they shared some private joke.

Amanda did not return his smile. "I wonder, Dr. Montgomery, if we might discuss some of the issues of your book."

Hank was looking down at his plate in astonishment. No bowls or platters of food were served, just individual platefuls of what looked to be invalid food:

a pale, soggy fish, about six green beans, three slices of tomato. He was hungry and this wasn't going to fill a hole in a sock, much less the hole in his belly. He looked at the identical plates of Taylor and Amanda— except Amanda had even less on her plate. He'd have to get something to eat later.

"Dr. Montgomery?" Taylor said.

Hank looked at him, at the way he sat, shoulders back, neck stiff, and thought he took a lot on himself. He was just a fiancé yet he sat at the head of another man's table. And why was he waiting to marry Amanda?

"Oh yes, issues," Hank said and took a bite of his fish. It was as flavorful as eating a spongy piece of air. "I guess the real issue is, Who owns the land? Does the rich rancher or the worker? Does the rancher have the right to treat the worker as he wants or was slavery abolished? When are you two getting married?"

Amanda was speechless at the man's presumption and rudeness, but Taylor was very smooth. He acted as if he hadn't heard the last question.

"I believe it is the rancher's land. The workers are not slaves, they can leave when they want," Taylor said.

"And let their wives and kids starve?" Hank answered. "Look, maybe we better not get into this yet."

"Of course, you're right. This afternoon Amanda will take you on a tour of the ranch and you can see how a ranch of this size operates."

Hank looked across the table at Amanda and thought it would be better not to be alone with her. He wondered how long her hair was when it was down. He'd already finished his meager meal, so he watched Amanda and Taylor eat their tasteless food ever so slowly. They seemed so prim and proper, yet they were in love and about to be married. Did they kiss passionately beneath the palm trees? Did Amanda slip into Taylor's room at night?

"If it's all the same to you, I thought I'd find a hammock and doze for the afternoon," Hank said, then saw the two of them gaping at him. Now what did I say? he thought.

Taylor recovered first. "It has been arranged and there is no hammock," he said, as if he expected no further change of his plans. Hank wanted to defy the arrogant bastard, but if Taylor was forcing the lovely Amanda on him, why should Hank fight him? Besides, they could go into town and get something to eat.

Amanda had hoped Taylor would allow the man to waste the afternoon lying about in a hammock, but he hadn't, and Amanda knew he must have his reasons. She added laziness to the list of Dr. Montgomery's attributes. She already had clumsy, poor table manners, aggressive, slovenly dresser. How many others would she discover this afternoon?

At the end of luncheon, Amanda said, "I will meet you at 2:15, Dr. Montgomery, in the north vestibule."

His eyes twinkled. "Which end of the vestibule?"

"I beg your pardon?"

He smiled at her. "I will be there precisely at 2:15, not thirty seconds later."

When she turned away from him she was frowning. For some reason she seemed to amuse him. She went upstairs to get ready, and when she came down he was waiting for her, leaning against the wall as if he were too tired to stand up straight. "Shall we go?"

"Your wish is my command."

She didn't know why, but his every word seemed to

grate on her. The chauffeur waited for them, but Dr. Montgomery hesitated before getting into the back seat with Amanda.

Amanda did her best with him, oh how she tried, but he never seemed to be listening to her. Taylor had drawn a map for her that showed the route they were to take around the ranch and he'd listed facts she was to tell Dr. Montgomery, facts she'd memorized about how much it cost to run a ranch the size of the Cauldens'. She told Dr. Montgomery acreage, number of hops produced, number of employees fed and sheltered. She showed him the other crops grown on the ranch: figs, walnuts, almonds, corn, and strawberries and asparagus in the spring.

But he just sat in the back of the limousine and stared out the window and said nothing.

She showed him the grape fields and the small winery.

"How about a bottle?" he asked, pulling one from its holder.

"My family does not drink alcohol," she said. "This is for sale." She turned away from him and continued telling him the facts about the winery.

"You're a regular little encyclopedia, aren't you?" he said as they got back into the car.

Amanda, under other circumstances, might have thought his words were a compliment, but somehow his tone was not that of a compliment. She didn't know what to reply to him.

At 3:51, as Taylor's schedule said, she had the chauffeur return them to the ranch house so that they arrived back at precisely four P.M. Amanda suggested that Dr. Montgomery make use of their library, but he had given her an odd look, said he could take care of himself and had left the house. Later, Amanda had seen his little two-seater, topless car speed down the road toward town.

She sat down at her desk and tried to study her French textbook, but her hands were shaking. He was a *very* unsettling man. She had never been very good with strangers, but this man made her feel awkward and strange and, well, she didn't like to think this, but he somehow, well, made her feel angry. He didn't exactly sneer, he didn't ridicule, but somehow, she felt disapproval coming from him. Not disapproval of the ranch—at times he'd shown some interest in things, such as listening for the rustling sound a hop made when it was ripe—but she felt he disapproved of her.

She left her desk and went to the small mirror over the dresser. What was it about her that he disapproved of? Did he find her physically repulsive? Stupid? She had tried to be as accurate a guide as possible and had spent several days memorizing Taylor's facts about the ranch, but she felt she had failed. Were Dr. Montgomery's female students so much more erudite than she that by comparison she was a moron?

Again, she had that feeling of anger but she pushed it down and returned to her desk. Tomorrow she was scheduled to take him to a museum in Kingman and she had to tell him about Digger Indians, the Donner Party and early mining in the area. She had better review her facts.

Hank sat on a bar stool eating a three-inch-thick corned-beef sandwich and drinking a beer—his third.

What a little prig she was, he thought. What a

self-righteous, know-it-all, fact-spouting little prig! She lectured him as if he were an elementary school student. She was the lady of the manor and she had been given the onerous task of entertaining the town blacksmith, an uneducated lout who didn't know a knife from a fork. He'd seen the way she looked down her little nose at him while they were eating that tasteless meal.

No doubt she thought of him the way her father thought of the laborers, that they should be grateful to get to work for so illustrious a family as the Cauldens and how dare they ask for decent wages? Why, it should be enough that he allowed them to bask in his sunshine, to touch his crops. She, that sanctimonious little Miss Amanda, probably thought he was thrilled to get to stay in a house like theirs. Tomorrow she'll probably ask if I've ever seen a flush toilet before, he thought, slugging down the rest of his beer.

He wasn't sure what he should do. His instinct was to leave the Caulden house immediately, but he felt an obligation to the governor and, most of all, to the unionists. Maybe his presence *could* prevent trouble. Maybe he could watch out for the laborers' rights better if he were inside the Caulden house. Just being there, he might be able to stop something before it started. Logically, he knew he should stay. Emotionally, he wanted to get away from the cold little Amanda and her even colder fiancé. And to think that when he'd first seen her he'd—

He didn't know what it was that he'd felt, but she'd snowed on it and killed the seed.

He left the cool, dark bar and stepped into the bright sunlight, thrust his hands into his pockets and went to his car. It was about time for dinner at the

Cauldens'. Wonder what they were having? Boiled chicken and boiled rice and boiled potatoes?

Amanda had never seen Taylor so angry.

"That is not the dress I told you to wear to dinner," he said under his breath.

Amanda tried to keep her back straight and not cry. Taylor hated tears. "I forgot. Dr. Montgomery upset me and—"

"Upset you how?" If possible, Taylor made himself taller. "Was he forward with you?"

"No, he doesn't . . . I mean, I think he dislikes me."

"Dislikes you?" Taylor was aghast. "Amanda, I am surprised at you. I thought you above these female vapors. Did you follow the schedule? Did you explain to him each part of the ranch?"

"Yes, I did it exactly, to the minute as your schedule said."

"Then there can have been nothing wrong. Now go upstairs and change your clothes and do not tell me any more of your fantasies. You are going to make me think that I have chosen the wrong woman to marry."

"Yes, Taylor," she whispered and went to her room. Alone in her room, dressing as fast as she could, she felt it again, that little gnawing sense of anger. She hadn't felt anger since Taylor came to live with them. Before he came she often felt anger. She used to get angry at her mother, at her father, at her friends at school.

Then her father had hired Taylor and given him absolute control over Amanda. He had taken her out of school in Kingman and started giving her private lessons. Things had changed then. Amanda soon learned that anger and/or defiance was a useless emotion; Taylor didn't allow either. He had put Amanda on a schedule that didn't allow for anger (4:13 P.M. temper tantrum). No such thing was permitted. And he had hired Mrs. Gunston to make sure Amanda did what she was told.

Besides the classes, Taylor had said Amanda's mother was a bad influence on her. After all, didn't Grace Caulden have a "past"? J. Harker had agreed, and Grace had been sent to some expensive spas around the world, and when she returned, her daughter had not even been allowed to hug her hello. Grace had retired to a spare bedroom at the back of the top floor and had rarely come out since.

As Amanda started down the stairs again, she vowed she'd try harder to please Dr. Montgomery and therefore please Taylor.

Chapter Four

Hank was late for dinner and he felt Taylor's cold displeasure as soon as he walked in the door. Was this house run like a military school? Again, J. Harker did not appear and it was just the three of them eating. If you could call what was on the plate eating. He'd been wrong about the menu. It was boiled chicken, boiled rice and boiled *beets*.

He couldn't keep his mouth shut. "You feed your hands this well? No wonder unionists are choosing you to picket."

Taylor gave him a look to freeze. "It is better for the body to eat lightly. Amanda and I constantly fight gluttony."

"You've won," Hank said and pushed his plate away. "You mind if I'm excused? I have some reading to do."

"Amanda is finished also," Taylor said. "She would like to show you the almond orchard."

"That's all right. I've seen a lot of the ranch today." He got out of his chair and started toward the door.

Taylor gave Amanda a glare that let her know she was to follow the professor. With a yearning look toward her half-eaten food, she followed Dr. Montgomery.

Hank stopped when he heard her behind him. "Afraid I'll see something I shouldn't?"

"I have no idea what you mean, Dr. Montgomery," she said honestly.

"You wouldn't know where the kitchen was, would you?"

"Through there," she said, pointing, then followed him. She had not been in the kitchen for years, not since Taylor had found her there one day eating milk and cookies. He had been horrified at her impending obesity.

In the center of the big kitchen was an oak table covered with many dishes: roast beef, gravy, at least five vegetables, yeast rolls, butter, fruit salad, green salad, and on a counter were three kinds of cake. The servants were sitting down to dinner, food halfway to their mouths when they stopped at the sight of Hank and Amanda.

"Miss Amanda!" the cook gasped and sprang to her feet.

Hank just gaped at the food. "Mind if I join you?"

"No!" Amanda said, knowing that Taylor would be furious with her if she allowed him to sit with the servants. "I mean——"

The cook, who had been with the family since Amanda was a baby, knew a great deal of what was going on. She also knew what this big, strapping, healthy Dr. Montgomery had been given to eat today. "I'll fix you a plate," she said to Hank.

"Yes," was all he could say, his mouth watering. "And from now on, I want *real* meals."

She smiled at him. "If Mr. Taylor will allow——"

"*I* will allow it," Hank said, taking the heaping platter of food from her.

"Miss Amanda?" the cook said, holding out an empty plate.

Amanda didn't remember having seen so much food in her life and she felt fairly faint for wanting it. But Taylor wouldn't approve; he didn't like plump women. "No, thank you," she said at last.

"All right," Hank said, "take me to the almond orchard or someplace where I can sit down."

Amanda went out the back door behind Hank, leaving the delicious smells behind her and following his fragrant plate like a hungry dog.

"There," Hank said, his mouth full and pointing with a loaded fork toward the little summerhouse. It was a floor, a roof and four latticed posts, and inside seats all around.

She followed him into the summerhouse and sat opposite him and all she was aware of was the smell of the food.

"You aren't going to tell me when this was built?" Hank asked, wolfing down roast beef. "Or what kind of wood this is?"

"It was built in 1903, right after my parents and I moved here. It is made of cypress and is an exact copy of an English gazebo my mother saw in a magazine."

"Oh. Sorry. I guess you don't like to talk about your mother."

She was surprised that he knew. Everyone else in Kingman knew, so why not this stranger? He was eating a buttered roll. Taylor did not believe in bread and certainly not butter. "I'd rather not talk about her."

"I understand. When did she die?"

"Die?" Amanda asked. "My mother is not dead."

"But she doesn't live with you, then?"

51

"My mother stays in her room. Perhaps, Dr. Montgomery, we should change the subject."

She turned her head away and Hank sat there, eating, and watched her. Seeing her profile in the moonlight made him remember his first impression of her, as if she came from another time and place, as if he'd known her before. But her coldness, her haughtiness, her snobbery made him know he was mistaken. He wondered if her thin little body was capable of emotion.

He turned at a noise and saw the cook coming through the darkness and bearing two plates, each heaped high with three slices of cake.

"Thought you might like a little something else," she said, setting the desserts down and taking Hank's empty plate, then leaving.

Hank offered a plateful to Amanda, but she shook her head. "Suit yourself, but it's awfully good." Little prude, he thought, too cool to even accept a piece of cake. No doubt she thought her purity would be threatened if she touched devil's food cake. He wondered if she and Taylor kissed at all. Probably it would be a kiss as tasteless as that afternoon's fish.

Amanda didn't dare look at him while he was eating the cake. Her stomach was rumbling and the smell was making her mouth water. But she didn't dare eat any because Taylor might smell it on her breath or see bits of chocolate between her teeth. He wouldn't like her if she were so weak-willed as to eat cake that wasn't on the schedule.

"Better," Hank said as he put his cleaned plate aside and leaned back against the post, his legs stretched out. "What do you have planned for us tomorrow? I assume you do have my day planned."

She frowned at his tone then began to quote Taylor's schedule. "We go to the Kingman Museum in the morning, then home for luncheon, and then a scenic tour of the area. That should take us to dinner time."

"What do you do for fun?"

"I do watercolors and sew," she answered, smiling to herself. Taylor gave her excellent grades on the watercolors and they were used as a reward for other subjects well done.

"How do you stand the excitement?" he murmured. "What do you and your lover do on nights on the town?"

"We do not go into town," she said, confused. Taylor said Kingman was too provincial to be worthy of his time, that he'd not visit a city smaller than San Francisco, where he went once a year to buy clothes and other necessary items. Other than those two weeks, he rarely left the ranch.

"Too good for it, are you?" Hank asked and realized he was getting nasty. Something about her primness, her smugness, her refusal to even bend enough to eat a piece of chocolate cake, brought out the worst in him.

He stood. "I'm going to bed. You coming in?"

"Yes," she said softly, and gave one last look at the shadow that she knew was the second plateful of cake.

Moments later she was in her room, and on her desk were pages of notes on the history of Kingman that she was to commit to memory before going to bed. She sat down heavily in her chair and wished for the thousandth time that Dr. Montgomery had never come. For some reason he seemed to dislike her a great deal, more with each passing minute, and to earn this dislike she was having to work twice as hard, miss meals, and repeatedly incur Taylor's wrath.

So tonight she would have to stay up late studying, and tomorrow she'd have to take him to a museum, and no matter how hard she'd try to be a good guide, she'd no doubt displease him. Why was *he* so hard to please and Taylor so easy? If she did what Taylor had written down, in the exact order, exactly on time, Taylor was happy. Perhaps she should ask Dr. Montgomery what he wanted of her. But no, that wasn't a good idea, because if it conflicted with Taylor's schedule, she'd have to ignore Dr. Montgomery's wishes.

She glanced at the clock on the wall and thought she'd better stop pondering and get to work.

Hank stood on the cool balcony, looking at the stars and smelling the rich fragrances of the night, and wished he had a whiskey. To his left was Amanda's room and he could see a light through the curtains, could even see the shadow of her sitting at her desk. He knew he could step off the balcony onto the verandah roof and walk right across to her window.

And then what, he thought. Have Miss Amanda tell him how many feet it was from his balcony to her window? He wondered what she'd do if he kissed her. Tell him the history of kissing?

He went back into his room, took off his clothes and climbed into bed. He went to sleep right away, but a couple of hours later he woke and, on impulse, put on his robe and went to the balcony. Amanda's light was still on and she was still hunched over her desk.

Frowning, he went back to bed. However much a prude she was, she was certainly diligent at whatever she did.

When he woke the next morning it was late and he sensed that people were already up and at work. He dressed hurriedly, then raced down the stairs. Amanda and Taylor were standing in the doorway to the dining room, Taylor looking at his pocket watch, Amanda obediently behind him.

"I guess I'm late again," he said without concern, and walked past them into the dining room. On the sideboard were silver servers full of scrambled eggs, biscuits, gravy, ham, sliced pineapple, waffles and syrup. "Ah," he said in the tone of a hungry man confronted with delicious food.

He filled a plate and sat down, then looked up to see Taylor and Amanda watching him. There was a sneer of disgust on Taylor's coldly perfect features but on Amanda's . . . It was just fleeting, but he almost thought he saw wistfulness or maybe it was true hunger, but the look was gone instantly and she looked down at the watery poached egg in her cup.

After breakfast the limousine and chauffeur were waiting and Hank almost groaned. Another day of touring and lectures.

An hour later they were standing in the Kingman Museum, which, as far as Hank could tell, was a tribute to the Caulden family.

"My father bought four ranches at one time," Amanda was saying. "They were very inexpensive because the silt from the mines nearby had caused the Glass River to flood and deposit the silt over the land. At great expense, my father dredged the silt off the land and exposed the rich soil underneath. He also put a stop to the mining."

"I bet he did," Hank murmured.

"Then he irrigated the land and—"

"Became rich," Hank put in.

Amanda looked away. Again he was making it clear that he didn't like her or her family.

"When did your father buy this museum?" he asked on a hunch.

"Two years ago." She didn't understand why he laughed at that.

"Come on, I've had enough. Let's go outside."

"But it isn't time yet. We still have forty-two minutes in here."

"I plan to spend forty-two minutes enjoying the out-of-doors."

Reluctantly, she followed him outside. She hoped Taylor wouldn't find out that they had left the museum early. And now what was she to do with him? She started toward the waiting limousine but he wasn't with her. She turned and looked at him standing there with his hands in his pockets, looking more like a very large little boy than a man. She did so wish he would stand up straight like . . . like Taylor did.

"How far is it to town?" he asked.

"Two and a quarter miles," she answered.

"Somehow, I thought you'd know. I'll walk. I'll meet you at the Opera House."

Amanda felt a moment of panic. She just knew he'd never show up at the Opera House and she had a hideous vision of having to tell Taylor that she had "lost" Dr. Montgomery. "The driver can—" she began, then stopped because he was walking rapidly toward town. With a sigh, she told the driver where to meet them, then, holding her hat on, she hurried after Dr. Montgomery.

When the car went by and he saw she wasn't in it, he turned back to see her scurrying along after him.

Impatiently, he waited. You'd think I'd want a beautiful young woman along, he thought. But Amanda was about as real as a magazine photo. "I don't guess I'm to be trusted alone, am I? Might meet with some union leaders and do something awful, right?"

Amanda suddenly felt very tired, tired from staying up most of the night trying to learn what she needed to know for this man, tired of missed meals, tired of his snide comments. "I am doing my best to make your stay pleasurable, Dr. Montgomery. I'm sorry if I'm failing." She kept her shoulders back in the posture Taylor had taught her—taught her with the help of a steel brace.

He relented. Maybe she couldn't help being a cold little prig any more than he could help being what he was. It wasn't right to be angry with her because she wasn't what he wanted her to be. So she walked as stiffly as a poker with two legs, so she pulled her hair back so tight her eyes were stretched, so she spoke only in facts, so she dressed like somebody's mother, so she had no humor, no warmth, no passion about her. It wasn't his business.

"I apologize, Miss Caulden, I have been rude to you. It's just that I haven't had my days planned for me since I left my mother's house, and I'm afraid I'm too old to start over again. Look, there are some children playing. Couldn't we just sit still for a while and smell the roses, so to speak?"

"Roses?" she asked. "There are no roses in the schoolyard."

He groaned, then took her elbow and began to lead her toward the fenced schoolyard. School was out now, but there were three young children playing on the swings and seesaws, and a pretty young mother standing nearby. He left Amanda near a bench under a giant oak tree and walked toward the group. More than anything in the world, he wanted to see a friendly face.

"Hello," he said, and the woman turned. She was indeed pretty and she *smiled* at him. It seemed to be ages since a woman had smiled at him.

"Hello," she answered.

"I'm—"

"No, don't tell me." She looked past him to Amanda sitting primly on the bench. "You must be the Cauldens' guest Some teacher or something, right?"

"Close enough," he answered, holding out his hand, which she shook. "Hank Montgomery." He nodded toward the children. "Good-looking bunch. Father still alive?"

She laughed. "He was an hour ago."

"My loss," Hank said with a sigh.

She walked away toward the swings and her little girl and Hank followed her. "What's it like up there?" she asked softly, motioning her head toward Amanda. "The Cauldens treating you right? You here to teach Amanda?"

"It's all right, and Amanda seems to be teaching me." He paused a moment. "You know her?"

"I did. We went to elementary school together, but her father took her out of school just about the time she started liking boys, you know?"

Hank couldn't imagine Amanda liking anyone, but he nodded. "He hired her a tutor?"

"That man Driscoll. I've only seen him a couple of

times. He doesn't come into Kingman, but I've seen him ride through in the back of a car. Not my type," she said, smiling more broadly at Hank.

Not mine either, Hank thought. So, Amanda was going to marry her tutor. That made sense, what with her little mind being nothing but a catalog of information.

The woman started to say more, but the little girl fell off the swing and started to scream and the woman picked her up. She didn't seem to be really hurt, just scared, and she kept peeping around her mother at Hank.

Hank put out his arms to her and the child went to him.

"Flirt!" her mother said, laughing.

Hank held the little girl and they studied each other. He liked children and hoped someday to have several of his own.

"Miss your kids?" the woman asked, prying for information.

"No kids; no wife."

"Are you and Amanda . . . ?"

"Heavens no!" he said before he thought. "I mean, she's engaged to her tutor, Taylor Driscoll. I figured everybody in town would know. Usually in small towns doesn't everybody know everybody else's business?"

"Not the Cauldens'," she said, again lowering her voice. "They may be rich as Croesus but there are some things that can't be bought. Not that I care, but to my mother's generation it mattered a lot."

"What did?" Hank asked.

The woman looked past him and he saw Amanda

approaching. She took her child and stopped her confidences.

"Hello, Amanda," she said.

"Hello," Amanda answered, and by her blank face it was easy to tell that she had no idea who the woman was.

"Lily Webster. We went to school together."

"Yes, of course," Amanda said. "How are you?"

"Overworked. Well, I better be going. Nice to meet you, Hank."

"Same here," he said, and smiled as she walked away, all three children hovering around her. Hank turned back to Amanda. "You ready to go?" He paused, for she was staring after the woman as if she'd seen a ghost. "You all right?" he asked.

Amanda recovered herself. "Yes, I'm ready." She remembered Lily. When they were in the fourth grade together they had sneaked into the cloakroom and tied and buttoned every piece of clothing together. They had just finished when the teacher caught them and made them unfasten everything then stand for two hours with their noses in a circle on the chalkboard. When her father heard of it he had been horrified but her mother had laughed delightedly.

But that had happened before Taylor came. Sometimes she didn't seem to remember anything that existed before Taylor came. It was as if his presence blotted out everything that had happened before his arrival.

Now her fellow prankster, Lily, was married and had three little children and Amanda didn't even know when her own wedding was to be.

She frowned at Dr. Montgomery's back. His questions were beginning to bother her. He was making her wonder what Taylor had planned for them. She *knew* when the wedding was to be—when Taylor felt she was ready and not before. And at the rate she was going in doing what he wanted her to do with Dr. Montgomery, she was *never* going to be ready to be married.

She walked just behind him the rest of the way into town and breathed a sigh of relief when she saw the limousine waiting in front of the Opera House. But to her chagrin, Dr. Montgomery turned away from the car. "Here it is," she called, hoping that perhaps he just hadn't seen it.

He ignored her and kept walking toward a restaurant. Amanda dodged two old Ford pickups and crossed the street after him. He had to go back to the ranch for luncheon because she had to pick up the schedule for the afternoon.

At the restaurant, he held the door open for her.

"Luncheon will be waiting for us at home," she said.

"Why drive all the way back there? Besides, it might do you good to eat somewhere else." He firmly took her arm and led her inside the cool restaurant, where the smell of years of meals permeated the place.

Amanda couldn't remember the last time she had eaten out. It had been here with her mother and she had been wearing white gloves. A waitress handed them menus and Amanda read of rolled fillets of veal, rib roasts, leg of lamb and stuffed chicken breasts. The selection made her mouth water, but she knew there was nothing of which Taylor would approve.

She put the menu down.

"Made up your mind already?" Hank asked.

"I'm not eating here."

Angrily, he slapped his menu down on the table. "What is it you have against food with flavor? Or is it that you're too good to eat in a public place?"

Again, that little feeling of anger rose in her. "It is neither. It is just that I do not wish to get fat."

He gaped at her, openmouthed. "Fat? You'd have to gain twenty pounds to be considered *thin.*" He picked up her menu and handed it to her. "I'm your guest and you're supposed to keep me happy, remember? I want you to eat."

She felt very frustrated. She wasn't supposed to get fat; Taylor didn't like fat women. But, too, Taylor wanted her to entertain Dr. Montgomery. Only Dr. Montgomery didn't like museums or tours of the ranch or healthy food. He liked to talk to women in parks and hold children, and walk, and eat. He seemed to like eating best of all.

Amanda tried to choose the least fattening thing on the menu, but when the waitress came, Dr. Montgomery chose for her: chicken breasts stuffed with creamed spinach, spiced peaches, sage dressing, watercress salad, yeast rolls and butter.

"Miss Caulden," he said, "if I swear not to run away or interfere in your father's business, tomorrow could we spare each other our company?"

"I . . . I don't know," she answered. What would Taylor say? She was to go with Dr. Montgomery to see where he went. But she was also supposed to make him *like* the Cauldens and she wasn't doing very well at that, was she? Taylor said he would be in awe of their house and ranch, but so far nothing seemed to awe him. She didn't know what to do. "Do you have any plans of your own?" she asked. Maybe he meant to stay at the house.

"I want to get in my car and drive. After that, I have no idea what I want to do." Except get away from this woman who unsettled him and made him alternately nervous and angry.

Amanda felt a moment of panic. Taylor would be angry if he went away by himself. "Would you possibly like to read tomorrow? If I repulse you I'm sure I could occupy myself elsewhere."

Damn, damn, damn, he thought. Honey, you don't repulse me. You drive me crazy. That hair of yours. Those big, sad eyes. That body that would be real nice with some meat on it. How could the interior of such a beautiful package be so awful?

"I do have some essays to grade and some letters to write," he said at last. "I'll stick around the house tomorrow."

She looked so relieved that he thought she might cry, and just for an instant he thought that she might get into trouble if he didn't do what she wanted. But that couldn't be. She was an ice lady or she wouldn't have fallen for stone-faced Driscoll. They were a perfect match. Maybe they made love to each other by reading love sonnets aloud.

The waitress put their plates of food on the table, and the expression on Amanda's face made Hank smile.

"You look like you're about to worship it rather than eat it. Dig in. Enjoy."

It had been years since Amanda had eaten food like this. Taylor said the body was a temple and must be treated with reverence, therefore it was not to be filled with unhealthy, greasy food.

Her first bite was heaven, absolute, sheer heaven. She closed her eyes and chewed and let the flavor roll about in her mouth.

Hank looked up from his plate to see Amanda with her eyes closed and wearing an expression that he had only seen on a woman's face when he was making love to her. He dropped his fork and her eyes flew open.

"Like"—his voice broke—"like the food?"

"Yes, thank you, I do."

She went back to eating, her eyes open, thank God, but Hank had a little trouble swallowing. Calm down, Montgomery, he told himself. She's just a pretty girl, that's all. You came here to talk to the union leaders, not get yourself in trouble like you did with Blythe Woodley.

"Miss Caulden, could you tell me a little about Kingman?"

Like a little box that you put a nickel in, she began to spout facts. She told about the five railroad tracks (one main one and four sidings) and the seven mail deliveries a day. She told about the Digger Indians, the Spanish land grants, the copper mines. She told about the Donner Party arriving just east of Kingman at the Johnson Ranch and she rattled off facts and dates about the rescue parties and the number of survivors and deaths. She told of dates when the town flooded and when it was burned down. She told of dams built, bridges built. She gave numbers of population, dates schools built, dates—

"Stop!" he said, gasping for air. She was a wind-up

toy that never ran down, but at least his ardor was cooled. Taylor Driscoll could have her. She was all looks and nothing else. "Eat your cherry pie," he said, pushing the plate toward her. He smiled at the way she cleaned her plate. For someone who was worried about getting fat, she sure could pack it away.

Chapter Five

Taylor Driscoll stood behind the desk in the library staring intently out the window toward the front of the house. He looked at his watch again. 2:13. Where was she? He had given her a schedule this morning and she was to return by noon, so why was she over two hours late?

He looked at his watch again. 2:14. Still no sign of the car. Damn her! he thought. Damn her for making him feel like this. He cursed her and he cursed himself for caring so much. He'd sworn long ago that he'd never love another woman—women were too untrustworthy. They said they loved you and then they deserted you.

As he stared out the window he seemed to be transported back to his childhood when he used to stand by the window and wait for his mother to come home. She'd come staggering up the steps, two young men holding her up, her red-dyed hair frothy about her face, her big breasts heaving, her fat hips swaying, with a man now and then squeezing an ample buttock and making her laugh raucously. Young Taylor used to watch as his father, who always waited up for his wife, came out the front door and helped her inside. The young men would make taunting remarks to Mr. Driscoll but he never seemed to hear them.

Taylor would leave the window and go back to bed, but he'd lie there, his little fists clenched at his sides, and hate both his parents: her for being the fat, loud, stupid, uncaring woman she was and him for being refined, educated, and for stupidly loving this unworthy woman.

Taylor spent every moment he had reading and studying, trying to get away from his mother, who lolled about on a sofa and ate chocolates and never lifted a finger to help manage the household servants or even to talk to the child who was her son. Sometimes Taylor would stand in the doorway and glare at his mother, but this would make her laugh at him, so mainly he stayed in his room. His books came to represent love to him, for there was no love anywhere else in his house. His mother openly admitted she had married his father for his money, and her main concern was rich food, revealing dresses covered with flounces, and "having a good time," which involved whiskey and good-looking young men.

Taylor's father's only concern was suffering and feeling miserable because he loved a woman like his wife. He seemed to regard loving her as an incurable disease that he'd contracted.

When Taylor was twelve his father had died, and within a year his mother had spent every penny he'd left to both of them. Without regret, Taylor had packed a bag of dirty clothes—all the servants had left months ago—and had taken a hundred dollars he'd managed to steal when his mother was drunk and gone in search of his father's relatives.

For years he'd begged for an education. He had

developed a strong sense of pride when he was living in his parents' house—he needed it to survive the abuse, shame and degradation—but he put his pride aside as he asked for a little from this relative, a little from that one. After a few years, they began to regard him as an obligation, and they knew that if they didn't send money or letters of introduction, or whatever Taylor was requesting, they would be bombarded with letters from Taylor and from other relatives who he had asked to intercede.

By the time he was twenty and was graduating *summa cum laude,* each relative was taking full credit for having put him through school and having encouraged him when Taylor would have given up.

After college, he tried one job after another, but nothing appealed to him and he was considering going back to school to get his Ph.D. and teach when he got a letter from a distant cousin-by-marriage, J. Harker Caulden. Caulden said he had a wayward daughter who he was afraid was getting out of control. Her mother was useless at discipline and he hadn't the time. He wanted Taylor to come and privately tutor the girl until she was of marriageable age.

Taylor had immediately visualized his mother and had imagined a fourteen-year-old harridan who sneaked out the window at night to go to parties. Taylor hoped he could save her, and, if he were strict enough, he might be able to prevent another being such as his mother from developing.

He accepted J. Harker's offer and went to California and the huge Caulden Ranch to start his taming of young Miss Amanda.

Taylor almost laughed when he saw Amanda. He had expected a young version of his mother and instead he saw a tall, gangly, almost-pretty girl who looked at him with big, eager eyes. And it took only two days to find out that she had an excellent brain—a brain empty of learning but stuffed full of clothes and boys and gossip and other frivolous things.

At once he saw the potential. She was as malleable as a piece of clay. He could make Amanda into a lady, into the exact opposite of his mother. He could teach her so that she could converse on something besides the latest dances. He could dress her in a refined, sedate style. She would *never* be fat under his guidance.

She was an excellent pupil, so eager to learn, so eager to please. He didn't mind the hours he spent writing out her daily schedules because then he knew where she was. Amanda would never have *time* to leave him.

As the years passed, Amanda grew into a very pretty young lady who wasn't remotely like his mother. And he began to fall in love with her. He didn't want to and fought it at first, because women were unfaithful creatures who used you when they knew you loved them. So he had kept his love for her to himself but he had bound her to him so she couldn't get away, and someday, when the idea didn't frighten him so much, he planned to marry her. Right now he feared that if he married her, she might change, she might become his drunken, fat, stupid mother.

He looked at his watch again. 2:18. Still no sign of her. He hated allowing her to go out with that barbarian Montgomery but he had no choice. Montgomery could cause a great deal of trouble on the ranch and he needed to be kept away, and Amanda was the only one available to do it. The ranch had come to be very important to Taylor, for J. Harker had said it was someday to be his. Amanda was Harker's only child and he meant to leave everything to Taylor through her. The security of money was something Taylor needed. His childhood, especially after his father died, had been one long time of begging for money, books, tuition, shoes, clothes. The years of begging for even necessities had deeply hurt his pride.

So now he was torn between doing what he could for the ranch and keeping Amanda isolated.

He almost allowed himself to smile when he remembered Amanda saying she thought Dr. Montgomery didn't like her. Didn't like Amanda? A woman who could converse on nearly any intellectual subject in four languages? Not likely. But then perhaps he was one of those lower-natured men who preferred scullery maids and night-club floozies.

It was 2:22 now and still no sign of Amanda.

He stared out the window so hard his head began to ache.

Amanda's feet were hurting and she was so worried about being off her schedule that her stomach was feeling a little queasy. Dr. Montgomery wanted to walk around the town of Kingman and look in shop windows and talk to people and, in general, waste time. Taylor had repeatedly told Amanda how precious time was and that it was not to be wasted on frivolous matters, yet here she was doing nothing to improve her mind. And also, Taylor had told her what awful people the citizens of Kingman were. Hadn't they ostracized her mother? They didn't like the Cauldens and she was better off not associating with them. Yet here she was, standing behind Dr. Montgomery and nodding in recognition to passing people, some of whom knew her name.

"Hasn't hurt you to speak to a few of the common folk yet, has it?" Dr. Montgomery said in an angry tone to her when she mentioned returning to the ranch.

And another thing that made this outing so unpleasant was this stranger's attitude toward her. He smiled at passing women but at her he glared and frowned and made very disagreeable remarks. She wanted to go home to the safety of Taylor and her books.

She almost bumped into Dr. Montgomery when he stopped in front of the drugstore. There was a sign there telling of a dance next Saturday.

"You and Mr. Taylor going?" he asked her. "Planning to paint the town red?"

She understood his meaning if not the slang. "We do not attend dances," she said stiffly.

"Is it the dances or the townspeople who aren't good enough for you?"

Again she felt anger. "Dancing is a waste of time, and as for the townspeople—" She was on the verge of telling him about her mother but she didn't. She was not going to be rude merely because he was. "Dr. Montgomery, I would like to return home now. It is late and there are other things to do."

"You go back, then," he said angrily, thinking that he *had* to get away from her and the whole Caulden clan. The two cold fishes of Amanda and Taylor, the rude, belligerent J. Harker and the mother who was locked away somewhere and spoken of in mysterious half-sentences, was more than he could bear.

But as he looked at Amanda, standing there absolutely straight, her thin little shoulders thrown back, her eyes with just a spark of fire in them, he knew he couldn't leave. Something was holding him.

"All right," he said, "we'll go back."

Amanda could have cried with relief as they walked back to the waiting limousine. He didn't speak to her on the drive back and she was grateful. She needed to gather her strength for the coming meeting with Taylor.

Once in the house, Taylor came to the hall to meet them, and Amanda could tell he was angry. He waited for Dr. Montgomery to go upstairs, then he called her into the library.

For a moment he stood with his back to her, then he turned on his heel and faced her, his dark eyes glittering, his cheeks pulled in in fury. "I am disappointed in you, Amanda. Very disappointed. You knew you were to be back here at noon, yet you were not. No! Do not give me excuses, I will listen to none of them. Don't you realize how important your assignment is? If unionists come here and make trouble, we could lose this year's crop altogether. And all because you did not keep to the schedule."

Amanda looked down at her hands. *How* could she keep Dr. Montgomery to the schedule? Somehow she *had* to. It seemed that everything—the whole future of the ranch—depended on her.

"Now, go to your room and think on what you have done. Do not come to dinner tonight, but later come to the parlor and read for Dr. Montgomery. Perhaps if you are here with me you can keep on schedule." And I will not be worried about you, Taylor thought, frowning at her bowed head. "Go on, Amanda," he said, controlling the anger in his voice.

Amanda went up the stairs slowly, feeling as if she

had gained fifty pounds. Mrs. Gunston was waiting for her. Amanda was to go to the basement to do her exercises, then a bath, no dinner, and reading for Dr. Montgomery in the evening. She was beginning to despise that man!

Hank stayed in his room until dinner, trying his best to read a couple of his students' essays. Sometimes when a student had done well, but not as well as he liked, Hank allowed him or her to raise his grade with a research paper. So, between terms, Hank sometimes had papers to grade. But he couldn't keep his mind on the papers; all he could think about was Amanda. He wasn't sure what about her infuriated him so much, but something did. He remembered the way she had looked at lunch, her eyes closed, that look of sublime happiness on her face. "I wish I could cause her to look like that," he muttered and turned back to the essay.

Amanda didn't come out of her room for dinner, and Hank was sure it was because she couldn't bear his company. He sat in unnatural silence beside ol' stiff-necked Taylor, eating veal cutlets while Taylor ate more boiled fish. Hank wondered what Amanda ate in her room when she was out of Taylor's sight. Boiled fish or perhaps fried chicken?

After dinner, just as the clocks all over the house chimed 7:15, Amanda appeared in the parlor. Hank looked around his newspaper, nodded curtly to her, then hid behind his paper again. He wondered if she'd leave when she found her beloved Taylor wasn't alone.

Taylor announced that Amanda was going to read for them.

"Don't let me stop you," Hank said from behind his paper, but he was aware of the heavy silence in the

73

room and knew he was supposed to give proper attention to the show. Slowly, he folded his paper, put it aside, then sat primly with his hands folded in his lap like a proper young gentleman.

Amanda, wearing a prim little blue dress with a sedate lace collar, was standing perfectly straight before the two of them, holding her poetry book open. As he would have guessed, she read the most boring poems ever written: William Collins's "Ode to Evening," Shelley's "Hymn to Intellectual Beauty." He would have fallen asleep except that her reading gave him a chance to look at her: long, thick, lush lashes, a full mouth that moved enticingly as she talked. He listened to her voice, felt it caress the lovely words and wondered how it would sound if it were murmuring love words to him.

But any love words she said would be to Taylor. Hank looked at Taylor and saw the man wasn't enjoying her reading so much as judging it. He looked like a teacher with a student—not like a man listening to the woman he loved.

Hank was aware that Amanda had stopped reading and he watched while she walked toward Taylor and handed him the book. She gave him a soft, tentative smile and said, "Please," in almost a whisper. Hank felt a pang of jealousy as cold, unsmiling Taylor took the book from her. Hank thought that if Amanda had smiled and said please to him, he'd certainly smile back; in fact, he just might do *anything* she wanted. But Taylor just took the book, opened it and began to read John Milton's "On the Morning of Christ's Nativity."

While Taylor read in a monotonous voice, Hank

watched Amanda, saw the way she looked at Taylor as if he were a god, as if he had the power of life and death, yet Taylor seemed to be oblivious to her adoration. It suddenly made Hank angry that Amanda should give so much and get so little in return. If she were his he'd give to her. He'd give all she could take and then some. If he were engaged to her he'd not spend his evenings reading poetry to her, he'd take her into the lanes where the jasmine grew and he'd kiss her while slipping that awful dress from her shoulders. He'd—

"Dr. Montgomery?"

He came out of his reverie to hear Amanda. She was holding out the book of poetry to him.

"Perhaps you'd read something for us?"

Hank was so deep in his thoughts that at first he didn't understand what she was saying.

"Dr. Montgomery is an economist," Taylor said in that brittle way of his. "I doubt if poetry interests him."

Hank didn't take the book but looked at Amanda, his eyes as hot as he was feeling, and he began to quote from William Butler Yeats.

"A sudden blow: the great wings beating still
Above the staggering girl, her thighs caressed
By the dark webs, her nape caught in his bill,
He holds her helpless breast upon his breast.

"How can those terrified vague fingers push
The feathered glory from her loosening thighs?
And how can body, laid in that white rush,
But feel the strange beating where it lies?"

There was silence in the room when he stopped speaking, and he was aware only of the lovely blush stealing up Amanda's neck and onto her face.

"I cannot say that that was to my taste, Dr. Montgomery," Taylor said in a remote voice. "Amanda!" he said sharply, making her turn her attention back to him. "I think you should read another selection."

Suddenly, Hank couldn't bear to be in the same room with them. "If you will pardon me," he said, and without waiting for anyone to do so, he left the room. He went outside, but even there he felt hemmed in, as if he were suffocating and couldn't get enough air. He went to the big garage where his car was, and before he thought about what he was doing, he was in the Mercer and driving away.

The cool wind on his face and body made him feel better. He drove down the rough dirt road, faster and faster still, pushing the Mercer to its limits, knowing that its brakes weren't worth a damn, but he needed the speed and the feeling of freedom. He needed to put some distance between himself and that house. ". . . her thighs caressed," he thought. ". . . fingers push the feathered glory from her loosening thighs."

The car was doing sixty when he saw the girl. She was standing in the middle of the road, startled by the car's headlights as she crossed. She just stood there, frozen in space, as Hank approached faster than she'd ever seen anything move.

Hank had the reflexes of a race car driver, and he swerved to the right a foot before he hit her and plowed into a fence, tearing up posts for fifty feet as Hank used all his strength to slam on the brakes, trying to stop the speeding car. He took up about twenty feet of a row of Caulden's hop plants before the car at last stopped.

It took him a second to recover as he just sat there, staring at the hop field illuminated by the car lamps. Then he began to move, to pull hop vines and strings from around him so that he could get out the doorless side. His legs were weak but they gained strength as he started back to the road, so that he was running by the time he reached the girl.

It was dark but he could see her sitting in the middle of the road. He didn't think he'd hit her, but now he wasn't so sure.

"Are you all right?" he asked anxiously, kneeling in front of her.

"I ain't never seen somethin' move that fast," she said in wonder.

As Hank inspected her, he smelled liquor on her breath and realized she was drunk. Gently, he took her arm and hauled her up. "Come on, let's get you home."

Smiling, she collapsed against him, her body like rubber. "You the one stayin' at the Cauldens'?"

"I am. Come on with me. If I can get my car out I'll take you home."

"Home with you? Amanda won't like that."

"She'll never notice," he said, his arm about her waist as he supported her and led her to the car.

He had to tear away more vines and string to make room enough to get her in the passenger seat.

"Nice," she murmured and leaned back against the leather seat.

He spent another few minutes cleaning off the front of the car and inspecting the ground. It was dry and he thought he could get out without help. He bent the broken fencing back, then got in the car.

The only light was from the moon and the headlamps, but he could see that the woman was young and pretty in a dark, flamboyant way. She wore heavily applied cosmetics on a face that was already strongly featured, but the red lipstick drew his attention to her lips.

When she saw him looking, she smiled in a slow, seductive way. "I like a man who drives fast."

He started the engine and began to back out. "Where can I take you?"

"Charlie's Roadhouse," she said.

Hank hesitated for only a moment, then said, "All right." It might make him feel better to see a little life. "Only if they don't have poetry readings."

She laughed in a way that made him know that she'd been to Charlie's Roadhouse several times before and knew there were no poetry readings.

He enjoyed the ride to the roadhouse with her, enjoyed seeing a woman relaxed in the seat, not sitting stiffly and inhumanly. He liked seeing a woman who looked as if she might be able to laugh.

The roadhouse was about five miles out of town, set a little back off the road behind a graveled parking lot, about three autos parked there now. The lights and the sound of laughter drew Hank inside.

The girl had already got out by the time Hank had walked to her side. She was wearing a cheap red satin dress and her lipstick was smeared at one corner of her wide mouth, but the drive seemed to have cleared her head because she was standing on her feet more steadily.

She took his arm and pressed her body close to his.

She was well rounded and pleasing now, but in a few more years she'd be fat.

"The gang's gonna be green with envy when they see you," she said. "What's your name?"

"Hank Montgomery," he answered, smiling down at her. "And yours?"

"Reva Eiler." She pulled a bit on his arm and guided him toward the front door of the tavern.

There were only four customers in the tavern, which was lined with booths around three sides, a long bar on the fourth wall. Half the floor space was taken up by tiny tables and lots of chairs; the other half was a dance area and bandstand. Reva greeted the man behind the bar, but no one else, as she led Hank to a booth in one corner.

"So tell me all about yourself," she said, taking a compact from a little beaded bag and beginning to repair her face. When she'd finished she removed a cigarette from a silver-plated case with most of the plating worn off. Hank took the matching lighter from her and lit her cigarette as she pushed her heavy hair back. It was cut to shoulder length, and Hank realized that he rarely saw women with hair this short and he liked it. He wondered how Amanda would look with hair like this.

"Not much to tell," he said. "I teach economics at—"

"Economics!" she gasped just as the bartender set two beers before them. "Thanks, Charlie," she murmured. "You don't look like no teacher of economics. I thought maybe you and Amanda were lovers or somethin'."

Hank took a deep drink of his beer. "You know Amanda?"

She looked at him for a long time. There was something about him that appealed to her. He was good-looking, extraordinarily so; dark blond hair, blue eyes, that nose that gave him the look of a prince—those lips. She liked those lips of his a lot. But there was something else, too. It was . . .

"You're rich, aren't you?" she said, picking a piece of tobacco off the tip of her tongue.

Hank was startled and didn't speak for a moment.

"Don't worry, I won't tell anybody if you want to keep it a secret. It's just that I can smell it on somebody. You develop the sense when you grow up as poor as I have. No, no sympathy, just buy me another beer and tell me what's going on at the Cauldens'."

Hank put his hand up to the bartender, then turned back to Reva. "You know Amanda? I mean, do you know the Cauldens?"

She smiled at him. She was young but he sensed that in another few years she wouldn't be. He didn't think she'd age gracefully.

"You meant Amanda," she said. "How is she? Still a brat?"

"Amanda?" he said. "Amanda Caulden a brat? You must mean someone else. Amanda is perfect. She walks perfectly, talks perfectly, discusses only perfect subjects; she eats perfectly healthy food; she loves a perfect man. Amanda is not a brat."

Reva finished her first beer and started on her second one. "When you were in elementary school, did you have one kid who was your archenemy? Somebody who rubbed you the wrong way no matter what he did?"

"Jim Harmon," Hank said, smiling in memory. "I

thought he was the meanest kid ever born. We fought all the time."

"Right. Well, Amanda and I were enemies from the first day of the first grade. I still remember it. My old man had been drunk for three days and my mother'd run off again, like she always did when he got mean, so there was just my big sister and me. She dressed me as best she could, but my clothes were torn and dirty and wrinkled and when I got to school the other kids laughed at me. I was used to being laughed at and it was something I understood, but then little Miss Amanda, all clean and white, came up to me and put her arm around me and told the others to stop laughin'. It made me crazy. I could stand bein' made fun of but I couldn't stand pity. I pushed Amanda down, jumped on her and started beating her."

Hank listened to this with great interest. "And what did Amanda do?" he asked, thinking that she no doubt went crying to the teacher.

Reva grinned. "Blacked my eye is what she did. She got in trouble but I didn't, because the teacher walked out when Amanda was sitting on me and slamming a right fist into my face. We were enemies forever after that—until ol' man Caulden took her out of school. Nobody's seen much of her since then. It's like she moved to another state. Has she changed much?"

Hank couldn't imagine the Amanda he knew being in a fist fight. What had made her change so drastically? Did she finally realize she was the richest kid in town and that she was better than everyone else?

"She's changed," he answered at last. "She's not the same Amanda she was then. You want another one?"

What I want, Reva thought, can't be found in a bottle. I want somebody like you: clean, smart, strong, somebody to take care of me. How involved was he with Amanda? "So," she said, "are you visiting her or somebody else at the Cauldens'?"

For some reason, he was reluctant to mention the unionists that said they were coming to Kingman. He didn't want the town frightened; people had fanciful ideas of what unionists were and what they hoped to do, so he decided to keep it quiet.

"I'm learning about the ranch. I didn't know J. Harker had a daughter before I came. And Amanda is engaged to her tutor."

Reva leaned back against the bench and smiled sweetly at him. "Then you should get to know the people of Kingman. There's a dance Saturday night," she said, and there was hope in her voice.

Hank knew Reva wasn't his type but in the last few days, since meeting Amanda, he wasn't sure what his "type" of woman was. No doubt he was fascinated by a prude like Amanda because she was the only woman he saw daily. It was as if they had been shipwrecked on an island alone. After a while, *any* woman would start to look good. Maybe if he went to a dance and saw other women, he wouldn't be watching the self-righteous, skinny little Amanda so much.

"Could I pick you up?" he asked at last.

Reva grinned broadly and pushed her hair back. "I'll meet you there. Eight o'clock?"

"Great," he said. "I better be getting back. The Cauldens may lock the door."

She almost said, you can stay with me, but she didn't. He drove her to the corner of Fourth and Front streets and let her off. She wasn't going to let him see where she lived. She watched him drive away toward the Cauldens' big, dark ranch and she knew that once again Amanda had something she wanted. Reva had often pondered and cursed the accident of birth that had given one person everything and her nothing. Amanda lived a life of ease, no worries, no cares, no drunken father threatening her every day, no one telling her what to do or how to do it, while Reva's life was the opposite. Amanda had always had everything good and Reva was handed all that was bad.

Reva started walking toward the railroad tracks. But maybe, this time, Reva could win. She began planning how she could scrape together enough money from her cashier job to buy a new dress for Saturday night. Wouldn't everyone be surprised to see her with someone like *him?*

Chapter Six

Amanda didn't exactly sneak out of the house but she certainly didn't make any noise either. She took her notebook with her and her fountain pen, but she didn't take a light. She hoped the moonlight would be enough; besides, she wanted to study the constellations and she could do that better in the darkness.

It had been an odd evening, as every minute had been since Dr. Montgomery had arrived. After reciting that . . . that poem he had left the house and she'd heard him drive away in his pretty little automobile. For a while afterward she had not heard a word Taylor had said. She kept remembering the way Dr. Montgomery had looked at her while saying those words, words she'd never thought could be put together in such a way.

She wished he didn't dislike her so much and that perhaps he would teach her poetry. She felt a pang of disloyalty to Taylor for even considering another teacher but, after all, the goal was for her to learn, wasn't it? And when she had learned enough, Taylor would marry her and they'd live happily ever after here on the ranch.

Once downstairs, she went to the summerhouse

where she and Dr. Montgomery had sat while he ate his plateful of food. Amanda thought it best not to think of food because her stomach grumbled from the missed dinner—missed because Dr. Montgomery refused to follow the schedule.

She leaned back against the post and gazed up at the stars. In spite of the fact that she hadn't been able to sleep for several nights in a row, she wasn't sleepy tonight. Something about the heavy, hot night air, the fragrance of flowers and the clearness of the sky made her feel very odd.

While she was stargazing, the quiet, deep rumble of a car came down the driveway and Amanda immediately tried to draw herself up as small as possible so Dr. Montgomery wouldn't see her. She held her breath as she heard the engine stop then the sound of footsteps crunching on the gravel. She'd wait until he was in the house, then she'd go in. She didn't want to meet him on the stairs and be subjected to more of his caustic remarks.

As she waited and listened, to her disbelief, he seemed to be not moving toward the house but toward her. She didn't dare move.

"I thought I saw someone," he said while still several feet from her.

Amanda let out her breath with a sigh. Caught! she thought. "Good evening, Dr. Montgomery," she murmured.

Hank walked into the summerhouse and sat down across from her, as far away as he could get. He'd seen just a corner of her white dress reflected in his headlamps. Ordinarily he wouldn't have noticed, but it was as if he had a second sense about Amanda. Go to bed, he told himself. You've had too many beers and you're feeling too good from the run in the car and you shouldn't be here with her. But his mind didn't tell his body to move, so he continued sitting there. "I met a friend of yours tonight."

Amanda couldn't imagine who would describe herself as a friend; it had been years since she'd seen anyone but Taylor and her family. "Oh?" she asked. She needed to get upstairs. Taylor would not like for her to be here. This wasn't on the schedule; in fact, she wasn't even studying constellations right now.

"Reva Eiler," he said.

For a moment Amanda didn't place the name, then slowly she began to remember her fights with Reva. Was that Amanda the same person she was today? Thank heaven Taylor had saved her from what she was.

"Don't remember her?" Dr. Montgomery asked. "She remembered you, black eye and all."

In spite of herself, Amanda smiled. "Yes, I remember her. I felt sorry for her, but she stopped that. She always—"

"What?" he coaxed.

"Always seemed to want what I had. If I wore a blue dress with little hearts on it, two days later she'd show up with a blue dress with hearts on it. Once Mother put a big pink-and-white-striped ribbon in my hair and the next day Reva wore a ribbon just like it. I . . ." She trailed off.

"You what?"

"I threw my ribbon in the river."

He smiled at her in the darkness. "I'm taking Reva to a dance on Saturday," he blurted before he thought.

"Good," Amanda said. "Reva has had too little joy in her life."

"Unlike you," he couldn't resist saying. She was so damned pretty in the moonlight, looking a bit like a fairy maiden, somehow ethereal, with her white dress and her pale oval of a face.

She stiffened. "I have had a great deal of happiness in my life. I have my family, my fiancé, my books. It is all one could ask for."

It probably was enough for her, he thought, but for most women it wouldn't be. "Why don't you and Taylor come to the dance with us and make it a double date?"

"I hardly think so," she said and couldn't imagine Taylor dancing. She stood, gathered her notebook and pen and started toward the doorway. "I think I better go in."

As quickly as a cat, he blocked her way. He was standing very close to her and he could smell the fragrance of her. Without thinking what he was doing, he reached out to touch the hair at her temple. "Don't go," he whispered. "Stay here with me."

Amanda swallowed hard. He was looking at her the same way he had when he'd quoted that poem to her, the poem about loosening thighs. No man had ever looked at her this way or spoken to her this way. It was frightening, yet at the same time she couldn't move away.

"How long is your hair?" he whispered.

"Long?" she asked stupidly. "To my waist. It is difficult to keep neat."

"I'd like to see it not neat. I'd like to see it long and full and thick."

Amanda was feeling quite strange. Perhaps it was the missed meal. Perhaps it was several missed meals over the last few weeks, but she did indeed feel light-headed and limp-limbed. "Dr. Montgomery, I don't think . . ." she began but trailed off as she took a step backward and he stepped forward.

"What are your shoulders like, Amanda? As white and as smooth as the skin of your cheek?" He touched her cheek with the back of his fingers.

Definitely strange, she thought, her eyes locked with his. His words were not right, she thought, and he shouldn't say these things to her. Perhaps she should cry for help. But she only took another step backward and he took one forward.

"Those eyes of yours could eat a man alive," he said, his voice pouring over her like something hot and thick and creamy. "And lips. Lips made to be kissed. Lips made to whisper love words. Lips made to kiss a man's skin."

Oh my, she thought, but no words came out. Oh my, oh my, oh my. She was afraid of him, and that's why she didn't scream or run from him. Only this emotion didn't feel like fear, it felt . . . There was nothing to describe it or compare it to.

"Amanda," he whispered and put his hands on her neck, his thumbs caressing the line of her jaw.

She had never been touched like this and it was as if she were starving. She closed her eyes, leaned her head back and let herself feel his hands on her face.

Then, one minute he was there and the next he was gone. For a moment she stood there, all alone in the night, and wondered if she'd dreamed it all, but then she heard the door of the house shut noisily and she knew he'd gone inside.

Heavily, she sat down on the seat, her pad and pen, which she'd clasped to her the whole time, falling to her lap. Wrong, she thought. This was absolutely, completely wrong. It was wrong to have done and even more wrong to have *felt*.

She thought of Taylor and her chest tightened. He trusted her so much, he believed in her so much, yet she'd betrayed him as if she were a wanton creature with no morals. How could she ever be worthy of Taylor if she acted like this toward this stranger who was toying with her? Dr. Montgomery might seem like a man of high character, what with his degrees and all, but he wasn't. He quoted vulgar poems and drove too fast and invited women he didn't know to dances, then made improper advances to an engaged woman practically under her fiancé's nose. This was not the behavior of a man of high moral character such as Taylor was. Taylor *never* drove too fast (or drove at all, for that matter). Taylor didn't indulge in unseemly pastimes like dancing, and Taylor would never, *never* drive out in the middle of the night and meet someone like Reva Eiler. And he didn't make improper advances, not even to the woman he was to marry. Taylor didn't tell a woman her lips were made to be kissed, or to whisper love words or to kiss a man's skin.

Kiss a man's skin, she thought. To kiss his bare shoulder or his throat or even the palm of his hand or his— No! she told herself, put those thoughts from your mind. Or at least, when she thought them, she was to imagine kissing Taylor's bare shoulder and not Dr. Montgomery's as she was doing. But for the life of her she couldn't even imagine Taylor in his shirt sleeves, much less bare-chested.

As she started back toward the house, she knew she had never been so confused in her life, and once again she wished Dr. Montgomery had never come. From now on she was going to do her best to stay away from him.

Hank didn't sleep much that night. He didn't know if it was guilt or just plain old-fashioned lust that kept him awake. Why did he always seem to want the women he shouldn't have? He hadn't been the least interested in Blythe Woodley while she was his student, but the minute she was engaged to another man, he couldn't keep his hands off of her.

Now here was Amanda, not at all the sort of woman to inspire great passion, yet he couldn't keep away from her. She was pretty but there were lots of women prettier. She was too thin, too perfectly proper, too much of a little old maid. So why was she driving him stark, raving crazy?

He got out of bed, and before he could change his mind he packed his clothes. Tomorrow he would leave the Caulden house and go into Kingman to stay. That would be better anyway, because the unionists would be able to reach him there. He'd stay at the Kingman Arms and every night he'd go out with a different woman, a warm, real, flesh and blood woman, one who ate pork chops and drank beer and didn't believe dancing was a mortal sin. He'd find a woman he could *talk* to.

It was three A.M. before he fell asleep.

"Amanda," Taylor said sternly. They were in the dining room, waiting for Dr. Montgomery to join them for breakfast. "Mrs. Gunston says his bag is packed, that he means to leave today."

Amanda swallowed guiltily. It was her fault that Dr. Montgomery was leaving.

"Perhaps you don't understand what this means. This Dr. Montgomery is practically a socialist. All his writings indicate that he believes in giving everything to the poor people. He wants to take away your house, your pretty clothes. Amanda, he wants you to work in the fields, to be a servant. Would you like that, Amanda?"

She remembered the meal of roast beef and mashed potatoes the servants had been eating in the kitchen, but she pushed that vision away. "No, I wouldn't," she said solemnly.

"It may happen if Dr. Montgomery has his way. When these union men come, they will go to him and he will side with them and he will incite them to strike."

Amanda looked down at her hands. And if that happens, it will be my fault, she thought heavily, but she couldn't figure out what to do. One minute Dr. Montgomery seemed to detest her and the next he was making improper advances to her.

"Amanda!" Taylor said sharply. "Why is your hair in disarray?"

A strand had fallen from the tight bun she wore. She pushed it back into place. "I was rushed this morning because Dr. Montgomery was in the bathroom." Suddenly her restraint broke. "Oh, Taylor, I wish you'd give him a schedule. He is so erratic! He comes and goes at the oddest times, goes into the bathroom whenever he wants, eats when he's hungry and eats whatever he wants. He makes life difficult for everyone else."

Taylor was startled and disapproving of her outburst at first but then he smiled. Here was proof that Amanda was a woman who understood logic. She was never going to come home at two A.M. staggering from drink, or sleep until noon, or disappear for three days at a time. Amanda would never abandon her children or her husband.

To Amanda's utter disbelief, Taylor bent slightly and kissed her forehead. He had never kissed her before.

"Come, my dear," he said softly. "Perhaps you'd like a little strawberry jam this morning, and in a few weeks, when the hops are picked and Dr. Montgomery and the unionists are gone, perhaps we can talk about our marriage plans."

Amanda was too stunned to speak. What had she said? What had she done? A moment ago he was upset because she was not doing what he wanted with Dr. Montgomery and now he was planning their marriage.

Amanda sat down at the table. Whatever had happened, she was glad of it. She put jam on her toast and, as she had done at lunch with Dr. Montgomery, she closed her eyes and let the taste flow down her throat.

It was Taylor's turn to be shocked. "Amanda!" he gasped.

"I'm . . . I'm sorry," she said, opening her eyes. "It just tastes so good."

He moved the jam jar to the other side of the table as if he were moving a liquor decanter away from an alcoholic, and Amanda tried not to look at it with longing.

Hank felt rotten when he woke, so he went to the bathroom and half filled the tub with icy cold water then sat in it. His teeth chattered and his skin tightened like a bandage about his body, but it did wake him up—and it helped him forget his dreams about Amanda.

One more meal with her, he thought, then he'd leave this strange household where four people lived but he saw only two of them.

Dressed, he started down the stairs but paused, his hand on the rail. Across the stairwell that extended to the first floor was the door to Amanda's room and it was ajar. To his left, behind the wall, he could hear the faint, descending steps of a maid on the back stairs. He was alone upstairs.

Without thinking about what he was doing, he walked the few steps to Amanda's room and pushed the door open. He didn't know why it surprised him, but the room had less character than a drawing of a model room for a magazine. There was nothing wrong with the room; it had furniture and pictures on the walls and curtains at the windows, but there was nothing personal in it. Guest rooms in his mother's house had tatted lace on the tables, a bright-colored shawl to spread across your legs if you wanted to read at night. She put embroidered pillows on every chair, novels by the bed, fresh flowers wherever she could and little scented pillows on the dresser.

But Amanda's room had none of these things. The surfaces of all furniture were bare. The bed with its blue cotton spread looked spartan, with no lacy little pillows heaped on top. The pictures were dull etchings of scenery that was too perfect to be real. The curtains were dark blue, not a deep, rich blue that could give some character to the room but a plain, boring, nondescript blue.

He walked to the far end of the room to the desk

where he'd seen Amanda silhouetted during the night. There was nothing on top of the desk. He opened the right-hand desk drawer and the contents were as neat as the outside. On top was a handwritten piece of paper headed: Schedule, and below that, today's date. Below that was a minute-by-minute account of where Amanda was to take Dr. Montgomery, what she was to talk to him about, even what she was to feed him and what to wear while doing it.

He shut the drawer in disgust. What a controlling little bitch, he thought. She not only had to put her own life into perfect order so that she had no freedom, she had to do the same for everyone else. Suddenly Hank felt sympathy for Taylor and wondered if he knew what he was getting into. Would Amanda make out a schedule for Taylor when he was her husband? 11:01 P.M.: *fourth attempt to breed a child.* If he failed in six attempts would she throw him out? He didn't imagine Amanda would put *11:01 P.M.: feel passion* on her schedule.

He walked out of the room and left the door open, not caring about covering his tracks. Another couple of hours and he'd be out of this place.

In the dining room Amanda and Taylor were already seated and eating, and after a curt greeting, Hank filled his plate from the silver dishes on the sideboard. He tried to control his anger but it wasn't easy. He felt like a free animal that had been caught and put in a zoo and a strict feeding schedule made out. She put him on a schedule; did she put Taylor on one too? If he didn't keep to it, was his punishment loss of the ranch? Marry me and do exactly what I say, to the minute, and the ranch is yours. Is that what she said to him?

Poor guy, Hank thought, glancing at Taylor with some sympathy. She didn't allow dancing or parties; she snubbed women who were once her friends.

"Dr. Montgomery," Taylor was saying, "Amanda would so like to go into Terrill City today and hear a lecture on Eugenics. She can't possibly go alone, and I have accounts to do. Would you mind terribly accompanying her?"

Hank opened his mouth to say no, but then he knew he wanted to tell her just what he thought of her manipulation of the people around her.

"I would love to," he said, looking across the table at Amanda, every bit of the anger he felt showing in his eyes.

Amanda looked at him, and when she saw the anger in his face she almost said she didn't want to go anywhere with him, but it was too soon after Taylor had mentioned their marriage to risk angering him. But something about the way Dr. Montgomery looked at her made the hair on the back of her neck stand up.

After breakfast she waited for him by the car—for thirty minutes she waited, until at last he sauntered outside.

"Mess up your schedule, missy?" he said nastily.

She backed away from him, away from the rage she could feel coming from him. "We . . . were to leave earlier, yes," she said tentatively.

"Then what's to keep us from going?" He turned to the chauffeur. "We won't need you today." He looked back at Amanda, his eyes glittering. "Either we go in my car or not at all."

"All right," she answered softly, and rather liked the idea of traveling in his pretty, open car.

"That's not on your schedule either, is it?" he said with anger, then stomped past her to the garage.

She stood still for a moment, looking toward the back of him. Had Taylor given him a copy of today's schedule? Perhaps Dr. Montgomery was angry at himself because he saw how late he was or because he'd been in the bathroom when it wasn't on the schedule.

He went through the complicated motions of starting his little yellow car, then backed it out of the garage and quickly moved it so close to her that he almost ran over her toes.

"Get in!" he commanded.

Amanda was only too happy to obey. There was something wonderful about the little car, and she smiled as she sank into the black leather of the passenger seat then held on to her hat as Dr. Montgomery let out on the clutch and they started moving. But it wasn't moving like the limousine moved. She watched, fascinated, as he began to shift gears. The car began to accelerate. She had never traveled faster than 15 mph before and that had seemed fast, but now, with the wind tearing at her hair and face, her eyes batting quickly to keep bugs from flying in them—for there was no windshield except for a circle of glass before the driver—she knew she was traveling very, very fast. And she liked it. Oh yes, she liked it very much, liked the wind, the openness of the car, liked the way the trees and fields tore past them at lightning speed.

They hadn't gone very far, not as far as Amanda would have liked, when there was a loud sound and the car swerved quickly to the right. There was an angry expletive from Dr. Montgomery, and Amanda watched with interest as he fought the wheel of the car and began to slow it down. He kept his eyes, his feet and his hands busy and never once did she feel that he had lost control.

When, at long last, the car was under control, Dr. Montgomery turned and looked at her, his face, if possible, even more angry. "A blowout. This should mess up your little schedule real well."

Since the objective was to get Dr. Montgomery out of Kingman for the day, Amanda hoped Taylor wouldn't mind if they were late for the lecture. As for Amanda, she just wanted to ride in this fast car some more.

She leaned her head back against the seat, closed her eyes and smiled in memory.

Before she knew what was happening to her, he grabbed her from the seat and pulled her into his arms and then he was kissing her. Kissing her hard and passionately, just the way he drove.

She was so stunned she couldn't react. She didn't even have time to close her eyes, but just when she was beginning to realize what was happening to her and thinking she rather liked this, he thrust her from him so violently that her back slammed into the side of the car.

She put the back of her hand to her lips and stared at him wide-eyed.

"Was *that* on your schedule, Little Miss Prim and Proper? Did the ride scare you? Was something like speed too much for your perfect little world? You may think you can command every man around you but you can't. You may have poor old Taylor in your palm because he wants your daddy's ranch, but you don't rule all of us."

Furiously, he turned toward the back of the car and jerked one of the two spares off it and began to change the tire.

Amanda stood where she was. His speech, his kiss, indeed, his actions, were incomprehensible to her. She had no idea in the world what he was talking about and for a moment she was afraid of him. They were alone on a dirt road, ten miles out of Kingman, and there wasn't a house or car in sight.

Courage, Amanda, she thought. She walked to stand behind him and, holding herself as rigidly as possible, she said, "Dr. Montgomery, I am very sorry that I have displeased you so. I am sorry that breaking the schedule distresses you, but now I think I should return home." She turned and began walking west toward Kingman.

Hank slammed the tire on the wheel. "If you'll just hold your horses, I'll take you back and then I'll leave your precious ranch and—" He heard the crunch of gravel and turned to see her walking away.

Serve her right to walk, he thought. It might do her some good to have to do something for herself. His hands on the spare tire, he stopped and rested his forehead against it. He didn't think he'd ever been quite so angry in his life. Injustice was what made him angry, not pretty girls. He hated seeing people mistreated, hated tenements owned by rich landlords, hated to see poor sharecroppers, hated to see any person who lacked freedom.

Maybe that's what made him so angry: Amanda had tried to take away his freedom. She had set him on a schedule and expected him to do just exactly like she wanted. Just like her father, he thought, J. Harker believed that anyone who worked on his land had no rights.

He turned and looked at Amanda, growing smaller in the distance.

Just like her father, he thought. Just like her father, always trying to control people, and that Driscoll was cut from the same cloth. The two of them would like to control the world and everyone in it.

Hank sat up straight, as if startled. "Control the world," he whispered, "or just control one small daughter?"

He was on his feet and running instantly.

Amanda stopped when he blocked her way and hunched her shoulders as if prepared for a blow.

"Amanda," he said softly, disgusted with himself for frightening her. "Tell me about your schedules."

He didn't look angry anymore, but Amanda didn't trust him. "Taylor makes a schedule for me every evening."

"And how long has he been doing this?" Hank asked, his breath held. He wasn't sure what he was going to find out, but he had just a nugget of an idea.

Amanda was leery of him. Why was he asking questions about something as ordinary as a schedule? "Since I was fourteen. Taylor was hired to be my tutor."

"The schedule I saw seemed to list every minute of the day."

She frowned. "Yes, of course. It is what I do. Doesn't your schedule list what you are to do?"

Hank didn't answer but he let out his breath. "And your schedule also includes what you wear?"

"Yes."

"What you eat?"

"Yes."

"Even when the bathroom is yours?"

She looked away, blushing. "It makes for an orderly household."

Hank stood and looked at her for a long while, looked at her profile, the curve of her neck. When he'd first seen her he had thought she had sad eyes and now he knew the reason for the sadness. At fourteen she had been a butterfly just starting to emerge from a cocoon, but her father had snapped her up and hired a butterfly killer—ol' Taylor—to push her back into the cocoon. And there she had remained.

He wanted to take her in his arms and hold her and tell her that now things would be all right, but that wouldn't help, because, the truth was, Amanda didn't know there was anything wrong that needed righting.

"Amanda," he said patiently, the way one would speak to a shy child. "You are being held prisoner. Just as your father mistreats the people who work for him, so is this Driscoll misusing you. Other people don't have a schedule; other people are free to eat what they want, go to the bathroom when they want. Driscoll has taken all your freedom from you, and freedom is something that is granted to everyone under the American Constitution. Come with me now, Amanda, and I will take you away from here. I will see that you never again have to live by a schedule." He held out his hands, palms up, beseeching her.

Amanda was so stunned that for a few moments she couldn't speak. She looked up through the bright sunlight at this tall, handsome man who at this moment looked like an evangelist trying to save sinners from their wicked ways, and the anger that she had been feeling since he arrived erupted in a volcanic mass.

"How dare you presume to tell me about my life," she said through teeth clamped tightly shut. "How dare you criticize my father and my fiancé." She took a step toward him and her rage seemed to make her taller—or him shorter—as she looked him in the eye. "What do you know of me or my life? You come to my home as a guest and you have done nothing but sneer at us and look down your nose at us. For your information, I happen to *like* my life. I *like* orderliness. I *like* the feeling of accomplishing things, and most of all, I *love* my father and my fiancé. And as for your American freedom, I believe it also means a citizen has the right to choose, and I happen to *choose* to give some direction to my life. Now, Dr. Montgomery, I suggest you get in your fast little car and speed away as quickly as its wheels will turn. *I* will walk back to my home, and when I get there the first thing I will do is see that your clothes are sent to you."

With her back stiff, she stepped around him and started walking down the road, her every step showing her anger.

In a state of shock, Hank stood where he was, listening to her angry steps behind him. He felt like a fool. Since the moment he saw her, he had felt that there was something between them. He had been angry at her for not seeing it. He had been jealous of Taylor and he had looked for a reason to believe she didn't *really* love Taylor. He felt like a vain, strutting fool, so vain that he couldn't believe she would love someone other than him. He could feel his face turning red as he remembered his arrogance in telling her he was going to rescue her and save her from big, bad Taylor.

He ran his hand over his face and wiped away the sweat. Ever since he'd met Amanda he hadn't been himself. He'd been behaving like a schoolboy who gave presents to the girl he liked then an hour later he was hitting her. Looking back at the last few days, he was mortified at his behavior. He remembered walking down streets and leaving her behind, making snide comments and sometimes downright rude ones. He had forcibly kissed her, something he'd certainly never done before.

And what had Amanda done to deserve such treatment? Nothing but be herself. She had taken him to museums and he had sneered. She had offered to talk with him on subjects she thought might interest him and he had been contemptuous. She had even let him join in a simple after-dinner reading of poetry and he had ridiculed her by reciting a licentious poem.

He had never felt so small in his life.

He turned and walked down the road toward her, halting her by standing in front of her. "Miss Caulden," he said before she could speak, "there is nothing I can say that will fully express the depths of my apology. You are right in everything you said to me. My behavior has been abysmal, beyond any level of decency. I do not expect you to forgive me, so I will leave your house at once, but please, may I drive you back to your home?"

Amanda's anger was beginning to cool now and she thought of Taylor's fury when she told him she had screeched at Dr. Montgomery to leave her house at once.

"I should apologize to you," she said, knowing she

was lying but also knowing that her future marriage to Taylor might depend on this lie. "My behavior, too, has been inexcusable. Please do not leave."

Please, he thought. She looked at him with those big eyes that exuded sadness and said, please. He should go; he knew that. He knew she wasn't good for him. She was as tempting as cake to a fat person, as irresistible as liquor to an alcoholic. Yet he knew he couldn't leave her. He was going to stay and he was going to learn to leave her alone. He had a job to do with the unionists and he was going to do it.

"Yes, I'll stay," he said at last. "Will you come back to the car with me and wait in the shade while I finish changing the tire? I'll take you into Terrill City for your lecture and I promise I won't drive fast."

She murmured consent and sat under a tree while he changed the tire. She had been right in what she'd said. Every word, every syllable had been right, but she kept hearing his words. Was it true that other people didn't have schedules? Were people free to eat when and what they wanted?

She tried to push the thoughts from her head. She was *choosing* to follow Taylor's schedule.

Chapter Seven

Hank drove ten miles an hour to Terrill City. The town was about three times the size of Kingman and much more modern, with many stores and places of interest, and the people on the streets were more fashionably dressed, several of the women wearing cosmetics.

Some of the women eyed Hank appreciatively in his sporty yellow car, but he was too glum to notice them. He stopped before the Masonic Hall where Amanda's lecture was being held, got out and opened the door for her.

"What time will it be over?" he asked in a dead voice.

"At one. You aren't coming?"

"I'm afraid Eugenics isn't my cup of tea."

"The library is—"

"I saw that there's a matinee on. I think I'll go see it."

Amanda's eyes widened. "A motion picture?"

Hank had his hands in his pockets. "Yeah, sure. I'll see you at one."

Amanda stood on the sidewalk and watched him drive away. A motion picture, she thought. He was actually going to *see* a motion picture. What would it be about?

In the Masonic Hall, the woman lecturer was talking with enthusiasm about the selective breeding of people to create a pure race of intelligent, perfect beings, and all Amanda could think of was the motion picture.

Afterward, she went outside, and Dr. Montgomery was leaning against the side of his car waiting for her.

"Would you like lunch, then go home?" he asked.

She agreed, and he drove her to a pretty little restaurant on the outskirts of town. Amanda's mouth started watering the moment they stepped inside. The last time she'd had lunch with Dr. Montgomery she had eaten the most delicious meal.

As the waitress came for their order, Amanda's stomach rolled in anticipation, but Dr. Montgomery spoke before she could.

"The lady is on a special diet. Could you give her some plain boiled potatoes, no seasoning, boiled green beans and fish, also no seasoning?"

The waitress looked at Amanda, and Amanda hoped the young woman would say that no, that wouldn't be possible, but she didn't. "Sure, if that's what you want. And what about you?"

"I'll have the house special," Hank said.

Amanda tried to conceal her disappointment. It was better, of course, that she eat good, honest, wholesome food instead of greasy, butter-dripping, sauce-coated— She made herself stop that line of thought.

"Did you see your motion picture, Dr. Montgomery?" she asked.

"Sure," he mumbled, not looking at her. The truth was, he hadn't paid much attention to it because all he'd been able to think of was Amanda. He *had* to get away from her. He couldn't bear to continue seeing her hour after hour.

"Was it enjoyable?" She wanted to ask him hundreds of questions but she didn't dare. Motion pictures were frivolous things, not at all mind-improving.

"The same ol' thing," he said. "Bad guy, good guy, and an innocent girl with too much eye makeup."

"Yes," she murmured, not knowing how to get him to elaborate.

Their food came and Amanda's eyes bugged as she looked at the dishes spread around Dr. Montgomery: a salad of strawberries and pineapple, trout broiled in butter, creamed potatoes, cucumbers with French dressing, asparagus soufflé, popovers and coffee. Her own plate looked bland and tasteless, and she was afraid she wouldn't be able to keep the envy out of her eyes if she didn't get her mind on something besides his food.

"Shall we have a conversation?" she asked.

Hank looked up, startled. Her eyes were wide, her features soft. It would be better to never speak to her again, but he mumbled, "Sure."

"What shall we converse on?" she asked. "I have been studying President Wilson's new tariff reforms. Or perhaps you'd like to discuss the economic reconstruction in the Balkan States?"

Whenever she talked, he knew she wasn't for him. He gave her a little smile. "Know nothing about them."

"Oh," she said, and watched as he cut into his trout. There was butter glistening on it. "American income tax?" she asked with hope in her voice. "I also know about English and Danish income tax."

Hank smiled broader. "Not me."

He broke open a popover, and Amanda could smell it, and when he buttered it the butter melted and ran into the soft little holes of the dough. "Servia?" she said quickly. "Adrianople? Janina? Turkey?" Maybe talking about a war would take her mind off the smells and sights.

"I know nothing about any of them," he said happily. Now he was remembering what he didn't like about her. "Why don't you tell me?" If he could keep her talking, maybe he could remember long enough to get back to her house and get *out*.

She talked while he ate. She talked about the Bulgarians having taken Adrianople after a three-day assault. She talked about Austria's reaction to the takeover and then hypothesized whether Servia and Montenegro would unite.

The more she talked—lectured—the better Hank felt. This was the Amanda he despised. He could imagine this Amanda and Taylor together with ease. Maybe they'd give birth to a set of encyclopedias.

The waitress came back with two desserts of thick-crusted peach cobbler. Hank started to tell her to return Amanda's portion but then Amanda grabbed the plate and began to eat it. She ate like no one else he'd ever seen: sensually, with pleasure in her eyes, almost as if she were making love.

"Is that all you know about the war?" he asked angrily.

Amanda was used to having her knowledge quizzed but it was difficult to think when flavors such as these peaches and this divine crust were in her mouth. "R . . . Russia is angry at Austria and Austria is . . ." She trailed off for a moment and closed her eyes.

"Austria is what?" Hank snapped.

"Angry," she said at last. "Austria is angry at Russia."

"Good," he said. "Are you finished yet? We have to get back. The schedule, remember? Don't you need to study something to improve your mind?"

"Yes," Amanda said, coming back to reality. Tomorrow she was to have a test on the history and present consequences of the Panama Canal and she would need to study. She looked at the clean plate with regret. Taylor was right: unwholesome food was bad for one in more ways than one. The peach cobbler had just made her hungrier. "We should go."

He drove back to the Caulden Ranch very slowly and Amanda arrived without a hair mussed. The first thing she knew she must do was find Taylor and tell him they had returned and perhaps he'd like to revise her schedule since she was back from Terrill City earlier than planned. But at least she'd get her studying done and not have to stay up late tonight doing it.

A servant told Amanda that Taylor was in the library.

Hank left his car in the garage and stayed outside while Amanda hurried inside. No doubt she couldn't wait to see her beloved Taylor, he thought, and realized he was getting angry again. At the moment, he couldn't bear to see them together.

With his hands in his pockets, he strolled to the side of the house, idly looking at the plants and the building. The door to the conservatory was open, and he went in. For a few moments he enjoyed the heavy fragrance of the jasmine, then he heard voices behind him in the library. He started to leave, but he knew it

was Taylor and Amanda and he stayed where he was
and listened.

"You have returned early, Amanda," Taylor was
saying in a cold voice. "You were to keep him out until
evening."

"I apologize, but he seemed to want to return."

"What he wants is of no consequence. Or doesn't
the welfare of the ranch mean anything to you? You
are willing for all of us—me, your father, your mother, yourself—to be thrown out with no means of
support merely because you cannot occupy one rather
ordinary working-class man?"

"I am sorry," Amanda whispered. "I don't know
what to talk to him about. We have nothing to say to
one another."

"Nothing to say!" Taylor exclaimed. "Do you forget everything you have learned when you're with
him?"

"No, I don't, but he isn't interested in scholarly
pursuits, he . . . he goes to motion pictures."

"But the man is a college professor," Taylor said,
his voice puzzled, then he changed. "You must be
doing something wrong."

"Should I . . ." Amanda said hesitantly,
". . . should I go to a motion picture with him? Or a
dance? I believe he likes to dance."

Taylor's voice was cold enough to freeze the plants
in the conservatory. "Is that the kind of woman you
are, Amanda? Have I proposed marriage to a loose
woman? Have you been hiding your true self from me
all these years? Perhaps next you would like a bottle of
gin sent to your room."

"No, sir," she said, slipping back to the time when
he was just her tutor and not her tutor and her fiancé.

"Or perhaps you'd like to wear short dresses and take a typewriting job."

"No, sir," she said softly. "I want only what I have."

"It doesn't sound so to me. Amanda, you have no idea how fortunate you are. You have everything life has to offer. You'll never have to beg for money or for an education, yet you are willing to throw everything away." He paused a moment. "Or perhaps it is me alone who you wish to thwart. Perhaps you want me off the ranch. Is that it, Amanda? You do not want to marry me and this is your way of telling me so."

"No," Amanda said, and there were tears in her voice. "I want more than anything in the world to marry you, but I don't understand this man. I don't know how to please him."

"Nor does it seem that you know how to please me, either." There was another pause. "You may go to your room and you will stay there the rest of the day, through dinner, and you will devote yourself to your books and you will find a topic that will interest this man. If he leaves here and meets with his unionists it will be your fault and you will be"—he lowered his voice—"punished for your disobedience. Now go. I can no longer bear the sight of you."

Hank heard Amanda's steps leaving the library and his first impulse was to go to Taylor and hit him in the face, but Hank held up his hands and saw that they were trembling. What he had just heard made him sick to his stomach. He remembered being angry when he saw Blythe Woodley with her fiancé because the man was overbearing with Blythe, but Blythe's intended had been nothing compared to Taylor Driscoll. Taylor had assumed absolute control over another human's life.

Hank left the conservatory and walked outside, trying to get enough air to breathe, but there didn't seem to be enough oxygen on earth. This is what he'd seen in Amanda's eyes, this sadness, this look of a caged animal—not frightened but resigned. Taylor owned her mind, her thoughts, even her body. He controlled her as if she weren't an autonomous human being—as if she were something he'd created.

Hank began to understand things that had happened since he'd arrived: the rigid timetable of Amanda's. Of course she knew that she had three and a half minutes left in the bathroom because that was how much time Taylor had allotted her. Her dresses were of somber colors and cut, and her hair was pulled back tightly. Taylor wanted her that way. She spoke only of things she'd learned in books because Taylor didn't allow her to take her nose out of them.

Hank thought back to the times he'd seen Amanda sitting at her desk late at night. She had to entertain him all day yet keep up with her studies at night. This was a woman who was old enough to have graduated from college yet she was still being sent to bed without supper if she didn't obey her master.

Master! Hank thought. How he hated the word. Each man was master of his own fate, but some men, because of their wealth or ancestors, set themselves up as better than others. Taylor had said that Hank was working class, as if there were classes in America. And he'd told Amanda that if unions were brought in, their ranch would be taken away from them. The union was the boogy-man of the owners.

Hank closed his eyes for a moment and thought of all Taylor was doing to subjugate Amanda, to keep her in line, to deny her her God-given freedoms: the freedom to choose, the freedom to love, to like or dislike, the freedom to laugh or frown or cry. He had taken all that away from her, holding over her head threats of bankruptcy and of withdrawing from a marriage.

Hank walked to the front of the house and looked up at Amanda's window. He understood now, understood why he had first been drawn to her. It was his hatred of oppression and injustice. Some part of him had recognized it in her and knew he needed to help her. He would help her realize that she had just as many rights as another person had and that she didn't have to eat, sleep and breathe according to a schedule made by someone else. He would teach her these things, and when he was finished, she'd be able to tell Taylor Driscoll to go to hell.

He smiled up at Amanda's window. "Sleeping Beauty," he said, "I'm going to wake you up."

He turned away from the house and started toward the garage. He needed to get away and make plans— plans about how to bring Miss Amanda Caulden to life.

Hank stood in his room on the second floor of the Caulden house and put the canvas rucksack he'd just bought on his back. He left his jacket in the closet and wore only his shirt with the sleeves rolled to his elbows, his trousers held up by suspenders. He walked out on the balcony and stood there a moment looking up at the starlight. To his left he could see a light behind the curtains of Amanda's bedroom and just the faintest shadow of her bent over her desk.

Making as little noise as possible, he threw a leg over the balcony railing and stepped onto the porch roof which ran just under Amanda's open windows. The roof was steeper than it looked and his shoes slipped, but he caught Amanda's windowsill with one hand and the frame with the other. He was halfway inside the room before she looked up and saw him. She was as primly dressed as always, every button fastened, every hair in place, in spite of the fact that it was ten o'clock at night and she was alone in her room.

Amanda looked up from her book on economic history to see Dr. Montgomery coming through her window. Shocked was not the word for what she felt. Her first thought was, Taylor will not like this.

She stood, her body stiff with disbelief, and, again, that rising feeling of anger. "Dr. Montgomery," she said, "you cannot possibly come into my room."

"Sssh," he said as he stepped inside. "You'll wake everybody." He nodded toward the bare floor in the center of the room. "That looks like a good place. Here, take this." He removed the canvas bag from his back and handed it to her.

To Amanda's utter disbelief, he went to the bed and removed the spread. "Dr. Montgomery!" she gasped. "You cannot—"

"You really are going to wake everyone." He lifted the cover, let it billow in the air, spread it on the floor, then sat on it. He reached up for her to hand him the rucksack and, as Amanda watched, he began to pull food from it.

There was a salad of lettuce and what looked to be lobster or crab meat, another salad of chopped chicken with peas, little sandwiches, olives, stuffed celery, pickles, strawberries and pretty little white cakes.

Dr. Montgomery held up a bottle of a thick, red liquid. "Strawberry sauce for strawberry shortcake."

Amanda just stood where she was, looking down on the food in wonder.

"You aren't hungry? I missed dinner and I thought you did too, so I hoped we could share this. I don't really see any difference between eating here together or in the dining room, do you? If you do, we could go downstairs and wake the servants and they could boil something white for you. Maybe we could wake up Taylor and he'd join us."

"No," Amanda said quickly, and blanched at the thought of waking Taylor. The smells of the food were drifting up to her and making her knees weak. She sank down to kneel on the spread as a general might kneel when surrendering his sword to an enemy.

"Sandwich?" he asked, holding out the plate full of tiny crustless sandwiches to her. "They're minced ham with just a hint of mustard."

Amanda took the sandwich and made a nibbling bite, then the whole thing disappeared into her mouth. The flavor of it, tart and salty, was delicious.

Hank, smiling, handed her a pretty little porcelain plate. "Help yourself. It's not much but it's the best I could do on such short notice. I hope you like lobster."

"Yes, anything," she murmured, reaching for food and eating too fast, but everything tasted so divine and she had this feeling that it was all going to be taken away from her.

"You were studying?" he asked.

"Economic history," she mumbled, mouth full of chicken salad made with a rich, creamy mayonnaise.

"Ah, yes, I guess that's because I'm here. Or have you always studied economics?"

"I thought it would be something to converse on. I didn't realize you—" She stopped because she meant to say that she hadn't realized he would be more interested in fast cars, motion pictures and women from the wrong side of the tracks.

"But we haven't spent much time talking of economics, have we?" he said. "Or speaking of anything else, for that matter. I have been terribly rude to you, Miss Caulden, I do hope you'll forgive me. More lobster salad?"

"Yes, please," she said. She was beginning to relax somewhat. It was, of course, outrageous for this man to be in her bedroom late at night, but he certainly didn't seem dangerous and he did seem genuinely contrite over his past behavior.

"You like economics so much you miss meals to study it?"

"No, Taylor—" She started to tell him the truth but caught herself. "It was better that I stay here and study."

"I admire your dedication. I was in school for years but I don't believe I ever missed a meal while buried in a book. I get hungry and I want food. Nor could I eat what you do. You have enormous self-discipline, Miss Caulden."

"I guess I do," she murmured, but at the moment she didn't feel very disciplined. She felt as if she might sell her soul for a heaping plateful of that strawberry shortcake.

"When do you graduate?"

"Graduate?" she asked, looking at the strawberries.

"Yes, you're what? Twenty-three, twenty-four? Most women have finished school by now, yet you still have a tutor."

"I will finish when I marry," she said, reaching for a strawberry.

Hank began to heap her plate high with cakes and strawberries, drenching it all with thick strawberry sauce. "When you marry Taylor, that is? Tell me about your wedding plans."

"We haven't made any yet."

"Isn't that unusual? How long have you been engaged?"

Abruptly, Amanda set down her plate of half-eaten food and glared at him. She was beginning to understand now what he was doing and why he was in her room. Just as the devil enticed people, so was he enticing her. "Dr. Montgomery, contrary to your opinion of me, I am not a fool. Will you please leave my room and take your things with you at once?"

"There are more strawberries."

"I do not want more strawberries," she said, lying. "Now will you please leave?"

He sat where he was, knowing she would call no one. When she was angry the quiet sadness left her eyes. "Where do we go tomorrow?"

"I think perhaps you and I will not go anywhere. I have things I need to do here." A lump of fear formed in her throat as she thought of telling Taylor she would not keep Dr. Montgomery occupied tomorrow.

"Taylor wants you to keep me away from the house. He wants you to take me somewhere where the unionists can't find me, right?"

She hesitated. "I am merely to make a guest's stay comfortable."

"Uh-huh," Hank said, munching on a strawberry.

She glared down at him, her half-eaten strawberry shortcake glaring back up at her. "Dr. Montgomery, you *must* leave."

"Not until you tell me what you have planned for tomorrow."

She was afraid he'd do something embarrassing if she didn't tell him what he wanted to know. She went to her desk to get the schedule Taylor had given to her at eight P.M. "We are to go to the Pioneers' Museum in Terrill City tomorrow."

"That sounds like a barrel of laughs. I should be glad it isn't to the library to memorize dates of the Spanish-American War."

She narrowed her eyes at him. "Where did you get your Ph.D., Dr. Montgomery? From a mail-order catalog?"

He chuckled. "I just like to do things in life besides study, that's all, and it might do you good to look at something besides the inside of a book. Could we compromise? I'll go to your museum with you if you go where I want in the afternoon."

"I do not waste my time on motion pictures," she snapped at him. "I want to improve my mind and—"

He jumped to his feet. "You ought to try improving your *life.*"

For a moment they stood glaring at each other, then Amanda backed away from him. No one had made her angry since she was a child, but this man did. But there was something else, too, as she looked into his deep blue eyes, something she didn't understand at all, something that she was feeling deep inside her.

"Please leave," she whispered.

He turned away from her and began shoving left-overs and dishes into the rucksack. He had been right, he thought. Somewhere under her icebox exterior was a woman. He could make her angry, and that was a step in the right direction, and just a moment ago he'd seen something else in her eyes. Something that for the first time made him think she'd seen him as a *man*.

He picked up her plate containing the half-eaten shortcake and set it on her desk.

"Take it," she said. "I don't want it. I shouldn't have eaten with you in the first place."

"You'll save all your meals for Taylor? Is he the only one fit to eat with?"

"*You* aren't fit to sit at the same table with him."

"That's the best compliment I've heard this year. I'll see you tomorrow morning and, remember, the afternoon is mine." He put his rucksack on his back and left her room through the window.

Amanda sat down on the bed, her body feeling heavy and weak after her encounter with that man. What an utterly bizarre few days it had been, with everything turned upside down. Taylor was telling her he couldn't bear the sight of her, and this awful man, Dr. Montgomery, was making her act like a schoolgirl again. It was as if he were making her forget all her years of training with Taylor. Twice she had looked up from her studies and caught herself thinking of food —not good-for-you food but the kind Dr. Montgomery kept forcing on her.

As she thought, she looked across the room at the strawberry shortcake on her desk. Telling herself she was *not* going to eat it, she went to it and picked up the plate. There was no fork but, in spite of that, in spite of telling herself no, she picked up the sticky cake in her hands and began to eat as if she were starving.

When she was finished she looked at her gummy hands in horror, and even while refusing to believe what she was doing, she began to lick her fingers. Once finished, she sighed in disbelief of herself, then went to the door and silently opened it. She made her way down the dimly lit hall to the bathroom, making as little noise as possible in the hopes that Taylor wouldn't hear her.

When she came out she glanced nervously at Taylor's door, but there was no light. Nor was there a light on under her father's door or Dr. Montgomery's. Turning, Amanda saw a light shining from under the door of the spare bedroom where her mother spent her days. For just a moment, Amanda wondered what her mother was doing at this time of night. Years ago Taylor had forbidden Amanda to spend time alone with her mother as he thought Grace Caulden was a bad influence on her daughter. And Grace soon learned her daughter's precise movements, so they rarely saw one another.

Amanda shook her head. This, too, was Dr. Montgomery's fault for disrupting her orderly life. Her mother *was* a bad influence on her, just as Dr. Montgomery was a terrible influence on her. But she had to put up with him until the hops were harvested and all danger of a strike was past. When that was done, then she could return to her normal life. Once again she and Taylor could sit in the parlor after dinner and discuss intelligent, meaningful things.

They could eat food that was good for one's body. And she would know what was going to happen during a day. There wouldn't be any more riding in speeding cars or having a man climb in your window during the night. And there wouldn't be any more anger in her. She was calm and quiet when she was with Taylor, but when she was with Dr. Montgomery she was constantly having to repress her anger.

Back in her room, she changed into her nightgown, put the spread back on the bed, then hid the dirty plate Dr. Montgomery had left behind. It wouldn't do for Mrs. Gunston to find it in the morning.

She cleared the top of her desk because Mrs. Gunston reported on the condition of her room each day to Taylor. Amanda felt a little guilty about not studying more, but she felt so tired and sleepy with her full stomach and, besides, what was the use of studying? Dr. Montgomery never talked about anything intelligent. He merely ate and drove his little car faster than the wind. Both of which she detested, she reminded herself.

Tomorrow she'd do better than she had today. Tomorrow she'd act as if Taylor were standing beside her. She would direct their conversation to intelligent, enlightening matters, and nothing he could do would make her show her anger at him.

And she'd not eat his food, either! And when he drove fast, she'd demand that he slow down. She'd have to deal with him firmly and show him that she was indeed master of her own life. How dare he say she was oppressed! She'd show him that she was capable of making her own decisions.

She went to sleep and dreamed of creamed corn and fudge and roast beef, and when she woke she was ravenous, and the thought of a single poached egg and a dry piece of toast revolted her. But she stamped the feeling down so that she was in control again when Mrs. Gunston came to wake her.

Chapter Eight

When Hank woke the next morning he felt great. Last night with Amanda, he had done just what he meant to do: he had made her show emotion. If he could rouse her anger, he could rouse other emotions in her, and emotion was the key to making her realize she was being controlled by someone else.

He was whistling when he went down to breakfast, and he was greeted by a scowl from Taylor Driscoll. "Good morning," Hank said cheerfully. "Ready for another hearty breakfast of ham and eggs?" Smiling, he passed Taylor and went into the dining room. How in the world could Amanda think she loved that ramrod-stiff caricature of a man?

He smiled warmly at Amanda, who was already seated at the table behind her meager breakfast, and went to the sideboard to help himself to the feast laid out there.

"Bacon?" he asked Amanda before Taylor entered the room. "It's awfully good."

"And bad for your body," she said coolly.

"'Fraid he'll catch you eating it? Well, don't worry, you can make up for it at lunch. I'll feed you something good."

Amanda wanted to say something scathing to this man but Taylor came into the dining room. She was beginning to genuinely hate Dr. Montgomery. There seemed to be no end to his vanity. He presumed that he knew what was good for everyone else in the world.

She looked from Taylor to Dr. Montgomery. They were both good-looking men, but she liked Taylor's dark handsomeness better than Dr. Montgomery's blond boyish good looks. She liked the way Taylor sat up straight, the precise, clean way he ate. Dr. Montgomery ate with too much enthusiasm and he had a lazy, slouching way of sitting. He was too big, too . . . too masculine. Yes, she definitely liked the reserved strength of Taylor. Taylor was a man who knew exactly what he wanted in life and went after it. And Amanda knew what Taylor wanted from her, whereas Dr. Montgomery seemed to want . . . Well, she didn't really know what he wanted—but whatever it was, he wasn't getting it from her.

At the end of the silent meal, Amanda went with Dr. Montgomery to his car. She didn't even bother to ask him to go in the limousine. He started in on her at once. "Are you hungry?" "Do you want to stop somewhere and eat?" "Would you rather go swimming than to the museum?" "Did Driscoll give you a test this morning?" "Did Driscoll buy that dress for you?" "Would you like to pick out some new clothes for yourself?"

On and on the man went, but Amanda refused to get angry. He was a foolish, egotistic, overbearing man who liked to believe he knew everything about everyone else's life and he wasn't worth getting angry over.

He drove slowly to Terrill City, and Amanda used

the time to watch the way he shifted gears. By the time they arrived at the museum she was able to anticipate when he was going to make a gear change. At least she was learning *something*, she thought, rather than wasting her time with this frivolous man.

At the Pioneers' Museum he was rude and impatient. She was telling him about the tragedy of the Donner Party that was represented in the museum. "It was then that the rescuers found the remains of the others," she said, hinting at the cannibalism but not wanting to speak directly of it.

"I guess it beat shoe leather," he said irreverently. "Look, I have to make a phone call to arrange for this afternoon. Wait here for me."

He doesn't like others ordering me about but *he* is perfectly free to give me orders, she thought. Defiantly, she left the museum to stand outside in the cool shade of the porch. Brilliant fuchsia-colored blooms hung from a bougainvillea vine that draped one side of the porch. Suddenly she felt a wave of homesickness to be back at her desk with her books. What awful thing was this man planning for this afternoon?

"There you are," he said from behind her. "Have you seen enough of this place? Let's get something to eat. I'm hungry."

"That seems to be the usual state with you. Tell me, Dr. Montgomery, how *did* you earn your Ph.D.? From out-eating the other students?"

He gave her a hostile look. "I impregnated all the female students and they gave me a doctorate to get rid of me." He took her arm as she got in the car, then when he was seated he turned to her. "Look, I don't mean to be rude, it's just that you don't ever talk about anything besides what's in books. There's a whole world out there," he said, gesturing, "and I think you ought to see some of it."

"I don't know why you assume I'm stupid, Dr. Montgomery. I have seen enough of the world to know what it's like. It is a dirty, angry place full of dirty, angry people."

"And who told you that?"

"Taylor said—" she said, but stopped. "It is my own observation."

"Right, and I'm Christopher Columbus," he said, putting the car in gear. "You haven't been outside that house long enough to know what the world is like."

She knew that if the world was composed of people like him she most certainly didn't want to see any more of it.

He stopped in front of a restaurant and came out a minute later laden with a big cardboard box that he strapped onto the back of the car between the spare tires and the gas tank.

"We're going on a picnic," he said, as if he dared her to contradict him, then slammed the car into gear and took off.

Another waste of time, she thought. She was going to be so far behind in her studies that Taylor was never going to marry her.

He drove through the countryside, toward the Sierra Nevada mountains, past farmhouses and orchards and planted fields toward a dense grove of trees. There was a pretty pond in the center of the trees and he parked the car in the shade nearby. It was an isolated place, made private by the circle of trees, only a cow path leading into it.

Amanda looked around and began trying to identify the wild flowers and the birds. If Taylor asked her what she had been studying, she could tell him.

"Pretty, isn't it?" Hank asked, removing the box from the back of the car. "They told me about it at the restaurant. Here, take the end of this."

Amanda took the opposite end of the cloth he held. It hadn't crossed her mind that the place was pretty, but it was. The grass was greener here than in the full sun and the water was blue and the buzz of the insects was pleasant and— She pulled herself together. She was going to act as if Taylor was with her, remember?

"Are we to sit on the damp ground?" she asked.

"No, on the dry cloth. A little dampness won't hurt you. That's what skin is for—to protect you." He began to unload containers of food.

Amanda swore to herself that no matter what he brought out of that box she would not eat it. If she kept eating meals with him she'd get fat in a week, and Taylor would despise her. It took a great deal of self-control to watch the food being spread before her. There were strips of chicken breast in a golden sauce, cold roasted guinea hen, bread sticks, a grapefruit and endive salad, cold, seasoned boiled potatoes, sautéed eggplant, strawberries and tapioca, pretty little meringues, and candied almonds on top of a gorgeous chocolate cake. He poured glasses of lemonade from a big, frosty jar.

Amanda swallowed but turned her head away.

"Where do you want to start?" Hank asked, holding out a plate to her.

She took the plate, then put on it a small helping of potatoes and began to eat in tiny bites. She didn't even take the lemonade because she knew it had sugar in it.

"That's it?" Hank snapped at her.

She ignored his words and his tone. "Dr. Montgomery, could we discuss something less personal than my eating habits? Why don't you tell me what has made you believe that there is any good to come of unions? Were your parents, perhaps, migrant workers?"

"No, they weren't. Are you going to carry this subjugation of yours to the point where you don't eat?"

She ate a tiny piece of potato, hoping her body would ignore the tantalizing aroma of the food before her. "I think you have me confused with your migrant workers. I'm one of the rich tyrants, remember? It is people like me who give them jobs and thereby cause them enormous amounts of pain and misery." She kept looking at that chocolate cake. The icing was only on the top and dripping fatly down the sides, exposing seven layers of cake sandwiched together with thick, rich, dark chocolate cream.

"You don't know what you're talking about," Hank said. "Have you ever been in the fields during harvest time? Did you know that a lot of farmers *sell* drinking water to the workers? A hundred and ten degrees and they can't even get water."

"I'm sure you must be exaggerating. Of course the workers could go elsewhere if they don't like the way they're treated. This is a free country, yet you make it sound as if they were slaves owned by their master." She was looking at the cake, watching the way the light made the icing sparkle, and didn't see Hank's eyes turn dangerously dark. She was talking about the thing that meant most to him.

"It's people like you," he said softly, "that make a union necessary. The workers are simple people. They

127

don't have the education and resources to fall back on so they can change jobs on a whim. They have kids to feed and clothe and they can't afford to quit a job. So they work in the heat and save a dime by not buying water and they faint from heat exhaustion."

Amanda frowned at his words. She didn't like to think of the picture he was painting. What would Taylor say? she asked herself. "I cannot be responsible for all the poverty in the world, Dr. Montgomery. My family merely offers jobs. If the workers do not like the conditions they can go to another ranch."

Rage filled Hank. "You pompous little prig," he said under his breath. "You sit there in your silk dress surrounded by food and you're too good—too superior—to even eat it while others are out there fighting to make enough to buy a loaf of bread. People like you make me so mad I could—" He broke off, so angry he could no longer speak. Without thinking what he was doing, he shoved his right hand into the cake she seemed so fascinated by and grabbed a quarter of it, then lunged across the food and slammed the cake in Amanda's face. "There!" he yelled at her, grinding icing and cake and chocolate cream filling into her face. "You can eat and won't. They want to but can't."

He was trembling with rage. Amanda's face and most of her hair were black with chocolate, her eyes wide in horror.

"I'm going to wake you up, Amanda Caulden," he yelled at her. "I'm going to pull you out of that cocoon of yours no matter how hard I have to fight."

It was very difficult to keep one's dignity when one's face was covered with chocolate cake, but Amanda did her best. "Did it ever occur to you that some of us are happy the way we *are?*" she said, her own rage making her tremble. "You set yourself up as a god and decide to change me, change the workers, yet maybe we *like* the way we are. If I'm asleep I'd rather stay asleep than participate in a world where men bombard women with food." With that she got up and went to the pond to wash her face.

She felt like crying; she felt like screaming. But most of all she felt as if she'd let Taylor down. He would be horrified beyond description if he saw her now. She turned when she heard Dr. Montgomery walking up behind her.

"If you do another thing to me I shall press charges," she said, cringing away from him.

He winced, then held out a clean handkerchief. "I thought you could use this."

She snatched it from his hand and wiped her face. She thought she'd got most of it off but black smears came away on the cloth. Taylor was going to *kill* her. She'd have no supper for a month. How she wished the earth would open up and the flames of hell swallow Dr. Montgomery!

"Here, let me," Hank said, kneeling beside her.

"Don't you touch me," she said, seething.

He snatched the handkerchief from her and washed it in the pond. "Amanda, you are a mess. You have cake all over your face, your hair, even your clothes."

Amanda could feel the color draining from her face. She had never done anything to really, truly anger Taylor, but if she came home looking like this, what would he do?

Hank's face changed as he looked at her. "You're scared, aren't you?" he asked softly. "Do they beat you?"

"Of course no one beats me," she said, but her tone showed her uncertainty.

He stood, then took her hand and pulled her up. "All right, we'll fix everything. We'll wash your hair and your dress and everything will be dry by the time we return. You'll be as good as new."

"Wash my dress?" she gasped, horrified. "My hair?"

"Sure," he said. "It's either that or go home to your beloved Taylor looking like that."

For a moment she weighed the consequences and she decided that most anything would be better than having Taylor see her like this.

Hank watched the emotions play across her face and he was reminded of the migrant workers, torn between wanting to cause no problems and wanting to join a union and protest. Was Amanda really that afraid of Driscoll?

Hank made her decision for her as he slid his suspenders off, unbuttoned then removed his shirt and held it out to her. "Go into the trees there and take off your dress and put this on. We'll wash the chocolate off and it'll dry in no time."

Amanda looked up at him, standing there in an undershirt, exposing broad shoulders and muscular arms. Contrary to what she would have thought, he wasn't repulsive-looking or frightening. In fact, he looked rather pleasant.

"Go on," he said, and his voice was a bit lower than usual.

Amanda stood and walked around the pond and into the deep shade of the trees. She was wearing a severe, straight suit of boyish cut, and right now she wished it were two pieces so she could leave her skirt on, but it wasn't. She removed it to expose an ankle-length slip of flesh-colored chiffon trimmed with wide borders of ecru Chantilly lace. It felt odd to be without long sleeves and a high collar but it also felt cool and unrestrictive. She glanced down at the skirt and frowned at the lace. The skirt was semi-transparent from her knees down, her black silk stockings peeping through. Once again she reminded herself of Taylor's wrath if she appeared at home with a chocolate-encrusted suit and face.

She pulled the pins out of her hair and let it hang loose to her waist, then shook it and smiled. Sometimes her hair was pulled back so tightly it hurt her head.

When her hair was free, she picked up Dr. Montgomery's shirt and for a moment she held it out and looked at it. To her knowledge, she'd never held a man's shirt before and she was surprised at how large it was. She wondered if Taylor's shirt would be so large.

Ridiculous! she told herself and hastily put the shirt on. Next she'd be comparing Taylor and Dr. Montgomery. The shirt only reached to her knees, and below that were several inches of lace that played peek-a-boo with her black, silk-clad legs.

Hesitantly, she walked into the clearing, her suit over her arm.

Dr. Montgomery was stretched out on the tablecloth, still wearing only his undershirt and trousers. He was gazing up at the trees, looking to be half asleep. Lazy, she thought. The man was lazy. But she didn't think of it angrily.

"Ready?" he said and turned toward her.

He had an expression on his face that she'd never seen a man wear before. Taylor had certainly never looked at her like that. She didn't understand his look but it was making her blush.

"I think the chocolate will . . . will come out easily," she said hesitantly, for the man was gaping at her. He sat up, then slowly turned toward her, his eyes barely blinking as he looked at her.

"Amanda, you are beautiful," he whispered.

"Beauty isn't important. It is one's mind that matters," she said, then felt a little absurd to be standing there in her underwear and lecturing him. But she conquered her feeling. His looks might make her blush but he was a man who'd just slammed a cake in her face.

She turned on her heel away from him and went to the pond to try to wash the cake off her suit and out of her hair. The suit was easy, and she felt many pounds lighter when the cake stains blended with the brown twill of the suit. Her hair was another matter. She needed a mirror to see what needed washing.

"Allow me," Hank said from behind her, making Amanda jump.

She didn't trust him. "If I don't agree with you, do I get the tapioca poured over my head?"

He knelt beside her and used his handkerchief to wash cake from her hair. "It wasn't that you disagreed with me, it was—"

"Yes?" she asked. "What *did* make you do this despicable thing?"

He had his hand on her jaw and he stopped washing and looked down at her mouth, then moved his thumb along the curve of her lower lip.

Amanda's heart began to beat faster. You shouldn't allow him to do this, she thought, but she didn't move. "Unions," she whispered as he watched her mouth.

He looked back at her eyes and seemed to recover himself. "You don't know what you're talking about. You're just parroting your father and that man you think you love."

"*Do* love, Dr. Montgomery."

He took his hands from her face and rinsed out the cloth. "You know nothing about love."

She snatched the cloth from him. "You have no idea what I know about. I happen to know a great deal about love, as I have been in love with Taylor since I was fourteen. It is an abiding, enduring love."

"I've seen the two of you together. He's your *teacher,* not your lover. How many times has he told you you're beautiful? How many times has he been so overcome with passion that you've had to shove him out of your room?"

"Taylor is a gentleman. Of course I've never had to shove him out of my room. I don't want a man who is so . . . so . . ."

"Passionate?" Hank asked. "Here, let me do that." He started to use the cloth to get the now-drying cake from her hair but it didn't work. "It's in there pretty good. Here, stretch out there, put your head on the rock and I'll have to rinse it."

Amanda didn't like the idea but she obeyed. Hank went to empty one of the glass food dishes and when he returned she was lying on the grass in the shade, her head on a rock, hair spread out around her. He groaned aloud, making her look up at him in surprise.

"I assure you that I can wash my own hair," she said, starting to rise.

"No!" he said quickly. He filled the container with water, then knelt by her and poured water through her hair. There was part of him that didn't believe what he was doing. In the past, if he'd found himself alone with a young woman who was wearing her underwear and silk stockings on long, beautiful legs, it would have been because he had removed her clothes to make love to her. But here he was, innocently washing her hair.

"What were we talking about?" he asked. Maybe talking would make him stop *looking* at her.

"You were insulting me, as usual," she said, but there was no anger in her voice. She closed her eyes and felt his hands on her hair and head. This whole day had been awful, of course, an absolute waste of time. Dr. Montgomery hadn't cared about the museum and had rudely let her know it. Then he'd yelled at her and hit her in the face with cake—really an awful day, but right now she didn't want to be anywhere else but right here in the drowsy heat with the warm water pouring over her hair.

It seemed the most natural thing in the world when Dr. Montgomery kissed her. She didn't open her eyes but just enjoyed the sensation of his warm lips on hers. She put her hand to the back of his head. Just the tip of his tongue touched hers and it was very sweet. She might have lain there forever if he hadn't put his hand on her breast.

The sensation was so startling, her eyes flew open. She pushed him away and sat up, wet hair clinging to the shoulders of his shirt. "How dare you!" she gasped.

"Rather easily," he said, grinning, "and with great pleasure. The same pleasure you felt, I might add."

"You attacked me!" she said, standing.

He grinned at her in such a knowing way that she

looked away, her face red. "You have to take me home," she said stiffly.

Hank stood. "Sure. We drive up with me shirtless, you in your underwear and my shirt and your hair wet."

Amanda couldn't even imagine what would happen if Taylor saw her like that. He would leave her, leave the ranch. She'd ruin her own life and her father would hate her for making Taylor leave. Sometimes Amanda thought her father liked Taylor more than he did his own daughter.

Heavily, Amanda sat down on the grass. "No," she said softly, "I'll have to wait until my dress and hair are dry."

Hank turned away rather than say another word to her about her fear of the man she said she loved. How could he make her see that fear and love didn't go together?

"You have a comb in that little purse of yours?"

"Yes," she murmured, and he walked toward the car. She was feeling very confused at the moment and again she wished Dr. Montgomery had never come into her life. She had to get away from him. This evening she would tell Taylor that the professor was an impossible man and she didn't want to spend more time with him. Taylor would understand. He would understand and give permission— No! she told herself. They were in love, not student and teacher, so they'd discuss this situation and—

"Hold still," Hank said, and knelt behind her and began to gently comb the tangles from her hair.

"Dr. Montgomery, you cannot continue touching me," she said, moving away from him.

"Because that's your lover's right? Look, I'm sorry

about the cake, and this is my apology, all right? Now turn around and hold still. Besides, your fiancé doesn't do this, does he?"

Amanda turned around, and his combing felt wonderful, so relaxing, so gentle. No, she thought, Taylor had never touched her hair—or held her chin in his hands, or kissed her lips. Yet she knew that he did love her. Love wasn't just touching. It was also respect and being able to look up to the one you love. And neither of those qualities were in Dr. Montgomery.

"Are you married?" she asked abruptly, surprising herself.

"No, nor engaged, nor in love."

"Ah, so you don't know what it means to be in love."

"Neither do you, so I guess we're equal on that score."

"Taylor and I are—" she began. "Oh, what's the use? You have your mind made up, and nothing I say will be able to change it. Could we talk about something else?"

"You mean one of your 'conversations'? Something about some foreign policy or a list of the causes of the War Between the States?"

"That's a very good topic. You know, of course, that slavery was only one of several causes. As an economics professor—"

"Quiet, or I'll kiss you again."

Amanda almost smiled at that but she controlled herself. "Do you know anything about botany?"

"Do you know anything about your mother?" he shot back.

Amanda started to move away from him but he held

her hair in his hands and she couldn't move. "I believe that is personal, Dr. Montgomery."

"Could I bribe you with lemon meringue pie?" he asked, his big hands gently combing the tangles from her long, thick hair.

In spite of herself, she did give a little smile. At the moment she couldn't seem to remember Taylor. As she sat here in the grass wearing a man's shirt, a man's hands in her hair, Taylor and her father seemed far away. "My mother used to brush my hair and we used to eat lemon meringue pies together," Amanda said softly. She hadn't thought of her mother very often in the last two years.

"And when did it stop?" Hank kept stroking her hair, running the comb through it, letting it wrap around his bare forearms. He just wanted to touch her. He wanted to put his arms around her and kiss her neck and slide the shirt from her shoulders and—

"When I was told—" she said, "I mean, when I found out the truth about my mother. She was not a good influence on me."

Hank could hear the wistfulness in her voice. So Taylor had taken her away from a mother who brushed her hair and fed her food with taste. "I had a cousin like that, one who was a bad influence on me, I mean. He gave me whiskey and cigarettes, took me to a . . . well, a house of wayward ladies, taught me lots of curse words, taught me how to drive too fast. If it was bad for my health or could possibly kill me, ol' Charlie had me do it. It's a wonder I lived to be sixteen. I guess your mother was like that, huh? Drank, did she? She didn't take drugs, did she? Opium dens? Or men? Did she take lovers in front of you? Or—"

"Stop it!" Amanda said angrily. "My mother never did any such thing in her life. She was wonderful to me. She used to make all my clothes, pretty dresses with embroidered collars, and she bought me wonderful shiny shoes, and every Saturday she took me into Kingman and bought me ice cream and—" She stopped abruptly because she was aware of pain. More pain caused by Dr. Montgomery, she thought.

"I see," he said, his voice heavy with sarcasm. "She does sound like a terrible influence."

She turned away from him, then jerked her hair from his hands. "You know nothing about it. You are judging—and condemning—something you know absolutely nothing about."

"Then explain it to me, Amanda," he said, using her first name for the first time.

She put her hands to her temples. "You confuse me. Why should I explain anything to you? I don't know you. You're a stranger. You'll be gone in a few days, so why should I tell you anything?"

"Is that it or are you afraid to tell me? Tell me what hideous thing your mother has done, so I can hate her too. I hate oppression. I despise tyrants who hurt those weaker than themselves. Tell me what awful thing your mother has done to you so that you two live in the same house but never see each other."

"She never did *anything* to me," Amanda half blurted. "She never hurt anyone in her life, but she used to . . . to *dance!*" She glared at Dr. Montgomery in defiance. Now he knew.

"Oh," he said after a long pause. "Professionally? With or without clothes?"

Amanda could only gape at him. She had told him this deep, dark secret about herself, a secret that

Taylor said tainted her blood and made Amanda not quite "good," and yet Dr. Montgomery paid no attention to it. He was a dense man! *"With* her clothes, of course," Amanda snapped. "Don't you understand? She was on the *stage."*

"Was she any good?"

Amanda made a sound that was half anger, half frustration and got up and started toward the car. The man had the sensibilities of a rock!

He caught her arm and turned her toward him. "No, I *don't* understand. Maybe you could explain it to me. All I hear is that your mother loved you and you loved her, then somebody told you she used to dance and suddenly you hate her."

"I don't hate her, I—" She jerked her arms from his grasp. He confused her so much. He made her question things she knew to be true.

Hank saw the pain and anguish on her face and he calmed. "You know, you never did eat. Why don't you come over here and eat and explain to me about your mother? I can be a good listener and sometimes it helps to talk about things."

Obediently, Amanda followed him to where the cloth was spread on the ground and where the food was waiting. Suddenly, she did want to explain things to him. He kept condemning her, but if he heard the whole story maybe he'd understand—and if he understood, perhaps he'd stop making her angry with his sly innuendos.

He poured her a glass of still-cool lemonade and heaped a plate full of food and handed it to her. "Eat and talk," he commanded.

"My mother was good to me as a child," she began, her mouth half full, "but I didn't know that the reason she spent so much time with me was because the other women of Kingman would have nothing to do with her."

"Because she was a dancer?"

"Yes. You see, my father had no idea of her past when he married her. My mother comes from an illustrious family. They came over on the *Mayflower* and he was introduced to her in good faith."

"Meaning that he thought she was pure and innocent and had been kept secreted away until he met her?"

Amanda frowned. "Something of the sort. It was only later, after they were married, that someone recognized Mother. It was a man who'd been forward with her, I believe, a man who she had repulsed. He told everyone in Kingman." Amanda looked away. "He had a photograph of Mother in . . . in tights." She almost whispered the last.

"So then what?" Hank asked. "The whole town ostracized her?"

"Yes," Amanda said softly, and looked back at her food. "When I was in the third grade a girl said I thought I was so good because my mother rode on the *Mayflower* but she was just a cheap dancer."

Hank was beginning to understand a great deal. "Who had told the townspeople of your mother's background?"

"My father was very proud of his wife."

Hank watched her eat silently, her head bowed. So, J. Harker had married a woman who he thought was pure, innocent and blueblooded and he'd later found out she had spirit and personality—and probably legs as good as her daughter's, he thought with a smile.

"Dr. Montgomery, I do not believe this is a matter for amusement."

"So your father had bragged to everyone about his wife being better than anybody else, then he finds out she had been on the stage where, I might add, she had turned away the advances of too-forward young men. So the town turned on her, did they? I'll bet they were glad to snub someone they were afraid would snub them first. What did your mother do?"

Amanda hadn't thought of the town being wrong, only of her mother's scandalous behavior. She had run away from her family when she was eighteen, just after she'd become engaged to a man fifteen years older than she, and her father hadn't been able to find her for two whole years, during which time Grace had supported herself by dancing in a chorus with seven other young women on stage in San Francisco. Grace's father had forcibly returned her to his home, and six months later she was married to J. Harker Caulden—a man who wasn't at all of the same social background as Grace, but Grace's father believed that only the bottom of the barrel was good enough for a fallen woman such as Grace was.

"My mother stayed home with me," Amanda answered. "We dressed dolls together and she read stories to me and she let me try on her jewelry and—" She stopped because her words were causing an ache inside her. She remembered the soft, powdery smell of her mother, the goodnight kisses of her mother, the times she woke from a bad dream and her mother came to her and held her.

"So Taylor Driscoll came into your life and told you

your mother was a bad influence and you've stayed away from her ever since. Is that right?"

"Yes," Amanda said softly, still thinking of her mother.

"I guess your mother encouraged you to go on the stage," Hank said. "Did she let you try on her tights? What about her stories about life on the stage? Were they glamorous?"

"She never mentioned her time on the stage to me. And she certainly didn't try to entice me to run away from home as she did."

"Then tell me, Miss Caulden," Hank said softly, "just how was she a bad influence on you?"

Chapter Nine

"I don't want to talk about my mother anymore, Dr. Montgomery," Amanda said sternly.

Hank was watching her. "I don't blame you. Terrible person she must be. Let's talk about something pleasant, like when you're getting married."

"Soon," she said, finishing the food on her plate.

"Cake?" he asked. "Or have you had enough?" His eyes were twinkling.

Amanda felt she should have refused the cake he offered but she didn't.

"Let's discuss something neutral," he said. "Such as love and courtship and your wedding night with ol' Taylor."

Amanda choked.

"Lemonade?" he asked innocently, holding out a glass. "But I guess you know all about sex, what with a mother like yours and all the studying you've done. Tell me, does Taylor put lovemaking on your schedule or is it something he does spontaneously?"

"He doesn't—" she said angrily, then stopped. "Taylor is a gentleman."

"I'm sure he will be on your wedding night too. Did you ever think that as much as he likes educated women he's going to be disappointed with a bride who knows so little about . . . shall we say, the physical side of marriage?"

"Taylor is my teacher and I'm sure he'll teach me what I need to know."

"So he'll be your teacher even after you're married? It won't stop at the ceremony? Will you be given a schedule every day of the rest of your life?"

Amanda stood abruptly and glared down at him. "You are despicable, Dr. Montgomery."

Hank sat with his eyes fixed on her legs—long, slim legs with those black silk stockings. "Amanda," he whispered, putting his hand out to touch her calf.

But Amanda was already headed toward the pond to retrieve her still-damp dress. Within minutes she had it on and her wet hair pulled back into a tight knot. She walked back to the cloth where the food and Dr. Montgomery were sprawled. "I want to go home now," she said as coldly as possible.

He looked up at her with angry eyes. "Home to the open arms of the man who loves you?"

"Dr. Montgomery, my life is none of your business. How can I make you understand that?"

In one rolling motion, he came to his feet to stand in front of her, his face close to hers. "I'll understand when I see that it *is* your life. All I see now is a puppet, not a woman, and Taylor pulls your strings to make you do whatever he wants you to do."

"That's absurd! I control my own life. I—"

"Prove it!" Hank snapped. "Prove to me that Taylor wants you and not just your father's ranch and I'll leave you alone."

She took a step backward. He had said, out loud, her most secret fear. "Of course he wants me," she said in little more than a whisper. "Taylor loves me and he proves it every day. Every night he writes my schedule. He cares about what I eat, what I wear; he directs my learning, he—"

"Keeps his job," Hank said, jaw clenched. "Your father can't dismiss him as long as he's still teaching you. You're twenty-two years old, Amanda. When do you get to graduate? When do you get to cut your strings and be free?"

He was confusing her and making her angry at the same time. "You are making my head hurt, Dr. Montgomery. Please take me home."

"Home to that automaton you say you love? My *car* has more feeling than Taylor Driscoll has."

The confusion was beginning to leave Amanda and all that was left was anger. "What proof do you need?" she snapped at him. At that moment she felt she would do *anything* to make him stop antagonizing her. "Tell me what I need to do to prove to you that Taylor is the man I love."

"Passion," Hank said quickly. "The man is incapable of passion. Even if you marry him you'll die an old maid. Make him prove he can cut the mustard."

Her face turned red, embarrassment overriding anger. "I will ask him—"

"No, don't *ask* him anything. Invite him to your room. Throw yourself at him. Sit on his lap and run your hands through his hair."

Amanda stared at him for a moment, trying her best to visualize sitting in Taylor's lap, but she couldn't. She turned away from Dr. Montgomery and headed toward the car. "You are a frivolous man," she said under her breath.

Hank grabbed her arm and spun her about, pulling

her close to him. His mouth came down on hers with a mixture of hunger and anger.

Maybe it was Amanda's anger, too, that made her respond to him, but her arms went around his chest, pulling him closer as his mouth opened over hers and she tasted of his tongue with all the pleasure she gave to the food he'd introduced her to. Her breasts pressed against his chest, her hips against his as he pressed into her. His knee moved between her legs, and Amanda slid her body upward, letting him support her weight, with only the toe of her left foot touching the ground.

Hank moved from her lips, his mouth searing its way down her neck.

Amanda's whole body was throbbing and pounding, her heart pumping wildly, but she managed to push away from him. "Is that what you mean by passion, Dr. Montgomery?" she was somehow able to say.

The rage in his eyes was enough to kill a person. He didn't say anything as he grabbed the edges of the cloth and began rolling dishes and food together, then dumped it into the cardboard box and strapped it on the back of the Mercer.

"Get in," he commanded her as he held the car door open, and Amanda obeyed.

He drove too fast back to the Caulden Ranch, then had a devil of a time getting the brakes to halt the car. At the garage Amanda started to get out, but he stopped her. "We have a wager, remember?"

Amanda didn't want to look at him. His hands, his lips, his food, his words were all making her life hell.

"You're to make Taylor show passion," he said.

"Dr. Montgomery, I think—"

"It's Hank," he snapped. "I think you could be that intimate with me."

She kept looking straight ahead, wishing he'd get out of her life so she could go back to what she knew and understood. "It was something said on the spur of the moment, and I don't think—"

"If you win, I'll leave Kingman."

She turned to look at him then and the hope in her eyes made him angrier.

"If I win, you go to the dance with me tonight."

With you and Reva Eiler, she almost said, but there was no reason to even think of the dance because she was not going to lose. She was quite willing to climb into most any man's lap if it meant getting rid of the obnoxious Dr. Montgomery. "And what of your unionists?"

"I'll send someone else, someone who couldn't care less about Caulden's pretty daughter, someone to whom it won't matter that you throw your life away."

"How melodramatic you are," she said, concealing her anger. "Tell me, how do you plan to ascertain the winner of this idiotic wager? Do you plan to hide behind the door and spy on us?"

"I'll trust your word for it. You have until 7:30 this evening to entice Taylor into some sort of primitive display or—"

"Such as yours?" she interrupted.

"Or you go to the dance with me," he said, ignoring her.

"You had better pack."

He gave her a smug smile. "I'm going into town to buy you a dress for tonight. I doubt if Driscoll's bought you anything suitable for a night of tangoing."

She stepped out of the car. "I hope you know

someone else who can wear it, because I won't be needing it." She shut the door and gave him a malicious smile. "It's been interesting meeting you, Dr. Montgomery, not pleasant but interesting. I will meet you at 7:30 in the gazebo and I expect you to have your suitcase with you." She turned on her heel and walked back to the house as the car drove away behind her.

Amanda kept her courage all the way up the stairs and into her room, but when she shut the door behind her, every ounce of strength left her and she fell back against the door, her eyes closed. In the woods, alone with that awful man, she'd turned into another person—a swaggering, courageous young woman who wasn't like the real Amanda at all.

She looked around her sedate, tidy, colorless room and knew this was the real Amanda. She walked to the desk and picked up Taylor's new schedule. She was already off course, and the moment she touched the paper, she felt Taylor's power over her return.

Heavily, she sat down on the chair. What in the world had she done? She was to *entice* Taylor? Make improper advances to Taylor? She'd rather walk across burning coals.

But if she didn't do it, she'd have to go to a dance. Of course she could always tell Dr. Montgomery she'd been joking. And he, being the civilized man he was, would no doubt throw her over his shoulder and carry her out the door. Then everything really would be over between her and Taylor.

She put her elbows on her desk and buried her face in her hands. What awful thing had she ever done to deserve the curse of Dr. Montgomery? God gave the Egyptians the twelve plagues and to her He gave Dr.

Montgomery. Job would have thrown in the towel if he'd had to deal with *this* man.

She opened her eyes to look at the schedule again. She was late getting back with Dr. Montgomery, and right now she should be studying the current battle between the Greeks and the Bulgars so she could discuss it at dinner tonight with Taylor—if she was still alive at dinner. Taylor might kill her if she did what Dr. Montgomery had goaded her into trying.

If only there was someone to talk to. *How* did one entice a man like Taylor? With Dr. Montgomery all one seemed to have to do was stand in one spot for a moment or two and he was enticed. Amanda's mind drifted back to this afternoon. The warm air, the birds, the food, Dr. Montgomery's lips and hands all seemed to be rolled into one long, delicious sensation.

No! she told herself, stop those thoughts. Dr. Montgomery was an overbearing lower-class moron who wasn't fit to clean Taylor's boots. But he certainly did make her feel—

Mother, she thought suddenly. Her mother would know what to do.

Before Amanda could give herself time to consider what she was doing, she left her room, went down the hall and knocked on the door to the room where Grace Caulden practically lived.

"Come in, Martha," Grace called to whom she thought was the maid.

Amanda opened the door and found that her heart was pounding as if she were doing something very wrong. Her mother sat at a little desk, her pen moving rapidly over a piece of paper, her back to Amanda. Amanda had, of course, seen her mother in the last few years but she'd always averted her eyes. Taylor could be rather harsh when he caught her talking to her mother.

"It's me," Amanda whispered.

Grace turned around in her chair, her eyes eating her daughter, but she didn't move toward her. It wasn't easy to suppress the urge to envelope Amanda in her arms.

"Something has happened," Grace said in a soft, carefully pronounced voice. She was as pretty as her daughter, with her dark hair and eyes, but there was no sadness in those eyes. For a woman who was nearly shunned by her own family, she looked remarkably happy.

Amanda felt terribly guilty being in her mother's room but at the same time it felt so good. She knew this confusion was Dr. Montgomery's fault. "I need some advice," Amanda said softly.

Grace put down her pen and gave her full attention to her daughter. "I will do my best."

"I . . . I have done a very stupid thing." Amanda looked down at her hands.

Grace resisted the urge to say, Good! but just waited while Amanda stood there and fidgeted. Her awful, unstylish, boxy dress was stained and rumpled and her hair was a mess.

"I made a wager," Amanda said, and went on to explain as quickly as possible.

When she finished, Grace's mouth was open. "Dr. Montgomery is . . ." she trailed off.

"He is an awful man! I wouldn't consider this ridiculous wager except that if I win he'll leave Kingman. Taylor has no idea what he's like or he wouldn't ask me to spend time with him."

Grace's eyes brightened as she began to think

quickly. "What you must do is win this wager. For the good of everyone on the ranch you must win. Now is not the time to think of yourself. You must throw yourself at Taylor and let nature take its course. I'm sure Taylor will understand—and respond. After all, he's a normal, healthy man and you are a beautiful young woman. And it's perfectly all right since you're engaged to be married. I'll bet Taylor has had to restrain himself from touching you. He's merely being respectful."

"You don't think Taylor will dislike me if I'm too . . . too forward? He doesn't seem to like forward women."

"I told you, he respects you. Just show him you need a little less respect and a little more lovemaking and you'll not only win your wager but you'll probably get a marriage date set—and you'll get rid of your dreadful Dr. Montgomery. What more could you ask?"

Amanda smiled at her mother. "I guess you're right. Thank you." She turned to go, but Grace called to her.

"Amanda," she said softly. "What made you come to me?"

"Dr. Montgomery asked me questions about you and I, well . . . I guess I . . ."

"I understand. Go on now. You only have two and a half hours to win your bet."

Amanda smiled at her mother and left the room.

Grace leaned back in her chair and rolled her eyes skyward. "Please God," she prayed, "I need Your help. I don't know how I'm ever going to get into heaven hating Taylor Driscoll the way I do."

She looked back at the room and smiled. If Amanda made advances to that cold fish he'd be horrified. This

Dr. Montgomery was right: there was no passion in Taylor. Grace hoped Amanda flung herself on him and she hoped Taylor was disgusted enough to break the engagement, maybe disgusted enough to leave the ranch.

"The bastard'd never do that," Grace muttered. Taylor wanted the ranch so much he'd subjugate Amanda, banish Grace and make Harker think he couldn't run the ranch without this stranger.

Dr. Montgomery, Grace thought before returning to her writing, she'd have to pay some attention to that young man.

Amanda stood looking in her closet. Two and a half hours, she thought, and she'd already wasted fifteen minutes trying to choose the right dress. She wasn't used to choosing her own clothing since Taylor told her what she was to wear. She didn't guess she could ask him what to wear for his own seduction.

At last she grabbed a plain pink dress, since pink was the closest thing she had to red, and as she dressed she wondered what constituted winning this disgusting wager. A kiss on the lips, she thought. That's all it would take. For a moment she paused and thought that if she reacted to Dr. Montgomery's kisses with so much fervor, how in the world would she react to the kiss of the man she loved? Just thinking about it made goosebumps on her arms.

When she was dressed, she made an unscheduled trip to the bathroom, then went downstairs in search of Taylor. The maid said he was in the library. Amanda paused before knocking and took a deep breath. She was doing this for the ranch, she reminded herself.

At Taylor's "Come in," her hand was trembling on the latch as she slid the door back.

Taylor looked up from the desk, obviously surprised to see her, then he looked down her body coolly. "I do not believe that is the dress I chose for you."

"There was an accident," she answered glibly, as if she were used to lying. "At the museum a child fell against me with a piece of cake. Chocolate cake."

"Disgusting," he said. "Children today have no manners."

Amanda took a breath. "Not like our children."

Taylor looked shocked at her words, and Amanda felt a little surge of power at having so much effect on him. "Why aren't you studying?" he asked softly.

"I wanted to talk to you," she answered as she took a few steps closer to the desk. "I thought . . ." She hesitated. "I thought perhaps we could talk about our marriage plans."

Taylor took a while to recover. He didn't like this one little bit. Amanda was not supposed to be in the library; she was not supposed to be wearing that dress; and she most certainly was not supposed to be talking to him about marriage and . . . and children! He had to stop this. If she started going where she wanted when she wanted, where would she go next—to roadhouses? He stood.

"Amanda, you are to—"

"I'd like to talk about our marriage," Amanda said quickly, cutting him off. She hid her shaking hands behind her back.

Taylor walked around the desk and looked down his nose at her, his back rigid. "We will discuss our marriage when *I* say we will."

For the first time ever, Amanda felt anger at Taylor. It was that odious, interfering Dr. Montgomery, she thought. He was twisting her thoughts, making her doubt what she knew to be true. "I'm twenty-two years old, I'm a *woman*, not a little girl," she said in the voice of a ten-year-old.

"You are not acting like a responsible adult," he said, his jaw hard. "You are acting like a demanding, whining, controlling shrew. You are not behaving like a woman who any man would want for a wife."

Amanda remembered her mother's words: that Taylor was merely being respectful to her and that he was a normal, healthy man—and she also remembered her wager. Quickly, before she lost courage, she stood on tiptoe and pressed her lips against Taylor's.

Nothing happened. Perhaps Dr. Montgomery's barbarism was tainting her view of life, but every time she got within ten feet of him, his hands were on her body. But Taylor didn't bend, didn't respond, didn't move. She opened her lips a little but still nothing happened.

She opened her eyes and looked at him, saw him staring at her with rage. She pulled away from him. He was livid. His face was red, a vein pounded in his forehead—and Amanda was frightened. She remembered Dr. Montgomery's words of, Do they beat you? She stood there paralyzed, looking up at him.

It took Taylor a moment to recover enough to speak. He was really, truly horrified. The woman he had so carefully taught was turning into a harlot just like his mother. Were all women alike? Were women interested in only one thing?

"Are you finished?" Taylor said at last, his voice

cold enough to make his breath seem frosty. "Or perhaps you want more? Shall we copulate on the carpet? Is that what you're after?"

"No," she whispered. "I . . ."

"Have I misjudged you, Amanda? All these years I've thought you were different, that you were a woman worthy of love, a woman who had higher goals in life than merely procreation, and now I find that you're no different. Tell me, have you always been lying to me? Have you ever been interested in learning?"

"Of course I have," she said, and she felt like a harlot. "I didn't mean—"

"Didn't mean what?" he snapped. "Didn't mean to act like a woman from the gutter? What kind of woman throws herself at a man?"

"But we are engaged," she said pleadingly. "Shouldn't engaged couples show affection for one another?"

"I haven't shown you affection? You don't think planning your lessons, the time we spend together, the hiring of Mrs. Gunston to take care of you isn't a display of my affection?"

"Of course it is," she murmured. She had never felt so low in her life. How could she have been so crude? "I'm very sorry. It won't happen again. I apologize."

"I find your apology difficult to believe. Perhaps I am not the man for you. Perhaps I should leave the ranch and—"

Amanda's head came up. He *didn't* want the ranch more than he wanted her. She almost smiled. "No, please don't leave. I'll behave; you don't have to worry. I'll never do anything so . . . so brazen again.

Please forgive me. I'll go upstairs now and study all night with no dinner, and tomorrow I'll make you proud of me."

"That will be difficult."

"I will, you'll see," Amanda said, backing toward the door. "This won't happen again, I promise." She slipped through the library door and ran up the stairs.

Inside the library, Taylor sat down heavily and was horrified to find that he was shaking. He had almost lost everything: the ranch, Amanda, future security, everything. But something else that bothered him was that he hadn't been the least bit tempted by Amanda's kiss.

He stood. That was perfectly proper. He shouldn't think of her any other way except as his pupil until they were married. Even so, the whole episode had left him shaken. To come so close to losing the ranch and to see Amanda, the only female he'd ever come to trust, acting like a woman of the streets, had left him feeling as if the foundation had been knocked from under his feet.

For the first time in his life, he went to J. Harker's whiskey decanters and poured himself a two-finger-deep shot of whiskey, then downed it. He was sure his throat was burned raw, and his eyes teared as the hot liquid hit his stomach, but he felt better as he went back to the account books. Whatever had got into Amanda? Maybe she had too much free time. Maybe her lessons weren't difficult enough and didn't challenge her active mind sufficiently. He'd work on tightening her schedule and on giving her something to occupy her.

* * *

Amanda tried to keep her composure but she couldn't. Once inside her room, she flung herself on her bed and cried as if her life were over. She had almost made Taylor leave her.

She beat her fists into the bed and kicked her heels. She hated, hated, *hated* Dr. Montgomery. He was ruining everything in her life. Why didn't he go back to where he came from? Why didn't he just leave her alone?

She cried for nearly thirty minutes until a knock sounded on her door and she opened it to Mrs. Gunston. Amanda averted her eyes so the woman wouldn't see that she'd been crying.

"He sent this to you," the big woman said, looking smug and pleased about something.

Amanda took the book and paper and practically closed the door in the woman's face.

"Beginning Calculus," she read aloud, then looked at the new schedule. She was to study this book and there would be a test on the first four chapters at six o'clock the next morning.

"But tomorrow is Sunday," she whispered, then her shoulders drooped as she flipped through the book. It looked awfully complicated, and if she was to do well she'd have to stay up all night. And she would do well! She'd make Taylor see she wasn't frivolous, and wasn't a wayward woman.

She went to the desk and opened the book to page one.

She was so engrossed in trying to understand the basic principles of calculus that she didn't hear Hank enter her room through the window, so when he spoke, she jumped.

"Lost the bet, did you?" Hank said from behind her.

Amanda put her hand to her heart as she turned toward him. "Really, Dr. Montgomery, must you skulk about like a burglar? Couldn't you come to the door and knock like an educated, mannered person? Or perhaps I'm asking too much. Maybe you grew up in a stable with the rest of the animals."

Hank grinned at her. "Turned you down so bad he made you snippy, didn't he?"

She gave him what she hoped was a look to kill. But he didn't even so much as stop grinning. She turned back to her book.

"Ready to go? I bought you a new dress. It's supposed to be the latest thing for a young lady to tango the night away in."

She gritted her teeth and kept her face turned toward her book. "I'm afraid something has come up. I can't go." She waited for his explosion, but there was no sound from him for so long that she turned. He was sprawled on her bed, his long body taking up the whole bed. For just a second, he looked rather appealing, but she stopped that thought.

"Well?" she said. She might as well get the argument over.

"Well what?" He continued looking at the ceiling.

He had more ways for angering a person than most people had hairs on their head. She stood, her fists clenched at her side. "Dr. Montgomery, I want you to leave my room and I never want you to enter it again. Also, I want you to stop interfering in my life. As for this afternoon, I was . . . well, I was not myself and I said things I didn't mean. If you misunderstood and thought I meant to go to a dance with you I'm very sorry, but I have work to do and I cannot leave the house."

He just lay there, not saying a word, his hands behind his head.

"I asked you to leave!"

"What kind of work?" he asked at last.

She sighed in exasperation. "If you must know, it's *Beginning Calculus* and I have a test on it early tomorrow morning, so I have to use every minute to study."

He rolled off the bed and came to stand in front of her. "So you got punished, did you? A test early Sunday morning. What did you do? Wrestle him to the floor? Climb in the bathtub with him?"

"Get out of my room."

"Or did you just try to hold his cold hand?"

She looked away from him.

He leaned close to her, his lips near her ear. "Or did you maybe kiss him?"

Amanda sank onto the chair. "Would you *please* leave?" she whispered.

He put his hands on her shoulders and lifted her up to face him. "You ready to admit I was right? Your Taylor doesn't have any blood in his veins. He's incapable of anything resembling passion."

She twisted out of his grasp. "He's a good man and I want to please him."

"Why don't you please yourself?"

She gave him a false little smile. "It would please *me* to get back to my studying. And it would also please me if you left my room. Better yet, it would please me if you left America."

He pulled his watch from his vest pocket. "We're going to be late. I'm supposed to meet Reva at eight, so that gives you about ten minutes to dress. You'll like this dress I bought you."

"Does it have a bodice? Or is the skirt missing? Dr. Montgomery, I am *not* going to some loud, beer-swilling party with you and your equally disgusting friends."

He grinned at her. "You've already lost one bet today; what d'you want to bet you lose this one too?"

Chapter Ten

By the time Hank entered the dance with a woman on each side of him, he was ready to enter a monastery. Reva was angry because he'd shown up for their date with another woman and Amanda was angry because he'd threatened her until she had to attend the dance with him. Added to this was the fact that the two women were natural enemies and they'd had to share the passenger seat in his Mercer and Hank was beginning to think pleasantly of Amanda's suggestion that he leave the country. Maybe a long cruise on a ship. Maybe a cruise on a Navy ship where he'd see only men for months at a time.

"There's a table," Reva said over the noise of the ragtime music. "Of course it has only two places." She gave Amanda a withering look. Reva thought she could cheerfully kill Amanda right now. She finally got a chance at a gorgeous, rich, educated, rich, respectable, and, most of all, rich man like Dr. Montgomery and who should show up but Amanda? And to make it worse, Amanda was wearing a stunning white satin dress with a slant-cut overskirt that dripped with a fringe of crystal beads. Reva didn't know dresses like that existed, and it made her frilly blue dress that had cost her a week's salary look cheap and gaudy.

"It doesn't look like there's room," Amanda said. "You two go on. I'll find another table."

Hank's hand clamped down on her upper arm.

"Maybe I should be the one to leave," Reva said, then Hank took her arm, too, and began pulling both women toward the tiny table.

No cocktails were being served but beer and wine were abundant, so Hank ordered a bottle of champagne for their table. The three of them sat in silence, laughter all around, music playing, couples dancing, and waited for the wine. When it came, Reva and Hank drank greedily, but Amanda ignored her glass.

"Drink," Hank commanded her.

"And what will you do to humiliate me if I don't?"

"I'll make you dance with me," he said so just she could hear.

"I'll drink out of the bottle to escape that," she said, picking up her glass. The wine was heavenly, sour, effervescent, cold. She emptied her glass and the waiter refilled it.

"You don't have to get drunk. Is there any food you don't like?"

"There are just *men* I don't like."

"Excuse me," Reva said, "but I don't think I'm needed here. There are some people over there I know. I think I'll join them."

"Wait," Hank said, "let's dance." He took Reva's hand, and as he rose he looked down at Amanda. "You leave and you'll be sorry."

She just looked into her third glass of champagne and smiled.

"And slow down on that stuff."

Hank led Reva onto the dance floor and she nuzzled as close to him as was decently possible, but she didn't think he was aware of her. He kept looking at Amanda and frowning. Reva took his chin in her hand and turned those beautiful blues so they looked at her. "What's with you?" she said. "Are you in love with her or something?"

"God no," Hank said in horror. "I happened to have been cursed with a social conscience. I hate to see anyone who's under the rule of someone else."

"You mean Amanda? Some ruler she has, all that money, that big house of hers. Just that dress she has on is enough to make a woman forget any problems she ever thought she had."

"Yeah? You like that dress? Amanda thought it looked like something a saloon girl might wear."

"She was lying. Believe me, she was lying." This remark seemed to please Hank, and Reva smiled when he moved a little closer to her. He was an excellent dancer, and she loved the feel of all those muscles under her hands and those legs of his touching hers. If Amanda was going to get this man she was going to have to fight for him.

Amanda started on her fourth glass of champagne before the tension left her body. Or maybe tension wasn't the word for it. Maybe stark terror was what she was feeling. Dr. Montgomery had threatened to tell Taylor everything that had gone on between them since the professor's arrival if Amanda didn't go to the dance with him. Amanda was faced with definitely losing Taylor if Dr. Montgomery told or just the possibility of losing him if someone checked her room and found she was gone. She didn't even want to think about what her grade would be on tomorrow's test.

She took another swallow of the wine and began to look about the room. It wasn't as garish as she'd first thought and the music was much nicer than it had sounded at first.

"Amanda?"

She looked up to see a divinely handsome man leaning over her. Not as good-looking as Taylor, of course, or even Dr. Montgomery for that matter, but very pleasant, with dark brown hair, dark brown eyes and a nicely full lower lip under a fat mustache. She kept looking at that lower lip as he sat down beside her.

"It is you, Amanda. I haven't seen you in years. Remember me? Sam Ryan."

She looked back at his eyes. "Sam Ryan, the love of the whole elementary school. I remember we girls used to take turns swooning when you came by." Amanda was shocked that she'd said such a thing but she felt so relaxed that it didn't really matter.

Sam ducked his head in embarrassment. "I don't know about any of that, but you look great. I like that dress."

"Do you? I've had it for ages." It seemed that he was better-looking with every sip of the magic drink.

"Would you like to dance?"

"I'm afraid I don't know how."

"Oh." He smiled at her and leaned forward. "Are you here alone? I mean, is that guy you came with your date or Reva's?"

"Reva's!" she practically yelled. "He's nothing to do with me. He just drove the car. He's Reva's and no one else's. At least not mine. I hardly know him. I don't *want* to know him." She shut up.

Sam looked at her for a while. She had grown into a beautiful woman, with her hair soft around her face, her beautiful white shoulders exposed under the transparent sleeves of her dress. "It's awfully noisy in here, don't you think? Why don't we go somewhere and get somethin' to eat and talk about old times?"

"Food would be lovely," she said, thinking that she hadn't eaten since that disastrous picnic with that odious man. When Amanda started to stand up, she nearly fell, but Sam's strong arm caught her and she smiled at him as if he'd just saved her life. She was very happy to see a look in his eyes that she'd seen several times in Dr. Montgomery's. She didn't want to think about the way Taylor looked at her. His rejection of her today had hurt more than she wanted to admit.

"Thank you," she murmured, holding on to him, and the warmth in his eyes increased. He was making her feel very good. She clung to his arm as if she were an invalid as he led her toward the doors.

The tango ended and Hank turned toward where he'd left Amanda. The table was empty except for an empty champagne bottle and three glasses. Frantically, he looked about the room only to see Amanda clutching the arm of some big athletic-looking guy and gazing up at him with a simper and fluttering eyelashes. It took a moment before Hank could react, then he walked off and left Reva standing alone. Amanda and her overgrown boyfriend were already on the steps outside.

"Just where the hell do you think you're going?" Hank demanded, clamping his hand down on Amanda's arm.

"Wait just a minute, mister," Sam said, pulling Amanda toward him.

"You always did love to fight, didn't you, Amanda?" Reva said from the top of the stairs.

Amanda smiled at all of them and decided she was

going to drink champagne every day for the rest of her life.

Hank looked into Sam's eyes. They were the same height, but Sam was heavier and his face didn't have the intelligence in it that Hank's did. "This woman is under my protection," Hank said, as if he were talking to one of his stupider students. "I cannot allow her to run off with some—".

"Just one minute!" Sam said. "I've known Amanda all her life and I thought Reva was your date."

"So did I," Reva said.

"She is," Amanda said, smiling.

"You're drunk," Hank said with disgust and pulled Amanda toward him. "I'm taking you home."

She jerked away from him. "I *want* to get drunk. I *want* to run away with Sam. Isn't that the objective, Dr. Montgomery? To make me do what I want to?"

"Yeah, well I didn't mean for you to get drunk."

Sam started forward, but Amanda put her hand up. "You just wanted me to do what *you* wanted, didn't you?" Quickly, she spun about on her heel and planted her lips on Sam's. She didn't feel anything except anger, and when Sam's hands grabbed her waist she pushed him away and looked back at Hank.

"There! That's something *I* wanted to do. Now Sam and I are going to get something to eat."

Reva clutched Hank's arm. "That's just great, because we're going dancing." Reva pulled, but Hank didn't move as he watched Sam and Amanda start walking down the street, the streetlamps making them look isolated and intimate.

"I think I'm hungry," Hank said and started after Amanda and Sam.

Gritting her teeth, Reva followed him. "I thought you said Amanda was nothing to you."

"Merely a responsibility," Hank said, then turned into a diner behind Amanda and Sam. "Mind if we join you?" he asked as he took the opposite side of the booth, across from Amanda, Reva beside him.

"Could someone tell me what's goin' on?" Sam asked. "Who is this guy?"

"I would love to know the answer to that," Amanda said. "Just who are you, Dr. Montgomery? And why have you taken me to raise?"

"Good question," Reva said.

Hank picked up a menu and buried his face in it. "What's good to eat here? Not that it will matter to Amanda; she'll eat a wagonload of anything."

Everyone was quiet for a moment, three of them staring at Hank, but he didn't look up until the waitress came. He didn't know what made him angrier, prim little Amanda running off with this bonehead or the fact that she kept smiling so invitingly at him. She seemed to go from one extreme to another: Taylor, who was all learning and nothing physical, to this galoot, who probably had muscle for brains.

"Sam and I are going for a walk," Amanda said.

"Over my dead body," Hank said pleasantly.

"Maybe that can be arranged, Doc, although I hate to take advantage of an older man."

Hank nearly came out of his seat at that, but Reva put her hand on his arm. She was liking Hank more by the minute. If she could just get him away from Amanda.

"I think a walk's a grand idea," Reva said. "We'll all go. We'll walk out toward the museum." That was a long, dark road and there were hop fields on one side and maybe she could persuade Hank to walk under the dark rows with her.

"Maybe Amanda can get the museum opened for us," Hank said. "Then she could give us a tour."

Amanda gave him a cool look and moved closer in the seat to Sam. "Tonight I prefer to have fun. That's the objective, isn't it?"

Hank looked at the way Sam was gazing down at Amanda and the fork in his hand bent.

"You better be careful you don't hurt yourself, Doc," Sam said. "It takes longer to heal at your age. Come on, Amanda, you ready to leave this place?"

"Yes," she said, smiling maliciously at Hank.

Hank had to pay the check, and then Reva wanted to go to the restroom and she made him feel so rotten that he waited for her and he nearly lost Amanda and that schoolboy.

"Come on," Hank said impatiently to Reva.

"This is turning into the worst date I have ever been on," Reva muttered as they started walking. She did her best to coax Hank into the dark hop fields, but he didn't even seem to be aware of what she was doing.

Finally, she planted herself in front of him. "Look, I want to know what's going on. You invite me out to dance but you arrive with another woman who you say is nothing to you, then I get one dance and we're off chasing Amanda as if she were the love of your life. I just want to know where I stand. If you want Amanda, then don't invite *me* out." She knew she was risking losing him, but at this point her feet, in shoes made for dancing, hurt too much to care.

"Amanda's lived in a glass case all her life. She has

no idea what men are capable of, and she's been throwing herself at that football player all night."

"Sam's a good guy. Amanda will be all right with him."

"Hah!" Hank said and started walking again. "She's my responsibility. I made her come out tonight and I'd never be able to live with myself if anything happened to her."

"You sure that's all it is? You're not interested in her yourself?"

"Only as a student. She's not my type."

She was nearly having to run to keep up with him. "Prove it," she said daringly.

Hank paused for a moment and looked at her in the moonlight. Her makeup was too heavy and the dress she wore was cheap and he doubted if she had any idea what was going on in Servia but, at the moment, she was appealing. He put his hands on her shoulders and pulled her to him for a quick, perfunctory kiss. His mind was totally on finding Amanda.

"I think we've lost him," Amanda said, breathless from running to escape Hank.

"Is he your watchdog or somethin'?" Sam asked.

"*Something* is right. He thinks he owns me."

"But I heard you were engaged to some guy that lives with you."

Maybe it was the wine, but Amanda's memory of the humiliating scene with Taylor in the library came back vividly. If he was a red-blooded normal male, maybe it was just she who nauseated him. Dr. Montgomery didn't seem to find her physically repulsive but then he seemed to like all women. He flirted with

Lily Webster in the park, he took Reva to a dance. There didn't seem to be a woman he didn't like.

She leaned a little bit toward Sam. "Tell me, did you ever notice me when we were in school together?"

"Sure. You were Caulden's daughter. You were the richest kid in school."

"Oh," she said flatly. "Is that why you came up to me at the dance? My father's money?"

Smiling, he took her hand in his and led her to the edge of the road. "I didn't know who you were at first. I just thought you were the prettiest girl I'd seen in years."

"Really?" she whispered up at him, eyes wide. If she was pretty, why didn't Taylor want to touch her? She wondered if Sam would be repulsed if she kissed him. She put her face up toward his and she was pleased to hear his breath taken in sharply.

"Let's go look at the hop fields in the moonlight," he said and pulled her behind him. When they came to the fence, he swept her into his arms and lifted her over.

The sudden movement made Amanda feel a little dizzy, but the moonlight, this big, handsome man, the wine and his obvious interest in her were making her skin glow. She watched as he climbed over the fence and she saw a big muscle outlined in his thigh. When she looked up at his face, she saw he had seen her look.

"Come on, sugar," he said softly and caught her hand and began leading her under the overhead curtain of hop vines.

Amanda followed him, feeling good about herself, feeling that she, for once, wasn't a freak. Here was a man who *liked* her, a man who didn't want to teach her anything or give her a test. Here was a man who wasn't angry because she was displeasing him.

Suddenly, Sam turned and pulled her into his arms and began to kiss her. It felt so good to be kissed. He wasn't Taylor, who hated her kisses; he wasn't Dr. Montgomery, who only kissed her when he was proving something to her.

She stood on tiptoe and kissed him back, her arms going around his neck.

His lips went to her cheek, her ear, her neck. His hands began to roam all over her body, clutching her buttocks and jamming her hips against his.

"Oh yeah, honey, give me," he murmured, his mouth moving down to her shoulder.

She felt his hand on the filmy shoulder of her dress, then she heard a little tear.

"Sam," she said, pushing at him, but he didn't budge. His mouth was making her shoulder wet and the grinding of his hips into hers was beginning to hurt. "Sam, please let me go."

"Not yet, honey. Not till I get what you been promisin'."

Amanda was beginning to get concerned. His arms were tightening; his hands were moving. One big hand grabbed the side of her breast.

"No!" she cried, but he put his mouth over hers again. She didn't like his kisses. They weren't nice like Dr. Montgomery's kisses. She moved her head away. "Stop it! I want to go home."

"You *are* home, girlie."

He put one arm under her knees and lifted her as he sank to the ground.

She was frightened now and she began to struggle in

earnest, but she was half his weight and she had no effect on his strength. "No!" she screamed, pushing at him, pummeling any part of his body she could reach with her fists.

He grabbed her sleeve and she felt the fabric tear away as he began to run hot kisses down the front of her. She leaned her head back to scream for help but he put a thumb to her windpipe.

"No reason to make a fuss, baby," he said. "I'm just givin' you what you been wantin' all evenin'."

His mouth fastened on her breast and all Amanda could do was fight for air. She knew she was losing consciousness.

And then, all of a sudden, the thumb was removed. She opened her eyes to see that Dr. Montgomery had Sam by the hair.

"You bastard," Hank said, seething. "You're just what I thought you were."

Sam jerked out of Hank's grasp. "She wanted it. She's been askin' for it all night. You mad because she won't give it to you?"

The next second Sam was on his back, blood running from his split upper lip where Hank had hit him.

"I'm gonna massacre you, old man, then I'm gonna take her," Sam said, coming to his feet and preparing to run at Hank.

"You and what army?" Hank said softly before sidestepping Sam's head-down charge. He laced his fingers and brought both fists down on the back of Sam's head.

Sam kept going for a second, then fell facedown in a hop plant.

"So much for old men," Hank said from above Sam's inert body, then he turned to look at Amanda. Her face was whiter than the silk of her dress and she was holding the bodice together with her hands.

"Come on, let's go," he said as gently as he could, considering the fact that he could easily wring her neck. He put out his hand to her but she walked past him, her little nose in the air. All right, if that's the way she wanted it, she could have it. He wanted to comfort her but she didn't look like she needed any comfort. He didn't glance at the unconscious football player but rubbed his aching hands and followed Amanda back to the road.

Reva was waiting for them, but Amanda walked right past her and started back toward town and the car.

"Sam do that?" Reva asked, referring to Amanda's torn dress.

"Yeah," Hank mumbled, watching Amanda as she stalked ahead.

"I guess our date's over," Reva said. "It sure has been interesting."

Hank wasn't listening to her. He'd barely heard Amanda's cry of no. If he'd been two hop rows farther away, he wouldn't have heard her. Thinking about seeing that jerk's body wrapped around Amanda made him want to go back and kill him.

Amanda didn't stop until she was at Hank's Mercer, then she stepped inside, sat down and looked straight ahead.

"Move over and let Reva in," Hank said with more anger than he meant.

"No thanks," Reva said. "I think I'll go back to the

dance. But thanks a lot, Doc. Maybe we can get together again sometime." She practically ran across the street to the steps of the Opera House.

Hank started the car, got in the driver's side and turned toward the Caulden Ranch without saying a word to Amanda, but he silently cursed her all the way back. She had no sense about men, or sense about anything else for that matter. All she knew about were books and schedules. Why did she think she could handle some lusty young man like that Sam? And Hank didn't really blame Sam after the way Amanda had thrown herself at him.

He turned an angry look toward her just as another car passed them, and when he saw Amanda's face, his anger left him. She looked scared to death, as if her life were over. He pulled the car down a side road, stopped under an oak tree, then went to her side of the car.

"Get out," he said.

"I want to go home," she said in little above a whisper.

He put his hand on her arm but she flinched away from him.

"Don't touch me!" she said in a high-pitched half-scream.

"Amanda, I'm not a rapist and I'll be damned if I'll let you think all men are." He put one arm behind her back and another under her knees and scooped her out of the seat and into his arms.

When he touched her, she came alive, pounding his chest, kicking, pulling his hair. But he held her tightly, only grunting a few times when she hit some sensitive spot. After a long while she began to cry, and Hank moved with her to sit under the tree, where he held her close to him and stroked her hair while she cried.

"Are you hurt?" he asked softly.

Amanda was beginning to recover. "My pride."

Hank handed her a handkerchief. "Nothing else? Just an ugly dress torn?"

"It's a *beautiful* dress. The prettiest one at the dance."

"Think so?" Hank said happily.

Amanda blew her nose again. "I don't know what happened. He was so kind at the dance. And it was nice to have a man want to kiss me."

Hank felt personally insulted. "I keep kissing you and you don't seem to think it's so nice."

"Yes, but you just want to teach me a lesson. You want me to change myself into what you want me to be, and Taylor wants me to be whatever he wants. Sam just thought I was . . . that I was pretty."

Hank knew there was more truth in her words than he liked to admit. "But you flirted with him and made him think you were easy."

"I just wanted to feel wanted."

"I see. You want to tell me what happened today with you and Taylor?"

She shuddered at the memory of the scene in the library. "No, I don't."

"That bad, was it?"

She sat up in his lap, and for all the intimacy of their contact they may as well have been sitting in a parlor on chairs.

"Something I'd like to know is, if you wanted a man to make you feel desirable, why didn't you come to me?"

"You?" she asked. "But you don't make me feel desirable. You make me feel stupid. You make me feel that everything I do is wrong. You yell at me, ridicule me, threaten me, tell me I have no idea what life or love is. Taylor may not make me feel like a *femme fatale* but he thinks I'm smart."

She got off his lap, stood and tried to pull the torn parts of her dress together. "Taylor chooses my clothes; you pick out a dancing dress for me. I really don't see any difference except that Taylor does it without shouting. I must say, though, Dr. Montgomery, I do like your food better than Taylor's, but as for day-to-day contact, I much prefer Taylor's quietness, and after tonight I am further convinced that he's the man for me. Tell me, are dates always this much 'fun'? I think I'll stay home next time if you don't mind. Now, may we return to my home where I'm safe?"

She turned away and got in the car, trying to conceal that her body was still trembling from Sam's attack. During the years she'd stayed at home with Taylor as her tutor, she seemed to have missed out on part of her education. Taylor never kissed her, but then along came Dr. Montgomery and he did. Yet Dr. Montgomery didn't maul her or hurt her, nor did his hands feel like slime on her skin like Sam's had.

She turned her face to the wind and tried not to cry. For the thousandth time she wished she had never met Dr. Montgomery. If Taylor rarely kissed her, it wouldn't have mattered because she never would have known about kissing or fast little cars, or dancing, or succulent food if she hadn't met Dr. Montgomery. And she wouldn't have become reacquainted with Sam or Reva, who had given her dagger-looks all

176

evening. How different her life would be now if he'd never come.

And now she needed to get it back where it had been. She had to get home, sneak into the house (something else she'd never done before he came) and get to her calculus book so she could pass her test in the morning.

Hank stopped the car some distance from the house so no one would see the lights or hear the motor. "Amanda," he said, turning toward her, "you really can't blame me for what happened tonight."

"Of course not. I asked you to please take me to the dance. I even begged you to buy me a dress with half the bodice transparent. And I've told you how much I love your little picnics and all the other entertainments you've planned for me. Why should I blame you for any of the dreadful things that have happened to me since your arrival? My fiancé can barely stand the sight of me; I'm attacked by an old friend. But I'm sure it's all been my fault, not yours."

Hank didn't answer her but turned and started walking with her back to the house. He knew that what he was doing was right, but sometimes she made him doubt himself. Maybe he should take her at her word and leave her alone.

At the door to her bedroom, Hank took Amanda's hand and kissed her palm. "Good night, Miss Caulden," he said softly, then went into his room before she could speak.

He didn't sleep well that night but kept hearing over and over Amanda's words that he had no right to interfere in her life. She was right when she pointed out that all the bad things that had happened to her had been caused by him. Tonight she had been nearly raped, and if she had been, it would have been his fault. She had not wanted his help, yet he had forced himself on her.

At three A.M. he got out of bed and walked to the balcony outside. He could see Amanda's light still on and see the shadow of her bent over her desk. She was no doubt studying her calculus, trying her best to please the man she loved.

Hank walked back into his room and began to pack. He wasn't sure what he'd been trying to prove with Amanda, but right now he felt like a complete failure. The missionaries who went to Hawaii had felt they were right, but in the end they had brought disease and destruction to the Hawaiians—just as he was destroying Amanda, the woman he— He stopped. He didn't know how he felt about Amanda but he did know he'd do most anything before he hurt her. Maybe it had all been vanity, to see if he could take her away from Taylor Driscoll. And what if he'd won? Would she become another Blythe Woodley, who thought he should marry her? Would Amanda also tear up wallpaper samples and throw them at him? She was better off where she was, with Taylor, and if she wanted every minute of her life put on a schedule, then it was her choice.

He wrote a thank-you note to Mr. and Mrs. Caulden for their hospitality, although he'd never seen her and rarely seen him, then he tried to write to Amanda but couldn't. What could he say? Forgive me for trying to take control of your life when you have given control to someone else?

At 5:30 he heard movement upstairs and knew that it was nearly time for Amanda's punishment test. He swallowed his anger at such an injustice and closed his suitcase. It wasn't his problem any longer—never had been, for that matter—and went downstairs. As he left his thank-you note on the hall table, he noticed a light on in the library and that the sliding doors weren't quite closed.

Telling himself it wasn't any of his business, he peeped inside. Amanda, looking small and fragile, sat behind the massive desk, a paper and pen before her. But her head was on the desk, her hand palm up beside her. She looked like a sleeping child.

He felt a pang of remorse. She was asleep because he'd kept her out late and she'd spent the rest of the night studying. Silently, he slid one door open, then shut it and went to her. She was so soundly asleep she didn't hear him and didn't move as he took the test paper off the desk and looked at it. It was a difficult, complicated test and Hank cursed Driscoll once again.

It didn't take Hank but a moment to decide what to do. He took Amanda's pen, some pieces of Caulden's expensive stationery for scratch paper, sat down in a leather chair, a book for a desk, and began to work the problems. Thirty minutes later, he had finished and Amanda hadn't moved. He put the paper on the desk just as he'd found it, then, on impulse, wrote Amanda a short note and put it in her lap. Also on impulse, he kissed his fingertips and touched her hair, which was once again tightly drawn back. "Goodbye, Sleeping Beauty," he whispered and left the room and the house.

Chapter Eleven

Well, Amanda," Taylor said loudly, startling her awake so that she nearly fell out of the chair. "It looks as if my assignments bore you, as if you do not care whether you pass a test or not. Perhaps it's me who does not matter to you."

Amanda took a moment to adjust to where she was and what was happening, then she felt a sense of panic. She'd so wanted to do well on this test that she'd stayed up all night studying, which had caused her to fall asleep the moment she'd sat down to take the test.

Her fists clenched at her sides and she once again knew that Taylor's anger was caused by Dr. Montgomery. If he'd never come to Kingman she'd never have ended up going to a dance and being nearly raped, nor would she have had a test at six o'clock on Sunday morning. Nor would she have to see Taylor picking up the blank test paper.

"I can explain," she began, then fell silent. Explain how? she thought desperately, trying to make up a story other than the real one. "I . . ."

Taylor turned surprised eyes on her. "You have done very well," he said quietly. "I had no idea you were so good at mathematics." He had never given her much tutoring in mathematics, not because she wasn't good at numbers but because he'd never done well at the subject himself. He much preferred the arts and literature. He'd been so angry at her for her disgusting sexual display that he'd wanted to give her the most difficult assignment possible. Her study assignment had been from a beginning book of calculus but her test had come from a third-year book, yet, according to his answer sheet, every answer was perfect. According to this test, she was well past his knowledge of any form of mathematics.

"Good?" Amanda asked stupidly. "But I didn't even understand the questions."

He gave her a cold look. Was she making fun of him? "You have proved your point," he said. "Now go and change your dress. Wear the mauve silk. I do not like that dress at all. And fix your hair. It is coming undone. After breakfast I will inspect your sewing."

He put her test paper on the desk, then turned and left the library so abruptly that Amanda thought he was angry about something other than her sleeping. He hadn't said a word about her blank test paper.

She reached across the desk and took the test paper, then stared at it in astonishment. Neatly, concisely, each problem was answered in what looked to be her own handwriting. Even the fives were made the way she made them. Had she answered the questions in her sleep?

Even as she thought that, she knew it was impossible. It was while she was staring at the test in bewilderment that she saw the folded paper in her lap. She opened it.

Dear Miss Caulden,

Forgive me for interfering in your life; I was wrong. The test can in no way make up for my presumption but I hope it helps.

I wish you and your fiancé the best in the future.

Yours very sincerely,
Henry R. Montgomery

P.S. My doctorate did not come from a mail-order catalog.

It took Amanda a few moments to realize that Dr. Montgomery had saved her with Taylor and that the tone of the letter said that he was gone. At once she felt a great sense of relief. He had somewhat redeemed himself for the horror of last night, but nothing could fully make up for all he'd done to her in the past days.

She leaned back in her chair for a moment and breathed a sigh of relief. Now she could get her life back to the orderly, calm pattern it had been. Now she could make Taylor want to marry her. She'd follow his directions, keep to his schedule and study without stop, and before long he'd mention marriage again, and after their marriage they'd . . . What? she thought. Continue following Taylor's schedule? Study forever? Would she be delivered of a baby in the morning and have a French test in the afternoon?

Stop it! she commanded herself. She'd marry Taylor and live happily ever after is what she'd do. And she'd start right now by going upstairs and changing her dress and pulling her hair back into place.

She slipped Dr. Montgomery's note into her pocket

and meant to tear it into a hundred pieces and flush it, but when she was alone in her room she found herself carefully folding the note and putting it in the very back corner of her top drawer, in with her underwear. She told herself she could use it as evidence if needed. Evidence of what she didn't know, but she kept the letter just the same.

She went to her closet and took out the mauve dress and frowned. It was a color she did not like. The pale bluish purple made her skin look sallow and her eyes colorless. On impulse, she took down a hatbox from the top of the closet and removed tissue paper until she reached the beaded white-satin gown she'd worn last night, then held it up before her to see herself in the mirror. The fringe of beads would have been lovely if she'd danced.

Her heart nearly stopped when Mrs. Gunston gave a perfunctory knock on the door and entered. Amanda was standing in her slip and she hastily thrust the beaded dress behind her.

"You are not dressed," Mrs. Gunston said, looking shocked. "You were to have been downstairs three minutes ago."

"I was busy," Amanda said, holding the white dress at arm's length inside the closet. "I will be down as soon as possible."

"As soon as—!"Mrs. Gunston gasped, her big ugly face looking even uglier. "You are not on schedule. The master shall hear about this." She turned on her heel and left the room, nearly slamming the door behind her.

"The *master?*" Amanda said, then recovered herself. She had to get ready to go downstairs to breakfast and she had to get back on schedule. Then she remembered she hadn't even looked at her schedule that morning.

She dressed rapidly, tried to memorize the schedule and get downstairs as soon as possible, but something seemed to be slowing her down. Maybe it was the heat; maybe it was the fact that it was Sunday, but something was making her late.

Taylor was standing at the doorway to the dining room, his pocket watch out, a scowl on his face. "You are very late, Amanda."

"Yes, I know, but I was up all night studying and everything has been off since then. What's for breakfast?" She sailed past him and didn't see the way his mouth dropped open as he watched her.

Taylor closed his mouth. Yesterday the kissing and now she was off schedule. He had to get her back under control.

Amanda looked down at her poached egg and dry toast and nearly recoiled. She was so very, very hungry and this wasn't enough to fill a rabbit's belly. But she wanted to get back to her safe little world and this meager breakfast was part of it. She picked up her spoon.

"Well, Amanda, are you going to start this morning's conversation or must I?"

"I'm sorry, what did you say? Oh yes, the conversation. I'm afraid I forgot what's on the schedule. It has been a most hectic morning." She looked up as the maids began carrying in one covered dish after another for Dr. Montgomery's breakfast and set them on the sideboard. Amanda's stomach let its yearning for the food be known to her. She gazed at the silver dishes with longing.

"Amanda!" Taylor said. "What do you mean, you didn't read this morning's schedule?"

"I read it; I just don't remember it. Perhaps if you told me what was planned I could start the conversation."

Taylor didn't have time to recover from his astonishment because J. Harker burst into the room, a cigar jammed into the corner of his mouth.

"He's gone," Harker announced without greeting. "That professor and his fancy car are gone."

Both Taylor and J. Harker turned toward Amanda, their eyes accusing.

"I did the best I could," she said. "He didn't like having his days scheduled for him."

Harker turned to Taylor. "You put him on one of those damned schedules of yours? What'd you do? Tack it to his door? You tell him when he was allowed to pee?"

Taylor kept his back rigid. "I did not. Amanda was to stay with him, that is all. I merely suggested a few amusements for them."

J. Harker switched the cigar to the other side of his mouth. He'd always been in awe of Taylor's education, but right now he wondered if Taylor's brain was a book, with no common sense in it. "What kind of amusements? Libraries? Museums? He have to listen to Amanda reeling off facts?"

Amanda's face turned red at this, but neither man looked at her.

"Dr. Montgomery is a professor. I'm sure he enjoyed—"

"Enjoyed, hell!" J. Harker spat. "I was afraid to trust you on this. I didn't think you knew what you were doing. I told you not to send Amanda out with him. Montgomery is a big, strapping stallion, not a broken-down old gelding. Damn! Why did I trust you? Now he's gone, and instead of getting him on our side, he'll probably run to the unionists."

"I doubt that. We have shown him every hospitality. He had someone of intelligence to converse with. Just this morning Amanda made a perfect score on a calculus test."

For a moment, Harker could only sputter. "You expected a young animal like Montgomery to sit around with a pretty girl and talk about . . . about book learnin'? Have you got ice water in your veins? For God's sake, I can't stand to be around a little prude like Amanda for more than ten minutes, and she's my own daughter, so how can I expect a hot-blooded man like Montgomery to be able to stand her?"

No one saw the way the blood left Amanda's face.

"I'm sure Amanda made every effort to entertain Dr. Montgomery. Perhaps some family emergency drew him away."

"Yeah, some emergency like fear of dying of boredom." Harker put his cigar between his fingers and pointed it at Taylor. "You want this ranch, boy, you gotta do somethin' besides run my daughter's life. Those unionists cause me the loss of even a penny and I'll set you out of here on your ear. You understand me?" He stormed out of the room.

Taylor stood where he was, while Amanda remained seated, looking at her empty cup. Now Dr. Montgomery had caused her father to say these awful things about her. In the short time since that man had arrived, Taylor had shown he had no physical desire for her, and her father had admitted he couldn't stand to be near her. Some part of her had wondered why her father never ate breakfast with her and Taylor or why he never joined them in the parlor after dinner. But she'd never dreamed it was because he didn't want to be near her.

She looked up at Taylor as he stood paralyzed, staring at the doorway. Was he upset at what Harker had said to his daughter? Amanda didn't think so. She knew that it was fear on his face, fear of losing the ranch.

But Dr. Montgomery would be angry about J. Harker's words about his daughter, she thought, then squelched the thought.

She stood. "I am going to my room," she said softly and started toward the door, but Taylor beat her there.

He closed the door, then put his back to it, barricading them in. "What did you do to offend him? Why did he leave?"

Amanda's head reeled with answers. She offended him by doing what Taylor wanted her to do. She pleased Dr. Montgomery only when she ate what wasn't on the schedule, went places not scheduled and did scandalous things like attend a dance. But she couldn't say any of those things to Taylor.

"I am waiting, Amanda," Taylor said.

"I tried my best to keep to the schedule, but Dr. Montgomery doesn't like museums."

Taylor's eyes were cold and angry. "Perhaps you didn't make them interesting to him. Perhaps you weren't concerned enough with the welfare of the ranch to study enough to make the visits interesting."

It was all so very unfair. If Taylor loved her, didn't he care what her father had just said to her? She had rarely been allowed out of her room before Dr. Montgomery came, and then, without asking her, they had thrust him upon her and expected her to know how to handle a man who stared at her legs and kissed her and shoved chocolate cake in her face. How was a lifetime of study supposed to prepare her for this man?

"Your laziness is going to cost us the ranch," Taylor said. "The unionists will take it away from us. The hops will rot in the fields with no one to pick them, and it will all be your fault."

"I did the best I could." Tears of frustration sprang to Amanda's eyes. She hoped Dr. Montgomery ran off a cliff in that car of his and no one ever had to see him again.

"Your best was not good enough," Taylor said with a half sneer on his lip. "I want you to spend the day in your room. Do not come out until tomorrow morning, while I try to think of some remedy for what you have caused. And since you seem to find calculus so easy, let us see how well you remember your Greek. I want you to begin translating *Moby Dick* into Greek." He stepped away from the door. "Now go, and do not let me see you again for twenty-four hours."

Amanda went, but instead of feeling contrite she felt angry. Taylor had not been fair at all. He didn't know what Dr. Montgomery was like. He had no idea what she'd been through with that dreadful man.

But wait! she told herself. Taylor was good; he wasn't wrong. She *had* failed in the task he'd given her. For whatever reason she'd failed, the result was the same, and he had a right to punish her.

By the time she got to her room she had convinced

herself that Taylor was absolutely right, and she did her best not to think of what her father had said. But as the day wore on, some of her original conviction left her. It was hot in her room, and her dress of heavy silk broadcloth was stiff and made her even hotter. Lunch time came and went and she was famished. Twice she glanced toward her windows as if she expected Dr. Montgomery to come into her room bearing canvas bags full of food. But the house was quiet and no one came to interrupt her study.

By two o'clock she was faint with hunger and she was oddly restless. She couldn't seem to keep her mind on her translation. Instead, she kept remembering last night at the dance. She remembered the music, the champagne, the couples dancing. She pushed her chair back and began to try to imitate the dancers' steps. What would she have thought if she'd gone to a dance alone or with a woman and met Dr. Montgomery there? When he wasn't being an utterly obnoxious man, he was awfully good-looking. Would he have asked her to dance? Would he have been interested in her as a woman and not just as a specimen to study and change?

She whirled about the room, then felt so dizzy she had to sit down on the bed. She put her hand to her head for a moment as the dizziness passed. This is ridiculous, she thought. As Dr. Montgomery said, she was twenty-two years old and she was still being punished as if she were a schoolgirl.

She kept her head high and ignored her pounding heart as she left her room and went down the stairs to the dining room. Perhaps she could find a maid to bring her a sandwich that she could secrete back up to her room. To her chagrin, her father sat alone at the head of the dining table, a huge meal of roast beef, about eight vegetables, a pork pie, three kinds of bread and two salads spread before him. Amanda stared at the food for so long she didn't have time to get away before J. Harker saw her.

"Well?" Harker said belligerently.

"May I join you?" she heard herself saying, then practically floated to the table before he could answer. A maid set a plate and utensils before her.

"Did you come to explain or apologize?" he asked.

"I merely wanted to eat," Amanda said, heaping her plate full. She wanted to eat with her hands from the platters, but she managed to control herself.

Harker watched her for a moment, and for the first time in years he looked at his daughter as a human being. She usually acted like such a little know-it-all and this made him feel every year of his neglected education. "So why did the professor leave?"

Amanda dug into candied carrots. "He didn't like being put on a schedule. He likes motion pictures and dances and picnics. He did not like museums or lectures on Eugenics. Nor was he impressed by the size of our house or cars." Amanda couldn't believe she was talking this way to her father, but perhaps it was the delicious food that was her main interest.

Harker considered this for a moment. "And you couldn't bring yourself to go to a dance with him?"

"I am an engaged woman and, besides, I had enough trouble fitting the museums in with my other studies." The peas with little pearl onions were heavenly.

Harker was watching her. Usually the meals he'd seen her eat were tiny and extremely unappetizing, but today she was eating like a mule train driver.

Taylor had blamed Amanda for Montgomery's leaving, but at this moment Harker wondered whether Amanda had perhaps been responsible for the young professor staying as long as he had. As a child she'd been headstrong and willful—just like her mother—but he'd hired Taylor and within months Amanda had settled down. At first Harker had been relieved, but as the years went by and he saw Amanda turn into a prim and proper little machine, he began to wish she'd pull some prank. But he had too much work to do to concern himself with the education of a daughter. It was only when she got to be about twenty and she was still reciting verses like a ten-year-old that he was unable to bear the sight of her.

Now as he watched her eat like a field hand, he sensed that something was different. This morning Grace, who usually avoided him like the plague and had pretty much hated him since Taylor had arrived, smiled at him. And Harker had been looking at Taylor differently lately. He was no longer in awe of Taylor's education and had begun to wonder if the man knew as much as either one of them thought he did. Years ago, when Grace had demanded that Harker get rid of Taylor, Harker had refused on sheer principle if for no other reason. He'd made his decision and he was sticking to it—right or wrong—and even if Grace did refuse to sleep with him until Taylor was gone, he wasn't going to let that influence him. But this morning, when Grace had smiled at him, he'd remembered what a damned good-looking woman she was and he'd wondered at the way he'd chosen Taylor over a beautiful wife.

"Bring some of that peach pie," Harker said to the maid. "My daughter is hungry."

Amanda gave him a weak smile. "You don't think I'll get fat?"

"I like women with a little meat on their bones."

"That's what . . . I mean . . ." she stumbled, remembering what Dr. Montgomery had said. "Thank you, I'd like some pie."

Involuntarily, Amanda looked at the empty seat opposite her and thought, I miss him. She told herself that was a stupid thought and utterly incorrect but remembered the punishment work she had upstairs, and she wished she could go on a picnic with Dr. Montgomery. No! with Taylor, she corrected herself.

She tried to imagine Taylor stretched out on a cloth on the ground, tried to imagine him driving a car like the Mercer. She wanted to think of Taylor washing her hair, then kissing her, but none of the images would come to her.

J. Harker saw her looking at the empty chair as if she were seeing a ghost. "You, ah, like that professor?"

Amanda straightened in her chair. "He was a—" She started to say that he was a frivolous man, but he had cared about her and the way he'd answered the mathematics questions showed he wasn't uneducated. "He was an unusual man," she said at last. "Completely unpredictable. One never knew what he'd do from one moment to the next."

"No schedules, huh?" J. Harker asked, watching her.

Amanda smiled in delight. "Dr. Montgomery doesn't even understand the concept of schedules. He believes in personal freedom for everyone."

When she smiled like that Harker was reminded so strongly of Grace that he felt quite weak-kneed. He had carried a grudge against his wife for so long that he'd been able to almost forget about her. How dare she tell him who he could and could not hire! Especially after she'd betrayed him by not telling him she'd been a dancer before they'd married. And he'd bragged all over town about how her family had come across on the *Mayflower,* then they'd all laughed at him.

But now, looking at Amanda, he remembered Grace's lean, firm body in his bed. She'd been wonderful in bed but he'd given it up when she'd demanded he fire Taylor. Right now he felt that his stubborn pride had cost him his wife and his daughter.

"Do you know where your mother is this afternoon?" he asked abruptly.

"Why, no, I don't see her too often." Not since I asked her advice when I kissed Taylor, she thought, and the memory made her face turn pink.

J. Harker pushed back his chair and stood. "I think I'll go find her." He started for the door, then turned. "Maybe you'll have dinner with me tonight."

"Yes," she said, astonished. "I would like that."

When she was alone in the room, she gave a puzzled look at the empty chair. Somehow, this invitation was caused by Dr. Montgomery. He had caused her to be nearly raped, true, but he'd also brought about her father seeking out her mother and her father asking his daughter to dinner. Of course, she thought with a grimace, he was also the cause of her having to translate *Moby Dick* into Greek. At least now, with a full belly, she'd be able to get something done. Slowly, she went upstairs to her hot room.

* * *

"And you found this in her room?" Taylor asked Mrs. Gunston as he held the torn white satin dress in his hands, the crystal beads glistening in the sunlight.

"I knew she was hiding something," Mrs. Gunston said in a self-righteous way. "I saw her arm inside the closet, so when she went downstairs I searched. She had it wrapped in tissue paper and hidden inside a hatbox. It's not a dress you bought her, and you can see that it's torn right across the front. She's been doing something she's not supposed to, and it's my guess it has to do with that Dr. Montgomery. There's been strange things going on in this house since he came. I found a dirty plate hidden in her room, and one day—"

"That's enough!" Taylor said sharply, wadding the dress up in his hands. "You may go now."

"But there's more."

Taylor was getting sick of her sneaking ways. "That's all. Go now."

With a grimace of disgust, the big woman left Taylor alone in the library, sliding the door closed after she left.

Taylor stood still for a long while, staring sightlessly out the windows, and all his old fear came back to him. It was as if everything he'd ever worked for was collapsing about his head. Harker was threatening to kick him off the ranch; Amanda was doing things in secret, possibly with another man.

He looked at the satin dress. When? How? Where? *What* had she done? Was she so miserable before that she wanted to get away from him?

Yesterday she'd kissed him and he'd been very angry about it, but today he wondered if he should have been. Maybe she needed a different kind of attention than he was giving her. Maybe she needed to be . . . to be courted.

Amanda was a sensible young woman and she'd never be fooled by the bravado of someone like Dr. Montgomery, but then she was, after all, a woman, and women did like that sort of thing.

What sort of thing? he asked himself. Exactly how did one court a woman? With flowers and candy? He swallowed. Certainly not with Greek translation assignments. Was Montgomery courting her? Was the white dress part of his courting? Perhaps Amanda had ripped it apart, then hidden it until she could find time to discard it.

The more he thought about courting, the more sure he was that he should do it. In fact, he should have done it long ago. He would court Amanda for a few weeks—flowers, candy, hand kissing, all that—then they'd set the marriage date, which would be as soon as possible. After they were married the ranch would safely be his and Amanda would also be his. He'd keep her in *his* room where he could watch her all the time and she'd never be able to receive beaded dresses from other men.

He wrapped his fist around the dress and the tension began to leave his body. He hadn't planned on the courting, since Amanda was already engaged to him, but now he seemed to remember that men were supposed to court women, so perhaps Amanda was somewhat disappointed that he hadn't done so.

When he thought of the engagement, he remembered that he'd never bought her a ring. He thrust the dress in the bottom drawer of the desk, then went outside to the garage. He'd have the chauffeur take him into Kingman and he'd buy Amanda a diamond, nothing gaudy, but something refined and elegant.

Reva Eiler was still smoldering about the dance. It seemed that Amanda Caulden was put on this earth to make her life miserable. Reva'd had a chance at a dream like Hank Montgomery and who shows up but Miss Lady of the Manor, acting as if she didn't even *want* to go to a dance with Hank. Ha! Reva thought. Amanda would have done everything she could to get his attention, such as throwing herself at a drunken Sam Ryan, then acting like Sam was trying to attack her. Dear Hank had fallen for all of it.

As Reva started to cross the street she saw one of the Caulden limousines stop in front of the jewelry store and the chauffeur get out and open the back door. Out stepped the man Amanda was supposed to be engaged to—when she wasn't chasing after Hank, Reva thought bitterly. She watched as the tall, thin, dark man tried the jewelry store door then looked puzzled when it was locked. He went to look in the empty window where Mr. Robbins displayed the jewelry during the week. He was awfully good-looking, Reva thought, and grudgingly admired Amanda's taste in men.

Quickly, Reva crossed the street. "It's Sunday," she said, and the man turned to look at her. Reva felt a little chill run down her back. He was a haughty-looking man, almost as if his spine were steel instead of flesh and blood, but there was something else in there, too, that Reva recognized as a kindred spirit. He looked cold on the outside but she imagined there was passion underneath. He was trying his best to look down his nose at her bright lipstick and the brilliant turquoise hat she was wearing, but she felt his interest in her. Wouldn't it serve Amanda right if she had a fling with her boyfriend?

"It's Sunday and the shop is closed," Reva said again.

"Yes, of course," Taylor said and looked away from the woman. She was making him feel quite strange. He started back toward the car.

"Mr. Robbins lives just a block over and he'll be home from church now. I could take you to him and maybe he'd open the store for you." She looked up at him. "That is, if you wanted to buy something important—like, say, a diamond engagement ring, maybe." She'd noticed that Amanda wore no ring, and it made sense that he'd want to put his brand on her after seeing the way Amanda came home last night. Reva saw a flicker in those dark eyes and knew she'd guessed right.

"If you'll give me directions," Taylor began.

"No, we'll walk. Give your driver the day off. Besides, you'll need somebody to try on the ring. Amanda and I are about the same size."

Taylor frowned. This young woman was entirely too forward, too garishly painted, and obviously not of his class, but he allowed himself to be led away toward the jeweler's house. Getting the ring was very important to his future.

Two hours later, when he left the jewelry store, he was smiling. Miss Eiler really was a vulgar, loud, uneducated person, but there was something about her . . .

"You want to get somethin' to eat?" Reva said. "Maybe as a celebration of your last day as a free man? The diner always has chicken-fried steak on Sunday night."

Taylor started to protest in horror, but the words didn't come out. "It sounds delicious." He held his arm out to her and together they crossed the street.

Chapter Twelve

Amanda sat on the seat of the gazebo in the darkness and listened to the night sounds. She'd had a delicious dinner with her father and it had been pleasant even if neither of them said much. She was afraid to open her mouth after what he'd said that morning about her boring him to death. She somehow didn't think he'd like to discuss the President's new tariff laws. As the meal progressed, she found herself wishing Dr. Montgomery were there. He would know what to talk about. He'd be able to talk about the weather without comparing cirrostratus clouds with cumulonimbus clouds, as Amanda would do. In the end, all she'd said was, "It's hot," and J. Harker had said, "It sure is." But even without conversation, it had been nice sitting with her father and eating real food.

After dinner she hadn't gone to her room to do more Greek translation but instead had turned and walked outside in the growing darkness, and now she sat in the gazebo looking at the stars. She began to remember the times she'd sat here with Dr. Montgomery. She remembered watching him eat three slices of cake; she remembered his kissing her and asking to see her hair down. She remembered how he'd returned to the house one night and seen just the shadow of her dress yet he'd still come to her.

She straightened on the bench and told herself she should be thinking about Taylor, not Dr. Montgomery, but right now all she could think about was the unfairness of Greek translation. Taylor had merely blamed her for Dr. Montgomery's leaving without allowing her to explain, and not believing what little she had told him.

A car pulled into the garage and for a moment Amanda held her breath. It wasn't Dr. Montgomery returning, of course, and she certainly didn't want him to return, but just maybe, perhaps it *was* him.

By the time she heard five footsteps on the gravel, she knew it was Taylor. Dr. Montgomery's footsteps were heavier, more . . . more predatory, while Taylor walked light and quick, almost as if he were running.

He didn't see her, as she knew he wouldn't, and he went on into the house. She was supposed to be in her room, having had only one tiny meal all day, deep into *Moby Dick,* but instead she was outside enjoying the quiet darkness.

She listened as doors inside the house opened and closed and she knew her absence had been discovered. Thank heaven no one had wanted her last night when she'd been at the dance.

After a while the house quietened and the back door opened and closed and she could hear Taylor's footsteps on the gravel. "Amanda?" he called in a reserved way.

For some reason, Amanda almost didn't answer him. She told herself it was because he'd been unfair, but part of her said that Taylor was not the sort of man a woman wanted to sit under the stars with. This feeling was Dr. Montgomery's fault, she reminded herself. If he hadn't come . . .

"Here," she called to Taylor, then watched as he approached.

"Do you mind if I sit down?"

"Of course not," she answered, then began to explain. "It was so hot in my room that I couldn't seem to think. I was just taking a break." She stood. "I'll get back to work now."

"Wait," he said, and when she paused at the doorway, he continued. "Amanda, maybe I was a little harsh this morning. You have always done your best with any assignment I have given you and I suppose Dr. Montgomery was no different. I'm afraid I was angry at myself as much as at anyone else and I took it out on you."

Amanda stood motionless where she was. Taylor had never admitted to any fault before. "I understand," she whispered. "Dr. Montgomery has made us all on edge."

"I think I sent you off with him because I quite frankly couldn't abide him."

"Oh?" Amanda said, turning back into the gazebo. Taylor had never been this personal with her before.

"Such an insolent, lazy man. He's obviously never had two nickels to rub together, and I guess I resented his being in your father's fine house. Can you forgive me?"

"Why, yes, certainly." She hesitated. "Do I have to do more translation of *Moby Dick?*"

Taylor winced. "No." They were quiet for a moment. "Amanda," Taylor said at last, "I have something important to say to you."

Amanda prayed it was no more calculus. Since "she" had made 100% on the test she was afraid Taylor would want her to take up mathematics full time.

"I think it's time we talk about marriage."

"Oh," Amanda said, not having expected this, and sat down heavily on the bench on the other side of the doorway.

"You're becoming a young woman now and it's time to seriously consider when we'll be married. I have given it some thought and I believe we should be married two months from today. If that suits you, of course."

Amanda's mind was reeling. This morning her father had threatened to throw Taylor off the ranch and tonight he was proposing that they marry very soon. She couldn't help wondering if this was an attempt to secure his place on the ranch.

"You have nothing to say?"

Amanda almost answered that it didn't seem to be up to her. "That sounds fine to me."

Taylor frowned in the darkness. This afternoon had been so pleasant when he and Miss Eiler had chosen the engagement ring together. She'd said how overjoyed Amanda would be and how lucky Amanda was to marry someone like Taylor, but right now Amanda didn't look overjoyed. He took a breath. "Amanda, perhaps you don't want to marry me."

Before she allowed herself to think, Amanda blurted, "Do you want me or the ranch?" She put her hand to her mouth in horror.

"Oh, so that's it," he said and sounded relieved.

"Has this man Montgomery put such thoughts in your head?"

"I apologize, sir, it was an awful thing to say. Of course I'll be most happy to marry you any time you say. If you will give me a date I will begin preparations, or no, you will want to do that. But the groom isn't supposed to see the bridal gown beforehand, so someone else had better choose it, but you can if you want. I'll do what I can to help. My lessons keep me busy, but I'll—"

"Amanda!" Taylor said sharply. "Of course you may plan your own wedding. Sometimes you make me feel like a jailor, that I keep you under lock and key. I have merely tried my best to give you an education. I apologize if you have felt yourself to be a prisoner."

Only since Dr. Montgomery arrived, she thought, but murmured, "Of course I haven't been a prisoner."

Taylor reached inside his coat pocket and withdrew the little ring box. "May I have your left hand?"

Amanda had no idea what he was going to do. She was afraid she'd get a ruler in her palm, so she was speechless when he slipped a ring on her third finger. The diamond sparkled in the moonlight. She could only stare at it blankly.

"Does it fit?" he asked anxiously. "We tried to get the size right."

"It fits perfectly." Amanda still could barely speak. This was an engagement ring. Now it was official and she was committed to marry Taylor. So why wasn't she feeling like running and shouting for joy? "Who is 'we'?" she asked idly, stalling for time.

"A friend of yours, Reva Eiler, helped me pick it out. Actually, I wouldn't have the ring if it weren't for her. It's Sunday and the jewelry store was closed, but

Miss Eiler took me to the jeweler's house and got him to open it. Miss Eiler said the ring would fit."

It was all Amanda could do to keep from pulling the ring off her hand. Another woman had worn her engagement ring before she had! Wasn't it enough that Reva had Dr. Montgomery? Did she want Taylor and Amanda's ring also? "How helpful of her," Amanda managed to say and stopped looking at the ring. She wanted to throw it into the dark night.

"Amanda," Taylor said after a while, "about yesterday evening, when you . . . when you kissed me."

Abruptly, she stood. "I'm sorry. I apologized then and I apologize now." She felt herself getting irritated and the ring was burning her finger.

Taylor stood also. "That isn't what I meant. It's just that I sometimes have a difficult time thinking of you as an adult. I still tend to remember you as that gawky girl I first met."

Amanda began to relax somewhat. This made sense. Perhaps she wasn't repulsive to him after all.

"If I may?" he said and held out his arms to her.

Amanda was hesitant but she went to him and put her cheek against his chest. He was thin and she could hear his heart pounding against her face, and instantly she began comparing him to Dr. Montgomery. Dr. Montgomery was bigger, stronger, and his arms and body seemed to envelope her, and by now his hands would be all over her, with his lips on her hair and neck, moving down to her mouth.

Taylor moved away from her to look down at her, then he pressed his lips to hers.

Nothing, she thought. I feel absolutely nothing. I don't feel warmth or interest or an inclination to do anything more. I might as well be kissing a statue.

Taylor pulled away to look at her. "There, does *that* convince you that I want you and not the ranch?"

She gave him a little smile and a nod. What was wrong with her? This was Taylor, the man she loved. Perhaps if she tried kissing him again, this time she would feel something. She stood on tiptoe and put her face up to his, but Taylor drew back and gave what to her was an infuriating little chuckle.

"I think that's enough to begin with, don't you?" He dropped his arms from her. "Too much excitement and you'll not be able to sleep."

Anger choked Amanda so she couldn't speak, but she wanted to say that his kisses certainly weren't going to excite her.

"Now, Amanda, it's time for you to go to bed. Tomorrow is a workday and you have a history test. I do hope you've studied for it. Tomorrow, perhaps we can talk again." He smiled at her, then put the tip of his finger to her nose. "And if you're a good girl maybe there'll be more kisses. And, best of all, as soon as the hops are in, we'll start planning our wedding. That should make you smile."

Amanda didn't dare open her mouth for fear of what would come out. Now *Taylor* was making her feel stupid. Did all men, at some point, turn into patronizing, overbearing know-it-alls? Every man seemed to think he knew exactly what was right for her. Her father took her out of school and kept her at home with a tutor. Her tutor took her away from her mother and put her on a schedule. Then along comes Dr. Montgomery and he makes her stop studying and start eating.

"Yes, I'm going to bed," Amanda said and turned away quickly before she said something awful, such as asking Taylor if he meant to grade her paper with kisses: You miss four questions on Edward I's Scottish campaign and no kisses for you, Amanda.

Once in her room, she burst into tears. She wrenched the engagement ring from her finger, tossed it onto the bedside table, then flung herself onto the bed and cried desperately. Everything in her life was so confused. A month ago she'd known everything she wanted out of life. She'd wanted Taylor and nothing else. But now she'd met Dr. Montgomery and nothing seemed to be the same. She was discontent about *everything*. Instead of feeling as if she were educating herself with her studies, Dr. Montgomery had made her feel like an aging schoolgirl.

Toward midnight, she got up, put on her nightgown and went to bed, but she didn't sleep much. If only she had any idea what to *do*. If there were only some way she could get rid of the confusion in her mind.

Morning came and Mrs. Gunston gave Amanda Taylor's latest schedule, but Amanda hardly looked at it. And she realized that she didn't like Mrs. Gunston's attitude either. After all, who was the employer and who the employee?

Amanda felt very discontent with the meager breakfast she shared with Taylor and the equally meager lunch. He sent her back to her room after lunch to get her engagement ring which she'd forgotten to wear. At two o'clock she'd barely passed her history test and Taylor had said nothing at all. His cold silence was worse than his berating her. "I guess this means no more kisses," she murmured under her breath as he returned her paper with its low grade.

She went back to her room and glanced at the rest of her schedule, and a great, heavy sinking feeling overtook her. If she wasn't a prisoner, she certainly *felt* like one.

At 3:30 she walked to the window and saw her mother sitting in the shade of two almond trees, reading the newspaper. Amanda didn't even think about what she was doing but left her room, right in the middle of when her schedule said she was supposed to be studying Vermeer's paintings, and went downstairs and outside to her mother.

"Hello," Amanda said softly.

Grace looked up from her paper and saw immediately that her daughter had been crying, and crying quite a lot from the look of her swollen face. She wondered what that bastard Taylor Driscoll had done to her now.

"Have a seat," Grace said, "and the lemonade's cold."

Amanda poured herself a cool glass of lemonade, sat down and sipped it. There was a pile of cookies also and she ate two of them before she spoke. "Have you ever been so confused that you had no idea what to do?"

"Daily, but why don't you tell me what's confusing you? That is, unless it's Latin verbs. I'm no good at schoolwork."

"It's men," Amanda said, blinking back tears.

"I might be able to help you there."

Amanda didn't know where to start. "I'm afraid that dreadful Dr. Montgomery has ruined my life."

Grace's eyes bugged and she envisioned her first grandchild being born out of wedlock. She'd take Amanda to Switzerland. She'd—

"He seems to have made me—well, restless," Amanda was saying. "I love Taylor, I always have, and

I know I want to marry him. He gave me an engagement ring last night. Oh drat! I've left it upstairs again. Anyway, I know I love Taylor, but ever since Dr. Montgomery came I can't seem to enjoy anything. My studies are harder for me now. My mind keeps wandering."

"That sounds normal," Grace said.

"Normal? Normal for an engaged woman to think about another man?"

"Yes, of course. You know what you really need is to get Dr. Montgomery out of your system. You see, he's a novelty to you, that's all. It's like when a child first eats ice cream. The child should be allowed to eat until he makes himself sick, then the next time he'll use some judgment and not gorge himself."

"You think I should get *more* of Dr. Montgomery? I thought it would be the best thing for me when he left."

"Just the opposite," Grace said. "You saw him just enough to be fascinated with him. After all, you have led a rather sheltered life, and this kind of man is different enough to intrigue you. If you were to spend more time with him you'd soon see that he really isn't half the man Taylor is. After a few days of parties and dances and whatever else young people do today, you'd be back here hungry for Taylor and the way of life you've always loved."

All Amanda wanted was the confusion to stop. She didn't want to look at an empty chair and wish Dr. Montgomery were in it. She didn't want to compare Taylor with another man and have Taylor lose.

"Dr. Montgomery is a frivolous man," Amanda said. "He goes to motion pictures instead of lectures and he'd rather go on a picnic than to a museum."

"He sounds awful," Grace said, her eyes sparkling. Now she knew for sure that she'd lost her chance to get into heaven.

"But how do I see him again? Should I invite him to dinner? I don't think Taylor will like that."

And Taylor must always be appeased, Grace thought, rather like an ancient hungry god. She folded the newspaper back. "I just happen to have noticed an ad in today's paper." She handed the paper to Amanda and pointed.

Translator Wanted. Needs to speak and/or write as many languages as possible. Needed to help with incoming hop pickers. Five dollars a day. Apply Kingman Arms. Dr. Henry R. Montgomery.

"How many languages do you speak, dear?" Grace asked.

"Four," Amanda answered, "and I write three others. Mother, do you think I should apply for a *job?* I don't think Taylor would approve of—"

"But you'd be doing it *for* Taylor. As soon as you spend a little time around this riffraff and see what wasteful lives the others in the world lead, believe me, you'll come running back to the serenity of life with Taylor. You'll be *glad* to get back on a schedule and study something that has some meaning. And then, too, you'll be sure of your love for Taylor. You'll get this restless feeling out of your blood. You'll be a better wife and mother when you're ready to settle down."

Amanda wanted to believe her mother because the idea of the job excited her. And, also, what her mother said made sense. She would be a better person if she got Dr. Montgomery out of her mind. As it was, she found herself getting more impatient with Taylor by the hour.

She sighed. "I don't believe Father or Taylor will allow me to do this."

Grace clenched her fists. Years ago she'd lost out to Taylor, she'd lost her husband and her daughter to that man's need for possession, but she wasn't going to lose again. This time she'd fight until she was bloody. Amanda was beginning to love her again, beginning to come out from under Taylor's rule, and Grace wasn't going to let this transformation stop. Thank you, Dr. Montgomery, she thought, thank you for breaking the spell over our house. "I'll take care of your father," Grace said, "and your father will take care of Taylor."

"Are you sure?" Amanda whispered in awe.

Grace leaned forward and clutched her daughter's hand. "I'm very sure."

"A job?" Taylor gasped. "Amanda is to *work* outside her home? As a translator for those . . . those . . .?" His upper lip curled into a sneer.

J. Harker chewed on his cigar. Less than an hour ago Grace had come to him and talked about Amanda working for that Dr. Montgomery. Grace had looked so good and smelled so good, fresh out of a bath, and as she'd sat there her dress kept creeping up over her legs. "If we can't get the professor to stay here where we can keep an eye on him, we can send Amanda there."

Taylor seemed to hear crashing in his ears and knew it was more building blocks of his life falling down around him. He wished he'd never heard the name Montgomery. And to think! *He* was the one who had wanted him to come to the Caulden Ranch in the first place. "But *field* workers," Taylor said in disgust. "A woman of Amanda's sensibilities couldn't deal with such men."

"I'm beginning to think my daughter has more of me in her than I thought. She'll go to see about whatever the professor's doin' and she'll come back and report everything. We'll always be two steps ahead of the unionists. I'll get my hops picked and I won't have any union problems. She's goin' first thing in the mornin' to get that job." Harker didn't give Taylor time to reply before he turned away. "And she'll be havin' breakfast with me in the mornin'. I want her to have some strength tomorrow." He left the room.

Taylor sat down and put his head in his hands.

Amanda had never been so nervous in her life. She gave a quiet burp from the enormous breakfast her father had insisted she eat and looked out the car window. She hadn't seen Taylor since yesterday, and she knew his absence meant disapproval of what she was doing. She would have liked to have explained to him that she was doing this for the good of both of them but he'd never given her the chance.

Her father had certainly seemed pleased, though. He'd smiled at her and given her second helpings of everything. Perhaps her mother had explained what Amanda was doing.

"We're here, miss," the driver said.

Amanda looked out the window and saw the long line of people standing in front of the Kingman Arms.

She'd never spoken to the chauffeur before, except to give directions (Taylor said that one did not speak to underlings unless absolutely necessary), but now he seemed almost like a friend. "Why are all those people there?" she asked.

"Five dollars a day is a lot of money and an awful lot of people speak more than one language."

Amanda was surprised that he seemed to know exactly why she was there.

"Shall I get you to the head of the line, miss? I could go in and tell Dr. Montgomery you want the job. I'm sure he'll give it to you."

Amanda wasn't as sure. He'd already said some awful things about her money and her snobbery. "No, thank you, I'll just wait in line with the others." She grimaced at that because most of the people in line looked as if they hadn't had a bath in all their lives. A man with a missing front tooth grinned and winked at her.

"I'll just wait over here for you, miss, and I'll keep watch that no harm comes to you."

"Thank you very much, uh . . ."

"James, miss."

"Thank you, James." She waited while the chauffeur came around to open the door for her, then she got out and walked to the back of the line.

The people in the line weren't very pleasant to her and said several unkind things about her clothes, the car she came in, and whether she needed a job or not.

"The *lady's* come down to us," one overpainted young woman behind Amanda said. "Think a silk dress will get you the job, honey?"

Amanda said nothing. What had made her think she wanted to do this?

"Maybe it's the handsome college professor she wants," another woman said with a smirk.

Amanda turned to face the jeering women. "How many languages do you speak?" she asked coolly.

"It's none of your business," the first woman said.

"I speak four and can write three more," Amanda said quite loudly, so that most of the people in the line could hear her. James, waiting in the car, smiled encouragement at her.

"What's that?" said a young man with a notebook who was moving down the line. "Did someone here say she could speak four languages?" He looked at Amanda and the other three women.

"I do," Amanda said.

The young man looked her up and down. "What are they?"

"French, Italian, Spanish and German. I can read and write Greek, Russian and Latin."

He was writing as she spoke but he crossed the Latin out. "Any Oriental languages? Hindu?"

"I have only a rudimentary acquaintance with Chinese but I'm afraid I'm not fluent in it."

The man gave her a quizzical look. "Any other 'rudimentary acquaintances'?"

"A bit of Japanese, a bit of Hungarian."

People in the line were beginning to leave as they gave malevolent looks to Amanda.

"Come with me, honey," the man said and grabbed Amanda's arm and began pulling her into the hotel.

The lobby was a mess, with people running everywhere, people shouting, people sitting on every available surface. There were bundles and suitcases piled along the walls. Children were screaming; men were smoking and frowning; women were looking exhausted and ignoring the demands of husbands and children. The air was blue with smoke; the noise was deafening and it must have been a hundred and twenty degrees in the airless room.

"Stand right there," the young man said to Amanda. "And don't leave. Whatever you do, don't leave."

Joe Testorio pushed his way past the people in the line and into the room that was supposed to be Dr. Montgomery's bedroom. Hank, in shirt sleeves that he'd sweated through, was interviewing one applicant after another. Reva Eiler, his secretary, stood behind him—or maybe hovered was a better word.

"I found her," Joe said, putting his head between Hank and the applicant. "She speaks four languages, can read and write three others and knows 'a little' of three more."

"Yeah?" Hank said. "So where is she? You should have tied her to the door to keep her from getting away."

Joe ran back into the lobby. Amanda had not only not walked away, it didn't look as if she'd moved a muscle. Can follow orders, he thought.

"He's waiting for you," Joe said and took Amanda's arm and began pushing people aside to get her into the hotel room.

Amanda's breath caught as she saw Dr. Montgomery bent over some papers and asking questions of a nervous, dirty little man. It seemed like ages since she'd seen him.

"Here she is, Doc," Joe said.

Hank looked up and saw Amanda, resembling a spring flower growing out of a dung heap. She looked cool and fresh and pretty and oh so wonderfully desirable. "No," Hank said, then turned back to the man on the other side of the desk. "And what do you speak besides Italian and English?"

"My English not so good but my Italian is very good," the man said with a heavy accent.

"But what *other* languages do you speak?" Hank asked angrily, knowing too well that his anger was for Amanda. Why couldn't she just get out of his life altogether?

No, Amanda thought, he was not going to dismiss her just like that after all she'd gone through to get here. She couldn't bear the idea of facing either of her parents if she failed to get the job.

"But, Doc," Joe wailed.

Amanda stepped forward. "May I be of assistance?" she asked. She could feel Reva's eyes boring into her but she wasn't going to let herself be defeated. In perfect Italian she said to the little man, "Dr. Montgomery would like to know if you speak any languages other than Italian or English."

Grateful to at last be able to understand someone, he poured out his problems to Amanda: that he had seven children to feed and he needed a job and five dollars a day was an enormous lot and he hoped he could get the job but he only spoke Italian and English only a little bit.

Amanda thanked him and wished both him and his family well. She turned to Hank. "English and Italian and that's all. Shall I help with the Mexican family next in line?"

"You can't help at all. Joe, take Miss Caulden out of here."

"Caulden?" Joe gasped and looked at Amanda as if she were the devil himself. "Come on, let's go."

Amanda moved away from Joe and put her hands on Dr. Montgomery's desk. "I thought you needed help. I thought you believed in equality and fairness, but I guess you have to be poor to deserve fairness. One set of laws for the rich and another for the poor. Pardon me, I didn't understand." She straightened. "I wish you luck, Dr. Montgomery, in whatever you're trying to do." She began to make her way through the crowd to the door.

Hank watched her go and he was torn between wanting someone to help him translate and never wanting to see Amanda again. He'd thought of nothing but her since he'd left her house. He could see her, feel her, smell her.

"You're right, Doc, we don't need no Caulden working for us," Joe said. "She'd probably give away all our secrets to her old man."

"What secrets?" Hank muttered and then he was running after her. He caught up with her before she left the hotel, grabbed her arm and pulled her into the first door he saw, which happened to be a tiny, smelly broom closet with one bare, weak light bulb overhead.

"Dr. Montgomery," Amanda said, rubbing her arm, "I would have known your grip anywhere."

"What do you want, Amanda?" Hank demanded.

"A job. I saw your ad in the paper and I do have some knowledge of languages. I've always been rather good at languages. Of course I probably *should* have spent my life learning the latest dances instead of wasting it learning what's inside books, but now I seem to be cursed with knowledge, so I thought I might put it to use."

"And help me start a union? Do you realize that I'm trying to get the people to join the ULW? I want them to join together to demand better working conditions. The enemy is people like your father."

"Is that what you tell them? To personally hate anyone who owns land? They wouldn't have jobs if it weren't for my father."

Hank hated her attitude. She didn't have any idea what poverty was. Except for self-imposed hunger, she didn't know what it meant to go without a meal. "Did Taylor give you permission to apply?"

"I didn't ask him," Amanda answered truthfully. "Dr. Montgomery, do I have the job or not? If not, I'd like to go home."

"You won't last a day," Hank said.

"And what sort of wager do you want to make that I will last, and that I'll do a good job?"

"Amanda, you make it through today and you can have anything of me you want."

"Oh?" she said, one eyebrow raised. "I'll take you up on that, but you should worry that what I want will involve guns and knives and incendiary bombs."

He opened the door to the broom closet. "I'll chance it," he said softly. "But you won't last past noon."

He was almost right. Many times during the day Amanda wanted to go home. She was given fifty jobs at once. She was to write translations and do oral translations at the same time. Every hour more people arrived on trains into Kingman, and Dr. Montgomery had hired people to meet the trains and tell them to come to him so he could explain what a union was.

At eleven A.M. they moved out of the Kingman Arms and into a house that Joe had rented. There were big signs in front saying that this was the union headquarters.

All day long Amanda told people that they had rights, that if they bonded together they could peacefully make changes. Peace was the key word, she began to realize. Taylor and her father had said that the unionists wanted to burn and kill, but nowhere did she hear mention of violence.

By three o'clock she was very tired and she wanted a bath and a cool drink, but she kept going. Twice she looked at Dr. Montgomery and he looked more tired than she did.

The people were making her feel awful. Their eyes were hungry and tired. One woman's baby cried from hunger, and Amanda opened her purse and gave the woman the little bit of pocket money she had. She gave another woman the enameled comb in her hair. At four o'clock she sent Joe to get her chauffeur, then sent James to the diner to order three hundred sandwiches and distribute them—and to send the bill to her father.

Repeatedly, she felt Dr. Montgomery's eyes on her but she looked away.

The children were what upset her the most. How could toddlers be expected to pick in the fields? How could she bear to see them hungry? The children wanted to touch her because she was so clean and pretty, and several times Amanda held a baby in her arms while she explained to a father what a union was. Two babies wet on her, one threw up on her shoulder.

By eight P.M. the house began to clear out. The workers were beginning to find campsites along the roadsides or wherever they could.

Amanda just sat in her chair behind the little table that was littered with papers and pencils and stared dully around her. She didn't seem to have any thoughts at all. Today she had been through hell and back—or maybe she wasn't fully back.

"Let's get something to eat," she heard Reva say to Dr. Montgomery.

Dully, without conscious thought, Amanda stood. Home, she thought, home to a hot bath and a hot meal.

Hank was watching Amanda and he knew what she was feeling. The first time he'd worked with field workers he'd felt the same way. The poverty was stunning, and he had been as ill prepared for it as Amanda. Maybe this is what he'd first sensed about Amanda, that she was a person who *cared*. She cared about Taylor; she cared about her father, about her mother. She didn't stand up for herself because she believed that other people were more important than she was.

"You go with Joe," Hank said to Reva. "I have something I have to do."

Reva knew he meant he had something to do with Amanda. "I could have sent sandwiches if I had a rich father," she said bitterly. "She just has the money to do what we all want to do."

"I don't see any kids' vomit on you," Hank said and walked toward Amanda. He put his hand on her arm. "Come with me."

"I have to go home," she whispered, not looking at him. "James will be waiting for me."

James, he thought, not "my chauffeur" or "my car." "I'll tell him to go. I owe you an apology and I want to give it."

She looked up at him and she saw understanding in his eyes. She nodded. "I want to go somewhere clean and quiet," she whispered.

He took her hand in his, not the formal taking of her arm, but the more intimate palm and fingertips entwining, and led her to his car. He told her chauffeur, who'd spent most of the day sitting in the car waiting for her, to go home and that Miss Caulden would be returning later.

Chapter Thirteen

Hank drove Amanda to the secluded area inside the trees around the little pond where he'd taken her on a picnic. He had to almost pull her out of the car, then she just stood there.

"Amanda," he said, but she didn't respond, so he took both her hands in his. "Talk to me, Amanda. You've never seen poverty like that, have you? You've been isolated in your pretty house and you never knew people like them existed. They're the people who pick the crops that put food on your table. It's the sweat of these people that puts silk on your back and diamonds on your fingers."

She tried to pull away from him but he held her hands. "I want to go home and burn my clothes and I want my schedule back." Tears were coming to her eyes. "Let me go, I said! I want to go home!"

As she struggled, he pulled her into his arms. "Go ahead and cry, Amanda. Cry all you want. You deserve it."

She fought against him. She didn't want to cry and she didn't want to ever see him again. "Let me go. I want to go *home!*"

"I think maybe you *are* home," he said, holding her

to him, pinning her arms as she struggled. She didn't have the strength to fight, and after a while she clung to him. He seemed so healthy. She'd seen sick people today, people who couldn't afford a doctor. She began to cry in his arms, and he sat down, his back against a tree, and held her.

"I worry about test scores while they have no food," she said through her tears.

He unpinned her hair and stroked it as it hung down her back. "You can't blame yourself."

"But my father—"

He touched his lips to hers to quieten her, and to the astonishment of both of them, it was like the setting off of a bomb. Amanda opened her mouth under his and pressed her body against his. Neither of them thought as Hank's hand sought her breast and found it, and as Amanda felt his hand, her body went limp in his arms, opening herself to him.

"Amanda," he whispered against her lips, "we have to stop or I won't be able to."

"Please don't stop," she said desperately. "I couldn't bear it if another man turned me away. Make love to me. Make me feel whole and clean and as if I'm worth more than a test score."

Hank started to say no. She was upset and emotionally spent and she might regret this in the morning.

"Please, Hank," she whispered. "Please."

He had once thought that if Amanda ever asked him "please," he might do anything she wanted. He'd guessed right. He couldn't deny her anything, and all rational thought fled.

He stood with her in his arms and walked toward the spring-fed pond. "How about a bath, baby?" He moved with her into the pond, clothes, shoes, wallet and whatever else was on their persons and all.

The cool water sobered Amanda. "Dr. Montgomery," she said nervously, "regarding what I said a moment ago—"

He kissed her. "You can fight me or help me, but the result will be the same. You won't be the same when you leave here tonight, Amanda."

She was standing on the bottom, the water to her waist, and she knew by the look in his eyes that he was telling her the truth. She wondered if she'd wanted him from the first moment she'd seen him. Tonight she was going to do what she wanted to do. Tonight she wasn't going to rely on a schedule or someone else to tell her how to act.

"Yes," she whispered and began unbuttoning her filthy dress.

Hank pushed her hands away and deftly unfastened the buttons, then slipped the dress off her shoulders. There was an intensity in her eyes that seemed to go through him like a knife.

"I've never wanted anything in my life like I want you right now, Amanda," he said and grabbed her to him, her feet coming off the bottom of the pond. Neither of them noticed her dress catching water and sinking.

Hank opened his mouth over Amanda's until he almost swallowed her, as his hands pushed the straps of her undergarments off her shoulders, and when they wouldn't slide, he tore them off.

Amanda was too bewildered to think. There had been an absence of passion in her life and she responded to him with all her pent-up desires. He was every flirtation she'd ever missed, every dance, every social, every romantic novel she hadn't read; he was every piece of cake, every glass of champagne, every handholding she'd never experienced. "Yes, yes," was all she could say, her head leaning back, her hands in his thick hair.

When her breasts were bare, he fastened his mouth on the pink tip, drawing her into the hot, wet cavity of his mouth.

Amanda's knees gave way and he supported her, one hand clutching her firm, round buttocks. He picked her up and her loose, torn garments fell away into the water. She was wearing only black silk stockings and black, lacy garters.

Hank put her legs about his waist, his hands cupping her buttocks as his mouth stayed on her breast, sucking, his tongue hard and firm, running across her hard nipple. He set her down in the grass, her back at an angle against a mound of earth. He ran his tongue down her belly, nipping with his strong teeth at the fleshy part around her navel.

"Let's see how all of you tastes," he said, and he buried his tongue in the most intimate part of her.

Amanda's eyes came open; she grabbed the hair of his head and started to push him away, but then his tongue was moving, his lips sucking. She arched her back and clasped his ears with her silk-clad knees. His hands came up to clutch her breasts, his thumbs flicking at her nipples, which were hard and sensitive.

Just when she thought she might die, he moved his mouth down to her inner thighs and his hands were rubbing on her skin, making her skin feel hotter and hotter and hotter. She moaned under him as he ran his hands down over her legs, over the silk of her stockings. Silk and skin.

He paused with his hands on her ankles, then withdrew them from her body.

Amanda opened her eyes in horror. Was it over?

"Just a pause, baby," Hank said huskily, reading her mind. He was removing his clothes, and Amanda turned her head away.

"No you don't," he said and leaned into her, his body between her bent legs. She could smell herself on his face, and instead of repulsing her, it made him seem more intimate. "You don't turn away from me," he said. "You look at me like I look at you. You kiss me where I kiss you."

Amanda opened her mouth to say no to that, but he put his tongue in her mouth, ran it over her teeth, pulled her tongue into his mouth. She wasn't going to say no to anything he said.

He came out of his clothes quickly, and if Amanda thought she was going to die before, the feel of his bare skin next to hers almost did her in. His ribs were between her thighs as he once again kissed her breasts then began moving up. She kissed his lips, his chin, his neck, the soft spot in his collarbone; then the hair of his chest was in her face, and she turned her face back and forth, feeling the maleness of him, smelling him. His strong arms were by her head, big enough to crush her. He made her feel so small and yet so powerful because she could feel his heart pounding.

He moved up and her mouth opened onto his hard, flat belly. She could feel his manhood prodding her throat, so smooth, so strong. And then it was at her mouth.

"No," she whispered and turned her face away.

"I don't believe in double standards," he said throatily. "Taste me, Amanda."

She grabbed him in her hands and sucked him down her throat. He was hard and smooth, like hot marble, and she sucked on him until his skin nearly came off.

She groaned when he moved away from her, but she felt his frenzy as well as her own.

She was wet when he entered her, wet and ready, and he slid into her like a hand into a glove. Amanda bucked under him but he calmed her as he held himself back. He didn't dare move because he was ripe to bursting.

Amanda found her rhythm and began to move slowly while he held above her, supporting himself on his arms, his eyes closed and an expression of pain-pleasure on his beautiful face. Amanda was like a child with a new and wondrous toy, sliding up and down, in and out, gliding, silk and satin, hard and soft.

And then her body began to tighten and her fingers clawed into his back and she pulled him down to her. She wanted him closer and closer to her. She wanted his hot, tawny, male skin next to hers. She wrapped her legs around his lower back, the black silk on his skin, and pulled him deeper and deeper into her.

His reserve left him and he became an animal: a wild, violent, mindless animal as he thrust into her, holding her to him as if his life depended on her. Only she could give him what he had to have.

He came in one blinding, debilitating flash that made him shudder as if he might come apart, and Amanda clung to him as he lifted her with him. They were one.

It took long, long moments for Amanda to come to

herself. She held him fiercely, with her arms, her legs, held him inside her with muscles she'd just discovered tonight. She buried her face in his neck, touching him as much as she could.

Hank held her just as tightly. Never had he had an experience like this. No woman had made him come so hard, as if his whole body were pouring into her. When she began to relax her grip on him, he couldn't bear to release her. He pushed her legs down beside his and, doing his best to stay inside her, he rolled to his back and held her hot, delicious body on top of his. He wouldn't even let her foot hang off his body. He wanted all of her, every hair, every pore.

He thought maybe she dozed. She was as limp as . . . as a woman who was sated, and she fit every plane of his body, as if they had been carved out of one piece of flesh and somehow accidentally separated. But now they were together again.

He caressed her hair at her temple and lay as still as he could to let her sleep. If anyone deserved rest, she did. Ever since he'd met her he'd wanted to open her eyes to the world around her, but today, when he'd seen her eyes opening, he'd wanted to take her out of that dingy little rented house. She'd been so horrified at the poverty of the people. And he'd seen the way she had blamed herself. Why did she think the world's evils were *her* fault? Why did she think it was her responsibility to give Driscoll what he wanted? Or Caulden? Didn't she ever do what *she* wanted?

He pulled her closer, felt her snuggle near him like an infant—*his* baby, his precious, darling, beloved baby.

Amanda roused and looked up at him. "I think I fell asleep."

He pushed her head back down to his shoulder. "Sleep all you want."

Amanda was returning to being Amanda and not some blind machine of passion. She was also beginning to remember some of what she'd done. "Dr. Montgomery, I—"

"Hank," he said and held her head down. He never wanted to break this moment. Never wanted to leave here. Here was where he was meant to be, where he never wanted to leave.

"I think I should go home," Amanda said softly.

"Not yet," he answered and put his leg over hers, and at that moment their most intimate entanglement was broken.

Amanda knew she needed to get away from him. She had to go somewhere and think about what had happened to her tonight. And she was beginning to be embarrassed by where she was and what she'd done.

She pulled away from him, turning her back to hide her breasts from his view. "I think I should get dressed."

The spell was broken for Hank. She was Miss Caulden again. If she wanted to play formal, so could he. "The last I saw your clothes they were on their way to the bottom of the pond."

Amanda felt a little like a reveler the morning after. Now she was going to pay the price. Was she supposed to enter her father's house stark naked? Dr. Montgomery and I were talking and one thing led to another, she'd say. She took his shirt from the grass and slipped it on. "Now what do I do?" she said, mostly to herself.

Hank sat up, trying unsuccessfully to control his

anger. Her only concern was how she was going to conceal what she'd done from Driscoll. Sympathy for another person only went so far. There came a time when Amanda was going to have to think for herself, a time when she was going to have to say this is what *I* want. "I'll take you home," he said flatly. "We'll sneak you in like we did the night of the dance."

No word of, Stay with me, Amanda thought. No words of love. No words of, I want to spend the rest of my life with you. Just an animal coupling, then she was to go home. She deserved it, didn't she? She'd gone after him, sought him out. He'd left the Caulden Ranch, yet she'd followed him, had climbed into his car with him and had asked him to make love to her. What was that old saying? Beware of what you ask for, you might get it. Well, she'd got what she asked for, all right, and now she was going to have to pay the price.

She stood. "I'd be grateful if you'd return me to my house," she said coolly. She was very close to tears. Would he go back to Reva now or would he maybe visit that pretty little Italian girl she'd seen him looking at today? She couldn't bear to look in his eyes. For all Amanda's strict upbringing, she wasn't really any better than the women who lived on the edge of town. "I will find a way to get inside."

He drove her back to her house in silence, neither of them speaking, each of them occupied with his own thoughts, both of them angry and hurt.

Amanda sat in the passenger side of the car, wearing his shirt and her black silk stockings that stopped just above her knees.

"Stop here," she said, indicating the end of the long Caulden driveway. "I'll walk."

He was further angered that she wanted to get rid of

him as soon as possible. Would she go tearing back into her fiancé's cold arms? "He won't forgive you for this, you know," Hank couldn't resist saying.

"No, I guess not." She didn't know who he meant, but it didn't matter, because she doubted if anyone would forgive her. She got out of the car and he didn't bother to help her out, nor did he say a word before he sped away, leaving her standing in the darkness.

Amanda walked slowly up the long driveway and at the house she saw a light on in the parlor and her mother sitting alone reading. Amanda put her head up to the window. "Psst!" she said.

Grace Caulden looked up, saw her daughter, then went to the window. "Amanda, are you all right? You look as if you've been in an accident."

"Worse than that," Amanda said. "Mother, could you get me some clothes? I seem to have . . . well, lost mine."

"I would be glad to, dear," Grace said and left the room. Moments later she was outside in the darkness of the trees, a dress over her arm. "That dragon, Mrs. Gunston, was hovering about your room. I had to sneak past her."

"She is a bit of a dragon, isn't she?" Amanda said, staying in the shadows so her mother couldn't see the extent of her nudity.

"Would you like to tell me why you've come home wearing only a man's shirt? It wouldn't by chance be Dr. Montgomery's shirt, would it?"

Amanda didn't want to answer her mother. She just wanted to go to her room and be safe.

Grace watched her daughter for a while then smiled. "Whenever you want to tell me what happened, I'll be here to listen."

Amanda nodded. She was afraid she might cry if she started to talk. They walked together into the house. Taylor was standing at the head of the stairs, as if he were waiting for Amanda. He was formidably tall, his face as dark as a thundercloud.

"You are *very* late, Amanda," he said.

"And very tired," she answered.

"You are to come to the library. I want to talk to you. There was an exorbitant bill sent here today for sandwiches. You must explain yourself. And also explain why your hair is down."

Amanda couldn't bear any more. "I am too tired to go to the library, and the bill for the sandwiches can be taken out of the money that's been saved over the years from all the meals I've missed. Now, please excuse me, I am going to bed."

Amanda was too tired to think how revolutionary her words were. Behind her she left a stunned Taylor and a mother who was smiling broadly. Once inside her room, she pulled off her dress and hose and fell into bed, not bothering to put on her nightgown.

Mrs. Gunston gave her usual quick knock the next morning and walked into Amanda's bedroom. The room was a mess; clothes on the floor, shoes kicked into far corners, hose draped on a chair. The bedclothes were half on the floor, and sprawled in the middle of the bed was a nude Amanda, on her stomach, one foot hanging over the side.

For a moment Mrs. Gunston was too astonished to speak. "Get up from there!" she shouted at last. "How dare you throw your clothes about? How dare you—"

"Go away!" Amanda said angrily, turning over, the

sheet pulled across her breasts. "Go on, get out of here, and tell Martha to bring me some coffee. Strong coffee."

Mrs. Gunston obeyed.

Amanda sat up and put her hand to her head. It was aching, and the woman's shrill voice hadn't helped any. She looked up to see Taylor standing in her doorway. *Now* he comes to my bedroom, she thought. Not when she begged him to pay attention to her, but now when another man had . . . had touched her.

"I do not like this," Taylor said. "Ladies do not shout."

Amanda at last saw some interest in his eyes as she sat in her bed with just a sheet under her arms. And something about his interest made her a little sick. "I need to dress to go to work. Would you mind closing the door?"

Taylor stepped further into the room. "Amanda, I cannot allow you to go back to that place today. The chauffeur said it was full of filthy people."

"The chauffeur's name is James and yes they are filthy people, but it's because they have no money—or food or a place to sleep."

"Amanda," Taylor said firmly, "I forbid you to go. Last night you looked as disreputable as one of the field workers, and this morning—" He broke off and stared at her.

"And this morning, what? This morning I don't look like your pupil? Oh, Taylor, please go before we have a fight. I must get dressed, and please don't say you forbid me to go because then I'll have to defy you. Wait until the hops are in, when everyone is gone, then we'll talk again, but please don't make me say something now that I'll regret later."

Taylor didn't seem to know what to say as he backed out of the room and closed the door.

Amanda leaned back against the headboard. It was as if another person were inside her body. She'd yelled at Mrs. Gunston, who'd always terrified her, and told Taylor she was not going to do what he told her to do.

She reached over to her desk and there lay a new schedule, freshly made out by Taylor. Right now she was supposed to be downstairs wearing her pink-and-white-striped silk that made her look as if she were eight years old and eating two poached eggs and one piece of dry toast.

She tossed the schedule back on the desk. It seemed so frivolous to stay here studying when so many people needed help. Frivolous, she thought, a word she'd often used to describe Hank.

"Hank," she said aloud, trying it on for size. It didn't seem to suit him. It was too new, too modern, too unromantic. What was the name on his books? She took one out of the bookshelf beside the bed and opened to the copyright page. Dr. Henry Raine Montgomery.

"Raine," she whispered. It sounded like a knight of old, a strong, virile man who might fight for the common people. Raine, she thought, Sir Raine. Better yet, Lord Raine.

She got out of bed, scratching and yawning, and put on a blue suit. It was too dark, too severe for her taste, and she thought that today she might stop by her dressmaker's and choose a few new pieces of clothing, something Raine, er, ah, Hank might like.

She went to the bathroom—at the wrong time according to today's schedule—and on impulse, knocked on the door to the room where her mother

233

spent her days and invited her mother to breakfast. "Father eats about this time. Perhaps we can eat together, just the three of us."

"Like we used to, before—" Grace said but broke off. She didn't need to add, before Taylor came.

It was a pleasant breakfast, and Amanda didn't say much as her parents seemed to have hours' worth to say to each other. Amanda occupied herself with thoughts of last night. Perhaps she'd been hasty in her judgments; maybe Raine—she meant Hank—did want her. Maybe she wasn't just another woman to him.

With her mind occupied, she bid her parents good-bye, unaware of how different she seemed with every step. Taylor was waiting for her by the car and she braced herself for the coming argument.

"I would like to *ask* you not to go," he said softly.

"I'm needed there," she answered.

"And you're needed here."

"Here no one knows I'm alive. I stay in my room all day with my books and papers. I've hardly seen my own parents in years. Please don't make this harder for me, Taylor. I want to feel that I'm useful to someone."

Taylor put his hands on her upper arms. "You are useful to me," he said, and there was desperation in his voice.

Amanda almost said she'd stay with him but the memory of the hungry children stopped her. If she could help them in any way, she was going to do it. "It's just until the hops are in," she said. "I want to help see that there is a peaceful unionization."

"Unions!" he said, dropping his hands, the pleading look leaving his eyes. "You don't know what you're talking about. Those people want to take the food out of our mouths. They want—"

"So you beat them to it, is that it? You take their food first, before they can do it to you? Oh, Taylor, come with me. See these people. They aren't thieves. They're just—"

He took a step away from her. "You forget that I've run the harvest for eight years with your father. I've seen them. They're filthy—"

"Good day, Taylor," she said and walked away from him.

On the drive into town, her mind seemed to whirl with a thousand conflicting thoughts. So much had happened to her in the last few weeks. Before Dr. Montgomery came she was content and happy, and now everything was confused. She didn't know if Taylor was her teacher, the man she loved or her enemy. And Dr. Montgomery! Lover? Friend? Teacher? Enemy?

It was already chaos at the union headquarters. Joe told her the mess was her fault because they'd heard free food was being passed out. He didn't trust Amanda because she was a Caulden and he let her know it.

Amanda went up the stairs to the room that she'd shared yesterday with Dr. Montgomery. In spite of telling herself that yesterday meant nothing, her heart was pounding as she reached the doorway.

The man who'd made love to her last night was holding Reva Eiler in his arms and kissing her.

It was as if the bottom of Amanda's world fell out. She had been right about him. She was an experiment to him, nothing more. He'd wanted to see if he could "unionize" her, to see if he could make her stand up for her rights just as he persuaded the workers to stand up for theirs. Perhaps she should have had a translator explaining things to her as they went along. She thought of Taylor with longing. When the hops were in she'd be glad to go back to her schedule and an orderly way of life.

"Good morning," she said cheerfully and took her place at her desk. She heard Dr. Montgomery and Reva break apart but she didn't look at them.

"Good morning, Amanda," Hank said softly.

She didn't look up. "Dr. Montgomery," she said curtly, "shall we allow the people in? Or perhaps you'd like to use this room for private meetings? I could go down the hall. Yes, I think I'll do that." She started gathering papers.

"Amanda, please let me explain."

She looked at him, and as her eyes locked with his she remembered every caress he'd given her last night, every word he'd spoken. Blood rushed to her face and she looked away. "Explain what, Dr. Montgomery?" She thought she heard him groan. No doubt he was upset at having one of his women see him with another of his women. "Explain these new translations? Explain how I'm to tell the people this is a union and not a soup kitchen? I'll do my best."

"Explain about Reva. She—"

"Threw herself at you?" Amanda's eyes blazed. "You poor man. That seems to happen to you a great deal."

"Amanda, please, I—"

She grabbed a letter opener from the desk. "You take one step closer to me and I'll use this."

His eyes were angry now too. Calmly, he reached out, grabbed her wrist and squeezed until the opener fell to the desk. "Have it your way," he said. "Let's get busy. We have people waiting."

Amanda was glad for the noise, the confusion and all the people. They kept her from remembering last night. Reva kept smiling at her in an infuriating way, and a few times Amanda caught Dr. Montgomery glowering at her but she looked away.

At one o'clock Hank clamped down on Amanda's hand and said, "We're going to lunch."

"No, thank you," Amanda said. "I'm not hungry."

"The day *you* aren't hungry is the day the world ends. Come with me or I'll make a scene so bad you'll never be able to hold your head up in this town again."

"I'm not sure I care, if it means being alone with you. Or do we take your other lady friends? Your harem, to be precise."

"I'll carry you," he threatened.

Amanda stood and walked out with him but she wouldn't allow him to touch her. He stopped at his car. "I will *not* get in that with you," she said. "No matter what you do to me."

He almost smiled. "All right, then, we'll try the diner."

He didn't speak again until after they were seated and he'd ordered the special for both of them.

"Thank you," she said nastily. "I'm accustomed to having my meals chosen for me."

"What's eating you? Is it last night? Or is it this morning? If it's last night, I—"

"I'd rather forget that, if you don't mind."

"I'll never forget it as long as I live," Hank said softly and started to take Amanda's hand, but just then the waitress arrived with their food.

To the utter astonishment of both of them, Amanda burst into tears. The waitress heard and gave Hank a dirty look for whatever he'd done to cause her to cry in public. Embarrassed, Hank grabbed the tray from the waitress's hand, put their plates of food and drinks on it, took Amanda's arm and began pulling her toward the back of the restaurant. The kitchen workers looked up in surprise, and Amanda tried her best to keep from crying, but it wasn't easy. He didn't stop until they were outside, several feet from the restaurant and in the shade of a big oak tree.

He half shoved her to sit down. "Okay, talk," he said, putting the tray down and sitting in front of her.

"Dr. Montgomery, I—"

"Don't give me that doctor stuff, Amanda. After what happened last night we're past the formal stage. I want you to tell me why you applied for a job with me, why you wanted me to make love to you and why you're crying now." Even as he said it, he knew that some part of him wanted her to say that she'd come to him because she was in love with him. He wasn't sure what he'd do if she did say that, but after last night he was close to willing to ask her to marry him. To spend every night in ecstasy such as he'd experienced last night . . .

"I was rude to Taylor this morning," she said, and Hank's shoulders fell. "And to Mrs. Gunston."

"Pretty horrible," he said sarcastically. He'd hoped it was jealousy that had made Amanda so angry this morning. Reva had thrown herself at him, and Hank had wanted to see if another woman's lips made him forget himself as Amanda's had. They hadn't. "So," Hank continued, "you're mad at me and crying because you were rude to Taylor this morning?" What about us? he thought. What about last night?

Amanda was trying to get control of herself. Hank handed her a plate of food and she began to eat. She was beginning to associate food with this man. "I came to work for you because I think I realized you were right about something."

Hank gave her a hopeful look.

"I don't really seem to know much about life."

"Oh," he said flatly.

"I mean I do know about some aspects of life, but not about dating, and—well, Dr. Montgomery, I don't seem to know much about love."

"You did all right last night," he said softly, his eyes hot.

She looked away. "In a way, it has been very kind of you to undertake teaching me what you have. I know I've been resentful because I didn't want you for a teacher, but then when Taylor first came to me I resented having a schedule." She gave him a little smile.

"I can't imagine resenting something like that," Hank said.

"Please do not be rude to me, Dr. Montgomery. You are the one who wanted to be my teacher, not the other way around."

"So what's your point?" he asked angrily. "You came to see how the other half lives, right? So now you'll go back to your teacher/fiancé and you'll be better for having had your little fling. Is that it?"

Tears came again to Amanda's eyes and she set down her plate.

"Oh damn," Hank said and handed her his handkerchief. "All right," he said softly, "tell me what's bothering you."

"Everything!" Amanda said, and the word came from her heart. "I feel so discontent, so restless. I used to be so *happy* before you came. I studied all day, Taylor and I had such lovely evenings of poetry and music, but now—" She blew her nose. "Now I hear ragtime music in my head and I don't want to stay home all the time and I want to *use* my knowledge. And I question what Taylor says and what my father says. And the poverty of those people who came to pick the hops! I feel like a princess who has been isolated in a tower all her life."

Hank wasn't going to lecture her, wasn't even going to tell her she had been isolated. "So you came to work for me to see some more of the world. Was last night part of the cure for your restlessness?"

"I don't know what last night was," she answered honestly. "Last night just added to my confusion. I don't seem to know who I am or what I want anymore. And Taylor seems so different. One minute he treats me as a little girl—he said he thinks of me as a little girl—and the next he's promising me kisses if I do well on my lessons."

"He what?" Hank asked, astonished.

Amanda didn't answer him directly. "I think Taylor may be as confused as I am. I'm not sure he knows if I'm a schoolgirl or a woman. He's been stuck with me so long that I'm not sure he remembers how to treat a woman."

Hank didn't say that it was something one never forgot. He tried to look at her problem from a distance, as if she were his student and not a woman whose mouth had— Student! he thought. Think student. "Which would you like to be, Amanda?" he asked in his teacher-voice. "A woman or a school-girl?"

She picked up her plate of food again. "I have been attracted to you, Dr. Montgomery, I can't deny that."

Hank gritted his teeth to keep from saying anything.

"But I don't think I would have been if I knew how to make Taylor think of me as a woman." She glanced at him and saw he wasn't looking at her with anger and it made her relax. "There is a great deal of truth in some of what you've said to me. I am somewhat of a prisoner in my house, but it's only because it hadn't occurred to me to break out. When I decided to stop my studies and come to work with the union, I was able to do it. And this morning, Taylor . . ."

"Taylor what?" Hank asked, keeping his voice cool.

"This morning I was—well, I slept without my nightgown on and the door was open and Taylor walked by and he . . . he looked at me with interest. He looked at me as if I were a woman and not a child."

Hank set aside his plate. He couldn't eat any more. "Oh?" he managed to say. Was that what last night meant to her? That at last ol' steel-spined Taylor had realized she was a *woman?* "So he looked at a half-nude woman in bed and showed some interest, did he?"

"You always manage to make Taylor sound less than human. Don't you realize that he's been my teacher since I was a child? Of course he'd think of me as a schoolgirl. That's why when I kissed him he—"

"He what?"

"He was repulsed by me," she answered softly, remembering the hurt. "He has kissed me since, but it wasn't the same."

"The same as what?"

"Well, you know," she answered, her face turning red.

"Perhaps you should tell me."

"Last night, what we did . . . It was as if I couldn't help myself. You are so much more experienced than Taylor. I mean, women are everywhere around you. Reva kisses you, Lily Webster looked as if she wanted to do with you what we did, and I'm sure you have many women at your college."

"Hundreds," he said. "Thousands. Everywhere I go women fall all over themselves to go to bed with me." He couldn't keep the sarcasm out of his voice. She was making him feel like a gigolo while Taylor was a respected citizen with morals—someone worth having. "Where is this heading, Amanda?"

"I wonder if maybe you'd teach me. I mean, you have been teaching me, but I've been a reluctant student but perhaps I could become a willing student."

"Teach you what? How to make love?" His eyebrows were nearly in his hairline. This is how a prospector felt when he struck gold.

"No, of course not. You taught me that last night, and I'm grateful. I won't be afraid of my wedding night now and I'll know what to do."

"You're welcome," Hank said, and refrained from telling her he doubted if Taylor knew about the things they'd done last night.

"Would you teach me the part of life that's not in books? Such as dancing and motion pictures and whatever else men and women do together? Maybe if I quit acting as a schoolgirl, Taylor will stop treating me as one."

Taylor, Hank thought. He was beginning to hate the man. She looked on last night as a prelude to her wedding night with Taylor. So what else did Hank want? Did he want her to say that after last night she couldn't bear to live without him? Did he want her to be another Blythe Woodley? He'd wanted to sleep with Blythe, then have her find some other man to marry, and now Amanda was offering him just that, but for some reason Amanda's offer was making him angry.

"Motion pictures, huh? Anything else?" he asked at least. "No more sex lessons?"

She looked away, blushing. "I'm sure we covered everything last night."

"Tip of the iceberg," he said, as if he were talking about the weather. "There are many other positions, such as you on top or standing or sitting or—"

"Standing?" she asked curiously. "I mean, how . . . ? I just wondered, physically, how . . . ?"

"I'd stand and you'd wrap your legs around my waist and I'd support your—" He cupped his hands as if to hold her buttocks. "And I'd set you down on my old man."

"Your—?" Amanda laughed, then stopped herself. "I think last night was enough teaching in that area. I think I'll wait until my marriage to Taylor." Although she couldn't imagine Taylor setting her down on his . . ."Dr. Montgomery," she said softly, "do you think I could have a baby from last night?"

Hank choked on the iced tea he was drinking. "I hope not," he said sincerely.

"But I thought that what we did was meant for procreation. I am somewhat concerned about this."

"Amanda," he said, exasperated. She was talking to

him as if he were another woman. "I don't know too much about this kind of thing. I've been to bed with many, I mean a few women here and there, and I don't think any of them have had my children. In fact, I'm sure one of them would have mentioned the fact to me. And lovemaking is for procreation but it's also somewhat pleasurable. Didn't you enjoy yourself last night?"

Amanda couldn't look at him. Enjoy herself? She'd nearly died in pleasure last night. This morning she could have taken a gun to both him and Reva when she'd seen them touching. "Yes, I did," she whispered. "But I thought one . . . mating equaled one child. Married couples . . ." She trailed off as she had no idea what married couples did.

"Married couples," Hank said quietly, "make love often. For example, if, say, you and I were married, I'd make love to you every night and in the morning before I went off to teach and I'd probably come home to lunch, too. You couldn't possibly have a child every time."

"I see," Amanda said. She was trying to keep this conversation on an intellectual basis, but her skin was beginning to feel strange. At lunch? In the daylight? She wondered what he looked like when he had no clothes on. She knew the feel of him but not the look. Were those shoulders of his as wide as they felt? Were his thighs— She cleared her throat. "I had no idea. Thank you so much for telling me."

"Anytime," he said pleasantly. "I'll show you, tell you, whatever you want."

"Very, ah, kind of you." She smiled weakly and looked at the dirty platters on the ground. All she had to do was say she wanted a different kind of lunch and he'd take her away in that little yellow car of his and then his hands would—

"You ready to go back?" Hank said.

"Yes," she answered, swallowing and starting to rise.

Hank put his hand on her arm. "You want to tell me what happened between you and Taylor the day you lost the bet? What happened to cause him to be repulsed by you and to punish you with calculus?"

"I'd rather not talk about it," she answered.

"Maybe I could help you prevent its happening again, but I can do nothing if you don't tell me what went wrong."

She didn't like to remember that afternoon. "I kissed him. He was standing in front of me and I stood on tiptoe and kissed him."

"Just like that."

She didn't know what he meant. "What other way is there? We had that awful wager, and I thought I was doing it for the ranch, because you said you'd leave if I could make Taylor show passion, so I kissed him. How else was I to do it? If I kiss you, you—" She stopped. "You understand what I mean."

"I understand perfectly. You acted like a schoolgirl and he no doubt treated you like one."

"Schoolgirls don't kiss their teachers. Or perhaps your female students do."

"Never, but if one did, I'd treat her just as Taylor did you."

"Oh," she said, feeling that all the pain of the last few days really was her fault. "I'm not sure I know what you mean."

"Come on, let's go back. We can spare a few minutes and I'll show you how to seduce a man. The proper way to do it."

She hesitated.

"I thought you wanted me to teach you about being a modern woman."

"I had motion pictures in mind or maybe that you'd teach me to tango."

"Reva knows about men. I'll bet if Reva kissed Taylor he wouldn't punish her with calculus."

Amanda felt her ring finger with her right hand, meaning to feel her engagement ring, but she found she'd left it at home again. Reva had helped Taylor choose *her* ring. "Let's go, Dr. Montgomery," she said. "I'm not good at many things but I am an apt pupil."

He watched her pick up the tray of dirty dishes and walk toward the back of the restaurant. So far he hadn't found much of anything that she wasn't good at. Grinning, he followed her. He had a lesson to teach.

Chapter Fourteen

They walked across the dusty, hot street of Kingman in silence. Amanda found she couldn't speak in anticipation of what was to come. It was just a lesson, she told herself, a lesson she could transfer to Taylor. After all, it was Taylor she was interested in, wasn't it? Taylor was the man she'd loved for years. Taylor was the man she was going to marry. She *needed* to learn how to change herself in his eyes from a child to a woman. And Dr. Montgomery was kind enough to teach her.

"In here," he said, opening the door to the broom closet.

"Here?" she asked.

"Only place private. Come on, we've been away too long as it is."

She had the distinct impression he wanted to get this duty over with. The problems of the people upstairs were of course much more important than hers. She stepped inside the closet and he locked the door behind her.

Hank turned a big bucket upside down and sat on it. "First of all, you're at a disadvantage if he's standing, because he's taller than you. Wait until he's sitting down, then you have the upper hand. Now, pull the string and kill that light and come sit on my lap."

"But—" she began.

"Pretend I'm Taylor. You can do that better in the dark. Amanda, if you want a schedule after you're married, then don't learn what I have to teach you. It's up to you."

She pulled the string on the light and the room was absolutely dark, but Dr. Montgomery's hands found her and guided her to sit on his lap.

"Amanda! What are you doing? You should be studying your Latin."

"Yes, I— Oh, I see, you're Taylor."

"Pretending to be," Hank corrected. "Amanda, if I were me, I'd put my arms around you like this," he said, his arms caressing her back, "and my hands would do this." He ran his hands down her arms, his thumbs touching the sides of her breasts. "And I'd kiss you like this." He kissed her softly, lingeringly, in such a way that made her remember last night. Her arms went around him, her tongue entwined with his. She moaned when his hand cupped her breast. Sitting, he'd said. People could make love while sitting down. She turned more fully toward him.

He pushed her away. "But I'm not me. I'm Taylor." Hank was swallowing and he was painfully uncomfortable. She was going to drive him mad. "Taylor would sit here like this." He put his hands beside his thighs, not touching her. There was a little light coming in around the door and he could see enough of her to again realize how beautiful she was. There seemed to be less sadness in her eyes. "Now what are you going to do?"

"I don't know. With you I don't have to do anything. You always seem to be ready." She could feel how ready he was now, against her left thigh. Her heart was still pounding, but he seemed to be so cool and unaffected by their kissing—well, maybe not all of him was unaffected. "I guess I would kiss him," she said, leaning toward his lips, but he turned his head away.

"No, start more subtly. Here, kiss my neck a little and maybe use this hand to unbutton a few buttons and this one you can put in my hair."

"Oh," she said, "I see." This was the easiest assignment she'd ever had. His hair was soft and clean and seemed to twine around her fingers. The buttons of his shirt opened easily, and she slid her hand inside to touch his bare flesh. "Like this?"

"Exactly," he whispered.

She put her lips to his neck. Hot, smooth skin with just the faintest trace of whiskers. She touched her tongue to his whiskers. His skin tasted good.

"Ear," Hank said, and could hardly hear himself above his heart's pounding.

Amanda thought she was maybe getting the hang of this. She put his earlobe in her teeth and pulled it gently. He moved his hands from his thighs to hers. She ran her tongue around the rim of his ear, her breath warm against it. "Am I doing all right?" she whispered.

"Fine so far," he managed to say.

She began to get creative as she kissed his temple then his eyes and down his face to his cheeks. She had unbuttoned most of his shirt now, and she wanted to feel her bare breasts against his hot, dark skin, feel the hair of his chest against her smooth skin.

"This ear?" she whispered, and used her tongue to

caress his left ear. She had to stretch across him a bit and her breasts felt so good where they touched him. She wanted to open her dress and feel his mouth on her.

She kissed his lips. As if she were dying, she kissed him, plunging her tongue into his mouth, ravishing him, attacking him, sucking at his lips, biting his lips; then her mouth and teeth bit at his jawline, down his neck. Her hands began tearing at his clothes.

Hank quit playing a game. He turned her to straddle him, treating her as if she weighed nothing, as he shoved her dress up over her hips. Her tap pants tore at the crotch so that she was bare against him, the cloth of his trousers against her soft inner thighs and her engorged womanhood.

His left hand clamped down on the back of her head, turning her so he could invade the deepest recesses of her mouth while his right hand unbuttoned his trousers, his knuckles caressing her. She rubbed against the skin of his hand.

Someone started trying the doorknob.

"I think it's locked," Reva said from outside. "You have the key or does Hank?"

"I think there are some keys upstairs," Joe said. "I'll go look."

"I'll go with you," Reva said, then to someone else she said, "You stay here. You can clean up your own kid's vomit."

Inside the closet, Amanda and Hank became aware of who they were and where they were.

"We better go," Amanda said. "I don't think they would understand."

Nor do I, Hank thought as he mechanically began to refasten his trousers.

Amanda at last found the string to the light and pulled it on, and for a brief moment their eyes met, but she didn't dare look at him for too long. It seemed that all he had to do was pull her string and she lit up like an electric light bulb.

Hank unlocked the door and looked out. Reva and Joe were still upstairs but standing quietly was an Italian woman holding the hand of a green-faced little girl. "Hello," Hank said. "We, ah . . ."

Amanda began to talk to the woman, making up a long excuse as to what they were doing in the closet as they passed her to go upstairs.

Hank paused on the stair landing. "What language was that?" he asked.

"Italian. Isn't she Italian?"

"I think she is, but I'm not sure what your language was."

"Oh. Greek, perhaps," Amanda said helplessly. "Maybe Russian. Maybe Latin."

He looked at her and it was all he could do to not touch her. He could feel her tongue in his ear. "Go fix your hair," he said, "then come back to work. We have another train arriving at two. Your father advertised for workers in three states. The more people he gets, the greater the competition for the jobs. He can fire hundreds and still have enough workers to pick the crops. Go on now. One look at you and everyone will know."

Amanda hurried up the stairs to the restroom. The mirror showed her flushed face, her hair about her shoulders and puffy lips from having kissed so much. She did the best she could to repair the damage. At least no one would be able to see her torn underwear. For a moment she leaned back against the door. It seemed that all he had to do was touch her and she came apart. She did outrageous, shameless things.

Taylor, she tried to remind herself. She was in love with Taylor and she wanted him to think of her as a woman. That was her goal.

She left the restroom and went back to the hot office which was filled with people who were trying to understand what a union was. Amanda was to explain to them that they would not lose their jobs if they asked for a drink of water.

She glanced at Dr. Montgomery before she took her seat. The back of his hair was mussed and she wanted to smooth it down, but as she watched, Reva's hand ran over his hair and straightened it. As Reva walked past Amanda she whispered, "Why do you have to have two men? Give me one of them, will you?"

Guiltily, Amanda gave her attention to the Hindu family before her. She needed to find a common language so she could talk to them. She didn't look at Hank again.

But Hank couldn't keep his eyes off Amanda. There were times when he couldn't remember what a union was. He thought of how he'd believed her to be a prig, an anxious, nervous, judgmental little prude. But then he'd touched her.

Reva annoyingly kept reminding him of his work and Hank had to stop daydreaming.

"Is anything going on around here?" Hank asked. "Something I could take a girl to?"

Reva gave him her most becoming smile. "There's a fair outside of Terrill City, and I've been dying to go," she said as a hint.

"A fair. Great." Hank wrote a note to Amanda,

slipped it in between some other papers and had Joe put it on her desk.

Amanda was talking to a Spanish family when she saw the note and, after days of translating everything she read, she read Hank's note aloud in Spanish.

The pretty young mother smiled while the handsome father said he'd be glad to go to a motion picture with her tonight and a carnival tomorrow night. Amanda blushed to the roots of her hair.

At 4:30 Hank stopped by her desk. "Well?" he asked.

"I'm engaged to someone else. I can't date you."

"I thought I might teach you how to act on a date so you won't make a fool of yourself with Taylor by lecturing him all evening."

"Oh," she said. She *wanted* to go with him, wanted to see a motion picture, wanted to sit next to him. And she was very aware that in another few days he'd be gone. "Yes, I'd like to go."

"And the carnival tomorrow?"

"Yes," was all she could answer.

Reva stood not far away, watching and listening. It really wasn't fair that Amanda should have so much while she had so little. Then she smiled. She wondered what Amanda's fiancé would have to say if he knew where Amanda was spending her evenings.

For the rest of the day Amanda felt as if something wonderful were about to happen. A few times she reminded herself of Taylor, but she told herself she was doing this for him.

At six, Hank came to her desk. "Ready?" he asked. "There's a show starting at 6:30."

Amanda picked up her handbag and left with him.

Reva stood staring at the door.

"Jealous?" Joe asked, laughing at her.

"Yeah, maybe I am," Reva said. "The rich get everything."

"You think the Doc likes Amanda because she's rich? Then you haven't seen him look at her when she walks across the room. He's more interested in what *she* has than what her daddy has."

"Who asked you?" Reva snapped. "I know somebody who will be very interested in those two." She left the union headquarters and started walking toward the Caulden Ranch.

Hank walked beside Amanda toward the Opera House, where the latest motion picture was being shown. He didn't touch her—but he wanted to. "If we were an engaged couple, you'd take my arm now," he said, holding out his arm for her.

Amanda smiled up at him. "Anything else?"

"There's always the possibility that you might get frightened by the picture. I hear that the heroine's life is in danger from beginning to end."

"And what do I do if I'm afraid?"

"Hold on to me," he answered and lifted her fingertips to his lips. "I'll protect you."

She stared at his lips for a moment then recovered herself. "Please remember, Dr. Montgomery, that you're my teacher and not my fiancé."

"I never forget it for a second." He led her into the darkened hall and they took a seat in the middle close to the front.

Amanda wasn't sure what she had expected in a motion picture, but she'd never dreamed how gripping one could be. The dangers that threatened the pretty young actress were so *real*. The villain was so awful, always plotting to get the young woman, always sneaking and skulking, looking for opportunities to steal her away.

Hank watched Amanda, saw the way her emotions played across her face as a child's would. She grabbed his hand once when the villain made a play for the heroine, so he put his arm around her shoulders and hugged her to him. He was rewarded by Amanda burying her face in his shoulder when the heroine nearly got run over by a train. He had never enjoyed a film so much in his life.

When it was over and the lights came on, he was reluctant to leave, reluctant to stop touching her. From the way she continued clutching his arm, he thought she felt the same way.

"What would an engaged couple do now?" she asked at last, holding the hand of the arm he had around her. He had only asked her to the motion picture. Would he take her home now? Would she go home and find that Taylor had scheduled a poetry reading for this evening? How could she read poetry after seeing a woman nearly severed by a train?

"I'd probably take you to a quiet, intimate dinner somewhere, someplace with candles and violins, then maybe we'd go dancing."

He was just telling her, not asking her to go with him, she thought. "I don't guess I could do that. I don't know how to dance."

"You could be taught. You do seem to have a capacity for learning."

"I guess it depends on the teacher." His lips were very close to hers and she hoped he was about to kiss her.

"Hey!" a man yelled from the back of the hall. "You two gonna pay for the second show?"

Hank and Amanda untangled themselves from each other and started out of the hall. Once outside, Amanda was reluctant to speak. Now she should ask him to take her home to Taylor.

"You know," Hank said, "you really should learn how to dance. What if you and Taylor are asked to the White House and the President asks you to dance? What will you say? That you don't know how?"

Amanda's spirits began to lift. "I suppose you're right. But I can't learn to dance wearing this." She looked down at her severe navy-blue suit. "My dancing dress was torn and it hasn't been repaired."

He took her arm. "We can fix that. There are more dresses where that one came from."

"I believe you asked to see me," Taylor Driscoll said, looking at Reva as she stood in the fading sunlight of the Caulden parlor. He told himself she was garishly made-up and her dress was dreadfully gaudy, but he still felt attracted to her. He'd like to see her with her face washed and wearing something simple and expensive, perhaps in a light blue. "How can I help you?"

Reva could feel this man's desire for her. He was a stuffed shirt, of course, but she was sure she could unbend him. She would very much like to kiss him, like to see him lean down to put his lips on hers. She turned away from him.

"I feel a bit like the school tattle," she said. "I came here to tell you about Amanda, but now I'm not so sure I should. Perhaps I should leave."

He didn't want her to leave. He didn't like to admit

it even to himself, but he'd been lonely in the last few weeks. Amanda was always gone, he never saw J. Harker, and of course Mrs. Caulden didn't speak to him even when they happened to meet. "Wait," he said to Reva. "Won't you stay and have some tea, or some sherry, perhaps?"

Tea, Reva thought. No doubt served in a silver pot. She looked at Taylor and saw the yearning in his dark, handsome eyes. Watch out, girl, she cautioned herself, he's not for you. She had a feeling that outside of this house he was as poor as she was. He'd only have money if he married Amanda. "Yes," she heard herself saying, "I'd like to have tea."

An hour later Reva was warming to her subject of telling Taylor about Amanda. He seemed to take it in stride, but she could see pain in his eyes. And bewilderment. Amanda didn't know how to fend off a guy who got too fresh, she didn't even know how to dance. Was her fiancé as backward as she was?

"So, you seem to think there is a growing attachment between the two of them," Taylor said, trying not to allow his feelings to show. Amanda was the first woman he'd ever allowed himself to trust and she was betraying him.

"Can I be honest with you? Hank's a dream of a man but, between you and me, you're not putting up much of a fight. You're handing Amanda to him on a silver platter."

Taylor stiffened. "I did ask her to escort Dr. Montgomery, but I thought—"

Reva set her cup down with a clink. "Why don't you go punch Hank?"

"I beg your pardon."

"I guess that's not a good idea," Reva said. "After

the way he took out Sam Ryan, I don't guess you'd stand a chance. But, you know, you do have an advantage—you are engaged to Amanda. Tomorrow night she's supposed to go to the carnival in Terrill City with Hank. Why don't you invite her to the fair? She'd have to go with you since you two are engaged."

"To a fair?" Taylor asked, aghast. "I hardly think so. There is, however, a reading of Thackeray's work tomorrow night at—"

"Reading?" Reva gasped, then leaned toward him. "When you proposed, how did you do it?"

"I believe, Miss Eiler, that such things are personal."

"Was it personal? Did you get down on your knees and swear undying love to her and say you'd die if she didn't marry you?"

"I hardly think—"

"That's what I thought." She leaned back on the hard little couch. "Hank would. If Hank proposed to a woman, believe me, it would be romantic. He'd probably hire violins, have a tub full of champagne handy, and he'd make the woman feel as if she were the most beautiful, most desirable creature on earth."

"I see," Taylor said, and he did see somewhat. Romance was what Miss Eiler was talking about. "Do you think Amanda would like that?"

"All women like to be courted. *All* women want a man to be passionately obsessed with them. That's what romance is—a man showing interest in a woman. It doesn't have to be flowers and violins, it could just be a man wanting the woman to be near him all the time. Talking is romantic. A man being jealous is

romantic. If you love Amanda, then you have to show her."

"I gave her a ring," Taylor said, defending himself.

"Which I've never seen on her finger since we picked it out. You didn't by chance tell her I helped you choose it, did you?"

"I believe I did mention the fact."

Reva groaned. There was passion inside him, she could feel it, but he had it locked somewhere deep down. He needed someone to help him thaw out. "Mr. Driscoll, if I may be blunt with you, you are losing Amanda. Unless you put up some fight for her, she's going to run off with Hank Montgomery, or maybe with a traveling salesman."

Taylor just looked at Reva. How did one fight? Perhaps poems by Robert Burns would do it.

Reva could see his confusion. "Invite Amanda to the carnival," she repeated. "Take her to the carnival and show her a good time. Win her some prizes. Take her on a ride or two. Take her through the Tunnel of Love and kiss her wildly. Bring her home and try to force your way into her room. Make her think you're going crazy with wanting her."

Taylor stared at Reva. He couldn't imagine doing any of the things she mentioned with Amanda but he'd like to kiss Miss Eiler.

Reva saw his look, and more than anything in the world, she wanted to touch this man. There was something about the way he was so stiff and unbending that fascinated her. "Perhaps, Mr. Driscoll," she said softly, "you haven't had enough practice in kissing women wildly."

"Perhaps I haven't," he answered just as softly.

They leaned toward each other very slowly and when their lips touched, electricity shot through them. Taylor put his hand to the back of Reva's head, holding her skull tightly.

She broke away first and looked into his dark eyes. Poor, she thought. Remember that. He's as poor as a church mouse. Fall for him and you'll end up with six kids and nothing to feed them. "Not bad," she said, "but you need work. Take Amanda to the carnival and practice on her. I must go now." She had to get out fast before she began "practicing" with him. "Good evening, Mr. Driscoll."

"But the shop isn't open," Amanda said to Hank as they stood before the dress shop window. Hanging inside was a gorgeous silk charmeuse dancing dress with a bodice of Chantilly lace.

"You know the story of Aladdin? I happen to know the magic words to open the door at any hour, day or night."

She looked up at him. When he was smiling at her she felt a little weak-kneed. "And what are the magic words?"

"I pay cash," he said, and Amanda laughed. "Come on, the owner lives upstairs. Let's get her to open the door and find you some clothes."

Amanda felt a little jealous at the way the store owner so readily agreed to open the shop for Hank—again. He'd bought her other dancing dress there too.

As they were walking down the stairs, the owner in front of them, Amanda said, "You two certainly seem friendly."

Hank stopped on the dark stairs, then pinned her against the wall. "If you and I were engaged or were really dating, I'd think that was a jealous remark. Are you jealous, Amanda?"

"Certainly not. How can I be jealous of you if I am in love with another man?"

"Who would you rather see kissing the pretty shop owner? Taylor or me?"

"I am most used to seeing you kiss any number of women. It's a wonder you don't put that as a requirement to join the union: All pretty women must kiss Dr. Montgomery before being allowed to join."

He laughed at that and moved so she could continue down the stairs. Inside the shop, Amanda forgot about men altogether. She hadn't been inside a dress shop since she was fourteen and Taylor had arrived. She had been so busy since then trying to keep up with her studies that she hadn't given much thought to clothes Taylor had chosen sturdy, simple clothes that covered most of her exposed skin. But here were dresses of fragile fabrics, with laces and beading, beautiful transparent silk georgettes, satins, crepe de chines.

She turned to look at Hank.

"Go," he commanded, laughing at her expression. "Try on everything. Buy whatever you want."

"Send the bill to my father," Amanda said before touching a sumptuous blue satin dress.

"I'll pay for everything," Hank said quietly to the store owner. He very much liked the idea of having purchased what touched Amanda's skin. "And put a couple of those in with the dresses," he said, pointing to pink silk crepe underwear sets that were trimmed with satin.

Amanda tried on the dresses and modeled each one for Hank. She couldn't describe the way he made her feel, as if she were the most beautiful woman in the world. She chose five dresses and wore the one she'd first seen in the window. They walked together to his car, Hank carrying her packages.

"Do I look all right?" she asked. It was very dark, especially dark where his car was parked. "I mean, if you were a man and I were a woman, an unattached woman, that is, would you be interested . . . I mean, would you think I looked all right?"

Hank dumped the boxes in the passenger seat of his auto, then took Amanda's hand and pulled her under the deep darkness of three palm trees. "Amanda," he said softly, "if you were mine right now, I would be so overcome with your beauty that I'd . . ." He lifted her hand to his mouth and bit the soft, inside fingertip of her longest finger. It wasn't a kiss, it was more as if he were on the verge of devouring her skin. He began gnawing down her finger into her palm, biting the cup of her palm, sucking at it. His teeth and lips moved to the inside of her wrist, then up and up, pausing for a second at the inside of her elbow, then up again, kissing the most delicate, most sensitive parts of her arm.

Amanda had her head back, her eyes closed as his mouth moved over the lace on her shoulders then across her collarbone, over her right shoulder and down her right arm. He sucked at the palm of her hand then bit at her fingertips.

"Amanda," he said. He had two of her fingertips in his mouth and she could feel his tongue, his teeth, the hot wetness of the interior of his mouth.

"Yes," she said, and she meant yes to *anything* he asked of her.

"If you were mine, that's what I'd do to you," he said.

Amanda looked at him, and even in the darkness she could see the hooded look of his eyes, the slight flare of his nostrils. In fascination, as a cobra watches a flute, she watched him move her fingers about in the interior of his mouth. Her body was beginning to weaken, and just as she was ready to fling herself at him, he dropped her hand.

"Let's get something to eat," he said and walked to the car to help her in.

She got in, balancing the packages on her lap.

Hank didn't say much on the way to the restaurant. He knew he was playing with a deadly substance, but he was like an addict and couldn't help himself. He could take her away from Driscoll; he knew that. But it wouldn't be fair to either of them. Under Amanda's beautiful exterior was still the prim little lady he'd first met. She wasn't the woman for him, no matter how sweet she tasted.

Amanda was thinking nearly the same thing. He was a poor rabble-rouser and he wasn't the man for her. When he wasn't touching her she could see him as he was. He was the sort of man a woman had a fling with, but he wasn't a man a woman should love. The woman who loved him would have a painful future.

She tried to keep that in mind as she watched him driving, his profile outlined in the moonlight and the headlamps. But she kept watching his strong hands on the steering wheel, the way he gripped the shift lever. She saw the muscles in his thighs working as he moved from pedal to pedal.

Hank glanced at her, saw the hungry look in her eyes and forgot about common sense. He put his right hand on her knee and touched silk. "Do you ever wear anything except black silk stockings?"

"Taylor says black is the most refined, the most ladylike color."

Hank laughed. "He's either a fool or a connoisseur."

"I don't know which either," Amanda said into the wind.

The quiet little restaurant lay on the outskirts of town, and when Hank stopped the car he paused a moment to look at her.

When he started to say something, Amanda put her fingers to his lips. He looked as if he were about to say something serious. "Let it last while it can," she said softly. She removed her hand. "How would a fiancé help his intended from the car?"

He smiled at her. It seemed that she knew the rules, that it was a game they were playing and nothing more. "First he might kiss her."

"Oh?" Amanda said and leaned her cheek against the leather seat.

Hank touched her face with his fingertips, moving back to her hairline. Every day her hairstyle had become looser and softer. "And then again he might not."

Amanda had been teased very little in her life and had never been teased in a playful sexual way by a man. "You!" she gasped, then when Hank put up his hands as if to protect himself from a blow, she lunged at him, packages falling to the floorboard. She slapped at him while his protecting hands kept coming in contact with some of the more delicious parts of her body.

"I give up," he cried. "I'll kiss you."

"You will not, because I won't allow it," Amanda said haughtily and got out of the car.

Hank bounded out his side, caught her and spun her about in his arms. "Deny me, will you, wench?" he said, mocking the villain in the film they'd seen. "Either you give yourself to me or I'll throw your old mother into the snow."

"But, sir," she said, turning her head away, "it is eighty degrees outside."

"Into the desert then. With no water. Now, wench, are you mine?"

Amanda gave one great twist, kicked him on the shin and started running. "Not on your life," she called.

Hank caught her within a few feet, holding her, her back to his front as she tried to twist out of his grasp. "I want all of you, your lips, your eyes, your breasts. I want to kiss you and caress you, make love to you all night long."

Amanda stopped struggling and turned in his arms. "To hell with the hero, I'll take you, the villain." She kissed him deeply, plastering her body close to his, feeling the hard maleness of him against her.

"Amanda," he said, crushing her against him, bending his body so that she bent backward. His leg slipped between hers.

Her heart was pounding and she wanted nothing more than to disappear into the darkness with him. "Are you trying to get out of feeding me?" she said at last.

He pulled back to look at her. "You've been starving since the first day I met you," he said, smiling at her. "Starving for more than just food."

"So you like to think," she said insolently and pushed him away. "I must look a mess. Get my handbag and take me inside so I can do something with my hair."

He obeyed her as if it were what he was supposed to do, and Amanda smiled. How wonderfully pleasant to tease and laugh and to order a man around. She smoothed her dress as he returned and they went inside.

It was the first meal they'd shared that they weren't fighting. In the soft candlelight, he seemed almost as if he were the man she loved. For a moment Amanda wondered what they would talk about, but then it seemed as if there were a thousand things she wanted to know about him: where he grew up, how he came to teach economics, where he'd learned calculus, what his family was like, what he did when he wasn't saving migratory workers.

"You race cars?" she said when they were on dessert. "Do you win?"

"About as often as I lose."

"Do you think I could come and watch you win, or lose?" she asked, then remembered that soon he'd be gone and she would still be here. She looked at her plate.

"Maybe you and Taylor can come and watch the races," Hank said. He meant to sound unconcerned but his voice sounded bitter. "I guess I better get you home."

Her head came up. "But you promised to teach me to dance. Remember the White House? It's why we bought me a dancing dress."

He wanted to take her home, wanted to put some distance between the two of them, but at the same time he couldn't bear to let her out of his sight. "All

266

right. Dancing it is, but I warn you, don't get too fresh."

"Or you'll what?"

"Do anything you ask of me," he said more seriously than he meant to. He called for the check and they left the restaurant.

Chapter Fifteen

Amanda stretched in bed, then slid back under the light cover and closed her eyes again. She didn't ever want to get up, didn't want to have to face sunlight or other people. She wanted to stay in bed all day and think of last night.

After dinner Dr. Montgomery had wanted to take her dancing, and after a few inquiries they found that the only dance in the area was on a barge floating down the Glass River near Terrill City. The barge had already left and wouldn't be back until one A.M.

"We'll make it," Hank had said, and the two of them went on a wild ride over dark, rutted roads until they'd reached the river, where he rented a rowboat and started rowing toward the barge. He could row like a demon. "Grew up in Maine, remember?" he said to her as she hung on.

As they neared the barge, the people stopped dancing and came to watch them and cheer them on as they drew closer. There were many hands to help them on board and tie the rented boat on the back of the barge.

"The lady wanted to dance. What could I do?" Hank explained, making everyone laugh.

They were the hit of the evening, and Hank was

right—Amanda had no difficulty learning the dance steps. By the end of the evening she was dancing the waltz, the polka, the schottische, and square dances as well as the tango. Amanda knew she'd never had so much fun in her life. For once she wasn't a freak; she was no different from anyone else. The men liked her because she was pretty and energetic, and the women liked her because she laughed.

They ate oysters and drank champagne and danced until the barge came back to home base and the band packed up and went home. By that time everyone knew everyone else's name and they waved and called goodnight to each other.

Hank helped Amanda over the side of the barge and into the rowboat, then, slowly, in the moonlight, he rowed her back to the rental place.

"Tired?" he asked.

Her hand was trailing in the water. "I feel wonderful. I had no idea this is what other people did."

"Instead of calculus tests on Sunday morning?"

"I wonder how many languages those women speak."

"Touché," Hank said, laughing. "Am I proving to be a good teacher? You wanted to know something about the world."

She looked at him in the moonlight. He seemed to get better-looking every hour. What a heavenly night it had been. "You're the best teacher in the world," she answered softly.

He drove her back to the ranch slowly, as if he didn't want to part with her, then stopped the car at the end of the long drive. No two people ever walked more slowly as they made their way back to the house.

"I guess I better go in," Amanda said. She wasn't

touching him but she wanted him to take her in his arms. "If we were engaged, perhaps a goodnight—" she began.

"I touch you, Amanda, and in thirty seconds our clothes would be off and we'd be rolling around on your mother's lawn. You go inside and I'll go to my hotel room. I'll see you at headquarters, and tomorrow I'll take you to the carnival."

She stepped toward him. "Hank," she whispered.

He nearly jumped away from her. "Go on, Amanda, get out of here."

Reluctantly, she turned and went into the dark, silent house. Once inside, she got into her nightgown, snuggled in her empty bed and wished he were with her. When she went to sleep she didn't realize that it had been hours since she'd thought of Taylor.

Now, awake, she wanted to stay in bed and think about every moment of last night.

But it wasn't to be. After a brief knock, Mrs. Gunston barged into Amanda's room. Her face showed her anger, but this morning Amanda felt too good to care.

"Two A.M.," Mrs. Gunston said. "You were out until two o'clock in the morning, and I don't imagine I'm the only one who heard you come in. It's disgraceful. I doubt that Master Taylor will want you after this."

"You think not?" Amanda said languidly.

"Look at you, you're a sight to behold. Lazing about in bed half the day, your hair down like that. I know what's going on. I'm not blind. It's that Dr. Montgomery. You're like all the women in this town, chasing after a pretty face. Everyone in town knows he's been seeing one of those Eiler girls. To men like him girls are just conquests to be made. And what has he got from you, missy? Anything he wants? Did he buy you that dress? Did you give him what he wants for the price of a dress? You—"

"You are fired, Mrs. Gunston," Amanda said, not even raising her voice.

"You can't fire me. I work for Mr. Driscoll."

"Who works for my father and therefore, in essence, works for me. I repeat, you are fired. I will instruct Taylor to give you two weeks' severance pay, but you are to be gone by this evening."

"But you can't—" Mrs. Gunston said, but her voice had lost its power. She turned on her heel and left the room.

"Bravo!"

Amanda looked up to see her mother standing in the doorway and grinning broadly. "Aren't you going to be late for work, dear?" Grace said as she shut her daughter's bedroom door, and Amanda could hear her whistling in the hall.

Amanda got out of bed and hurriedly rushed through dressing. She didn't want to miss one minute of work. She supposed she should feel awful about firing Mrs. Gunston, and perhaps she should worry about repercussions from her father and Taylor, but all she felt was pleased that she'd gotten rid of the tyrannical old witch.

She hurried down the stairs and rushed into the dining room. All that dancing last night had made her ravenous. She stopped abruptly when she saw Taylor sitting at the table, a newspaper in front of him. It seemed like years since she'd seen him, but the moment she did see him she became Amanda-the-student again. Her back seemed to remember that

271

steel brace he'd made her wear and she held herself rigid.

"Good morning," she said in a cool, remote voice, with no enthusiasm or laughter in it.

Taylor put his paper down and looked at her as she seated herself beside him. The maid appeared with a poached egg and a dry piece of toast. Taylor waved it away. "Bring Miss Caulden bacon and scrambled eggs and biscuits with butter and honey. Tea or coffee?" he asked Amanda.

"T-tea," she managed to say.

When the maid was gone, Taylor looked at Amanda. "I believe we need to talk."

For some reason, Amanda felt a forboding about what was coming. She wanted to postpone hearing what he had to say. "I need to get to the Union Hall. The people will be arriving and I need to talk to them. By our calculation there are sixteen languages spoken. I really don't know too many of them, but sometimes we can find one person who speaks a language I do know and we can tell the person about the union. Sometimes it's almost humorous. It will take as many as five of us to reach a man who speaks, say, some Chinese dialect. It's really very interesting, and I'm needed—"

Taylor put his hand over hers. "Amanda, I love you."

"Oh," Amanda said. "Oh."

He removed his hand when the maid placed the heaping plate of food before her. Amanda began to eat, but the flavor of the food made her think of Dr. Montgomery. Usually, when she was eating delicious food, she was with him. Dry, tasteless food was what she ate when she was with Taylor.

Taylor started talking again when they were alone. "I don't think I've done very well in changing from being your teacher to being a suitor. There are things in life that are difficult for me, and one of them is expressing my feelings."

She could see how difficult this was for him, and part of her wanted to tell him not to express himself. She wished she could get away and go to the Union Hall, then to the carnival tonight. Please, she prayed, don't let anything ruin the carnival tonight.

"I was awake all night," he said. "I heard you come in."

Who didn't? she thought.

"I don't know and I don't want to be told what kept you out so late last night, but I can't help but feel that some of it is my fault. I don't know if you realize that the reason I have kept you under such strict discipline is because I have been afraid of losing you. I know you believe the ranch has a great deal to do with why I asked you to marry me and, to be honest, financial security is important to me, but I asked you to marry me because I love you."

He looked at her, and his dark eyes that Amanda had always feared were full of hurt and pain. "You have given me back my faith in women, Amanda. My mother—" He stopped and turned his head away.

Her eyes widened. Amanda knew *nothing* about his family. "Your mother?" she asked softly.

He looked back at her, and Amanda thought perhaps she saw tears in his eyes. She put her hand over his.

"My mother betrayed me, and I thought all women were like her, but you're not, Amanda. You're good and kind, and I . . . I have treated you abominably."

"No you haven't," she protested, squeezing his hand. "You have taught me so much. I am probably the best educated female in America."

He gave her a grateful little smile. "Then you don't hate me?"

"Hate you? Of course not. We're engaged to be married, remember?" She started to hold up her ring to show him, but she'd left it upstairs again.

His smile broadened. "Amanda, I'm going to be honest with you. I don't really know much about courting, but I'm going to try. From now on you're not my pupil and I'm not your teacher. No more schedules; no more lessons. We'll just do what other engaged couples do. Amanda, I want us to be happy."

So why aren't I happy? Amanda thought. Why do I want to run into my room and cry for about four years? "Th-that sounds wonderful," she said.

"You don't look very happy," he said teasingly. "Maybe you need some proof." He turned in his chair and patted his knee. "Come sit on my lap."

Horror was the only word to describe what Amanda felt at his suggestion.

"Don't look so shocked, Amanda. It's a perfectly proper thing for an engaged couple to do."

Stiffly, she stood, and he reached out his hands and pulled her onto his lap.

"Now, doesn't that feel nice? Amanda, you really are beautiful." His hands went up her arms and he began trying to pull her toward him to kiss her.

Images were going through Amanda's head: She was sitting on Hank's lap in the cleaning closet. "I guess I would kiss him," she'd said. "No," Hank had answered, "start subtly. Kiss my neck, unbutton my shirt, put your hands in my hair."

Taylor kissed her, but nothing about the kiss made her relax at all.

He pulled away and looked amused. "I can see it's going to take some time. Amanda, I know that you'd probably prefer to be in your room studying, but there's more to life than books. After we're married, there are certain duties a wife performs for her husband. Not duties, exactly, but I do believe you could come to enjoy what happens between a man and a woman."

Amanda sat rigidly on his lap and remembered Hank saying, "Taste me." "I believe I could learn," she said.

"Then relax, Amanda," he said in the voice of Taylor-the-teacher.

Acting out of reflex from years of being obedient, she slumped against him and put her head on his shoulder.

He snuggled her against him, seeming to be content, while Amanda had the absurd idea that they didn't fit together. She thought she might be too heavy for Taylor's thin body, and she also sensed that, although he said he wanted her to relax, he'd be appalled if she turned to him and caressed his ear with her tongue. She couldn't help thinking of Hank: she seemed to weigh nothing to him as he tossed her over fences and lifted her in and out of cars, and *nothing* shocked him.

"Are you willing to give me a chance at being your lover instead of your tutor?" Taylor asked.

"Of course," Amanda said. "If we are to be married—"

"If!"

"*When* we are married, we will be l-lovers."

Taylor chuckled. "My shy little flower. I will introduce you to love. I don't mean to brag, but I have had some experience."

Me, too, she wanted to say, but she was sure that wouldn't go over too well.

He held her away to look at her. "We'll start tonight. I'll pick you up at your Union Hall—I should see where you have your little job—and we'll go to the carnival in Terrill City."

"The carnival?" Amanda gasped. "But—"

"Is there something wrong with the carnival? Perhaps you'd rather go somewhere else. A dance, perhaps. A motion picture? We could just walk in the moonlight. Perhaps a moonlight picnic? That would be nice. We could take a chocolate cake. I know how you love chocolate."

Amanda could bear no more. She got off his lap. "The carnival will be wonderful. I really must go now to my"— she hesitated—"to my little job. I will see you tonight."

"No kiss goodbye?" he asked lightly.

She bent forward to kiss him and he put his hand to the back of her head and turned her head to give her a hard, openmouthed kiss while his other hand moved down her arm to touch the side of her breast.

She jerked away from him abruptly.

He chuckled. "See, I can be something besides a teacher. Go on now. I'll see you this evening."

Stiffly, Amanda left the dining room. Moments later she was in the back of the limousine on the way to the Union Hall. Now she had everything she wanted out of life: Taylor loved her; he was treating her as an adult and not a schoolgirl, and tonight she was going to a carnival with a man she had loved since she was a child. She was the most fortunate, the luckiest woman on earth.

So why did she feel as if her life were over? Why did she feel like hiding in her room and never coming out?

By the time she got to the Union Hall, her body and face were rigid with unshed tears. The first person she saw was Hank, and for a moment his eyes met hers and caught fire. She looked away.

He came to her desk and leaned over her. "You're late," he whispered. "Out late last night?"

Just his breath on her ear sent chills along her body. "You may take the time out of my wages," she said coolly, moving to the other side of the desk. "Wages which you haven't paid me, I might add."

Hank moved next to her. "Has something happened? If that bastard Taylor did anything to you, I'll—"

"Taylor told me he loves me and he's taking me to the carnival tonight, Dr. Montgomery. I really do thank you for your tutoring of me. It looks as if it's worked perfectly." She held out her hand for him to shake. "I will owe you my undying gratitude."

He looked at her, then at her hand. "You're quite welcome," he said just as coolly. "If you need any more . . . help"—he looked her up and down in an insolent way—"let me know." He took his wallet from inside his coat pocket and pulled out two fives and slapped them on her desk. "For services rendered. Now, are you planning to work or has the rich Miss Caulden more important things to do today?"

"I can do more work in a day than you can in a week," she said, wishing he'd just get out of her sight so she wouldn't have to remember kissing him or dancing with him, or making love with him.

"We'll see about that." He turned away and went to his own desk.

Everyone in the hall had heard, of course. Joe looked at Reva and shook his hand as if to say, hot one. Reva looked away and smiled, but the smile didn't last long. She'd got Amanda away from Hank, but she didn't like to think of that lovely Mr. Driscoll with Amanda. Either man, Amanda couldn't lose. The fact that she had *both* of them enraged Reva.

Hank knew he was being childish but he couldn't contain his anger at Amanda. She'd always told him the truth, that she only wanted Taylor. She'd wanted to learn about sex so she could entice her fiancé. It was just that it had somehow not seemed *real*. He'd never actually believed she meant to marry that cold, sanctimonious bastard.

He was slamming papers on his desk and snapping at everyone when Reva glared at him. "What did you want?" she asked. "Did *you* want to marry Amanda? If so, why don't you go ask her and stop making the rest of us miserable?"

"No, I don't want to marry her," he snapped. "She's in love with that cold fish Driscoll and besides, she's a little—" Prig? That was no prim and proper miss who danced with him last night. It was no prig who sat on his lap in the cleaning closet. And the woman who begged him to make love to her . . .

"Haven't you got any work to do?" Hank snapped at Reva, then when she turned away he grabbed her arm. "Go to the carnival with me tonight?"

Reva rolled her eyes. "Amanda is going to the carnival with her fiancé, so you just happen to show up with another woman. Right?"

"You want to go or not?"

"Why not?" she said in disgust. "It can't be worse than my other dates with you. Hank, when you leave, this town is gonna curl up and die from boredom."

Amanda was glad for all the work Dr. Montgomery piled on her, and she was sure some of it was contrived, but at least it kept her from thinking. She went to lunch by herself, and for the first time since she'd met Hank, she wasn't hungry.

When she got back to the Union Hall, two men had got into a fight over a very pretty young woman and one man had plunged a knife into the other one. There was an hour's chaos while the doctor and the sheriff were summoned.

The sheriff wanted to put Hank in jail.

"He caused it and he's gonna pay," Sheriff Ramsey said, reaching for Hank's arm.

"Unless you have some proof—" Hank began.

Amanda stepped between the two. The sheriff was a short, thick man with a neck as big around as his head and he'd had the nickname "Bulldog" since he was a child. Amanda had often seen him talking to her father. "Dr. Montgomery had nothing to do with the fight," she said.

Sheriff Ramsey gave the utmost respect to Amanda because her father secretly paid him a monthly stipend for "extra" protection. "Miss Caulden, I don't know what you're doin' here, but this man is a menace to our peaceful community. He wants to start a war between the pickers and the ranchers. I hear he's givin' out guns, and here's proof he's supplyin' 'em with knives."

Amanda was a bit bewildered at this, her first real

taste of prejudice. "No one has supplied any guns or knives, and I can assure you that all we're doing is telling people that they have a right to join a union."

"Miss Caulden, if you'll pardon me for contradictin' you, all these people want is bloodshed." He looked at Hank and pointed. "And yours'll be the first blood that's shed." He looked back at Amanda. "I advise you to get out of here before somethin' awful happens. I'm goin' right now to speak to your daddy. I'm sure he don't know what you're gettin' yourself into." He turned and stomped out of the hall, two men carrying the wounded picker behind him.

Amanda turned to Hank. "What did he mean, bloodshed?"

"Some people believe that the only way to have a union is with violence. They think no one in the world listens to problems until you first get their attention, and the best way to do that is with a little blood being spilled."

He was watching her intently as he saw her digest this information. She'll probably run back to her books and her safe little world now, he thought.

"But if we explain to these people about unions, we can form one without violence."

"Forming a union is easy. It's when the unionists present their grievances to the owners that the anger starts. How do you keep the owners from laughing at a petition?"

"Strike," Amanda said.

Hank laughed at her. "Strike and they can have their maids serve their meals in their rooms for a few days?"

Amanda saw that Joe and Reva were smiling at her too, as were a family of workers who spoke English.

Once again she was a freak and an outsider, someone who didn't belong. She had begun to feel that she was part of something, that she was *helping,* but they'd never considered her one of them. They thought she was the rich Miss Caulden who didn't understand that not everyone had servants and unlimited budgets.

"They really should have saved some of their money," she said as haughtily as possible. Let them believe what they would. "Perhaps they waste it on drink and motion pictures. Perhaps I should translate the story of the grasshopper and the ant." She flicked an imaginary speck off her silk dress. "Couldn't we get one of these women to clean this place?" She sat down at her desk, her back to them.

No one said anything for a while, and Amanda was torn between rage and tears. All of them thought they were so enlightened, but they judged her by the circumstances of her birth, not by what they could see to be true about her.

Behind her, Hank was puzzled by her outburst. He had snapped at her because he'd disliked the way she'd stepped between the sheriff and him, and the sheriff's attitude had reminded Hank that she was the daughter of the enemy. But her words were like nothing he'd heard from her before. She'd worked hard the last few days and she had never shown any distaste for the workers.

At six o'clock, Taylor Driscoll walked in, and Hank felt a surge of irrational hatred for the man. And as Taylor looked down at Amanda with soft, loving eyes, Hank broke a pencil in half.

"Are you ready?" Taylor asked quietly.

Amanda straightened her desk and left without saying a word of farewell to the others. She still hadn't spoken when she and Taylor were seated in the back of the limousine.

"So, that's where you work?" Taylor asked. He wasn't used to making conversation. For the last eight years he'd talked to Harker about the ranch and to Amanda about what she was studying.

"Where I work, but not where I belong," Amanda said with some bitterness.

Taylor smiled. In his new position of not being her teacher, he was determined not to tell her what he thought of that filthy house filled with those filthy people. He reached across the seat and took her hand. "No, darling, you don't belong with them. You belong with me and people of your own kind."

Amanda looked at him and wondered if she were like him. She didn't feel much like going to a carnival but she didn't want to go home either. Maybe she *did* belong with Taylor. Of course she belonged to Taylor!

The carnival was loud and dirty; it stunk; it glittered; it was garish—and Amanda loved it immediately. It was what she needed to forget people who thought she was a spoiled little rich girl.

Taylor stepped out of the limousine and wanted to get right back in. The place was as hideous as he remembered. There was a sign looming over his head:

Princess Fatima, a full-blooded Bedouin from the fabled City of Nineveh, will dance the mystic anaconda dance exactly as danced by Hypatia in the Holy Writ.

Next to the sign was a fifteen-foot-high picture painted on canvas of a plump, scantily clad woman with a snake wrapped around her. This is what he went to college for? he thought. This is what he went to college to *escape*.

"Amanda, we can leave if this place offends you."

Amanda's eyes were wide in wonder as she looked about her at the skill booths, the rides, the exhibits, the food vendors. Everyone seemed to be yelling at once. "No, it's wonderful, isn't it?" She took his hand. "Oh, Taylor, thank you so much for bringing me. What shall we do first? Are you hungry? How about some popcorn? I used to eat that when I was a child. What do you think a corn dog is? Shall we find out?"

"Oh yes, please let's do," Taylor said, thinking he just might get sick. Did other men go through this for the women they loved? If so, it's a wonder anyone ever got married.

An hour later Taylor was sure he was going to be sick. He'd eaten popcorn, peanuts, a nasty thing called a corn dog and, feeling that he'd done his duty, he had politely refused the chocolate-covered caramels Amanda had offered him. He had even acted awestruck when a fat, dirty fortune-teller had looked at Amanda's palm and said, "You will dance with a queen and have a son who will become king."

Now she was looking longingly at a booth in which a vile-smelling young man in a red satin shirt was trying to get Taylor to throw a ball at wooden milk bottles in order to win a hideously ugly doll covered in pink and purple feathers.

"Amanda, what if a person were to *win?*" he asked, aghast.

"It's just for fun," she said.

"Come on, mister," the young man called. "Three

balls for a nickel. Ain't a lovely lady like this worth a mere nickel?" He looked Amanda up and down. *"I'd pay a nickel to win her."*

Amanda looked at Taylor with pleading eyes, and while he was trying to think of a reason why he couldn't participate in this ignorant, loutish game, they were shoved aside by another couple as if they weren't there.

Amanda's good mood left her when Dr. Montgomery and Reva stepped in front of them. She saw Hank slam the first ball into the milk bottles, all of them falling.

"Shall we go?" Amanda said to Taylor.

Hank turned around with a false surprised look on his face. "Well, Miss Caulden, fancy meeting you here. Driscoll," he said, nodding at Taylor.

"You gonna throw again, mister?" the barker asked, still eyeing Amanda.

Hank threw another ball and knocked more milk bottles down, then turned to Taylor. "Didn't they teach pitching where you went to school?"

"I think we should go," Amanda repeated to Taylor, but he didn't move.

Hank knocked down a third set of wooden bottles.

"Your choice," the barker said to Reva, motioning to the kewpie dolls hanging from the ceiling and walls of the booth.

Reva's face lit up as she pointed to a pink feathered doll.

Something primitive broke open inside Taylor, and he realized that it wasn't the vulgar prizes that were to be won that made men play this game but it was a man exhibiting his skill to win a woman. In the years since coming to the Caulden Ranch, Taylor had almost forgotten his past, all those years of struggling to put himself through school. One of his early jobs had been working at night in a carnival just like this one. He would take over for anyone who, for some reason or other, couldn't work that night. He'd worked in every booth, on every ride, in every fake exhibit.

He reached into his pocket and pulled out a nickel.

"Taylor," Amanda said, "you really don't have to do this. I have no desire to own one of those . . . those . . ."

"Kewpie dolls," Hank supplied. "Afraid he'll lose and embarrass you?" he asked softly.

"He hasn't lost anything to you yet," she answered, but she held her breath. She didn't really want Taylor to make a fool of himself.

Taylor knew the trick was that the bottom row of bottles were weighted heavily. When he'd worked for the carnival, he'd had to demonstrate to the audience that the bottles could be knocked down.

Easily, he knocked all three sets of bottles down, and Amanda, with a triumphant look at Hank, chose a purple-feathered doll.

"Shall we try the shooting gallery?" Taylor asked Hank. "Or do you use only brute force and not skill?"

"Try me," Hank said.

"I'm not sure—" Amanda began, but the two men stalked ahead of the women. Amanda gave Reva a weak smile and looked at the garish, fragile doll. "It is kind of cute, isn't it?"

"Which? Their idiocy or the doll?"

"Definitely the doll," Amanda answered.

The men went from one booth to another. Hank had to work harder, because he had no inside information on how to win the games, but he tried as if he were competing for his life. Taylor won at the booths that required skill and knowledge, but Hank beat him badly at the strength test. He made the bell ring, shoved a stuffed animal into Reva's full arms, then rang it a second time to win an animal for Amanda—but she refused to accept it.

By nine o'clock the women were weighted down with dolls, stuffed animals, plates, ugly little cups and saucers, and "surprise" packages. The two men prowled ahead of them like lions on the hunt.

When they'd covered every booth, the men turned and glared at each other.

"May we please take these things back to the car?" Amanda asked. "And if it's all the same with you, Taylor, I'd like to go home. I can feel a raging headache coming on."

Reva stood there, her arms full to brimming, and looked from one man to the other. She didn't think that Amanda had any real idea of what was going on, but Reva did. She was sure that Taylor had been winning prizes for her—not Amanda. She'd seen the way Taylor had glanced in her direction every time he won. He'd shoved the prize into Amanda's arms but it had been Reva he had looked at.

I think I may be in love with him, Reva thought with horror. He was completely wrong for her—he had no money at all—and she figured he'd never in his life marry someone like her, but right now she wanted to leave the carnival and be with him. Don't do it, she told herself. He needs money as much as you do, and he'll sell himself by marrying Amanda so he can get the Caulden Ranch. But before he married Amanda, she meant to have him.

Reva doubled over as if in pain, dropping most of the gaudy prizes.

"What's wrong?" Amanda asked, trying to free an arm to help Reva.

Taylor was there instantly, his arms supporting Reva.

"Just a stomachache. I think I better go home."

"Come on, then," Hank said reluctantly.

Reva groaned and clutched her stomach. "The ride in that little car of yours! I hope it doesn't make me sicker." She looked at Taylor, saw the interest in his eyes.

"I'll take her home," Taylor said. "She can stretch out in the back of my car."

"But I hate to ruin everyone's fun." Her eyes locked with Taylor's and she sensed that he understood her meaning.

Taylor straightened, and when he looked at Amanda he was her teacher once again. "Amanda, I am going to escort Miss Eiler to her home, but it is not necessary to ruin your evening. You may stay, and Dr. Montgomery, I'm sure, will drive you home." He didn't wait for an answer from either of them. "Here, Miss Eiler, let me carry those things for you. Good night, Amanda, and don't stay out too late." He started walking away with Reva beside him.

Amanda gritted her teeth. "I should have blackened *both* her eyes when I had a chance," she said angrily.

Hank was laughing. "What's the matter? Somebody steal your boyfriend?"

"Would you mind taking me home *now?* This minute?"

"How about a trip through the Tunnel of Love?"

"I'd as soon walk through a pit of snakes," she said and began walking ahead of him.

He caught her arm. "What's wrong with you? It looks to me like we have a splendid opportunity here. Reva has run off with your ice man boyfriend—what she wants with him, though, beats me—and here we are alone. You want to go somewhere private?"

"Not with you I don't."

He spun her about so that two animals and one plate went flying. "What's wrong with you? Last night you danced in my arms so close we were like lovers. We *have* been lovers. All I have to do is touch you and—"

"Right!" she hissed at him. "I'm no better to you than . . . than a paid woman, but when it comes time to defend *me,* you're a stranger. You may know about my body but you know nothing about *me.*"

"Amanda," he whispered, "we're drawing a crowd. Let's go somewhere quiet."

She started walking, him beside her. "Your room, perhaps?"

"What's eating you? What's made you so all-fired mad at me? Was it showing up here with Reva? Is it jealousy that's making you so mad?"

Amanda opened her arms and dropped all the prizes. "Men!" she gasped. "Do you think that every time a woman gets angry she's *jealous?* I don't care if you date Reva Eiler; I don't care if you date a hundred women. What I'm so mad about is what happened this afternoon. I may not know all the ways a union works and I may be naive about a lot of the ways of the world, but I'll be damned—yes, you heard me— *damned* if I'll let you or anyone else treat me like an empty-headed society girl. I had *never* participated in society until I met you. I happen to care about those people I've met at the Union Hall. I've defied my fiancé and embarrassed my family in order to help with something I've come to believe in, yet you and the rest of them treat me as if I have no conscience or no brain. Now, Dr. Montgomery, take your prizes and your fast little car and put them someplace not many people see. I will *walk* home."

She turned on her heel, nearly tripped over a stuffed duck, then kept walking.

Chapter Sixteen

Hank managed to get her into his car. It wasn't an easy task. He wasn't really sure what she was so angry about, but it seemed her feelings had been hurt today at work. Twice on the drive to her house he tried to talk to her, but she wouldn't speak to him. Maybe she was feeling rotten because she was finally realizing that she didn't love that emotionless Driscoll. It was good she was at last coming to her senses, but Hank saw no reason for her to take her anger out on *him*.

"Look out!" Amanda screamed.

Hank saw the two men standing in the road just when Amanda did. There was no way he could stop the car in time, so he swerved to the left to avoid hitting them. Even as he was pulling on the hand brake, he knew who the men were and what they wanted. "Stay in the car, Amanda," he said softly. "Whatever you do, stay in the car. And don't tell them who you are. I don't want the Caulden name mentioned in front of these men. Understand me?"

Amanda realized that something serious was happening and now was not the time for petty private quarrels. She nodded at Hank.

The men had started running as soon as they saw

Hank's car and they reached it just as he was getting out.

"Hello, Doc," the taller one said. He had prematurely white hair and bright blue eyes that the car headlamps showed to be glittering. "You know Andrei, don't you?"

Hank didn't smile. "Your last partner was killed down in San Diego, wasn't he? Whitey, we don't want you here."

"That's no way to talk to an old friend," Whitey Graham said.

"We're forming a union," Hank said, "and we want no bloodshed."

Whitey put his palms on the back of the Mercer and leaned toward Hank. "Violence is the only way to get the world to look at us and you know it. Nothing will happen unless we spill a little blood—and Caulden's will be first. I've heard of the way he treats his pickers. This year we'll get the bastard."

Hank held his breath and hoped desperately that Amanda would sit silently in the car and not let these men know who she was. These men were fanatics, dedicated to a cause, and the cause meant more to them than their freedom or their lives or the lives of anyone else for that matter. They meant to show the world what was wrong with it and they had decided that the only way to do that was by first getting the world's attention. They believed that Americans would overlook a thousand stories about the sad plight of the migrant worker but they would listen to stories of death and violence and bloodshed. Whitey Graham and one partner after another had traveled around America inciting different groups of migrant workers to rage against the treatment they were receiving. The rages had cost the loss of property and lives but they had forced reforms to be made. Whitey believed the solution was worth the cost.

"Caulden has the local sheriff in his pocket," Hank said. "He's a treacherous little man named Bulldog Ramsey and he'll break you in half with his bare hands."

"If he catches me," Whitey said. He glanced at Amanda. "I hear Caulden's daughter works for you."

"She does and she's a good worker. She's helped a lot in forming the pickers into a union."

"Forming them into a union." Whitey laughed. "They have to take care of their bellies and Caulden knows it. Caulden holds all the cards. He can treat the pickers like scum and they can't afford to do anything but take it." Whitey's eyes burned in the lamplight. "Someday we're going to take the power away from people like Caulden. Someday a union will speak for the workers. But before that happens we have to light some fires."

"Your fires burn people!" Hank half shouted. "Go back to where you came from, Whitey. The ULW has sent half a dozen organizers and I'm telling the pickers what a union is. We don't need you and your guns."

Again Whitey turned to look at the back of Amanda's head. She didn't look as if she'd moved a muscle since the car had stopped. "I hear Caulden's daughter is real pretty. As pretty as this lady?"

Hank snorted. "Caulden's daughter is as pretty as he is. All she needs is a cigar in her mouth and she could be his twin. This lady is Miss Janet Armstrong."

"Too bad," Whitey said. "I'll bet Caulden would do a lot to protect his daughter."

As Hank looked at the wild, glittering eyes of

Whitey, those eyes combined with the unnatural glow of his white hair, Hank felt chills along his spine. Amanda would be a prime target of their fanaticism. Kidnap her and they could blackmail Caulden into doing what they wanted. Kill her, Hank thought, and they would get the world to look at the problems of the migrant pickers.

"I can handle this, Whitey," Hank said, doing his best to keep the fear out of his voice. "Go back to where you came from."

Whitey stepped out of the circle of light made by the car headlamps. "Sure, Doc. I'll leave as soon as I see there're no problems. As soon as I see that my people are treated right, first by Caulden then by the other hop ranchers, I'll go home. I won't cause no problems." His voice began to fade as he moved farther away from the car. "And you say hello to that Miss Caulden for me. What's her name? Amy, is it? No, it's Amanda. You tell her Whitey Graham says hello to her." There were footsteps, then it was quiet.

Hank stood where he was, and in spite of the heat even at night, he felt cold. He didn't speak to Amanda as he started the car and got back into it. He went from being cold to sweating, so that by the time he reached the Caulden Ranch he was sweltering.

He stopped the car and turned to Amanda. "I don't want any argument from you, but tomorrow I want you to stay home. In fact, don't even go outside. Have Taylor give you some lessons and spend the day in your room."

Amanda didn't bother to answer his patronizing tone. "Do you think they mean to kill my father?" she whispered.

Hank just wanted her safe. He cursed himself for

allowing her to work at the Union Hall, for exposing her to what could be a violent situation. "Whitey isn't really sane. He believes himself to be on the side of the workers, but I think it's an excuse to justify violence. Last year in Chicago he beat up an eighty-year-old—" He stopped abruptly. He was so upset at Whitey's threats to Amanda that he wasn't thinking clearly. "I don't think he means to kill your father. More likely it will be innocent people who get killed, some man who has six kids to support. Whitey just wants blood to flow so the newspapers will write about it. It doesn't matter whose blood it is." He lowered his voice. "Not even yours, Amanda."

"Innocent people," Amanda said. "My father may not be killed, but 'innocent' people might. Does this imply that my father is guilty."

"Amanda, I don't want to get into this. Your father is out to make a profit any way he can. He doesn't care what he has to do to make a profit. I told you that he'd advertised in three states for his pickers. That's so thousands will show up. Maybe two thousand of them will agree to a union and will walk out of the fields if the conditions are intolerable, but there will be thousands more who are so hungry they'll work no matter what the conditions."

"My father isn't an inhumane man," Amanda said softly.

Maybe it was having been near Whitey's intense emotions, but Hank felt his own rising. "Your father shunned his own wife for years because before they were married she danced on a stage. He turned his only child over to a cold machine of a man who withheld food from her if she didn't obey his every whim. I wouldn't say Caulden is a man who is capable of putting himself in the place of others. Caulden decides what he wants and goes after it. It doesn't matter how many people get knocked down on his way to obtaining his goal. He wants profit from the hops and the hops have to be picked. I don't imagine he ever considered that those are *people* in his fields. They are profit-making machines to him."

"My father isn't like that," Amanda said. "You don't know him like I do." She remembered their meals together for the last few days. She refused to remember his words that he couldn't abide her. That was her fault, not his. She got out of the car, not waiting for Hank to offer his hand.

Hank jumped out of the car and ran after her. He stepped in front of her, his hands on her shoulders. "Amanda, whatever you feel about your father, that doesn't matter. What matters to me is your safety. I want you to promise me that you'll stay home tomorrow and not come to the Union Hall."

"What would you do if Reva were threatened?"

"Reva?" he asked. "What has she got to do with this? You still jealous of Reva and Taylor leaving the carnival together?"

Amanda walked away from him but he moved in front of her.

"I want your promise, Amanda."

"If Reva's life were threatened you'd probably think she was courageous enough to stand up to it. But me, I'm supposed to hide in my room because I'm just a silly little society girl, is that right?"

Hank gaped at her. No man could ever live long enough to understand women. "If Reva's life were threatened I'd want her to stay someplace safe too."

"But Reva's poor and I'm rich and that makes all the difference in the world."

Hank felt as if he'd just drunk a quart of whiskey and jumped on a merry-go-round. "The unionists want *you* because you're Caulden's daughter. Amanda, promise me you'll stay home tomorrow."

She walked past him. "Do not concern yourself with me, Dr. Montgomery, I can take care of myself. If not, I'm sure I can buy my way out of any situation." She hurried ahead into her house.

Hank stood outside, his fists clenched in anger. If he had to tie her to the bed in her room, he'd not let her expose herself to the fanatics' violence. He didn't understand just what she was so angry about but he wasn't going to let some little feminine snit of hers endanger her life. He went back to his car.

Amanda leaned against the front door of her house for a few moments. She knew she hadn't made any sense, but lately it seemed that her emotions were always ruling her brain. Those union men had scared her, scared her a great deal. The man named Whitey had a voice that quivered with emotion and it grated on Amanda like a metal file on her skin. The man talked of murder the way a person would speak of reading a book. Today when bloodshed in connection with the union was mentioned it had seemed like something remote and not possible. But this man Whitey made violence seem not only possible but likely.

If only there was something she could do!

Suddenly she stopped slumping against the door. All the talk of bloodshed was based on the assumption that her father was going to force the pickers to work under hideous conditions. If there was some way she could persuade the unionists that her father was not the monster they seemed to think he was, she could prevent violence before it started.

Even at this hour of the night her father was in the library. She had never before dared to disturb him, but lately she seemed to be doing many things she'd never dared before. She knocked on the library door, and when he told her to come in she slid the door open.

When he looked up at her, a scowl on his face, she was ready to turn and flee. J. Harker Caulden was not a man who liked surprises, and his daughter's unexpected appearance was obviously unwelcome. Amanda braced herself.

"Father, I would like to speak to you about an important matter," she said, trying to still her pounding heart.

"If it's about your marriage to Taylor—"

"No, it's not," she said quickly. Did all men think that women only concerned themselves with emotions like jealousy and romantic love? "I have been working with the unionists, and the people seem to think you're a . . . a tyrant and I would very much like to reassure them that you aren't. I want them to know that you do care about your fellow man."

J. Harker put down his pen, leaned back in his chair and studied her. Things were changing in his household and he didn't know what was causing the changes. Some of them he liked and some he didn't like at all. He liked his wife flirting with him and he liked his daughter showing a little spunk. But he didn't like her thinking she had the right to ask what he was doing when he ran his ranch. In the last few days Taylor had been giving him problems too. What did people like Amanda and Taylor know about running a ranch? They'd had their noses in books all their lives. Harker was beginning to doubt his wisdom in choosing Taylor as a son-in-law. Maybe he should find someone else for his daughter to marry.

But now Amanda stood before him looking like a scared rabbit who was putting on a brave little face and demanding to know how he was running his own ranch. He was tempted to tell her to get the hell out of his office, but then he thought he'd be wiser to use his daughter's connections to that unionist rabble. Perhaps he could help prevent any trouble. Not that it mattered much to him. Bulldog was deputizing half a dozen more men and they were going to be all over the fields during the picking. They'd stop any trouble before it started.

"Have they told you that all I care about is profit?" J. Harker asked.

"Why, yes."

"That I don't care about the people in the fields?"

Amanda was beginning to lose her feeling of terror. "Yes, they have."

"I do hope, Amanda, that you didn't believe them. That you didn't side against your own father."

"No, sir, I didn't. But I did want to hear the truth from you."

"I'm glad you came to me. It's time you learned a little about the ranch that supports you. You see, this isn't the first year I've had problems. For the last eleven years there have been rumblings of strikes and shootings and I've borne it all without ever defendin' myself. Everyone thinks I make an enormous profit on this ranch, but the truth is I barely pull through. Those union men only think of what I sell the hops for, they never consider the expense I have to put out. Amanda, it costs twenty-four dollars to grow a bale of hops and twenty dollars of that goes to pay unskilled labor. Hell, it cost nine thousand dollars a year just for the *string* to trellis the hops. Nobody ever thinks of string, do they? I guess they think I get it free somewhere. And then there's the cost of dryin' and shippin'. And this year it's been so dry I have two thirds the crop of last year. All these things add up." He stopped and stared at her.

"I'd like to pay these people twenty dollars a bale," Harker continued. "I know they're poor and I know they think I'm rich, but I pay them as much as I can. This year the price of hops is down so low that I'm havin' to cut corners everywhere—but I'm not cuttin' in wages, Amanda. I'm cuttin' everywhere else so I can still pay these poor workers top wages. For instance, every year I've let the Kingman store owners set up little satellite stores out in the fields. The workers spend their money with the Kingman merchants while I provide the land as well as the opportunity, but I don't mind—I share wherever I can. But this year I can't afford to be generous. Taylor's settin' up stores full of supplies I've bought. That way, through the stores, I'll be able to make a *little* profit, but I won't have to cut the wages of the poor worker."

Amanda was feeling jubilant. Her father wasn't a monster as everyone said. They just didn't understand. "If the union leaders came to you asking for things such as water delivered to the fields, you'd listen to their requests?"

J. Harker smiled at his daughter. "I've already arranged for *lemonade* to be delivered to the fields. And food. And glasses of cool well water."

"Oh," Amanda said, smiling. She felt as if her whole body were smiling. There'd be no need for the unionists to demand anything. The workers would know they had a right to protest but they wouldn't have anything to protest against. Who could get angry at a man who had lemonade delivered to the fields? "Thank you," she said, smiling. "I shall tell the unionists." She started backing toward the door. "Goodnight, Father," she said and left the room.

She went up the stairs as if her feet weren't touching ground. Everything was settled. There would be no violence. Actually, there would not even be a need for a union. If every employer were like her father and delivered lemonade to the fields, the workers would have no need to form a union.

Amanda undressed and went to bed still smiling. Tomorrow she'd be able to tell that smug Dr. Montgomery that he could eat his words. And wouldn't that awful man Whitey be disappointed? It wouldn't do any good to draw the newspapers' attention to a man who paid his workers top wages and delivered food and lemonade to them in the fields. And there would be no need to fear going to the Union Hall tomorrow. She was safe, made safe by her father, who was, in spite of what others said, a good man.

She went to sleep, never once giving a thought to Taylor. Nor did she wake when, at three A.M., he came creeping up the stairs, his shoes in his hand.

"Lemonade!" Hank yelled at her. "You risked your life by coming in here today because of *lemonade?*"

As soon as she'd walked into the Union Hall, Hank had grabbed her arm and pulled her into the cleaning closet. Now he stood glaring down at her, his eyes on fire with rage, cords in his neck standing out from the force of his shouting.

"Why bother to try for privacy?" she said coolly. "When you shout like that everyone can hear you."

"I don't give a good goddamn who hears me. Just where do you think you're going?"

Amanda was trying to open the closet door but he'd locked it. "I won't stay here and listen to such language."

He grabbed her shoulders and turned her to face him. "What your father said to you was worse than any language I know. He lied to you, Amanda. Out and out lied. If he were good to his workers there wouldn't be any need for us to be here."

"That is what I have been trying to tell you. There isn't going to be any violence. You can tell your friend, that awful man Whitey, to go home. He can find some other rancher to harass."

Hank dropped his hands and his face changed. "Do you really believe that, Amanda?" he asked softly. "Do you really see us as the villains? Do you think the governor sent me here for no reason? Do you believe we are just out to cause an innocent, loving man like your father problems?"

"I think you have misjudged *him*. I'm not saying other ranchers aren't persecuting their workers, but my father is a good man. He does the best he can. He has enormous expenses, and no one takes those expenses into account. He—" She broke off when Hank pushed past her and unlocked the door.

He held the door open. "Go home, Miss Caulden," he said tiredly. "This is no place for you. You are merely a recording device and nothing more. If I wanted to hear Caulden's platitudes, I'd have asked him. Now go home and stay hidden inside until the hops are picked and what's going to happen has happened."

Amanda walked past him into the hall. "You have made up your mind and I can't change it," she said stiffly. "But you will see. I just hope you're man enough to admit when you're wrong. Good day, Dr. Montgomery." She turned away from him and left the Union Hall.

On the drive back to the Caulden Ranch, her anger rose to the boiling point. The union organizers wanted to believe something was wrong, wanted to sing their union songs, wanted to believe they were the equivalent of slaves building a pyramid for a power-mad pharaoh. Today the picking started and by tomorrow they would have had time to see that at the Caulden Ranch human beings were treated as such.

She smiled to herself as she thought of how Dr. Montgomery would react. Would he be disappointed when there was no reason for his union? He wanted to present a petition for water to be delivered to the fields. She'd like to see his face when he found water, food and cool, delicious lemonade was being handed out to the workers. Perhaps she'd ask her father if she could distribute the lemonade. She had a vision of offering Dr. Montgomery a tall, frosty glass and smiling at him graciously. She doubted very much that he would admit he was wrong.

She left the limousine to go into the house, and the first person she encountered was Taylor. His eyes looked a little tired but he compensated for it by holding his spine especially rigid.

"Amanda," he said sternly, "I was just coming to get you. Your job at that place is now ended. The picking began today, and I see no reason for you to further expose yourself to those people."

"They are not 'those people'; they are human beings. If you do not have the courtesy to think of them as such, at least my father does."

"I will not be spoken to in such a manner, Amanda."

Amanda started to contradict him but she closed her mouth. In a few more days Dr. Montgomery would go home, defeated, and she would be left here alone with Taylor. She had better do what she could to placate him. "I apologize. It's the heat. It makes me on edge. I have already quit my job and I won't be returning."

"Good," he said quickly. "Now I think you'd better stay in your room until this is over. You've been involved more than enough."

"Of course," she murmured and started for the stairs, but she paused and turned back. "Taylor, I wonder if it might be possible for me to go to the fields and help. I would like to distribute the lemonade, perhaps."

Taylor's eyes widened. "Distribute the—" He calmed himself. "The men will be in the fields and I do not believe it's a place for a lady."

"But I worked with those men at the Union Hall."

"Amanda! Do not defy me. I cannot allow you to go into the fields. You would be horribly in the way. Do you want to cause everyone more work?"

"No," she said and realized her hand was tightly clutching the banister. It didn't seem that she was needed anywhere. They didn't need her at the Union Hall and they didn't need her in the fields.

"I have written out a schedule for you and put it on

your desk. I cannot stay to test you as I am needed in the fields. And, Amanda, when the hops are in, you and I are going to talk about your dismissal of Mrs. Gunston. I could not persuade her to remain." He stood there and watched as she climbed the stairs.

Once inside her room, Amanda realized that her jubilant mood was gone. She held up the new schedule and remembered Taylor telling her there would be no more schedules. She also remembered his talking about their being lovers. But the Taylor who she had just seen was as formal and cold as she had ever seen him.

She tossed the schedule, unread, on the desk and flopped across her bed. It was so hot and she felt so restless. She tried to recapture her good mood by imagining Dr. Montgomery when he realized how wrong he had been, but she couldn't quite conjure the vision.

She stood, looked at the schedule, saw she was to translate *Caesar's Campaigns* from Latin and groaned. Out the window she could see her mother sprawled on a lounge chair under the shade of a tree, reading and eating what looked to be chocolates. Amanda grabbed her writing materials, her Latin book and went to join her mother.

She spent a very pleasant afternoon lazing about in the shade in the company of her mother. Her mother gave her a fascinating novel written by a woman named the Countess de la Glace. It was all about romance and passion and a woman suffering over the love of a man who wasn't worth suffering over. Amanda read it avidly and put away a pound and a half of chocolates.

The next day her father and Taylor were too busy to

notice that she wasn't where she was supposed to be, doing what she'd been told to do, so she spent more time with her mother. Amanda, feeling that she was greatly daring, asked her mother about the time she'd danced on stage. Grace talked for hours, and Amanda began to realize that what her mother had done sounded more like hard work than sinful.

"But you had courage," Amanda said. "I wish I had courage."

"I think perhaps you do," Grace answered. "You just haven't found what you need courage for."

"You mean like Ariadne?" Amanda asked, motioning toward the Countess de la Glace's novel. "To decide I love a man and fight for him?"

"Who *do* you love, Amanda?"

"Taylor, of course," Amanda answered quickly, but her face turned red. Her time with Dr. Montgomery had been an experiment, nothing more. But part of her imagined how he'd act when he found out he was wrong about the workers on the Caulden Ranch. Would he be so contrite that he'd propose marriage? "I was wrong, Amanda, my darling," she imagined him saying. "I want to spend the rest of my life with a woman as wise as you are." She loved the idea of his admitting that she wasn't stupid—the way he always made her feel. But did she love *him?* Would she marry him? Leave Taylor and the parents she loved to travel about the world in his little yellow car?

"Amanda," Grace said, interrupting her daughter's daydreaming, "is that possibly your Dr. Montgomery?"

Amanda turned to look. It was he, coming from the direction of the fields. This was it, she thought. He was coming to apologize and to . . . Dare she hope for more?

"Amanda," Grace said, and there was concern in her voice, "I don't know Dr. Montgomery personally, but it's my guess from the way he's walking that he's angry."

Amanda smiled. "Angry at himself, perhaps. I think he's found out his coming here was useless. He's a very proud man and I'm sure he'll hate admitting he was wrong."

Amanda stood and smoothed her skirt. "I hope you won't mind if I invite him to tea. I think I'll order lemonade. It's a little joke we share."

"Whatever you say, dear, but Dr. Montgomery looks to me to be—"

"There you are!" Hank yelled when he was several feet away. He was in shirt sleeves and he was so soaked with sweat he looked as if he'd been caught in a rainstorm. "I told you to stay inside for safety's sake but here you are for anyone to see. You believe anyone who lies to you but you can't believe me when I tell you the truth."

Amanda blushed crimson and refused to look down at her mother. She opened her mouth to reply but Hank's hand clamped down on her forearm and started pulling her. "Stop it!" she managed to say. "This is my mother and—"

"How do you do, Mrs. Caulden. Amanda is coming with me. I am going to show her how her father treats the people who work for him."

"By all means, do," Grace said, looking at this man with interest. No one had told her Dr. Montgomery was such a handsome, virile young man.

"I do not want to go with you," Amanda said.

"You go on your feet or bottom end up." His eyes were blazing and he hadn't shaved in days. He looked almost frightening.

"I will not—"

Hank bent, put his shoulder to her stomach and heaved her over his shoulder.

"Release me!" Amanda yelled, beating his back with her fists.

Hank slapped her behind. "I'm too tired to be beaten."

"Mother, help me!" Amanda cried.

"Cookie, Dr. Montgomery?" Grace Caulden asked, holding out the plate.

"Thanks," he said, took a handful, then turned on his heel and left.

Grace went back to reading, and it was hours before she stopped smiling.

"Put me down," Amanda said.

Hank set her to the ground then grabbed her forearm and began pulling her behind him. "I want you to see something," he said.

"I was told not to go to the fields."

He stopped and turned on her. "You still won't think for yourself, will you, Amanda? You believe what everyone tells you, no questions asked. How your father has treated the pickers in the past years has been so bad people are talking of murder in order to make it stop, but that doesn't affect you. Caulden spends five minutes telling you he's a good man and you believe him over hundreds of other people."

"But he's my father, he—"

"You can't make a person good because you *want* to believe it. You can't will it to happen." He turned and started pulling her again. "I want you to see why unions are being formed."

Amanda was as angry as he was now and thought she'd love to see him drive off a cliff in his little yellow automobile. Her anger kept her from at first realizing what was before her.

She smelled the place first. It didn't take a breeze to bring the smell to her. It was a hundred and five degrees and the humidity was high as they got closer to the irrigated fields. Suddenly she knew she didn't want to see what lay ahead in the tented city on the horizon. "Wait," she said, jerking back and halting. "I don't want to go."

"Neither do I. I want to take a bath and maybe get ready to go to a dance tonight, but they can't and I can't and *you* can't." He began pulling her again.

On the east end of the hop fields was an enormous flat meadow that was now covered with tents and crude little shelters. There were also piles of filthy straw here and there. Garbage was everywhere: bones, rotting meat, horse manure. The flies were thick, and Amanda saw the skinned head of a sheep at the door of one tent, maggots crawling over it.

Hank had her arm firmly in his hand. "Your father rents the tents for seventy-five cents a day. Considering that a grown man works all day in this sun and this humidity and makes about ninety cents, that's a little steep, wouldn't you say? The ones who can't afford the tents buy straw and live on it. There is no provision for garbage."

He pulled her down the road to the center of the stench, and for a moment Amanda could only stare. Here were the outdoor toilets. There was a line of fifteen to twenty people waiting before each toilet, and as Amanda watched, one pregnant woman in the back of a line stepped aside and vomited. Amanda's own stomach turned over and she was still yards from the toilet.

"Your father has provided nine toilets for two thousand eight hundred people," Hank said. "Each one's a two-holer. The men and women share the toilets—they're only laborers, so who cares about privacy? They're just animals. Yesterday the pickers tried keeping the grounds clean by disposing of their garbage in the toilets, but the holes are only two feet deep. They were full by last night. Caulden doesn't provide any cleaning. Would you like to go inside one, Amanda? There's excrement on the floor an inch deep. As you can see, the smell makes the people sick. Stay here long enough and you'll get to see someone soil his pants or her skirt. The filth is giving everyone dysentery."

Amanda's defiance was leaving her. She had never seen anything like this, never imagined anything like this. Hank didn't have to pull her when they walked away. He stopped by a well pump.

"There are two wells for all the workers, but they're pumped dry by sunup, and the next closest well is a mile away. They don't get much rest as it is, but they lose what little they have by going for water."

He began walking toward the fields, his hand still clutching her forearm. He led her to the hop fields. On one side the workers had pulled down the tall, steeple-like trellis that supported the hop vines and on the other side the trellis was still up. The field was covered with men, women and children hurriedly pulling down the vines and stuffing them into bags. It was unbearably hot here and the heat waves shimmered in the humidity.

"Would you like to work in that heat, Amanda? A man died from the heat yesterday. So far four kids have been taken out on stretchers. There're no toilets out here, so the pickers can either not go all day or take the hour or so to walk back to the camp and wait in line for the toilet. And do they drag their one-hundred-pound bag of hops with them or leave it and let someone steal it? They go there," Hank said, pointing to the unpicked rows. "Of course that means that when they reach that part of the field they have to pick while walking in human excrement."

Amanda could say nothing. She could barely stand up in the intolerable heat. She made no resistance when Hank began pulling her again. He led her to a wagon, took money from his pocket and handed it to the man standing at the back of the wagon. "How about a cool glass of lemonade, Amanda?" he asked and handed her a filthy glass with a hot liquid in it.

She didn't dare refuse him. She took a sip, then grimaced. With great difficulty she swallowed the awful-tasting drink.

"Citric acid," Hank said. "Lemons cost more. With citric acid your father can make gallons for pennies, sell it for five cents a glass and make hundreds of dollars of profit." He took the glass from her and offered it to a sweaty, tired-looking little girl of about eight years. The child drank it greedily and looked at Hank with adoring eyes before turning back toward the fields.

"Your father sells food too, and the only water they get is one glass for one bowl of stew. You want a second glass you have to buy another bowl of stew.

You can't buy the water by itself—and Caulden sure as hell doesn't give away the water for free."

He began pulling her again, but this time Amanda walked beside him. He didn't have to hold her to him. She had to see all of it, had to see part of the world she had never known existed. She had sat in her room year after year while the hops were picked and had never even wondered about the people picking them.

Hank led her to the weigh station but they couldn't get close because everywhere were men and women frantically dumping their heavy canvas bags full of hops on the ground and stripping the vines and leaves off. There was pain and anguish written on the faces of the people, as if they were fighting for their lives.

"It takes a man many hours to pick a one-hundred-pound bag of hops, and then he drags his bag to be weighed and have it credited to his name, but your father has set up inspectors to tell the pickers the hops aren't 'clean' enough. So the pickers have to waste precious hours pulling off vines and string and tossing out unripe hops. Usually a man can pick two hundred fifty to four hundred pounds a day, but your father has it so a man can only get a hundred pounds a day. He works all day in this sun, no water, no toilet, and he earns from ninety cents to a dollar ten."

He turned to face her. "You know why your father demands such clean hops? Two reasons: one, he doesn't have to pay for the weight of a few leaves and string, but, most important, the second reason is because he *wants* the worker to quit. Your father is awfully clever, Amanda. I wonder if you got your brains from him. He came up with an ingenious way to cheat these people. The going rate across the country for hop picking is a dollar a hundred pounds.

Your father, in his ads, promised top wages and a
'bonus.' His wages are ninety cents a hundred-pound
bale and a ten-cent bonus for every bale picked. This
'bonus' is to be paid to the people who stay the whole
harvest time. If a worker quits before all the hops are
in, he loses his 'bonus.' Already a thousand Japanese
have left. They wouldn't work in this filth. For every
person who quits, your father gains ten cents on a
hundred pounds. Multiply ten cents by thousands of
bales by thousands of people. What you'll get is one
hell of a lot of cigars for Caulden and"—he looked her
up and down—"one hell of a lot of silk dresses for
you, Amanda."

Hank's fury was spent now and his shoulders
slumped. "You can go home now, Amanda. Go home
and sit under a tree with your pretty mother and enjoy
what your father provides for you."

"Wh-what is going to happen here?" she managed
to say. Her voice was hoarse. The horror of what she
was seeing was just seeping into her.

"I don't know. This is worse than I was led to
believe. Whitey has been doing a lot of talking. The
workers are terrified of losing their jobs, but seeing
your six-year-old kid pass out in the heat does something to you. And as hard as these people are working,
what with the wages so low and the food and water so
expensive, they're spending what they're making.
Some of them are already in debt to your father.
Tempers are beginning to boil. I think they'll go to
your father soon."

"He won't listen," Amanda said, watching a little
girl pull vines off hops. She was about three years old,
and the seat of her pants, showing under her dirty
dress, was soiled. Amanda didn't feel like defending

her father. The man who could allow something like this year after year couldn't be defended.

Hank lifted one eyebrow at her. "No, he won't listen, but I'm going to try to persuade him. I worry what will happen if some changes aren't made."

"You?" Amanda said. "But this morning I saw Sheriff Ramsey come to our house. Sheriff Ramsey will . . ." She trailed off.

"Shoot first," Hank said. "I'm aware of that. I want you to go back now, Amanda. I don't want Whitey to know who you are. Stay in your room. Better yet, why don't you and your mother go to San Francisco for a few days?"

Amanda could only look at him. Coward, she thought, I have always been a coward. At fourteen I was afraid to stand up to Taylor, and at twenty-two I'm afraid to stand up to my father. She turned away from him and started back toward the ranch house. Maybe she could make up for lost time.

Hank watched her go. It wasn't her fault, he knew that, but he'd wanted her to see what he was fighting. He made a little prayer that she'd take his advice and go away somewhere. But he didn't have time to worry about Amanda. He had to find Whitey and see what that fanatic was planning. These people were just hot enough and angry enough that it wouldn't take much to push them over the edge.

Chapter Seventeen

The door to the library was open, but it wouldn't have mattered to Amanda if it were closed. She walked into the room. Her father sat at the desk, papers before him, Taylor bent over him.

Taylor straightened and frowned at her. "Amanda, you are supposed to be in your room. I told you—"

Amanda looked only at her father. "There is going to be violence if you don't change what is happening in the fields."

J. Harker looked at her, his only movement his mouth working on his cigar.

"Amanda, you are not to speak of things you know nothing about," Taylor said. "You are to go to your room this instant and—"

"Shut up, Taylor," Amanda said. "This is family." Her father leaned back in his chair and Amanda met his gaze equally. The smells of the toilets and the rotting garbage were still in her nostrils. "The union leaders are talking about bloodshed, and your blood is whose they want to see first."

"Amanda," Taylor said, recovering from his shock, "you cannot—"

She turned to look at him. "Sit!" she ordered, as if

he were a pesky little dog. She glared at him until he obeyed her, then she went to her father's desk, put her hands on it and leaned forward. "You've got away with your thievery for years now, but this year is different. I think the pickers could put up with the filth and the lack of water, but they won't put up with the way you're cheating them of their money. If you don't start paying, they're going to start shooting." She looked at her father and their eyes were alike, both angry and stubborn.

"Amanda, I—" Taylor began.

Amanda glanced at him. "You keep quiet or you leave." She looked back at her father. "Well?"

J. Harker gave a snort of derision. "I have fifteen men working for me in the fields. They tell me what's going on, and if they can't reach me to ask permission, they carry guns and they know how to use them. Bull has more men posted around the area. Let them talk all they want, but the blood spilled will be theirs, not mine."

Amanda stood back. She had no intention of asking why he had so little humanity and she could see it was no use trying to persuade him. She would have liked to threaten him. But she knew of nothing that mattered to him except the ranch. If she threatened to leave home if he didn't clean up the camp, it would mean nothing to him. Hank had been correct: a man who could shun his wife and exile his daughter was capable of anything.

J. Harker's eyes looked triumphant.

"Winning is everything to you, isn't it?" Amanda said. "No matter who gets in your way, who you have to step on to get there, you have to win. You're not going to win this one. You may starve a few poor, uneducated migrant workers today, but tomorrow you'll lose. Your day is over." She turned on her heel and left the room. She couldn't bear to be near the man any longer.

Taylor caught her on the stairs. "Amanda," he said softly, "I didn't mean—"

"Yes you did," she said, glaring at him. "You meant every degrading, humiliating thing you've ever done to me. For years you've tried to make yourself just like my father. He has thousands of helpless pickers to tyrannize while you had only one isolated, lonely girl who was eager to please. Well, Taylor, just like those workers are fed up, so am I."

"But, Amanda, I love you."

"No you don't. You don't even know me. You love a wooden doll you've carved into what you think a female should look like. When you want me, you pull me out of my room; when you have no more need of me, you send me back to my room with a little list to keep me busy." She didn't want to waste more time talking to him but continued up the stairs.

"Amanda," he said, moving in front of her, "what are you going to do? I mean, our engagement is—"

"Off," she said, then halted and gave him a look of great patience. "First I am going to do what I can to help the pickers. I will . . ." She paused, searching for an idea of what she could do. "I am going to make them lemonade—free lemonade. And when the hops are picked I'm going away."

"With him?" Taylor shot at her. "I'm not as blind as you seem to think."

She looked at Taylor as if she'd never seen him before. "You may not be blind, but I have been. If Hank will have me, yes, I'll go away with him, but it's not likely he'll want me. Now, will you please move out of my way? There are people fainting from the heat even while we stand here arguing about inconsequential matters." She moved past him.

"Inconsequential!" he half shouted up at her. "My whole future is being decided by the whim of a woman lusting after some two-bit—"

Amanda whirled to face him. "You'll get the ranch, I'm sure of it. Where else is my father going to find a mirror image of himself? Neither of you men need me. But let me give you some advice, Taylor. You ought to leave here. You ought to leave today. Now. You should go get Reva and keep going and never look back. Reva will be good for you. She's just loose enough to counteract that piece of steel you call a spine. Now, I must go, and to tell you the truth, Taylor, I don't really care what you do."

She hurried up to her room, tore off her heavy silk dress and put on the lightest-weight white blouse and dark cotton skirt she owned. When she was dressed, she pulled clothing from drawers and her closet. She had no suitcase, so she went to her father's bedroom and pulled his from the top of the closet. She stuffed her clothes into the case and went downstairs. She didn't look at the house, for there was no feeling of sadness at leaving it. There was only a feeling that there was freedom outside the door.

She set her suitcase down in the butler's pantry and went to the kitchen, where she borrowed a tall, lever-handled juice extractor from the cook and called the grocery in Kingman and ordered a truckload of lemons. "Then send to Terrill City for them," she said into the telephone.

She went outside, the suitcase in one hand, the

juicer in the other when she stopped. She needed to say goodbye to her mother.

Amanda stood beside her mother's chair under the tree for a moment, and everything that had happened came back to her. She felt overwhelming anger at herself. Why had she allowed Taylor to deny her mother? Why had she followed Taylor so blindly?

Grace looked up at her daughter.

"Mother, I—" There were tears in Amanda's eyes.

"Planning to leave?" Grace asked, nodding at the suitcase.

"I have been a terrible person to you, and I—"

Grace interrupted her daughter. "Mind if I run away with you? And what's that for? It's not a cudgel for someone's head, is it?"

Amanda held the juicer up. "Father promised the workers lemonade and I'm going to give it to them. I figure it will be a day or so before he gets the bill for the lemons and stops delivery."

"And the suitcase? Does that have to do with the pickers or one very handsome economics professor?"

"I . . ." Amanda knew she'd been so brave for the last few hours, but her newly found courage was leaving her. She fell to her knees and put her head in her mother's lap. "It was so awful," she cried. "Those poor people are fainting from thirst because Father charges them for water, and I feel like such a fool. I have spent years in my room and—"

"Hush, Amanda," Grace said sternly. "Lashing yourself isn't going to help at all. You were a sweet little girl who wanted to please her father. Now dry your eyes and let's get to work. It's almost sundown, so the pickers will stop for the day, and the lemons will never get here before tomorrow morning. You wait here while I pack a few things, then we'll spend the night at the Kingman Arms and tomorrow we'll make lemonade. Now dry your eyes so you'll look pretty for your professor."

"But, Mother, you can't leave Father just because I'm leaving."

"What's here for me? Your father and I haven't had anything between us since he punished me for what he saw as a betrayal by taking you away from me. I have just been waiting until you either married Taylor or came to your senses. I couldn't leave before; we couldn't *all* desert you. But now I can leave." She stood. "Stay here and I'll be back as soon as possible."

Amanda sat on a chair, her hands clasped in her lap. "If Hank will have me," she'd said. It wasn't difficult to see that she'd loved him for a long time. With a grimace, she thought that if nothing else about her was strong her willpower was. She'd willed herself to love Taylor, and in spite of his bullying her, in spite of his patronizing kisses and his punishments, she'd remained loyal to him. Yet Hank had shown he cared about her, had treated her as a person, but she'd willed herself to despise him. She'd almost willed herself into a miserable life that she would surely have had with Taylor.

Her first concern was the pickers, but when they were gone she'd go to Hank and beg his forgiveness on bended knee if she had to.

Her attention was taken off herself as, through the trees, she saw about ten men approaching the front of the house. At the head of the group was the man with the distinctive hair, Whitey Graham.

Amanda was on her feet instantly. This was no doubt the presentation of the grievances that Hank had said he was going to give to her father. She began running and reached the house just as Taylor, J. Harker and two of Bulldog Ramsey's deputies came out to stand on the porch. Amanda stood in the deep shade to one side. She didn't feel that she fit completely with either side.

"We have a list of grievances," Whitey said. "We ain't happy about things in the fields."

Harker didn't give any indication that he heard the man. He just glared, his eyes like coals.

Whitey stepped up on the porch so he was an equal height level with Harker. Taylor started to protest this insolence, but Harker pushed him aside.

"Say what you came to say," Harker grunted.

Whitey read a list of seven complaints that included a need for field toilets, camp toilets, drinking water delivered to the fields, pickers appointed as inspectors, lemonade made with lemons and, finally, one dollar and twenty-five cents paid for one hundred pounds picked, with no bonus.

Everyone held his breath as Harker made up his mind.

Please, Amanda prayed, please agree to this.

Harker at last spoke and he agreed to more toilets, water delivered three times a day, real lemonade, and even to pay two dollars and fifty cents a day to inspectors chosen by the pickers. But he refused to raise the wages.

It was Whitey's turn to be stubborn. "You have just dug your own grave," he said quietly.

Harker smacked Whitey across the face with the back of his hand. "Get off of my land."

In the next moment all hell broke loose. One of the deputies lunged at Whitey. Whitey ran down the steps, while the nine men with him didn't seem to know whether to run or fight. The second deputy yelled that Whitey was under arrest, to which Whitey said there was no warrant for his arrest. With that, Whitey and his men ran from the property.

Amanda leaned back against the porch railing. It was done now. The ball had started rolling down the hill. No humans could stand the conditions in the fields for very long without exploding.

Suddenly, Amanda stood bolt upright. Where was Hank? He said he was going to present grievances but he hadn't even been among the presenters. Did he decide to keep out of it? Had he at last come to his senses and realized it wasn't his fight?

She almost laughed at the idea. Hank Montgomery didn't have a cowardly bone in his body. He'd single-handedly taken on J. Harker Caulden, a man who terrified his own family yet Hank had always stood up to him. Hank dealt with crazy men like Whitey Graham. Hank set up a Union Hall in the middle of Kingman, California, and when the citizens had painted GET OUT OF TOWN on the building, Hank had just shrugged and had Joe paint over it.

No, the cause of Hank Montgomery's absence from the grievance committee wasn't cowardliness or disinterest. So what had made him stay away? Something awful must have happened in the fields.

Without another thought, she started walking rapidly toward the fields. Her mother caught her arm before she was out of the cool, shady garden.

"Decide to leave me behind after all?" Grace asked, trying to sound lighthearted, but her voice betrayed her concern.

"The union men gave Father an ultimatum," Amanda said.

Grace groaned. "I can imagine how well your father took that."

"He slapped the presenter, but, Mother, Hank wasn't with them."

Grace frowned, seeing her daughter's fear. "I don't understand. Do you think Dr. Montgomery could have done a better job of the presentation?"

"Hank said *he* was going to present the paper. But he didn't do it. Mother, there is something awfully wrong. I know it. I'm going to look for Hank."

Grace Caulden set down the suitcase she was holding. "Then let's go. We'll find him."

"The fields are awful," Amanda said, her eyes searching her mother's. "The people are—"

Grace took her daughter's hand. "It's time we did something, don't you think? It's time we both stopped hiding in our rooms."

"Yes," Amanda said and they started walking.

They searched for two hours. They walked around every tent, every squalid little hovel, stepped over unspeakable piles of stinking garbage, endured much abuse and lewd remarks. They asked everyone, used every language Amanda knew. They communicated with hand gestures. They asked any way they could, but no one had seen Dr. Montgomery for hours.

Whitey Graham blocked their path when they'd started on their third hour of searching. "You two are Cauldens?" His eyes gleamed in the growing darkness. "Feelings are running pretty high against the Cauldens right now. You two better get out of here."

"I want to know where Dr. Montgomery is," Amanda said, swallowing her fear of this man.

Whitey grinned. "Went off hours ago with a pretty lady. Haven't seen him since. Maybe he's . . ." He trailed off, letting his face make his bawdy suggestions.

Amanda hid her clenched fists in the folds of her skirt. "I'm going to get him. I'll drag him . . . out of bed if I have to, and then he's going to talk to my father. You'll get your wage increase. Hank will find a way to persuade my father."

Whitey smiled in a mean way. "You sure seem to think the professor's powerful. Personally, I don't think there's anything anyone can do to make Caulden listen, except maybe a few shots fired into somebody."

Amanda swallowed and hoped her face didn't betray her terror. "I'll get him. Hank knows how to talk. If anyone can talk to my father, he can."

"It may be too late for talk." He was looking her up and down in an insolent way.

Amanda turned away from him and started walking toward the road to Kingman.

Grace hurried to keep up with her daughter. "What an awful man. He makes my skin crawl. Dear, where are you hurrying off to?"

"Reva Eiler's house," she said bitterly.

"You think your Dr. Montgomery is with her?"

"Yes I do. He seems to need lots of women around him."

Grace was tripping over clumps of grass, her heels were snagging, her skirt kept getting caught, and her little hat was down over one eye as she rushed to keep up with her daughter. "I've only seen you with him once, dear, but it was my impression that he was quite mad for you."

Amanda hesitated, then resumed her pace. "He looks at all women like that."

"No man has enough energy to be that intense about *two* women."

"Hank has lots of energy," Amanda said over her shoulder. "Massive amounts of energy. Long-lasting, enduring, incredible energy."

Grace stopped, eyes wide, and looked at the back of her daughter. "How very fortunate for the woman he loves," she murmured and hurried forward.

Amanda climbed over the fence at the edge of the field then helped her mother over.

"Are we planning to walk all the way into town?" Grace asked, flexing her aching ankles. She thought she had the beginnings of a blister on her left little toe.

"We are going to hitch a ride."

Grace turned away so Amanda wouldn't see her horror. For years she had prayed that her daughter would someday break out of Taylor's rule, but to go from being a meek little lamb to thumbing rides was more than she wanted.

The first car that came down the road stopped for them, but it was heading out of town. Handsome young Sam Ryan leaned out the window and smiled at Amanda.

"So, we meet again," he said softly.

Amanda narrowed her eyes at him. "Sam, I want you to turn this car around and take my mother and me to Reva Eiler's house."

Sam drew back into the car. "Sorry, but I can't." He looked as if he'd just noticed Grace. "I have to run an errand for my father."

"If you don't take me to Reva's house this instant,

I'll go to your parents and tell them what you did to me the night of the dance. I still have that torn dress."

Sam grimaced. "All right, get in, but I'm not waitin' for you at Reva's house."

"No one asked you to," Amanda snapped.

Amanda didn't say a word on the way to Reva's house. She didn't even answer her mother when Grace whispered, "What did Sam do to you at the dance?" Amanda was too busy raging inside at Hank Montgomery. Here she'd been thinking she loved him and thinking what a noble person he was to try to help the poor, defenseless workers, when he was out lollygagging with Reva Eiler. And Amanda had told Taylor to go after Reva! What a fool she was about men—and women, for that matter. Reva had flirted with Hank at the Union Hall and conned Taylor into taking her home from the carnival.

Amanda began to imagine the terrible things she'd do to both Reva and Hank when she found them together.

"Here we are," Sam said sullenly, "and this makes us even. Dad'll have my head when I'm late."

"You deserve it," Amanda said, shutting the car door. "You shouldn't take advantage of defenseless women."

"You weren't exactly defenseless with that professor around. He knocked one of my back teeth loose."

Amanda smiled at him. "Maybe you'll remember next time."

Sam grimaced and drove away.

"Amanda dear," Grace said, "you and I are going to have to have a long talk after this is settled."

Amanda didn't answer but went to Reva's door and

knocked. It was a filthy little house, with a broken swing outside, rusted tin cans in a pile by a fence with missing boards. Hollyhocks that looked as if they were fighting for life grew from something that looked like a truck fender. A pane of glass from the front window was missing and newspaper had been taped over it.

At her second knock, Amanda heard shuffling footsteps inside.

"What'd'ya want?" a man's voice yelled.

"It's Amanda Caulden, Mr. Eiler. I want to see Reva," Amanda yelled back. "If she's here," she said under her breath.

"She's asleep," Mr. Eiler yelled.

"With whom?" Amanda muttered. "I really do need to see her," she yelled through the door.

A hand angrily tore the newspaper from the broken pane of glass. The rest of the window was so dirty it may as well not have been glass. Reva's face appeared at the window. "I am here, Miss Know-It-All Caulden," Reva said, "and I'm alone in my bed, not that it's any of your business. What brings you to this part of town? Need somebody to clean your toilet?"

"Where is Hank?" Amanda asked.

"Not with me."

Amanda glared at her. "Then when did he leave? I assume it was his visit that has exhausted you into an early retirement."

"It happens to be nearly ten o'clock. Some of us have to get up and go to work in the morning. Not all of us can be princesses like—"

"Just a minute!" Grace said, stepping forward. "Before you two young *ladies*"—she emphasized the word—"start pulling hair, I think we should find out

326

what we came here to find out. Reva, Dr. Montgomery seems to have disappeared, and we were told he might be with another woman and we assumed it was you."

"He hasn't been here. He's been out at the fields all day. I saw him for a few minutes yesterday and he was pretty upset. He said it was awful out there and for me to stay away."

"Do you have any idea where he could be?" Grace asked.

"Maybe he went back to his hotel and went to bed. Or maybe he went to the Union Hall. Or maybe he went to the diner for something to eat. Or maybe—"

"You have to help us look," Amanda said. "I think something has happened to him." Now that she knew he wasn't with Reva, she was beginning to calm down. Whitey had lied to her, but why? Was he, perhaps, lying merely because she was a Caulden? Or was there another reason?

"He's all right," Reva said. "Hank can take care of himself. Besides, it's late and I need my sleep."

"You either come voluntarily or I'll drag you out," Amanda said.

"Really, Amanda," Grace said. "I'm sure Reva's right and Dr. Montgomery is fine. Perhaps we should—"

"I get Taylor," Reva said, as if he were a piece of merchandise.

"Done," Amanda answered in the voice of an auctioneer saying, "Sold to the woman in the dirty nightgown."

"Give me five minutes to get dressed."

"Forget the lipstick and you'll save three minutes," Amanda said with a sweet smile.

Grace looked away to hide her smile.

In four minutes Reva was dressed and outside. Amanda wasted no more time on catty remarks but issued orders like a general—or like her father. Neither Reva nor Grace considered contradicting her. Amanda assigned them places to check and gave them less than an hour. They were going to have to search nearly all of Kingman at a run.

An hour later they met in front of the Kingman Arms.

"No sign of him," Reva said. She too was concerned now. "No one has seen him all day. He hasn't been back to the hotel. Joe's at the Union Hall and he hasn't seen Hank."

Grace had had no luck either.

"If we could only find his car," Amanda said. Her heart seemed to have jumped into her throat. Terror was what she felt, sheer debilitating terror. He would never leave the fields and the unionists unless something had . . . happened. She didn't like to imagine what could have happened. There was too much talk of bloodshed and violence. "He would never leave that car of his," she whispered. "If we could just—"

"But his car is back at the fields," Grace said.

Amanda and Reva turned to look at her.

"I tripped once and saw something yellow in the hop fields. It was almost hidden under the vines, but I knew what it was. There's nothing else quite the color of Dr. Montgomery's little automobile."

"They've done something with him," Amanda said softly, and she knew it was true. "They want their violence, and Hank meant to stop them. They have removed him."

"Removed him?" Grace asked. "What in the world do you mean?"

Reva took a step backward. "You know, it's awfully late and I'm real tired. I think I better go home and get to bed. I have to go to work in a few hours. Amanda, after the hops are in, let's have lunch."

Amanda grabbed Reva's arm. "You're going to the ranch with us. We're going to find that Whitey Graham—I know he's behind this—and make him tell us where Hank is." She swallowed. "If we're not too late. Reva, does your father have a gun we can borrow? I don't think a man like Whitey will listen to three women saying please."

"A g-gun?" Reva asked.

"A pistol, maybe. Better yet, a shotgun. Two big round barrels should get his attention."

Reva moved away. "Then again, Amanda, you can have Taylor. You can have both men. I think I better get home now, so goodnight, Mrs. Caulden. Goodnight, Amanda."

Amanda caught Reva before she'd gone ten steps and put her arm firmly through Reva's. "Don't turn coward on me now. We have to find Hank. Maybe he can prevent the war that's about to erupt at our ranch, but, more important, Hank might be hurt."

"Not to mention us being hurt," Reva muttered.

"Sometimes, Reva, a person has to do things one doesn't want to do. Isn't that right, Mother? Mother?"

The two young women turned back to see Grace Caulden still standing in front of the Kingman Arms. Her oval face was as pale as the moon.

"Reva, does your father have any w-whiskey?" she whispered hoarsely.

"I can guarantee he has whiskey," Reva said, and fear sounded in her voice.

"Come on, we're wasting time," Amanda said. "We have to find Hank." She walked off into the night, the two women following her hesitantly.

Chapter Eighteen

"Are you sure you know how to drive this?" Reva asked. "Or even start it?" Her voice was very quiet and there was a quality in it that could only be classified as respect. Yesterday she would have said that proper, always-use-the-correct-fork Miss Amanda Caulden wasn't capable of any of the things she had done in the last two hours.

The three women had "borrowed" a double-barreled twelve-gauge shotgun from Mr. Eiler (he had drunkenly snored through the entire event and only turned over when Grace took his half-empty whiskey bottle from the crook of his arm). Then Amanda had got them a ride in the back of a smelly old pickup to the Caulden Ranch.

In the back of the pickup, over the rattling and jostling, a pale-faced Grace had taken her daughter's hand. "If I don't get out of this alive, dear, I have a confession to make. I am the Countess de la Glace."

Amanda blinked at her mother. "*You* wrote the book about Ariadne and that man?"

"I needed something to occupy myself while stuck away in that room. There are royalties from the sale of the books, and you and your young doctor could live

331

quite well on them." Grace leaned forward. "And see that Reva is taken care of, would you, please?"

Amanda squeezed her mother's hand. "When this is over may I read all your novels? I need to make up for lost time."

Grace smiled at her daughter and they were quiet the rest of the way to the fields.

It had been easy to find Whitey Graham; he was on the little dance platform at the south edge of the field, giving one of his speeches about the evilness of the employers. There were bonfires all about and the people's angry, tired eyes reflected the fiery heat. As Whitey led the crowd into one of the inflammatory ULW songs, Amanda stepped to the edge of the crowd, got Whitey's attention and motioned for him to follow her.

Reva and Grace had stood by silently, too scared, too astonished to speak, and watched while Amanda pointed the gun at Whitey's head and demanded to know where Hank Montgomery was.

Whitey was a cool one, Reva had to give him that. He said he didn't mind telling Amanda where Hank was as it would take her too long to get to him to do any good. "It's going to happen tomorrow. Caulden's refusal to listen to us was the final straw. This place is going to explode within the next twenty-four hours."

Amanda shoved the shotgun closer to his nose. "*You* are going to explode within the next two minutes if you don't tell me where Hank is."

He looked at Amanda with a bit of respect and told her that his partner, Andrei, had taken Hank away, up into the Sierra Nevada Mountains to a shack where Whitey and Andrei had hidden for a few days before entering Kingman. At Amanda's urging, he gave her complete directions. He seemed to think her concern was amusing.

"You rich people stick together, don't you?"

"Rich?" Amanda said. "Hank spends all he makes on the union."

Whitey laughed at her. "The professor's family is so rich they make you Cauldens look like paupers. We tried to get the workers to strike his father's company, Warbrooke Shipping, two years ago but . . ."

"You weren't successful," she finished.

"Amanda," Grace said, "you could stop this whole thing now. We'll take Mr. Graham away from here."

Amanda hesitated and weighed the possibilities. "People have a right to protest, and only my father could stop it now—and only Hank could persuade my father."

Whitey laughed again. He knew Amanda wouldn't shoot him, and it didn't matter if she went after Montgomery—she'd never get him back in time. They'd had to get rid of the doc or he could have ruined everything. He turned his back on Amanda and her shotgun and went back to the crowd.

"That man really doesn't care if he lives or dies," Reva whispered.

Amanda didn't waste time thinking about Whitey Graham. "I have to go get Hank," she said and started moving quickly toward where the Mercer had been hidden.

So now the women had removed the torn hop vines that covered the car and stood staring at it. "Can you start it?" Reva repeated.

"I hope so," Amanda said. "No, I *will* start the thing." She went over every movement she'd seen Hank make when he started the car. She pulled out the spark and the choke, then ran to the front and turned the crank. It took her four tries before the engine came to life, then she had to deal with the gears. The shifting was hard, the steering was so difficult her arms felt as if they were coming out of their sockets, and when she put on the brakes the car didn't stop. She mowed down six feet of hop vines before she halted.

"Amanda, I don't think—" Grace said fearfully.

"I've got it now," Amanda said, putting the car in reverse. "I'll be back as soon as I can." She hadn't counted on the steering being a mirror image when in reverse and took out more hop vines before she got onto the road. She waved to Reva and her mother, then headed east, her foot mashing the accelerator to the floor.

Both Hank and Taylor had said she was an apt pupil, but she'd never learned anything as quickly as she learned to drive that car. After fifteen minutes she began to feel that she was born to be behind a steering wheel. She had studied Hank's driving so intently that she knew from the sound of the engine when to shift gears.

It was the middle of the night and there was no traffic on the wide dirt road leading up into the mountains, and she let the car go, the wind blowing in her hair. The speed of the car, being able to control such a machine, made her feel powerful.

She had only one bad moment on the trip and that was when two farmers with wagons decided to stop in the middle of the road for a chat. Amanda kept her head, tried to calculate the width of the road, the distance it would take her to stop, knew she'd plow into a wagon if she did try to stop, so she did a neat left turn that sent her skidding sideways toward the wagons.

The farmers stopped talking long enough to turn and look at a pretty girl in a little yellow car come toward them, the nose of the car pointed toward the roadside fence, rocks and gravel spitting everywhere. One pair of horses started acting up, but the farmer controlled them.

When the car stopped sliding, Amanda was just under the body of two horses, one animal's eyes rolling wildly, the other one too frightened to move. The three people on the road were speechless. Amanda recovered first. Her heart was pounding but she was awfully proud of having avoided a crash.

"Good morning," she said to the farmers. There was a wilted hop vine on the passenger seat and she offered it to the horse's head hanging over hers. The animal began crunching and calmed down.

The two farmers helped her get the car turned back around and wished her luck wherever she was going. She waved as she drove away again.

She had to get gasoline once, then she was off again, up into the mountains. She prayed Whitey hadn't lied to her about where Hank was, and the closer she got, the more she worried. When she came to the deserted mountain cabin with half the roof caved in, she was almost out of the car before she could get it stopped. She hauled on the heavy hand brake, shoved a rock behind the back wheel and went running.

The cabin was empty. For a moment she panicked and was sure Whitey had lied, but then she saw a stain on what was left of the floor near the back wall. She went to it and examined it. Blood. There seemed to be a great deal of it on the floor, as if a wounded person had slept there all night.

For a moment she wanted to cry. She was tired and hungry and scared—and there was dried blood on the floor.

"Looking for me?"

She looked up to see Hank standing in the doorway. With a cry, she leaped up and into his arms. "You're alive! Oh my darling, my love, I was so afraid." She began kissing his face and neck.

"Whoa, wait a minute," Hank said, drawing back from her. "What's going on and could you ease up on my arm a little?"

She pulled away from him and saw the blood on the right side of his body. "They shot you? I'll kill them! I'll use Mr. Eiler's shotgun and—"

Hank put his fingers to her lips. "Could we save this until later? I'd like to know what's been going on. I'm afraid I've been knocked out all nigh⁺. I just woke up when I heard the car. Who drove the Mercer, any-way?"

"I did. Hank, darling, I've been worried sick. I was afraid you were dead."

Hank was weak from loss of blood and a cold night without food or water, and he was afraid he might have enough fever that he was dreaming this. It couldn't be possible that Amanda was calling *him* darling.

He knew he needed to get back to the ranch to prevent what could happen, but right now all that seemed to matter was Amanda. He put his fingertips to her hair. "Why are you here, Amanda?"

"To get you. I've come to take you back." Embarrassment overcame her. The last time she'd seen him he was blaming her for the living conditions of the workers.

"To help with the union? Couldn't you have appealed to Taylor?"

She opened her mouth to lie, to say that she came for him to prevent violence, but she stopped herself. "Yes," she said softly, "I came to get you for the unionists but, more than that, I came because I love you."

Hank didn't say anything at all, just stood there and stared at her for so long that Amanda knew she'd made a fool of herself. "Excuse me," she said and pushed past him to go outside. She kept her back to him. "If you're ready, I'll drive you back to the ranch. Whitey presented a list of grievances to my father yesterday, and my father, of course, wouldn't agree to a pay raise, so Whitey threatened him and my father slapped Whitey. The sheriff plans to arrest Whitey, probably today, and so you can see that—"

She broke off because Hank turned her around, dug his uninjured left hand into her hair and kissed her so hard her toes curled up inside her tight little shoes.

"I love you, Amanda," he said. "I've loved you for so long I can't remember not loving you. I think I've been waiting for you, waiting for you to make up your mind."

"I have made up my mind," she whispered. "I want to leave Kingman with you. I want to go with you wherever you go. I want to be with you always."

He smiled as he caressed her cheek. Her arms around him were hurting his shoulder, but physical pain was nothing to the pain he'd felt since he'd met her. When he first saw her he'd thought she was the woman for him, but it was as if an automaton were inside the body of the woman he wanted. But it was a woman, a flesh and blood woman, who had come for him.

"How did you get Whitey to tell you where I was?"

"I held a shotgun to his face."

Hank smiled. "How did you learn to drive the car?"

"I've been watching you."

He smiled broader. "What about Taylor?"

"I suggested he spend more time with Reva, and Reva asked for him so I gave him to her."

"Oh, you did, did you?" Hank laughed. "So you and Reva divided us up. I guess I should be glad you didn't flip a coin."

She pulled away from him. "If you are through laughing at me, I suggest we go."

He caught her arm. "Did you really mean it, Amanda? Have you realized at last that you love me?"

She didn't quite like the way he put it, but truth was truth. "Yes," she said. "I have finally realized it."

He drew back a little, a grin splitting his face. "I guess all this stuff about you'll go with me wherever I go is a marriage proposal."

Her embarrassment was returning. Wasn't this a time for champagne and diamond rings? But he was standing here in a bloody shirt, lines of tiredness around his eyes, and she was filthy and tired. "I guess so." She looked down at her hands.

"Wait until I tell our grandkids about this," Hank said. "They'll never believe their grandmother did the asking."

She squinted up at him. "You ever tell anyone about this and you'll never beget children with me, much less grandchildren." She turned on her heel and walked away from him.

He caught her and pulled her against him with his one good arm. "I apologize, baby. I just wanted to give you some of what you've given me. You can't imagine the hell you've put me through, knowing you were mine yet having you fight me. I died some every time you looked at Driscoll. I gave up hope once that you'd ever realize that you belonged to me and I walked out, but then you came strolling into the Union Hall. You have made me completely miserable."

She smiled against his sweaty shirt. "I'm glad. You've upset my life too."

He kissed her forehead and held her a moment. "I think we better go. My arm's beginning to bleed again and it'll be hard driving back with one arm."

"I'll drive back," she said.

He pulled away from her. "You?" He grinned. "Amanda, do you realize what the steering is like on the Mercer? And the brakes? Why, you couldn't even—"

"Who do you think drove up here?" she asked angrily.

"That was different, that was . . ."

"Was what?" she demanded.

"Necessary." He wasn't smiling any longer.

"And now it's not necessary? You think you're a better driver with one arm and a fever than I am with two arms?"

"As a matter of fact, I do."

She stepped back. "All right, it's yours," she said, gesturing toward the car. She stood aside and watched as he worked on the intricate starting procedure. His wound opened and he looked dizzy a couple of times, but he kept turning the crank.

She went to him. "Please, Hank," she said. "Please let me help."

Hank looked at her. He'd always known he'd do whatever she wanted if she asked him with a please. He knew it was one of the most difficult things he'd ever done, but he let her drive. She was worse than he'd imagined. She drove too fast, her steering was erratic, she passed other cars when she couldn't see around them. She kept asking him questions about when Whitey and Andrei had kidnapped him. He mumbled that Andrei had never meant to shoot him but a tree on the mountainside had fallen and scared Andrei so much that the gun had gone off. Hank ducked, but not quick enough. Andrei thought Hank was dead and pulled him into the cabin to get the body out of sight, then he'd left him. Hank had slept until Amanda arrived.

"Does it hurt much?" Amanda asked, looking at him.

He got a little sick every time she took her eyes off the road. "Not as much as death would."

Amanda thought she heard him say something else, but it sounded too much like, "Taylor had the right idea about women: keep them locked up," so she was sure she was wrong.

They stopped for gas twice and bought sandwiches and coffee, then were on their way again. They didn't reach the Caulden Ranch until sundown.

And by then it was all over.

As soon as Amanda pulled into the service road near the pickers' camp they could see that many of the people were gone. Hank was pale and weak, and

Amanda wanted to get him to a doctor but he wouldn't go. "I want to see your father," he said. Amanda nodded, took his hand in hers and they started walking.

Joe Testorio saw them and came running with the news. Everything had happened within minutes. Whitey Graham had been giving one of his speeches when two cars drove up, one containing the sheriff, the district attorney and a deputy, the other car containing four deputies. The D.A. made a request for peace, but one deputy pointed out Whitey and said they had a warrant for his arrest and were taking him. The officers started making their way through the crowd.

But then something happened, Joe wasn't sure what, but later someone said that a bench with some men standing on it had tipped. The noise and the men's yells were enough to send the crowd into pandemonium. A deputy fired a shotgun over the crowd's heads to quieten them. It had the opposite effect.

Three minutes later the crowd began to pull back, and on the ground lay the sheriff, the D.A., a deputy and two workers, one a boy of thirteen, all of them dead.

If possible, Hank grew a little paler when he heard the news. Amanda tightened her grip on his hand.

Hank walked into the Caulden house without knocking and strode into the library, Amanda beside him. J. Harker sat at his desk, looking as if nothing had happened.

"Come to threaten me?" he asked, looking at a bloody Hank and a defiant Amanda. "So much for your campaign against violence. The governor's sending the State Militia out. They'll shoot your unionists on sight. You've lost, Montgomery, you've lost."

"You don't realize it, but you're the loser. All you had to do was give the workers a decent pay raise—money you could well afford—and you could have prevented this. Now the world will hear about the Caulden Ranch."

"Hear how your unionists killed the D.A. and the sheriff," J. Harker said. "The country will tear your union apart. The D.A. was a loved man, with a wife and kids."

"What this country will hear about is the inhuman conditions that *caused* them to riot. And I'm going to be the one to tell them. I'm going to describe in detail what went on here, what pushed these people over the brink."

"And I'm going to help him," Amanda said.

J. Harker snorted. "You can go to your room. I'll get someone to replace Taylor."

"Has he left you too?" Amanda said softly.

"Ran off with that two-bit Eiler bitch," Harker muttered. "But he can be replaced."

"Now you have what you wanted: you have this enormous ranch all to yourself. You have no wife with a past to embarrass you, no daughter to play childish pranks and make people think you're less than perfect, no future son-in-law to intimidate. But you've lost something else too: you don't know it yet, but you've lost control of this ranch. You've shown your greed to the world, and you may be willing to let people die so you can make money, but the world's not going to let you. Your day is over, and Hank and I are going to help see that it's finished."

"Are you through now?" J. Harker said, his eyes

angry. "Then you can get out. I don't need any of you." Even as he said it, he knew he was lying, but pride had ruled his life and he was too old to change now.

"Goodbye, Father," Amanda said and turned to look at Hank. "Ready, darling?"

Hank nodded and they left the library, but he stopped her in the hall. "Amanda, if I wasn't sure before that I loved you, I am now. Will you marry me?"

"Yes," she whispered, then smiled. "And our son will be a king."

"What?"

"When I went to the carnival with Taylor, a fortune-teller told me—"

"I am bleeding to death and you're talking about that frigid—"

"I wasn't talking about Taylor, I was talking about our son who will be—"

He kissed her. "Come on, let's go to the Union Hall. I want to interview some people about what's happened. The faster we get this down, the faster I can get it to the newspapers."

"We'll go *after* I've driven you to a doctor."

"You are going to drive in town? With other cars on the road? With *pedestrians* in the street?"

"Please?" she asked softly, running her finger down his cheek.

"Yes," he said. "Yes."

willing to die for a cause or just plain craz...
one knows, went from one place of abuse ...

Author's Note

I have based the people and events in this book on history more directly than I have in any of my previous novels.

Dr. Henry R. Montgomery is based on Dr. Carleton Parker, a professor of economics who trained in Germany. Dr. Parker was a man who cared: he cared about his students, he cared about the way people were treated by their employers. While he was in school, he spent summers working in mines all over the world to get firsthand knowledge of labor and laborers. After graduating with honors, he returned to the United States where he wrote about and taught against the horrors that were visited upon nonunionized workers.

Dr. Parker hoped that the labor problems of the workers could be solved without violence, but the IWW, the International Workers of the World, the Wobblies as they were called, believed that violence was the only way to get the world's attention. Several men, and whether they were true martyrs willing to die for a cause or just plain crazy no one knows, went from one place of abuse to another and incited downtrodden workers to revolt in protest. Unfortunately, they seemed to have been right because, when blood was shed, the world looked and listened and eventually did something.

The Awakening is based on the Wheatland Hop Riot that took place on one swelteringly hot day in August 1913, in Wheatland, California. Every word I wrote about the conditions in the fields is true. Usually a writer has to add to the actual events to give her story more drama, but in this case I just reported the facts with no embellishment. The facts were worse than I could ever have imagined, and just the reading of them and later the recounting of them was enough to make me ill.

The riot itself was as I described. The district attorney, by chance, happened to be visiting Wheatland that day, and when the call for the sheriff's men came, he decided to tag along. He was killed in the fracas. During the riot, the owner of the ranch hid inside his house.

After the riot, the State Militia was called into Wheatland and a manhunt was made for the IWW leaders. Four men—William Beck, Richard "Blackie" Ford, Walter Bagan and Herman Suhr—were charged with murder. They were tried in Marysville, California, which is very near Wheatland (the Terrill City in my novel), where feeling against the unionists ran high.

The trial was a farce. Alibis were thrown out as being "too good." "Evidence" consisted of a telegram to IWW headquarters asking for postage stamps.

Bagan and Beck were acquitted; Ford and Suhr were

sent to San Quentin for life. Their sentences were meant to let the unionists know what would happen to them if they interfered in a private landowner's business again.

But it backfired. Dr. Carleton Parker, having left teaching to become the Executive Secretary in the State Immigration and Housing Commission of California, went to Wheatland. He asked questions and wrote some powerful articles about what had happened there. It was largely through his efforts that plans were made to enforce existing laws that provided regulation of sanitation of the labor camps. The Board of Health was given the power to inspect, condemn and prosecute employers, and a commission was set up to educate the migrant laborers and inform them of their rights.

I hope my story has not been too one-sided. The private landowner does have rights, and too often I hear employee comments of, "Someday I'm going to be the boss and sit in a cool office and do nothing but answer the telephone." The year of the Wheatland Riot, hop prices were rock bottom, buyers' warehouses were full from the previous years, and many hop ranches were going under—and it did indeed cost an enormous amount of money to run a ranch. The owner had to save pennies wherever he could. It is a philosophical dilemma: does he offer thousands of people low-paying jobs with no water (for water delivery costs money) and save his ranch and offer more jobs next year, or does he pay good wages, provide expensive services for one year, go bankrupt and offer no jobs the next year?

Mr. Durst (my J. Harker Caulden) eventually went

bankrupt, and today Wheatland is a pale shadow of its former rich self. I'm not sure who won from the Wheatland Hop Riot.

Jude Deveraux
Santa Fe, New Mexico
August 1987